The Colour of Secrets

Vanessa Wiggins

Published by SatinPublishing

This novel is a work of fiction. Names and characters are the product of the author's imagination and any resemblance to actual persons, living or dead is entirely coincidental.

ISBN-13: 978-1548848934
ISBN-10: 154884893X

Author Biography

Vanessa Wiggins lives in North Buckinghamshire. 'The Colour of Secrets' is her first novel.

Dedication:

For my parents and Hokey.

AUTHOR LINKS:

https://www.facebook.com/vanessa.wiggins.18

Acknowledgement:

Thanks to Trish for first reading my novel (twice!), to the members of my local book club for also reading and for their encouragement; to my other readers: friends and relations Doreen, Jo, Linda, Stephen, Janet, Adrian, Nick, Laura, David and others – and for their helpful comments. Also to Trish, Tessa and everyone else who badgered me to do something with it. Finally, to Hokey – and Sparky – for encouraging, distracting and motivating me.

Publisher Links:

http://www.satinpublishing.co.uk

https://twitter.com/SatinPaperbacks

https://www.facebook.com/Satinpaperbacks.com

Email: nicky.fitzmaurice@satinpaperbacks.com

Table of Contents:

Prologue

26 July 1960

It wasn't that life was dull when John Norbert wasn't around, but it was undoubtedly more exciting when he was. Things just happened. Things always happened, and waiting to meet him off the train Robbie knew that the long weeks of summer that lay ahead would bring unexpected adventures, perhaps even danger. It was always like that then, in those years.

He was a lone figure on the hot station platform; scuffing restlessly at gravel spilt from amongst the gaudy flower beds onto the stone flags. Impatient, anxiously anticipating his friend's arrival, his excitement was tempered with apprehension. The two boys had spent the past three summers almost daily in one another's company. For Robbie, John bestrode the years of his childhood, and would continue to do so in memory throughout his adult years, and yet even after three long summers together, he still knew little about him.

That year would be the last they'd spend a summer together, although Robbie Bradbury had no idea of that then, any more than he knew about John's life away from the village. He simply knew John as he appeared; rakish, crazy sometimes, wild even. He'd do things without any thought for the consequences, revelling in the risk-taking and riling other people. John, who seemed to belong nowhere and to no one, except perhaps to Robbie, his great friend and companion of those summers. Robbie never really understood why John would attach himself to a plump village boy - someone who was frequently shunned by the more adventurous village gangs, and was considered ordinary even by the indulgence of his own parents.

Days of games and mischief-making, that's what Robbie's eleven-year old self remembered from his past summers with John, and that's what he hoped for once again as he jiggered about on the station platform, knowing John never disappointed, that he wasn't motivated by reputation or by other people's expectations; it was simply the way he was. Robbie and his friends loved his outlandish behaviour and sheer cheek, 'devilment' his mother called it, and they delighted in their companion's wildness. Finally now, after ten long months he'd be arriving. Ten long months: an autumn and winter and a spring and early summer to forget. But not to forget.

Two or three people emerged from the cool of Moreton Steyning's small brick station in anticipation of the through train from London. They stood silent at the platform edge, staring down at the rails, peering into the sun, and away to the far hills, blue and hazed in the harsh sunlight. Robbie strained to hear the engine, fiddling with the sand bucket strap, swinging round the cast iron pillar, hopping on one leg and then another, burning with anticipation. Anything to fill the wait. The dread.

The station clock finally read 3.55pm and Joe Perkins strode onto the platform, flag at the ready, cap held low over his eyes.

Then, far away to the left the first steam came into view, distant steady puffs of white; small at first, marking the line of the track as it curved through the vale, parallel with the distant line of the hills, its engine huffing up the slow and steady incline through its shallow cutting, making the final approach from Cullingham to Moreton Steyning.

At first the steam billowed above the hedges, then the dark engine hove into view; a shimmering blur in the heat haze, followed by carriages with panels burnished and windows glinting gold as they pulled round the long curving rise towards the village station. The few waiting passengers stepped forward, bags raised and expectant. The sound of a labouring engine expanded to fill the air and it rumbled past, massive and thunderous, shadowing out the sunlight, vibrating the platform beneath Robbie's feet, and blasting out steam as the brakes squealed it to a halt.

Few people arrived at that time of day, and only three carriage doors swung open. A man stepped briskly from one and two women emerged chatting, having clearly returned from a shopping trip to Cullingham. Beneath the farthest door, a small well-worn suitcase thudded as it skidded across the platform, then two thin legs sprang down and the door was carelessly flung shut and there he stood, somewhat taller than last year, but scraggy still, and every bit as dishevelled.

He booted the case towards Robbie and drawled, 'Y'orright?' eyeing him sideways, watchful.

Both boys were suddenly awkward in one another's company. Robbie shrugged, tongue-tied and uncomfortable.

'Train's on time,' he lamely remarked, casting about for something to say. The eager waiting to see his friend, and now all that stored-up anticipation and excitement was choking any attempt to bridge the months and miles that had separated them.

'Full of bleedin' dead-uns!' John jerked his head dismissively back at the carriage, then swung to pick up the battered case.

They fell in behind the three other passengers, all locals, and John fished deep into his tattered school blazer for his ticket and matter-of-factly offered it up. The boys marched out from the station building and into the warm July sun. Robbie glanced back, witnessing the ticket collector's aggravated expression as he struggled to disentangle his fingers from the well-worked chewing gum that enveloped John's ticket.

Part One

1957 - 1960

Chapter One: 1957

The boys were both eight in 1957, the year John Norbert spent his first summer at Moreton Steyning.

By late July, with school newly broken up, Robbie and Lizzie were delirious with anticipation for the weeks of holiday that stretched ahead. She lived almost opposite him and the two, who had been born just a short time apart, had been close all their lives, since their mothers had first pushed them side-by-side, in large black prams, around the village. As young children they'd played and exchanged secrets and whispers. Now older, they remained best friends and constant companions, even though they were separated by gender.

They emerged from Mrs Patterson's corner sweet shop with dripping ice lollies and stood outside, enjoying the enticing sugary smells from within that mingled with those of the dusty lane. Sucking the sticky orangey juice that slowly trickled down their fists, they were observing the steady approach of an unknown boy.

At that time it was rare to see people in the village who weren't familiar. Both of them knew the names of everyone in Moreton Steyning, their relations and friends, and their relations' friends, and this was definitely a stranger; a boy of about their own age, but scrawny and short, and quite unlike any of the other village children. He was loping towards them on spindly, bandy legs with a mass of untidy coarse dark hair above a small scrunched-up face. Lizzie and Robbie had never seen a real monkey before, but to them he was as much like one as any human could be.

'Who's that?' asked Lizzie, voicing her friend's thoughts.

Both sucked hard on their lollies in thought, extracting the last of the juice so that only the tasteless grey core remained.

At that moment the horse-drawn cart belonging to Luff, the village hardware merchant, turned into the lane returning from his delivery rounds; all pots and coppers rattling as usual, obstructing their view of the boy. Lizzie stepped out into the road, leaning wide, then returned to Robbie's side with a puzzled look on her face.

'He's gone, he's disappeared!' she cried, eyes wide with astonishment.

This was good; a disappearing boy. They hadn't had one of those in the village before and it surely bode well for the holiday amusements to come.

Robbie walked out to the centre of the lane himself, but the little monkey-boy was nowhere to be seen although he checked in all directions, even behind them, although it made no sense to do so, before stepping back onto the path beside Lizzie.

They exchanged blank looks, any chance of speaking now drowned out by Luff's passing cart that rumbled and rattled noisily above their heads. They swept the still-empty street with their eyes before turning to watch the departing cart and there he was, clinging to the back, all sinewy legs and arms gripping onto the wooden slats, laughter etched all over his monkey face.

The sight brought a thrill of excitement to Lizzie and, even before Robbie could digest what they'd seen, she'd darted away across The Green. She was soon pounding along in a side passage that led to the back garden of one of the houses on the far side. Smaller, nimbler and fitter, she was already clambering up onto a wooden gate to peer over before he could catch up with her.

'It's okay, they're here,' she called as he puffed up behind her and, lifting the latch, she skipped eagerly into the neat back garden where two boys were playing football on the lawn. They paused and gazed towards Lizzie; two blond boys in shorts, mirror images of one another.

'There's a monkey in the village!' she cried, bouncing enthusiastically between the two of them so that they had no choice but to abandon their game.

'Woah!' roared Finch who, instantly captivated by the image, easily matched Lizzie's eagerness. He was at once ready to rush out and see for himself although he had as yet no idea where to go. His brother's more measured reaction briefly dampened his enthusiasm, but any lack of impulsiveness rarely lasted long.

Nid however, hands on hips with one foot steadying the ball, had a tone of finality in his voice.

'Can't be,' he'd said. He was by nature, rather more cautious than his twin, with a tendency for pedantry.

'It was too! We saw him, didn't we, Robbie?' Lizzie was stung by Nid's disbelief and turned eagerly to her friend for support.

Robbie shrugged, looking from one to the other. Nid was unwavering, but Lizzie's eyes held his imploringly. 'Looked like a monkey,' he tried. The last thing he wanted to do was undermine her but his own common sense nagged at him.

'Where?' both twins demanded in unison, one in raised excited tones and raring to go; the other somewhat challenging.

'He leapt up onto the back of old Luff's cart and was hanging on like this.' Lizzie enacted the scene, which involved her hopping about on one leg, hands gripping onto an imaginary cart.

'Was he hairy?' asked Finch.

''Course.'

'Sort of.' Robbie wanted to offer support while not over-embellishing the story. 'Actually, he was a sort of monkey-boy.'

'Well, who does he belong to?' Nid asked, his foot still resolutely on the football.

'He just came from nowhere,' Lizzie panted, regaining her breathless excitement. 'He was walking along Main Street when Robbie and I came out of Mrs Patterson's. Maybe it's escaped from a zoo... or a circus!'

'I think it was a boy.' Robbie said, trying not to disappoint her.

'A half-boy, half-monkey,' suggested Finch, who by now was swinging restlessly on the gatepost.

'Yes! Human mother, monkey father.' This, Lizzie stated with some authority.

'Gosh,' murmured Finch, still swinging.

'Well, I'd like to see him.' Nid was ignoring Lizzie's steady gaze that challenged him to doubt her any further.

'Well, he can't have gone far, can he?' she said. 'Mr Luff just takes his cart to the yard. The monkey-boy must still be in the village. I bet we can find him.'

'Let's start a search!' and Finch launched himself into their midst with the momentum of a final swing.

'We'll get Maggie and Ann,' announced Lizzie and with long plaits flying, she was off again, down the passage, across The Green and onto the top lane. The others raced after her – it was infectious, and there was no holding her back in this mood.

Lizzie knew just where to find Maggie and Ann; on the swings at the playground. She was already there when the three boys caught up with her, swinging on the climbing frame, doing her monkey impression and relating the story to the two other girls who listened, enwrapt.

Maggie, long-legged and thin, was taller than any of the others, the boys included. She had a sallow complexion and lank shoulder-length hair that gave her the appearance of someone older and she immediately took charge. She always did. It was a mystery to them all that she and Ann, so small and timorous, her exact opposite in every way, were such close friends.

'It won't have gone far,' Maggie had said. 'Monkeys like trees. It'll be in the copse.'

As one, the six of them sped down the steep Snail Path which ran alongside the playground and emerged back into Main Street, behind Mrs Patterson's sweet shop. They then pelted down to the edge of the village, clambered over a stile into the meadow and thrashed through the tall uncut grass to Long Copse, releasing a haze of golden pollen about them. Maggie and Lizzie out-ran the others and were already at the wood's edge, standing panting and red-cheeked when the rest of them caught up, none sure now quite what to do next.

It had been warm and bright on the field-edge but, now that they were within the copse, beneath trees heavy with their dark canopy of high summer, it was gloomily shady and felt ominous. They looked at one another, which was enough to spur Maggie into taking control once again.

'We'll split up,' she said. ''Me and Ann'll go that way; you two,' pointing to Lizzie and Robbie, 'go there, and the twins that way.'

She'd got all corners covered so they separated as instructed, although not really sure what to look for, or indeed what to do should they find it.

'This is exciting, isn't it?' said Lizzie to Robbie, face still flushed and beaming. 'And we've only been broken up from school two days!'

He didn't like to say he'd gone off the idea already, but it pleased him to see her happy, and she thrashed about in the undergrowth with a broken branch, making more than enough racket to frighten anything away.

'Come out monkey, monkey, monkey. Come on out! Here monkey, here monkey,' she cried, beating on the tree trunks and thwacking the high bracken aside.

Away to their left, Robbie could hear Nid and Finch whistling and shouting and beyond them with fainter voices, Maggie and Ann hulloing. A great clapping and flapping above made them almost jump out of their skins, but it was merely two pigeons, frightened from their languor by all the noise. They continued to thrash and call and whistle for ages but only disturbed the jackdaws high in the canopy, causing them to clatter off, loudly calling their disapproval. Eventually they all met up again.

'I expect he's found a nest by now,' Maggie suggested. She was standing with her feet apart on the broad surface of a tree stump, stick still held in her right fist, surveying the copse about them from her vantage point.

'But monkeys don't have nests,' said Nid. Like Maggie, he expected to be right.

'They do!'

'He might die if we don't rescue him.' Lizzie was mournful, her interjection deflecting any conflict. 'And I'm sure he's here because he's got lost.'

'He won't die,' Robbie tried to reassure. 'He'll be used to the trees. Anyway, if he's a boy or a monkey-boy, I expect he'll find a house to sleep in, or a barn maybe.'

'We must check all our garden sheds,' Finch proposed, 'and report back in the morning.' He could be surprisingly practical at times.

'Yep,' confirmed Maggie, jumping down from her lookout, 'and we can all think up new plans overnight to find him.'

That seemed to be that and, truth to tell, they were all feeling hungry by now, the position of the sun showing them that it was already teatime. They sauntered back across the meadow, tearing off grass seeds to dart at one another and, at the lane, went their separate ways.

***

Robbie felt a little uneasy about it all, but also excited. Lizzie was enjoying the adventure and no doubt it would all resolve itself, or perhaps they'd just never know. You didn't always know in life, he'd found. He soon reached home and pulled open the lean-to door.

'Robbie! Tea's on the table!'

The tone in his mother's voice told him he was late, but he knew that anyway. As he sat down Digby licked his fingers and settled under the table amongst three pairs of feet, his coarse fur warm and reassuring against Robbie's shins. His older brother Jonathan was already halfway through his beans on toast and didn't pause or look up until he'd finished, the movement of his fork from plate to mouth and back again one continuous circular motion.

'Plate's hot,' their mother said, placing his food before him and returning to her own. 'It's been warm today,' and she tucked back some hair that had fallen across her brow as she looked over to them with a half-smile on her broad face, gently touched by the first lines.

Robbie speedily devoured his food. He hadn't realised how hungry he was. Beside him Jonathan made a noise like a braying donkey, having already finished his own.

'Stay there,' she said, reaching out across the table and touching Jonathan's wrist. He settled back in the chair, contented look about his face.

'Where's Dad?' asked Robbie.

'Down at the allotment. Here, there's cherry pie left from yesterday. I saw Mrs Ward today and she's got her great nephew staying; same age as you. A boy from London. I said you'd go and see him, he won't know a soul here.'

'What does he look like?' Had he asked that for a reason, he asked himself, but he wasn't sure.

'How should I know!' she laughed. 'Go round tomorrow. Take him up the hill or something, introduce him to your friends. His name's John.'

Robbie didn't like the sound of this at all, but knew better than to argue, hoping it might all be forgotten if he said nothing further. He helped himself and his brother to cherry pie, and when they'd finished asked to go back out and play.

'Take Jonathan,' she said. 'Back at seven.'

They were out of the door within seconds, and certainly before they could be asked to clear the table. 'C'mon,' he said, grabbing a jam jar from the lean-to. 'Let's go to Snake Pond.'

His older brother merely chuckled approval and, letting themselves out of the side gate, the two of them hurtled along the narrow passage to the street, their pounding footsteps echoing against the still-warm whitewashed walls of their cottage, and away towards The Green. Here there were older boys hanging around, so they decided to avoid them by taking the quiet lane round the back from where it was only a short walk to the pond. This involved cutting across the Churchyard and then along one of the many paths that led up onto the hill.

Lullington was a broad undulating whaleback of a ridge, beneath whose south-facing slopes rested the village of Moreton Steyning.

The path they took, although invariably boggy in winter, was now, at the end of July, dry and overgrown and overhung with tall wavering grasses and the starburst seed heads of cow parsley, which formed a tight passage and drew them into single-file.

Robbie walked ahead, shrouded from behind by the shadow cast from Jonathan's large bulk.

'Where did you go, Robbie?' Jonathan asked. 'What did you do today?' For Jonathan, his younger brother was his best friend by far. The two, although apart in age, had shared toys and experiences all their lives and were equal in their closeness.

'I went out with Lizzie. You know, games and stuff.' Robbie wanted to tell Jonathan about the monkey-boy, but didn't know himself what he'd seen. Perhaps by tomorrow he'd feel differently, he'd tell Jonathan then.

Several springs emerged around the base of the hill, one of which was responsible for the seasonal dampness of the path. Others fed into the pond, creating an almost perfect circle of limpid dark water. Fringed by gently waving reed mace and yellow flags, it was sheltered by large oaks and sycamores, and they called it the Snake Pond because long dark snakes were often to be seen slithering in the water or wriggling through the tangle of weeds in the silty shallows.

It was the brothers' favourite haunt, rich with dragonflies, damselflies, water boatmen, pond skaters, newts, diving beetles, whirligig beetles, water spiders and frogs. Robbie collected all of these from the pond, often carrying them home in matchboxes and jars to the horror of their older sister. His accomplice in this, as in so much in his life, was Jonathan.

He'd never known a time without his brother; two years and eight months older, a foot taller and fully twice his weight, and yet still just a child-boy, Jonathan's benign companionship was an enduring constant of Robbie's childhood years. Yet it was Robbie who was charged by their parents with the responsibility for their joint activities, not he.

Following the warm dry spell that July had brought, the pond had shrunk by nearly a third but there lay a large log, sun-aged to a silvery smoothness, half-submerged giving access to the deeper water in the middle. They crawled along it and settled down.

It was a warm, still evening, golden light illuminating the myriads of insects that shimmered and darted above the water. Swallows skimmed amongst them, feeding with ease. The brothers gazed down into the water, shielding their eyes from the low sun that sent oblique shafts of light into the murky depths.

'Pond skaters,' Robbie pointed out.

'Lots,' said Jonathan, nodding vigorously and causing the log to rock.

They watched as the pond skaters effortlessly skimmed the surface on the tiny indentations made by their feet. Robbie, at the further end of the log, stretched out his fingers into the cooling water, combing the weeds for creatures, disturbing water boatmen and diving beetles. Jonathan scooped three up in his large hands but, as there were already several in a tank at home, Robbie told him to let them go. What he really wanted was a Great Silver Water Beetle, but so far they'd had no success.

Once last summer they'd seen one but hadn't manage to catch it; not even Jonathan, with his big hands and long arms, although frankly he wasn't very quick.

The swallows came down again, diving low over their heads hunting for the flying insects drifting lazily in the warmth of the evening air, but they scarcely bothered, so great was the bounty. Suddenly Jonathan lurched, rocking the log under his weight so that Robbie's sandals dipped into the water. He was holding up a wriggling newt, triumphant.

'A newt, Robbie!' he cried, eyes shining with delight.

Robbie had caught several newts before, but didn't want to disappoint his brother. Besides, they'd got nothing else that evening and so they carefully slid the creature into the jam jar and watched him as he curled himself around, bracing his feet against the glass, peering back at them with his throat slowly pulsing.

'He looks happy, doesn't he?' said Jonathan with satisfaction.

After this they'd lain back on the grass at the edge of the pond, watching the dipping and diving swallows.

'I'm going to ask Mum for a net,' Robbie remarked, and flung a pebble at the pale circle of a sawn-off branch that hung from the ancient stag-headed oak opposite, missing it by miles. His brother took up the challenge, scooping up a pebble from the dried-out pond edge and flinging it with all the strength of his sturdy arm and thick-set shoulder.

They played this game often, using the circle as a target, and it was Jonathan who was far superior; big for his age, well-built and with a strong throw. His first shot fell short, into the grass, while Robbie's next hit the knobbly trunk, too low down.

Jonathan sucked in his breath. Robbie flung another, a big looping shot that weakly struck the branch above. He needed to raise his game and hunted around for the perfect pebble. He soon found one; not too heavy, not too small that weighed just right in his hand. Standing to take aim he squinted to get the line right, threw his arm over and the pebble flew wide, landing with a feeble plop amongst the reeds. Jonathan rocked back on his heels, laughing his strange braying sound.

'Got you now, Robbie,' he said, clutching his chosen pebble and squatting on his haunches.

He took aim and Robbie knew he was done for. A strong jabbing throw from the shoulder just like a baseball pitcher, the shot flew straight to its target, the perfect lob. Jonathan flung his arms out to the sky in silent triumph, mouth open in celebration as the pebble ricocheted off the tree and away to one side.

A sudden noise made them both jump. A stocky lad, a couple of years older than Robbie, burst from the undergrowth, red-faced under his tightly-curled ginger hair, briskly rubbing one temple. It was Malcolm Draycott, and he clearly wasn't happy.

This wasn't good. Bigger, older and a great deal tougher than either of them, Malcolm was someone Robbie wasn't eager to encounter. A regular playground tormentor, Malcolm enjoyed inflicting his size and roughness on weaker boys with shameless spite. He hung out with the sons of other farming families from Rushwood End and, together they had a deserved reputation for bullying, something they were invariably keen to uphold. The Bradbury brothers and their friends had as little to do with them as possible.

A pang of fear gripped Robbie at suddenly coming face-to-face with Malcolm when no one else was around, especially as Malcolm had just been struck by Jonathan's pebble.

'Hello,' he said warily, in the hope of deflecting any aggression.

Malcolm grunted, looking around in surprise and discomfit, confused and puzzled by the stinging blow that had left his temple smarting. He hadn't expected to meet anyone on the route down to the village when he'd stumbled from the long grass, and he now found the two brothers on the path blocking his way past the pond.

Seeing Malcolm approach, and afraid it would be knocked over, Jonathan took up the newt jar and abruptly stood up, clasping it. He was the same age as Malcolm and even bigger in size but, by complete contrast, his demeanour was, as ever, placid and unruffled.

Hesitating, and unable to proceed, Malcolm halted and glanced at them both with an expression of malevolence that was mixed with confusion and pain. Still seated on the grass at Jonathan's feet, Robbie felt a sense of dread for what the next few moments would bring. Grasping at something, anything, on which to vent his anger, Malcolm jabbed a finger at the jar which was safely clutched aloft in Jonathan's large fist.

'What's that?'

'It's a newt. I caught it for Robbie,' Jonathan proudly smiled, holding the jar in front of his head so that one of his eyes suddenly appeared round and fish-like through the curvature.

There was a pause as Malcolm attempted to digest the information. 'What for?' he barked, a little breathless.

At their feet Robbie stayed silent, wishing to melt away into the long grass. Malcolm wasn't the sort of boy you could talk to about collecting beetles and wildlife, and he wasn't going to try and explain now. But unfortunately, Jonathan was.

'Robbie collects newts, and he collects frogs and beetles, and we take them home, and he puts them in the tank in the lean-to. And he collects pond skaters... and diving beetles and....'

Jonathan was beaming, happily relating their shared pastime. He hadn't even got onto the dragonflies, water spiders and caddis flies, never mind the Great Silver Water Beetle – although no doubt he would, given the chance – when he was suddenly interrupted by Malcolm Draycott who, unable to further contain himself, had buckled under the grip of mirth, his upper body folding abruptly forwards.

'Robbie collects newts, Robbie collects frogs!' Malcolm mimicked, cackling scornfully. 'Robbie-frog, Beetle-Bradbury!'

Jonathan flushed a deep crimson, and purple blotches bloomed on his cheeks. 'Don't laugh, d-don't laugh at Robbie,' he stammered. 'It's... not nice. You mustn't call him names!'

'Robbie-frog, frog-faced frog, Beetle-Bradbury!' mocked Malcolm.

'It's alright,' said Robbie, rising and backing away to let Malcolm past and out of their way. He tried to pull Jonathan aside, but he was by now too upset and outraged; heedless of any danger, or of Robbie's attempt to evade further interaction with Malcolm.

'Don't you say that,' Jonathan chided. He looked bewildered, but his thoughts were very clear. 'Don't you say that!'

Malcolm stared. Not many people took him on. 'You dumbo,' he sneered into Jonathan's face. 'Simpleton. You're a spaz, you are!'

'Come on, Jonathan,' Robbie urged, tugging again at his brother's shirt, fear now gripping at his insides.

'Don't you talk to my brother like that,' Jonathan persevered, impervious to the danger. 'My brother... he knows about... beetles... and things,' and finally with exultant pride, 'He's clever!'

This was too much for Malcolm. He lunged forwards, snarling, 'You're a weirdo!' and snatched at the newt jar, knocking it clean out of Jonathan's hand, sending it flying to the ground where it tumbled, spilling both newt and water onto the grass.

Jonathan reeled back, shocked and upset, unable to speak. Seizing his opportunity, Malcolm stormed past kicking the empty jar into the pond and, as a last furious gesture, shoved at Jonathan's chest. Unbalanced, Jonathan teetered at the water's edge, then stepped backwards into the soft mud which held him tight so that he sank down in the water onto his haunches in silent surprise, unable to move either forwards or back.

'It's alright Robbie,' he reassured as the ripples of water settled back around him. 'It's alright. He's gone. He's gone away now.'

Robbie paddled in, grasped his brother's big hand and hauled him to his feet. The two of them picked their way out, surveying each other's dripping trousers, Jonathan's wet to the waist and black with foul-smelling pond mud.

'Mum won't be pleased,' Robbie remarked, and knew that to be an understatement.

'It'll be alright, Robbie,' Jonathan reassured him once again. 'It's alright.'

That Malcolm henceforth took on the role of their childhood arch-enemy was perhaps largely attributable to this one chance encounter on a glorious summer evening. Anxious, lest he should now be lying in wait at The Green with the other farm boys, Robbie and Jonathan ducked round by the Church once more to avoid being seen, and then ran back across Church Piece towards home. Jonathan's wet and muddy trousers made a loud flapping noise, clinging to his chunky legs as he ran, and their shoes squelched unpleasantly. Once home, they went straight to the back of the cottage. The shed door was open, so Robbie knew their father was still down at the allotments, and he could hear their mother safely indoors talking to a neighbour.

Quickly he kicked off his shoes, pulled Jonathan's off and then his trousers and ushered him swiftly upstairs. 'Quick, have a bath,' he said.

'I had one three days ago,' Jonathan complained.

'Doesn't matter,' Robbie urged, trying to get him to hurry. 'Go on, your bum's all muddy!' he shoved him into the bathroom and turned on the bath taps, and then ran back downstairs.

'Is that you two?' their mother called.

'Yes. Jonathan's upstairs washing.'

'Get ready for bed. I'll see you shortly,' she said.

First of all he had to deal with the evidence and crept back outside where their four shoes and Jonathan's trousers were heaped in a brown muddy pile, oozing pond water. He quickly scooped water from the greenhouse butt into the tin bath, plunged everything in together and swirled them about, turning the water into a thick brown muddy soup. Carefully he flung the mucky water onto the grass where it wouldn't be noticed and sploshed another can full in. That just about did it and he propped the shoes up where he hoped they'd dry overnight. He squeezed the grubby water from the trousers and raced upstairs two at a time. In the bath Jonathan was happy as Larry, whistling loudly to himself. Robbie hung the trousers over the back of the bedroom chair to dry and went into the bathroom to get ready for bed.

'Malcolm's not a very nice boy,' said Jonathan from the steaming bath before resuming his cheery whistling.

***

The following morning Robbie Bradbury stood outside the left-hand side of a pair of plain brick Victorian semi-detached houses beside The Green. It was never a homely-looking house, with heavily-curtained windows and drab paint, and seemed out of keeping with the other largely old houses and cottages which surrounded it. The day was warm again but cloudy and heavy, which only added to Robbie's sense of unease as he hung back, kicking at the daisies, delaying the moment when he'd have to go in.

Finally, he rapped on the door, listening to the hollow sound of the heavy brass knocker echoing along the hallway within. Footsteps sounded and Violet Ward pulled open the front door, revealing an inhospitably bare and rather dim hall, with a narrow faded carpet which formed a strip along the dark linoleum. In her early sixties and with already greying hair, she had a thin, rather pinched face onto which an expression of resignation had settled. Childless, she was now widowed too.

'Robbie,' she said with a movement about her mouth that indicated a slight smile, 'Come in.'

He stepped unwillingly into the gloomy unwelcoming passage, conscious of a certain kind of damp, stale smell that he recognised from older people's houses. There was no sound from within, no sign of another soul there. He stood awkwardly.

'Go in.' She motioned towards the dining room, which led off from the hall at the rear, and as she did so the crêpey flesh on her upper arms waggled.

Robbie pushed open the door and stepped uneasily into a small old-fashioned room where, seated at a square table against the wall, was a short dark-haired boy.

'Robbie, this is my great nephew, John; John, here is Robbie Bradbury I spoke to you about.'

She held Robbie behind the shoulder and he felt she must know that, given the chance, he'd back out.

'I'll get you both some squash and you can have a chat and get to know each other,' she said.

Left alone, John Norbert and Robbie Bradbury surveyed one another in silence. John was seated sideways on a wooden dining chair with one arm draped over the back and, despite the warm weather and school holidays, was dressed in dark school trousers and a long-sleeved shirt which, being far too large, made him appear even more under-sized than he actually was. His thin legs dangled and he wore heavily scuffed shoes. He gazed steadily back at Robbie, dense currant-like eyes almost hidden by the coarse dark hair that tousled messily about his small, creased face.

Suddenly he spoke. 'Wotcha!' and he winked. The monkey-boy winked at Robbie, and his little face crumpled into a puckish grin.

'Play cards?' he asked in a strange hoarse voice that seemed too old to come from one so small, and in one hand he held up a deck.

Robbie climbed onto the empty chair alongside and watched as John skilfully dealt two hands and then schooled Robbie as he played his first-ever game of Rummy. John won and, remembering that occasion in later years, Robbie couldn't be sure that John hadn't cheated. In fact, knowing him better by then, was almost certain that he'd done so, but on this occasion he'd let Robbie win a hand near the end and seemed almost as pleased as he was.

Violet Ward brought them lunch of boiled eggs and bread and butter, which drew a halt to their card playing session. John ate noisily and savagely and then turned to his visitor.

'Where'd ya live then?'

Robbie had never heard anyone speak as this odd boy did, rough and harsh-sounding, the words twisted and chopped and then spat out as if discarded.

He nodded his head in the direction of home. 'Round the corner, on the lane; Woodbine Cottage. What about you?' He was curious to know.

'Cricklewood.' This meant as much to Robbie as Timbuktu but he was a little reassured when the boy added, 'Railway Terrace.' That at least was understandable.

'Does your Dad work on the railway then?'

But John merely passed over the question. 'Sor'a. Yours?'

'He works for Mr Harrison-Bates.'

'Wha's tha'?'

'He's a gardener up at the big house in Netherington.'

'Uh.' John greedily polished off a fourth chunk of bread and then slid off the chair, seemingly unimpressed or disinterested. Indeed, how could he understand this so-different world.

'You boys can get down now,' called Violet from the kitchen, rather pointlessly. She knew Robbie was a responsible boy with a reputation for being sensible. After all, he took care of that poor idiot brother of his.

John jerked his head, indicating for the other to follow, and they went out into the small back garden. 'Wha' goes on round 'ere, then?' he asked expectantly, and with a contained restlessness.

Robbie was unsure what to say, or how to impress this newcomer; or even whether he wanted to impress him. Did he really want to spend his holiday with this strange boy?

'Oh, stuff,' he shrugged.

'You got many mates?'

'Six or seven I suppose.'

Without further comment, John unlatched the side gate and slipped out. 'You comin' then?'

'Shouldn't we tell Mrs Ward we're going out?'

'She knows,' was all he said.

It was quiet around The Green that afternoon, and Robbie was relieved not to see any of his friends and have to explain about his charge. He wasn't sure they'd understand, but he also had no idea how to interest John or what to do with him. He led the way past Morris's the Greengrocers and crossed over the lane at the bottom of The Green towards Lower Farm.

'Fancy a look at the animals?' he asked, noticing that John was now devouring an apple that resembled those on Morris's outdoor display.

John made a noise that may or may not have been agreement, so Robbie led the way into the farmyard anyway and peered over one of the stable doors where he often came to see the horses. None were inside today, so he skirted the old wooden barn and approached the pig sties on the far side of the yard. By now John was hanging back, gnawing on the apple core, displaying an air of casual indifference.

'Here! Look,' called Robbie clambering up to look over the sty wall.

Four large black-spotted gingery sows lay side-by-side, like sausages in a pan, quietly snoring in the warm fetid air within. John yanked himself up alongside, arms flung over the top of the wall to hold himself in place, his feet scrabbling for a foothold.

'Phwoah!' he yelled, gripping his nose. 'Wodda bleedin' pong!'

As one, the pigs leapt to their feet, snorting and squealing in alarm, peering back at them with startled eyes beneath flopping ears.

'Ugh,' John cried, face contorted in disgust as he leapt back from the wall.

Stung on their behalf, and rather wounded by this brutal rebuttal of his attempt at entertainment, Robbie stammered out, 'They don't mean any harm.'

'Yuk! Shitty stink!' John croaked, shuddering.

'Actually, pigs are very clean, and they're very clever animals too,' but this wasn't going to hold sway with John, who by now was making theatrical gagging noises.

The farm geese, alerted by all the noise, came strutting round the corner of the sty, heads lowered and honking aggressively. John saw them and leapt away so fast that he stumbled, sprawling backwards onto the ground and, with the geese bearing down on him, scuttled away like a crab, emitting a frightened wailing noise.

He'd now got himself cornered between the sty and midden wall, so Robbie grabbed a pitchfork from the manure pile and brandished it at the troop who had now turned to scold him instead. The geese had the boys pinned against the walls and kept up such a racket that the farmer's wife soon emerged from the farmhouse carrying a broom and, with practised efficiency, shooed them all away.

'Stupid things,' she tutted. 'Come on now, you boys. You're not up to mischief are you?'

'Sorry Mrs Hobbs, no,' said Robbie, and the two retreated from the farmyard, keeping a wary eye on the gaggle of departing geese who now bustled importantly back to their pond.

Robbie really didn't know what to do after that and, in need of moral support, suggested they go to see a friend. John shrugged compliance and followed in silence the short distance to Wheelwrights where Lizzie Rose lived. Robbie knew it would be tricky explaining to her how he came to be in the company of the monkey-boy that they'd all sought yesterday but, if anyone could make the best of a situation, she could. Lizzie was rarely angry and invariably saw the bright side of things. That was why he liked her.

Wheelwrights was a large brick-noggin and timber-frame house, still the village wheelwrights, and with a range of old workshops set around a rear yard. It was here that Lizzie's father Joe Rose and his brother Ted worked, mostly as Carpenters by that time, but their father and Grandfather before had all been the village wheelwright as long as anyone could remember.

Hearing voices, Robbie led the way round to the yard where they found all the men of the Rose family at work; Lizzie's father Joe, her Grandpa, her Uncle Ted and her older brother Ron.

To Robbie's immense relief, they'd arrived just as the Rose's were about to fit a new wooden wheel, which was laid out on the ground in readiness. The three men were tending a fire in which the metal rim rested, heated to a deep ochre red. About them the air was full of blue smoke, and the acrid smell of hot metal drifted across the yard. Robbie gestured John should go over to the workshop to watch from a safe distance, grateful for the diversion. With all the superior maturity of his sixteen years, Ron stood in the doorway, leaning sullenly against the door jamb, hands thrust deep into his trouser pockets. He grunted acknowledgement, barely glancing at the boys. He wasn't blessed with Lizzie's sunny outlook on life, or her friendly open face.

The two boys watched in silent absorption as the metal rim, glowing wine red, was lifted carefully and slipped over the wooden wheel. Sizzling flames encircled it, sending the smell of singeing wood to their nostrils. Robbie was aware of John leaning forwards for a better look, his face tense with studied concentration. Ron Rose pushed himself off from the door frame with a careless lunge of the shoulder and Lizzie's Uncle Ted threw the first bucket of water over the wheel. With a great whoosh and hissing, a cloud of steam enveloped the three men. Ron dipped a bucket in the water trough and threw its contents over, followed by her father and Uncle who emerged in turn from the steam cloud to dip and throw, dip and throw, sending hissing cloud after hissing cloud into the air.

Somewhere in the midst, with his unlit pipe, her Grandpa banged and hammered the cooling, contracting rim over the wooden wheel which creaked and groaned within it.

John crept forward, his eyes fixed on the men working in rhythm; banging and sloshing, steam rising and hissing.

'Woah!' he whispered.

'Nearly there, lads,' said Grandpa Rose, talking not to the boys, but to his own sons, who remained mere boys to him. A few more taps and bangs as the steam subsided and they all stood back to survey their work. He pulled the wheel upright, checking it, and then Ted rolled it to the shed where he propped it up.

Grandpa clapped and rubbed his hands together. 'Time for a brew, boys!' Walking briskly towards the house he called back over his shoulder, 'Put the fire out, Ron.'

Joe Rose stroked down his overalls. 'Lizzie's gone to Cullingham with her Mum, Robbie. Back shortly, I reckon. Coming in for a cuppa?'

He didn't know it then, but being invited into this circle of working men as if it were the most natural thing, which indeed it was amongst the village families, sealed Robbie's reputation with John. The two boys followed the men into the spacious old kitchen where Ted filled the kettle and placed it on the range, and the men sank into creaking chairs around the large pine kitchen table. Stretching out their heavy boots, their large grimed hands placed on the smooth-worn surface, leaving Ron to make the tea. Another reason to be sullen.

Grandpa knocked out his pipe on the table edge. 'Reg'll be happy with that.'

'It went well.'

'It did.'

'There'll be another one next week if Jones's comes off.'

'That's what he says. Timber's coming Tuesday any rate, I told Saddlers'. Soon as that's in we can get started on their job.'

'Get yourselves a seat boys.' Joe Rose waved a broad hand towards the spare chairs.

'Anyway, Taylors are coming in whatever. I gave them the quote. You know what he's like, always the wink. I'll get the frames ready in the next few days.'

'Catch him paying on time!'

Grandpa Rose broke off and leaned forwards to John. 'Bet you've never seen that before, eh lad? Not like it was, though. I did several a week with my Dad when I started, ain't that right, Joe?'

'Changing times now, father,' Joe replied.

Ron produced the teapot and cups.

'And the biscuits, lad. Don't forget the biscuits,' ordered Grandpa with a conspiratorial wink towards the boys, enjoying the opportunity to play to a new audience. John's eyes followed the packet of ginger nuts around the table as it was passed first amongst the men and then to Ron.

'Here you go,' and Joe Rose pushed them across the table. Like the men, Robbie dipped one in his tea and sucked the spicy, gingery sogginess. John hadn't said a word, but watched from the corner of his eyes and then he dipped his into his tea also.

They listened as the men talked about work and people, their loud rumbling voices and laughter filling the kitchen, the smell of smoke still clinging to their overalls, until the door from the yard opened and Lizzie and her mother stepped in. Lizzie, somewhat smaller than Robbie, had a tanned oval face and long ash blond hair in plaits. She was always lively with a restless energy, her open expressive countenance a window to a carefree nature. He enjoyed the companionship of other boys, but he was always grateful for Lizzie's enduring friendship.

She saw Robbie first, and then her eyes fell on John and she realised with astonishment that this was the monkey-boy, seated here in her own kitchen, and with her best friend. Her expression revealed her inner questions of how? and why?.

Hearing Lizzie's sharp intake of breath, Robbie tried to avoid her questioning gaze, her eyes wide beneath her level eyebrows. He merely shrugged, helplessly and wordlessly.

'This is John,' Grandpa announced, speaking to her over his shoulder. 'Come and say hello, Lizzie.'

She walked stiffly to the table and murmured a greeting to John, who replied, 'Wotcha,' in his odd gruff voice, which made all the adults laugh and both John and Lizzie squirm with embarrassment.

Her mother interrupted, nodding up at the clock. 'Don't you be late home, Robbie.'

Thankful for a reason to escape and be relieved of his charge, Robbie slid from the chair, with John following.

Lizzie sidled up to him. 'I'll walk along with you,' she said, eyes still determinedly questioning his.

They crossed the yard in silence, John loped ungainly ahead on his thin, sinewy legs. Robbie walked so briskly that Lizzie had to trip along to keep pace, all the while nudging him firmly, her eyes fixed on his face, compelling him to explain, and she continued to press her elbow into his ribs as they walked. He tried to ignore her, not knowing what to say or how to explain the situation, and unable to speak without John overhearing.

They approached Mrs Patterson's sweet shop at the corner and, with dismay, Robbie recognised the familiar figure of Malcolm Draycott. He was unmistakeable with his ginger hair and lumbering walk, and he was approaching rapidly from Station Road. After the previous evening's episode, Robbie really didn't want to get involved with him again. Whispering urgently to Lizzie to follow, he tried to edge into the shop doorway and out of sight, but his efforts were thwarted by a group of older children who just then emerged from the shop, forcing the two of them back out onto the pavement and in full view.

Robbie earnestly hoped they'd escaped Malcolm attentions, but he'd already been spotted. As Malcolm strode across the lane, he abruptly veered from his route and lunged at the pair of them, sneering right into Robbie's face, 'Fat frog!'

Behind him, Robbie heard the other children's callous laughter and cringed with shame.

A few steps ahead, sensing that his new companions had stopped, John had turned and had witnessed the incident. A short way from him, Malcolm was now marching on, leering back over his shoulder, savouring the effect of his remarks on the unexpected and appreciative audience outside the shop.

For a moment, John followed him with his small eyes and then he bellowed after him, 'Ginger nuts! Ya've got big great 'airy ginger ones, ya bleedin' tosser!'

The group outside the shop exploded with bawdy laughter. Even Lizzie clapped a hand over her mouth, astonished giggles spluttering through her fingers.

II

'Shweeeeeoooo!'

Robbie was almost home when his father swept past, whistling a greeting with his usual fluting call, already half-dismounted as he swung the pushbike into the side passage. By the time Robbie had entered the back garden, the noises from inside the shed confirmed his father was in there, putting the bike away while, from behind the latched kitchen door, came the comforting smells of cooking.

In the back room seated at the dining table, Jonathan was deeply absorbed in his favourite pastime of drawing aeroplanes. He had a compulsive fascination for them and would spend many hours at a time drawing different models, having memorised all their names and details and could draw each with extraordinary accuracy.

The boys' bedroom wall was covered with his drawings, each one meticulous and conscientiously signed 'Jonathan' in his thick child-like scrawl. Robbie never understood how it was that his brother could draw so precisely and yet write little better than a child of half his eleven years. But, of course he did know why and, in knowing, was expected to be part of that adult world of forbearance.

Tom Bradbury came in, face weather-worn and leathery, typical of a man who'd spent his working life out of doors, bringing about him the smell of his day's work on his clothes and person. He ruffled his younger son's hair and slumped into the fireside armchair, snapping open the day's newspaper.

'How's my special boy then?'

This was his familiar greeting to Jonathan, who made his customary braying noise and continued drawing, fully engrossed. The kitchen door opened a crack releasing steam and the enticing smells of grilling chops into the room, reminding them all that they were hungry.

'Food in ten minutes,' called Sally and, as they all settled into the quiet and contented anticipation of their evening meal, the lean-to door abruptly slammed open announcing Susan, the brothers' elder sister, who bursting in, flung her duffle bag to the floor.

'Miss Sandford says my pliés are the best in the class!' she announced to no one in particular and began to demonstrate, dipping down with knees splayed, arms held wide and, not waiting for a response, flitted about the room flinging her legs and arms about. She hummed an accompaniment and adopted a sort of dreamy expression as she wafted back and forth in a fashion that she imagined made her look like a ballerina.

Undeterred that her performance brought no response, Susan pirouetted until dizzy and then stumbled into the dining table, scattering Jonathan's pencils. Imperturbable, he heaved a sigh and wordlessly retrieved them. Calm tolerance was an abiding feature of his personality.

There never was a greater contrast between the siblings than at that time. Susan, at almost thirteen, newly conscious of how she might appear to the outside world, was self-absorbed, preening and brash, and no longer a child. While Jonathan and Robbie resembled their mother's side of the family, brown haired and tending to be thick-set. Susan, like their father, was spare of build and with his conspicuous dark hair. Yet while Tom had given much of his mild and measured nature to Jonathan, Susan was quick of movement, talkative and extrovert, ever a firework in their midst.

Home was Woodbine Cottage, a low white-washed, part-timbered building with an undulating red-tiled roof and ground floor windows set low in the thick front walls. About 300 years old, according to the date 1681 set above the front door, the old cottage was only two rooms wide, with the 'best room' to one side and the dining room to the other with a later kitchen and lean-to added to the rear. The front door opened directly from the lane to a small entrance lobby between the two main rooms, but only strangers ever used that. Everyone else came down the side passage to the back garden and entered through the glazed lean-to, straight into the dining room.

The cottage was on Main Street, the primary lane in Moreton Steyning which linked the large triangular Green and Church at one end of the village with The Square, where most of the shops could be found, at the other.

Like most of the older houses in the village, the cottage had a large garden with flower beds; an aged apple tree, damson and pear trees, a soft fruit garden with blackcurrants, gooseberries and loganberries, and a garden shed with a greenhouse, a rickety timber log store and an old brick outhouse.

Tom Bradbury spent his working life growing and tending flowers and vegetables up at the big house, and yet he still took great pride in the tomatoes that he cultivated in the greenhouse, and the vegetables and potatoes which provided for the family from their nearby allotment.

He came not from Moreton Steyning, but from nearby Netherington. His own father had worked all his life as a gardener for the Harrison-Bates family at Netherington Hall and, at 14, he'd joined him there. Now he cycled the two miles each day along the Sheep Path, a grassy bridleway between fields, on his daily journey to the Hall. While once there had been six full-time gardeners and a boy, now there was only Mr Higgins, Old Man Frobisher who couldn't see much anyway, and himself. He would say, there's always plenty to do up there, but it wasn't kept like it was in father's day when everything was immaculate, all the edges clipped just so and the bedding-out changed two or three times a season, and the pots washed and scrubbed by the boy every winter. In those days house parties were a regular feature, with more than a dozen guests to stay at weekends, and each Christmas a big party for the staff and villagers to which everyone was invited. But times had changed.

'My old Dad would turn in his grave if he could see the daisies in the lawns,' Tom would ruefully be heard to comment.

His life was up there in that garden, season upon season, performing the annual rituals.

Sally Bradbury had grown up in Moreton Steyning. Her father was the village shoemaker with a shop in The Square which her brother now ran, although he was simply mending and selling shoes these days, and no longer making them. The daughter of a local tradesman, she was the powerhouse of the Bradbury family; a true force of nature.

On the mantelpiece was a small photograph, taken at Moreton Steyning Fair in 1935. Tom was standing in his best double-breasted Sunday suit and Sally wearing a new floral print frock. They stood awkwardly next to each other in front of a coconut shy, smiling a little self-consciously, their shoulders almost touching. They'd just met and he held the teddy bear he'd won and was about to present to her. Two years later they would marry.

***

Dinner was Barnsley chops with new potatoes and peas from the allotment, and then a big jam tart with strips of pastry separating the segments; strawberry jam, bramble jelly and lemon curd. Jonathan thumped the table to show his enthusiasm, drawing a frowning look from his mother as the custard jug wobbled perilously.

That night, after a week of warm sultry days, the weather broke. At first the air seemed to thicken and the light over the garden turned gloomy. Tom had opened the lean-to door to let in some air and relieve the closeness indoors.

'Looks like we're in for some rain,' Sally said, looking over her shoulder to the dimming garden.

'It's been coming all day,' he replied, and nodded his head towards the fireplace above which hung his father's barometer. 'Pressure's dropped.'

Just as he spoke, a wind blew the lean-to door shut and sent the garden plants all a-shuddering.

'It's black as night up there!' Susan said, pointing to beyond the shed roof.

With that, the first flash of lightening seared through the room's gloom and her shriek was drowned by the boom of thunder rattling the window panes. A few moments silence, then the first heavy drops threw up puffs of dust on the bone-dry paving outside. Without warning, the real rain came, straight down, drumming on the lean-to and shed roofs, bouncing up off the paths and turning the windows into rippling sheets of water. Jonathan jumped up and pulled the outside door firmly shut.

Susan dropped down under the table wailing, where she remained hugging Digby, but Jonathan and Robbie stood in the lean-to watching the rain which was now flooding across the paving and flowing into the side passage. Tom joined them and put a hand on each of their shoulders.

'No play outside this evening, lads.'

***

It rained on and off throughout the night, each new downpour preceded by a breathless empty silence, and then came the sssshhhhh of falling night rain. They lay in bed listening to it.

All the next morning it rained so that they couldn't go outside. Susan went off to visit a friend, but the boys stayed at home where Jonathan was quickly absorbed in drawing planes and Robbie mounted insects on cards for his collection. Outside, the rainfall was steady and incessant and the sky grey and closed-in.

By early afternoon Robbie was bored, tired of being indoors, and restless. He sat in the armchair by the dining room front window with his book open on his lap, unread. Digby lay on the mat, for all the world asleep, but one ear was raised and occasionally flickered. Dogs always know when it's too wet to bother going out, but they never miss a trick either.

He turned a few pages of his book; a cartoon annual he'd read so many times that each drawing was imprinted on his memory, and their facial expressions and actions all frozen in an instant of time, seemed as real as life to him when he suddenly realised that the light coming from the window behind was different. A soft yellow luminosity now bloomed turning the grey world back into colour. Below the heavy clouds a narrow band of blue held the horizon and was flooding the village with a low afternoon sun. Within minutes, the fences were steaming and the birds had burst into song.

Robbie leapt to his feet and Digby flipped up like a fish.

'Sun's out!'

'Jonathan's coming with me to Uncle Arn's,' his mother said. 'He keeps outgrowing his shoes, and just about everything else,' she muttered, checking her bag and purse. 'You can go out if you want.'

He splashed across the lane, still running with water, and ran up Snail Path, a steep sunken route which ascended behind Morris's, Violet Ward's and the other houses on that side of The Green, towards the playground by the top lane. The path had acquired its name from the handsome banded snails which could always be found clinging to the vegetation on its high banks.

They were all at the playground: Maggie and Ann, Lizzie, Nid and Finch, plus several older kids from the village, all anxious not to waste any time in getting back out of doors. Lizzie and Nid were on the swings. At the roundabout, Finch was furiously scooting with Ann crouched in the middle while Maggie, clinging with her feet on the running board, swung out with her hair and skirts sweeping the ground. Ann waved, her small form rotating so fast that she couldn't hold her arm up. Nid took a dramatic leap from his swing and ran towards Robbie.

'Where is he?' he cried. Clearly Lizzie had wasted no time in updating everyone.

'Robbie says he talks different.' Lizzie had scampered over, anxious not to miss any revelations.

'Oh, he's alright, I suppose,' said Robbie. 'He showed me how to play Rummies.'

'What's Rummies?' Maggie had also joined them, along with the other two.

'It's a card game,' Nid answered. 'Our Dad plays it.'

'Anyway, he's not a monkey at all,' Lizzie confided. 'He had tea at our house, and Uncle Ted said he looked like a "right little tyke".' She repeated this adult-speak, looking round at the others from beneath her eyelashes to determine its effect.

'Did he do something wrong?' asked Ann, seeking either reassurance or confirmation. She was made anxious by any sense of doubt.

'Don't think so,'

'Yes he did,' Lizzie exclaimed, springing up and down, eager to impart her knowledge. 'He shouted something ever so rude to Malcolm Draycott!'

This grabbed everyone's attention because Malcolm, with a reputation for bullying, wasn't popular with any of them, and they all crowded in while Robbie related the encounter outside Mrs Patterson's. Maggie clapped her hands laughing, Ann coloured and Nid and Finch elbowed each other, sniggering.

The incident was forgotten while they all raced around splashing one another in puddles until eventually they grew bored and, at someone's suggestion, wandered off in the direction of the hill, along the upper section of Snail Path. Here they were halted in their tracks by the unexpected sight of John Norbert ahead, furiously busy.

Swollen by the hours of heavy rain, the ditch by the upper lane had burst its banks and a slurry of muddy water was beginning to eddy down the path. With great energy and concentration, and despite his small size, John was heaving rocks and stones from the path-side bank into the course of the water, forming a channel for it to run along.

'Quick!' he urged without looking up.

They all began to rip out more rocks, turfs, rubble, and bits of branch from the undergrowth on the bank and hedge-base at its crest; anything they could gather up using their bare hands. In no time their shoes and socks were wet and muddy, but no one noticed in their determination to control the surge of water that was growing ever stronger and deeper all the time.

John stood back barking instructions on where to concentrate efforts. Every few minutes a new surge of water would break through the barrier further up, and they would have to send someone with reinforcements to make good as the speed of water increased, sending leaves and twigs swirling within it.

Sometimes the angle of the path kept it within bounds, allowing them to hurry ahead and prepare their dams for the encroaching tide. They spoke hardly a word that wasn't necessary, working effortlessly as a team, with John and Maggie directing and alerting others to points of weakness, or sources of material for their barriers.

John ran to the top, then back down to the frontline, breathless and concentrated, checking everything. Suddenly, he plunged into the bank further down, hauling out several large rocks with quick unexpected strength, then ran up to the top of the bank, from where he flung down a big branch retrieved from the base of the hedge.

"Ere!' he called to Robbie, struggling bow-legged, face reddening with the effort, and launched a large rock into the centre of the swirling stream so that it sent a great spray of water up his legs. Robbie beckoned to the twins and the three of them helped to haul the other rocks to where John directed, some of which took two to lift.

He jammed the log between the rocks and began to rip grass and scoop earth from the bank to fill the holes between. The others splashed their way down and, all working together, soon made a reasonably watertight bund which began to turn the tide from its helter-skelter downward rush.

They watched with speechless fascination while the levels rose, breathlessly checking to see if the wall would hold. Within minutes, the water had created an eddying pool with leaves crazily circling until finally it took its new route, away from the downward slope of Snail Path and into the back yard of Morris's Greengrocers.

It swept across the cobbles where it paused and collected, rising inexorably, then tipped over the two steps down into the storeroom and shop level, quickly picking up speed, and then fanned out across the shop floor. John's face was all studied concentration, showing no sign of emotion. Lizzie glanced uncertainly at Robbie and then, as one, they raced down Snail Path and round to The Green. As they arrived, water was lapping over the front step and Ken Morris could be heard from inside shouting, followed by a shriek from his wife who was looking out from the living room window above.

John plunged into the shop, emerging a few seconds later, staggering, red faced and eyes bulging under the weight of a table laden with tomatoes and lettuce. Maggie rushed in next with Ann, and they emerged with baskets of eggs and oranges. John had gone back in again when Morris blustered out, hauling a trestle of beetroots and celery with the help of a customer. The rest of them then sploshed in. The water was over their shoes and swirling through with astonishing speed.

Inside was a chaotic scene with Mrs Morris, panicked and trying to retrieve dropped items, while the rest of them struggled to lift display tables and manoeuvre them through the door, where the flood water was spilling over the step and out along the lane, finally gushing into the gutters by The Green.

Eventually everything was brought out, tables were placed on the road and grass, toppled fruit and cabbages abandoned on the ground, where they'd been trodden and slipped on. The water began eventually to subside, no doubt having broken through John's dam, when other people arrived, alerted by all the shouting and activity and began to take over, using their brooms to sweep away the water and debris. Morris and his wife were looking shell-shocked and astonished, but thanked their rescuers and told each to help themselves to an apple or orange.

The gang wandered away to the top of The Green, where they could look down on the chaotic scene, and sat on the grass to enjoy their fruit. John kicked out his legs and fell back, pilfered cherries and part-pulped strawberries spilling from his trouser pockets, and a hoarse laugh, far too big and gruff for his wiry frame, burst from his throat. The others also lay back gazing at the sky, and laughed until tears ran down their faces.

From that day on, John Norbert threw in his lot with the friends.

III

For a few days they avoided The Green, just in case anyone should associate their presence there with the day of the flood at Morris's, but they needn't have worried, the force of the water had quickly swept away their handiwork, and any suspicion of mischief fell on several older boys who'd been spotted at the playground shortly before.

In fact, several days of ditch and drain-clearing activity ensued in the village, with extra help being drawn from the local farm labourers, for fear more rainfall would bring a repeat.

The next day Nid and Finch called round for Robbie, proudly bearing a box that contained the kite their parents had given them for their recent eighth birthday. After the weeks of very warm, still conditions, the storms had brought fresher, breezier weather and they were anxious to take the new kite out to the hill for its first proper flight. Jonathan, who didn't mix with boys of his own age, was as usual going too.

Robbie dashed past Morris's, head down, and anxious not to be noticed, when he called for John who simply sauntered out, hands in pockets, strutting cockily past the shop as if nothing had happened. As they walked back to the others waiting at the corner, Robbie felt a wary admiration for this strange and imperturbable character.

John nodded to the twins but his small dark eyes were cast sideways, coolly appraising Jonathan who he hadn't encountered yet.

'That's my big brother,' Robbie explained to John's hard questioning look.

Jonathan simply beamed back, his large face radiating contentment. John recoiled slightly.

They picked Lizzie up from Wheelwrights and, to stay clear of The Green, they took the longer route to the hill via The Square at the other end of the village. Here the buses pulled in and several shops looked out over a small cobbled market area with a stone cross: the shoe shop, Franklin's the Butcher's, a small Drapers, a Newsagents & Tobacconist, the Grocer's and Luff's Hardware, which was further around the corner. At the junction of Main Street stood the Horse & Hounds pub, which was run by Maggie's father, and it was here that they found her in the pub yard, playing marbles with Ann.

'Coming?' they called.

'Where you going?'

'Fly our new kite,' cried Finch, arms waving in imitation of kite flying.

The eight of them followed the footpath between two houses at the top of The Square and out into the fields behind; swapping stories of what their parents had heard or said about the episode at Morris's, all the while enjoying their secret notoriety.

Cows grazed in these lower fields, but after the last gate it was all open grazing. Sheep roamed the slopes and the ground rose quickly to meet the sky. The day was fresh but sunny, with puffs of clouds set in the deep blue that follows once the rains have cleared the air; they could see for miles across the open countryside.

Nid and Finch led the way, their blond heads bobbing along ahead of the rest, hauling the large box between them, while Jonathan brought up the rear, puffing a bit at the eager pace the twins had set. The girls were chatting and laughing, and John strutted silently a short distance away.

'This'll do,' said Nid, flinging the box down on the smooth sward above the old rabbit warren.

It was a favourite spot for them. Just below the summit and south-facing, sheltered from the worst of any wind, the ground levelled out on top of a sandy outcrop exploited by the rabbits. They flopped down onto the short, fine grass and watched with mounting anticipation as the twins, with a great flourish, pulled their kite from its packing.

They'd expected something special and weren't disappointed. The others' fathers mostly worked with their hands, but Frank Bird worked for a Bank in Cullingham and ran Moreton Steyning's local branch. Whatever toys and presents the rest of them had, Nid and Finch's were always bigger and better. The kite was massive. So large the twins had only been bought the one between them.

'Crikey!' said Lizzie, leaning forwards on hands and knees for a better look.

'Quick! Let's get it up while it's still good and windy,' Finch urged, ever eager.

They all pressed forwards to help, clutching at bits of fabric and string but were quickly pushed back by Nid. 'You have to do it like this or you get it tangled. Dad said.'

Admonished, they held back. It took several attempts and some bickering but the twins finally assembled the kite. Even in their sheltered position, the strong breeze snatched impatiently at the rainbow-coloured fabric as Nid and Finch manhandled the frame ready for launching.

'I'll run with it and you hold the string,' cried Finch, preparing to set off right away.

'No... you have to run holding the string while I hold the kite,' Nid corrected, face serious with purposefulness, ever the perfectionist.

Full of enthusiasm Finch was off, leaping over the edge of the warren and pelting down the steep slope below, his legs barely able to keep pace with his descent, one arm held aloft clutching the string. Standing on the edge of the warren, Nid held the kite above his head where the gusting breeze quickly tore it from his grasp and sent it soaring up into the air.

Way below, hearing Nid's cry of surprise, Finch stopped just as the kite picked up the wind from the summit of the hill and eddied into its full force, spiralling upwards, its long multi-coloured tail spinning out. Within seconds its ascent had taken up the slack on the string, and they all watched in astonished silence as Finch's arm was jerked upwards from his side in mimicry of a wave. He tumbled forwards to the ground, clutching the wooden handhold at the end of the kite string with both hands, as the others leapt as one off the warren and scrambled down to where he lay, rolling dramatically on the ground, grimly hanging on.

'Hold on, hold on!' Nid screamed, grappling to take a grip on the handle while the rest of them grabbed at one or other of the twins or at sections of the string, burning their palms in the process. The girls screamed and tumbled, Ann did a complete somersault over her head, unable to control her downward sliding, and Jonathan, scrambling down behind the rest of them, only came to a halt when he fell against John, who in turn was holding onto one of Finch's feet, almost dragging his sandal off.

'I've got it, I've got it!' cried Nid, planting his feet into the edge of a tussock and bracing himself impressively. High above them the huge diamond of the kite swung to and fro against the deep blue sky. They gathered themselves together and sat on the ground to gaze up in wonderment. At that moment it was one of the most beautiful things they'd ever seen, its rainbow colours iridescent from the bright sun behind, its long tail of bows streaming away.

'It's wonderful!' cried Lizzie. 'Robbie, look, look!'

Maggie, sitting back on her haunches, was laughing with delight and Ann, a few yards below, where she'd come to rest from her tumble, was gazing up rapturously, her little moon-face squinting into the sun.

Suddenly, the kite lost the breeze. It faltered, wheeling a few more times, but more slowly, and then gradually sank lower and lower in the sky until it fell from view somewhere above the warren.

They sprang to their feet and raced back up the steep slope to where it lay in the grass, fluttering lightly in the breeze like a wounded creature.

While Nid was collecting up the kite, Finch stood at the edge of the warren.

'Did you see?' he exclaimed. 'It lifted me right up!'

While this wasn't exactly true, the rest of them were caught up in the excitement and didn't demur.

'It pulled me right up like this,' and he held his arms and one leg up to suggest how he'd been carried along. 'I grabbed it...', and he snatched at the air. '... and...' here he flung himself down and rolled about. '... then I caught it and brought it under control and held onto it, and then I brought it back down. See!'

'No, you didn't. I caught it and then the wind dropped,' Nid corrected dryly without looking up, as he gathered up the kite, his long blond fringe obscuring his face.

'You didn't!' grumbled Finch from his prone position, head lifted from the ground to glare at his brother.

'What if we can really get it to lift one of us up,' Maggie suggested. 'I bet we can.'

'I'll do it!' Finch said.

'It would be best if it's someone quite light,' Robbie offered. 'Like one of the girls. What about Ann? She's the smallest.'

They all turned and looked at Ann, who peered blankly back from under her bob of straight fair hair. 'Me?' she said.

'You'll need something to hold onto,' said Maggie. 'We can tie a stick onto the end of the string, then Ann can sit astride that.'

Ann looked pensive, but the rest of them were enthused and went scampering about to find something suitable. Lizzie soon appeared with a length of fence paling she'd found beneath the nearby hedge.

'Perfect!' proclaimed Nid, and firmly tied it to the string a few yards up from the hand-hold. 'Now, hold onto the stick and run down the slope while I keep hold of the kite, then you jump astride the stick when the kite takes off,' he instructed.

‘Who’s going to keep hold?’ she asked apprehensively.

‘Don’t worry,’ Lizzie reassured her. ‘Me and Robbie will, and Maggie’ll all hold onto the handle and make sure you don’t get carried away.’

Ann seemed unconvinced but, as Nid held the kite in readiness, she gingerly clutched the stick and the other three of them took firm hold of the handle.

‘We need a countdown,’ Nid said as the breeze ruffled the kite, slapping the tail about his legs.

‘I’ll do it!’ said Finch. ‘Three... two... one!’

Maggie, standing on the highest part of the warren and holding the handle, leapt first, followed by Lizzie and Robbie who, both gripping the string alongside her were suddenly yanked forwards by Maggie’s flying start and long legs. Ann, grimly holding onto the stick as instructed, slithered behind them, down the gravel face of the warren on her heels, and began to run and leap across the steep, hummocky grass slope as quickly as her short legs could carry her.

Robbie could feel himself being pulled faster than his legs could rotate, and beside him Lizzie had lost the rhythm of her run and was bumping and crashing into him. Within seconds they were a tangled mass of legs and arms, slithering down and sweeping Maggie before them to the ground. Above, Nid had already released the kite but, instead of soaring as before, it simply glided gently to the ground below the warren; watched by Ann who stood plaintively holding the stick, very much still on the ground.

They pulled themselves up, gasping for breath and rubbing grazed and grass-burned skin. At the crest of the warren stood Nid, hands shielding the sun from his eyes, and beside him twice his size, Jonathan, gazing down in concern. Beside them was John Norbert’s stick-like silhouette, hands on hips.

Again they toiled back up, gathering up the string while Finch collected the kite, and flopped down on the grass dejectedly; although not, in Ann’s case, disappointedly.

‘I know!’ announced John firmly.

They all turned to look. It was the first time he’d spoken.

***

With John on board for a piggy-back, Finch's legs were already unsteady. At a countdown from the rest of them, he staggered over the crest of the warren and wobbled shakily down its gravely face, and then he galloped awkwardly downhill before collapsing in a heap. John was sent sprawling over his head to land face-down in the grass.

Trudging back up, Finch was followed by a furiously red-faced but determined-looking John.

'Someone who won't bleedin' fall over,' John commanded.

'I'll do it!' cried Jonathan, leaping to his feet. His brother looked uncertainly at him, but Jonathan was pink with excitement and enthusiasm. 'I can do it!' he urged.

Once again they arranged themselves along the rim of the warren to watch. Jonathan dipped and John, stick beneath his bottom and string between his legs, sprang lightly into the piggy-back. Assuming his role once again, Nid held the kite aloft and proclaimed the breeze strong.

Taking up position on the warren's edge, Jonathan bent forwards with an athletic readiness belying his heavy build, the string's handle held firmly in one hand.

'I'll count you in.' Lizzie stood, arm raised, and they all joined in: 'Five... four... three... two... one... *GO*!'

Jonathan launched himself from the crest with a single-minded fearlessness, his eyes fixed on a spot way below them. Landing with two heavy thudding strides he raced forwards, bent low for speed with John, dwarfed and crouching upon his broad back like a race-horse jockey. With a light toss, Nid released the kite into the gusting breeze. Again it juddered and eddied, then met the strong winds across the top of the hill and quickly soared, taking up the slack of kite string.

'Now!' they all yelled, *'Now!'*

Jonathan glanced back over his shoulder as John's hands were jerked aloft by the tugging string, the pull of the rising kite lifting him effortlessly into the air, seated astride the stick. The others leapt to their feet, cheering and whooping as John Norbert swung to and fro, gently trailing the kite as it dipped and swooped and rose into the blue sky above. They couldn't hear him but could see he was laughing, throwing back his head and taking one hand from the string to wave as he slowly rotated.

Jonathan had slumped to the ground and sat, leaning back on his arms and with out-flung legs, a broad beaming smile of satisfaction on his face as he watched John drifting happily against the massive backdrop of blue sky, the kite now a deceptively small, brightly-coloured diamond way above.

Suddenly Robbie called out to Jonathan. 'Who's got the handle? The handle! Hold the handle!' he yelled as John drifted slowly above the slopes of the hill, ever higher from the falling ground.

Jonathan inclined his head, shrugging to indicate he couldn't hear. Lizzie and Maggie shrieked in unison, waving and gesturing, and Nid and Finch exchanged anxious looks. Already John was above head height and moving quite swiftly away from them all.

Robbie leapt from the warren with an athleticism that surprised even himself and thundered helter-skelter down the slope. Even through vision dislocated by the speed of his running over steep and uneven ground, Robbie could see that Jonathan still looked puzzled, but then saw that he suddenly jumped to his feet and ran with startling speed towards John. With one diving leap Jonathan disappeared into the bracken, just as Robbie stumbled and fell heavily forwards, still some distance away. Behind him he could hear the others but, glimpsed through the long grass stalks, Robbie watched as John suddenly stalled and was spun around. Clambering to his feet, he recognised Jonathan's arm protruding from the undergrowth, triumphantly clutching the kite's handhold.

When they all got to him, he was grimly holding tight.

'I've got it, Robbie, I've got it,' he called. 'It's alright.'

While Robbie hauled his brother to his feet, the twins grabbed the kite-string's handle. Above them, looking down calmly, John slowly rotated as they all worked together to play in the line.

Jonathan reached up and steadied the string and John took a bravura flying leap to the ground.

'Bleedin' brilliant!' he proclaimed.

They didn't fly the kite again that afternoon, stretching out instead in a grassy dip where fireweed and thistle down blew about them. Jonathan and John sat side-by-side, two strange cohorts discussing their kite-flying success and how to refine their technique, while Robbie lay on his front, parting the grass to discover tiny scurrying creatures. Lizzie and Ann were crawling about in pursuit of grasshoppers whose endless scissoring whirred in their heads; the others lay on their backs, hands folded behind heads, watching the fleecy clouds drifting overhead, talking together and laughing. High above, buzzards circled and soared, filling the air with their strange mewing cries.

It was some while later that they realised how time was passing and that they should be making their way home, so the Bird brothers packed up their kite and all headed off together. They were some way over on the western slopes of Lullington Hill, so they took a different way back into Moreton Steyning from their outward path, along the lower lane through Rushwood End which led past the outlying farms.

This path dropped down quickly then followed a narrow gully, drawing them into single-file before it emerged through a small copse into the yard at Rushwood End Farm. Although it appeared empty, this was not familiar territory and they all instinctively fell silent as they crossed the broad farmyard, past the end of the dark wooden barn, and then out into the narrow lane that led back down to the village. High stone walls lined the upper section of this deep lane which became increasingly rutted as they approached, about halfway down, the entrance to Lee Farm. This was where Malcolm Draycott lived. Here, the mature oak trees overhung; massive, dark and dusty at this time of late summer. It was shady and gloomy beneath their great canopies, even on a bright day.

All of a sudden Maggie let out a yelp, followed quickly by a shriek from Ann. Before the others could look round to see what had happened, a stinging thud knocked Robbie's head sideways with a jarring force, and Finch jumped back, crying out. Manure was raining down all about them in a series of thuds and splats. In sudden confusion they jumped and leapt about, trying to avoid the onslaught. Its source quickly made itself evident in the throaty guffaws of several lads from above the high wall, where they glimpsed Malcolm's unmistakeable hair. Helpless they ran, trying to deflect the wettest clods away from heads and faces with their hands, until they were out of range and down the lane towards the village.

They only slowed down once they were well away from the farm, reassembling to inspect one another. All bore the wet and grubby marks of their attackers' farmyard artillery. They mingled awkwardly trying to scratch and scrub away the dark and smelly manure clinging to their clothes and skin.

'Did you see who it was?' Nid exclaimed. He was red-faced with fury, fingers scraping at his grimy shirt sleeve.

'Malcolm Draycott,' replied Lizzie, tight-lipped, although they knew that only too well.

'And his mates,' Robbie added.

They looked at one another, silent in their fury. They'd been outwitted.

IV

Maggie loved cuddling the baby. Laura was plump and pink and she smelled nice, and she was always laughing and gurgling, flapping her fat little arms and kicking her baby legs up and down. Maggie was on the sofa, holding Laura on her lap. The baby had no socks on and was chewing on a biscuit with bits of soggy digestive stuck to her round cheeks. On the floor Maggie's younger brother and sister were rolling about, flinging toy bricks against the wall. They were eating their lunch – slices of bread – and were squabbling noisily. Maggie tried to eat hers too, holding onto Laura with one arm as the baby dangled; trying to prevent her from sliding off and onto the floor.

Their mother had gone out to the shops and their father was in the pub downstairs. The kids were running about now, their bare feet slapping on the lino floor. The wooden bricks scattered as Shirley shrieked, chased by Alan, and the pair of them stumbled into a dining chair sending it crashing noisily to the floor.

'Pack it in!' Maggie shouted, 'or Dad'll be up.'

The two younger children exchanged looks, dragging the chair back upright and returned to the floor, gnawing on their food, flinging bricks about again with their messy fingers. There was the sound of heavy steps on the stairs. The door opened; it was him.

'You kids! Keep the noise down. Maggie, you're supposed to be minding them. Keep those kids under control.'

The door closed noisily; thud, thud, thud as he clomped back down, his heavy frame juddering at each step. He was out of sight but she could see it in her mind's eye; the gloomy bar, smoke-filled and smelling of beer. Him squeezing back round behind the counter, surprisingly nimble for his size, and leaning there on his big bare forearms, swapping stories with his cronies. Nodder Potter, his skinny frame perched on a stool up at the bar, Mr Keach reading a newspaper and flicking ash on the floor, Gramps Norris smoking a pipe with his personal pewter jug that they kept hanging from a beam above the bar.

As children they weren't allowed in there. He said they'd get a thrashing if they went in the bar, but sometimes she crept in late in the afternoons when he was asleep. It was always so quiet, quieter than a normal empty room, even when the kids were making a racket upstairs. Perhaps it was because so many people had been in there over all those years and now, when they were gone, the room was at a loss.

Maggie liked to walk around the pub and look; cloths over the beer pumps on the bar, the big wall clock ticking loudly, cinders spilling from the grate onto the tiles, beer-smelling rugs in the 'snug' corner.

She knew where they all sat; Gramps Norris in the window seat nearest the fire, Mr-miserable-Keach with his back to the wall, face in a newspaper, skinny Potter with his lizard eyes and bobbing head propped at the bar with his back against the partition, I'm-better-than-you-Mr-Bank-Manager-Bird in the snug on Tuesdays and Fridays, when he opened the branch opposite. Old Dolly Parrott in the corner of the snug with her Mild, Jack Saunders with his cribbage board. She knew them all; she knew everything.

Sometimes Maggie found things they'd left: cigarette cards, a newspaper, some crisps left in a bag, a pencil stub.

It was sunny that afternoon when she'd slipped down to look, a narrow beam of sunlight crossing the gloomy bar and alighting on the chrome pumps. In its shaft, clouds of dust mingled, invisible elsewhere. The smell of stale beer had risen up the narrow carpet-less, window-less staircase to meet her as she'd crept cautiously down so as not to let any creaks give her away. Down there in the bar, the usual stillness, as much as fear of her father, made her tread silently. Ash and cigarettes spilled from the ashtray where Keach had been sitting. Gramps had returned his pewter pot with the big handle to the bar where it still sat, sticky with beer.

She moved to the middle of the room, breathing quietly, feeling the silence and absorbing the emptiness. Then something bright beneath the settle in front of the window made her turn. She stooped down as it lay there, glinting silvery from the reflected sunlight. She crouched right down on to the cold stone floor, then stretched out, snake-like, to reach under the settle. Her fingers closed around the cold hard metal, snug in her palm, and she drew back a shiny cigarette lighter. She kneeled back on the bare floor.

The beam of sunlight warmed her face and shoulders and sent dizzying whirls of dust around her head. In her hand lay the shiny silver item. She turned it over. There was a pattern around the base and two initials on one side in a smart script: *FB*. FB? Frank Bird; the twins' father. It was Friday, a Bank day, no doubt he'd been in.

Maggie weighed the lighter in her hand. It felt heavy, small and neat, but solid. She pulled back the top and tried the mechanism.

Instantly a spark fired and an elegant narrow flame burned. She snapped the top shut and looked round as if someone might discover her, but there was no one there of course.

Standing, she looked out of the low window to The Square where people were alighting from the Cullingham bus. Beyond, the awnings were out over the shops, with a few people moving between them or standing talking as people in villages always do. Not one of them knew; they were oblivious to her and her treasure. She weighed the lighter again, bouncing it in her hand, then thrust it into her dress pocket, skipped across the bar and mounted the stairs two at a time. She'd left the door at the top ajar and slipped silently back into the family's rooms.

There was a noise. Her mother was in the kitchen, shopping basket on the table, piling sausages into a frying pan.

'That you, Maggie? Put this away will you?' It was an appeal rather than a demand. 'Your father'll be awake in a minute and wanting his supper. There's eggs, tins, potatoes and milk. Now look sharp!'

The younger children burst in.

'I hope you two haven't been making a noise again.'

'What's for tea?'

'Nothing if you've woken your father. Maggie! I won't tell you again.'

Maggie pulled the groceries from the basket and shoved them into the cupboards. At the cooker, her mother stood jiggling sausages about in the blackened frying pan, her hair straggling forwards from the tie that attempted to hold it back. She was only thirty, but her face had frown lines, and darkening sags showed beneath her eyes.

'Open those beans,' she said, jabbing the fork towards two cans, 'and put some toast on for you kids.'

Stephen, her older brother, came in from playing with his mates.

'Tea won't be long,' their mother said, as he flopped wordlessly into a chair at the kitchen table.

Above them, the water pipes clanked, showing that her father was up and washing.

'Now look smart and set the table before there's trouble. Your father'll be here in a minute.'

There was no dining room in the pub's flat, and the seven of them had to squeeze around the kitchen table. Maggie could set the table fast, she did it every day after all, and it was ready in no time; toast on plates, butter in a dish, cups and saucers, sugar, milk bottle. She rushed out and reappeared with Laura, pink from sleep and pushed her struggling into the high chair. The others clambered onto chairs, scraping them into place, jostling for room along one side of the table as their mother heaped beans onto toast.

'I hadn't buttered it yet,' moaned Alan.

'Too late,' she said.

The kitchen door opened and their father heaved in breathing heavily, his thick, dark curly hair still awry from sleep. His wife put his sausage, egg and beans down, a plate of sliced bread, and poured steaming water into the big metal teapot as he silently tucked into his supper. They all ate without speaking until, after some minutes, he looked up at them from under his dark eyebrows and long lashes.

'I don't want to have to come up and tell you lot to be quiet again,' he said gruffly.

The younger ones looked glumly up.

'And you,' waving his knife in Maggie's direction, 'are supposed to be looking after them and giving your mother some help.'

Maggie didn't answer, but in her dress pocket the lighter hung heavily. She touched it for reassurance. When they'd finished eating she asked to go down to the yard.

'Help your mother wash up,' he said.

'Mum,' she pleaded with a sense of burning injustice. She'd baby-sat the three younger siblings all afternoon, apart from when she'd sneaked down to the bar, that is. She was always baby-sitting, or helping with the food, or the clearing up. She understood someone had to do it; her mother wasn't capable and Stephen was out whenever he wanted, which was always.

'Yes, alright,' she said, 'but tidy some plates away first.'

Maggie flung a few dishes into the sink and hurried to the main stairs at the rear of the flat, which led down towards the pub's yard, closing the upstairs door firmly behind her.

She was going out to the yard, but not just yet. At the bottom of the stairs, off the long dark passage that connected the outside door to the back of the bar, was the door to the pub's storeroom-cellar. Quietly she slipped the latch and sprang down the three stone steps into the closely racked room. Beyond this, another door led to the pub cellar with its beer barrels, but in here were bottles of beer, whisky, gin, lemonade, tonic, boxes of crisps and cigarettes, all her father's box files of paperwork and his desk, and everything else that was needed for the pub.

Slipping between two rows of tall racks, she ducked down and scrambled beneath, until she could bob up in a small alcove beyond, on the far side of a pillar. Here was her secret place, invisible from anywhere else in the room. Here she kept her special things, placed on the dark-varnished wooden shelves between the pillar and wall. Light came from a small square window high above, and she had a block of wood as a stool where she could sit and lean her back against the pillar. From here she could see them all; she could play with her special things and endlessly rearrange them.

In pride of place was her doll, Alice. Alice had long blond hair tied up in a pink ribbon and wore a long pink and white dress with frills at the hem and neck. One of her shoes was missing, but Maggie didn't mind, she thought her beautiful. The doll was hers now and she treasured it. She'd had Alice for nearly a year, ever since the day when Mrs Wheeler's little girl had dropped the doll from her pushchair. The girl's arm had dangled out and her blond head had peered round the hood, looking back, but she didn't cry. Mrs Wheeler had just kept walking on. Maggie had stood by the wall and then once they'd gone from sight, had darted forwards and picked it up. Then she took the doll home and put it on the shelves in pride of place and gave it her own favourite name; Alice.

Either side of where Alice sat were the coloured ribbons she'd found upstairs and a little fluffy dog, Jumbo, who was hers when she was a baby. On the other shelves were a little cardboard box, decorated with pictures of puppies and kittens which had once held chocolates, a present from Maggie's grandparents one Christmas. Some coloured pencils and two chalks, cigarette cards and pennies she'd found on the pub floor, her mother's old hairbrush, a metal toy cow and a plastic whistle from a cereal packet. Now she had her special silver lighter too. She moved the ribbons from the top shelf and placed the lighter there, just to Alice's right and with Jumbo to her left. She turned it a few times until the best side faced the front and then smoothed Alice's dress down, and with just one last check to make sure she was happy with the presentation of everything, Maggie slipped back under the racking, checking for sounds that no one was coming, and stole out of the storeroom door and then out into the pub yard.

It was early evening by now and the pub was opening up. He would be in the bar, cleaning glasses and checking the barrels.

On the opposite side of the yard from the pub were the old sheds and stable buildings. Maggie heard a scrabbling noise and stepped up onto the stone mounting block next to the pub, stretching upwards to see. It was that new boy John, the 'monkey-boy', looking even more like a monkey as he crouched on the corrugated iron roof of their woodshed. Edging forwards, he peered down as the first customers shuffled across The Square towards the pub. Nodder Potter of course, with his lizardy face, coming for his usual, and another local.

John saw her and winked. They both watched as the men approached the pub talking and stopped at the pavement's edge, engrossed in some subject. Nodder, his back to the shed, was droning away, waving his hand about as he jabbered on. John edged forwards on all fours, head barely two feet above Nodder's cap.

Maggie held her breath and kept completely still, watching John as he drew in his cheeks and then puckered his mouth. Something small and shiny appeared at his lips and then dropped, landing on Nodder's cap. John sniggered silently and looked across at Maggie, then signalled her to wait. This time he was making really sure. He sat back on his heels before repeating the procedure. A huge gob of saliva ballooned from his mouth. He positioned himself and released it perfectly onto the centre of Nodder's cap before creasing into silent manic laughter. Maggie found herself coughing to disguise a laugh as she jumped down from the block.

Potter turned, clearing his throat. 'Maggie,' he greeted hoarsely.

'Hello Mr Potter,' she said, and fled the yard.

V

Robbie spent most of his time with John Norbert in those school summer holidays of 1957, the new boy joining almost daily the group of friends on their activities and outings. They no longer found him so outlandish and, with time, came to enjoy the company of this brash and swaggering character with his impulsive and reckless behaviour.

By mid-August bunting had appeared around The Green, a sure sign that the highlight of late summer, the Moreton Steyning Fair, was only a few days away.

Robbie and John hung about The Green attempting to help; holding posts to be driven in, unravelling the rope to mark off areas, fetching and carrying things. In all probability they were a nuisance, but no one sent them away, and they were allowed to get involved. They were even sent on an errand to collect the tin tub from the Rectory garden for the apple bobbing, returning as they did straining and struggling with it between them. The Vicar brought his big lawn mower down to cut the grass, and Lizzie's and Ann's fathers, both Carpenters, erected frames for the stalls.

It was famously always sunny for the Fair and it proved to be so yet again. By eight in the morning the village was already bustling, with the stalls set up and the first visitors arriving. Special buses came in from Cullingham and the nearby villages, quickly filling the lanes with colourful wandering crowds.

There were swing-boats, roundabouts, a rifle range, coconut-shy, crockery smashing, skittles, wet sponge throwing, guess-the-weight-of the-cake and several other raffles, bottle stalls, plants for sale, donkey rides, fortune telling, a pet show and, at the top of The Green and run by the Vicar, games and fun for the younger children: egg-and-spoon and three-legged races and a Punch & Judy Show.

In marquees at the bottom of The Green and in Lower Farm's yard, the Moreton Steyning & District Allotment Society had their fruit and vegetable show, the WI their cake, jam and flower arranging competitions, and there was pet rabbit and domestic fowl judging. The village Butcher and Baker had their stalls out selling their produce, Luff the hardware merchant had a stand with his copper pans, saucepans and wicker baskets, and there were stalls and stands from traders in Cullingham and other local villages offering everything from clothes to bicycles. The Jug & Bottle on one side of The Green was open all day for refreshments, with tables and chairs outside under parasols, and there was a sandwiches and teas tent, and a hot pie stall as well.

By early afternoon the Fair was a cheery heaving throng and the air full of a hearty hubbub, above which the Netherington Silver Band could be heard performing popular songs. The Bradbury brothers had already spent most of their money on games and rides, knick-knacks and ices by the time they ran into Lizzie and the twins. All were being jostled by the crowds, and pressed in by the mass of people around the popular rifle range when, from nearby, a raw voice abruptly rang out.

'What you *dung* lately Bradbury-frog!'

The people about them turned to look for the source and their movement revealed, through a gap in the crush, the Rushwood End farm gang a few yards away, pointing and laughing with self-conscious menace towards the friends.

'*Shit yourself* then, you fat-frog?' mocked Malcolm Draycott, looking about for appreciation from half a dozen youths who stood with him, hands in pockets, faces twisted in sneering laughs.

Further ridicule followed from the group, which elicited yet more knowing laughter. Some of the crowd tutted but most moved away, largely indifferent or tolerant towards youthful high spirits on this festival day. With every new insult the farm gang egged one another on, finding the others' discomfort increasingly entertaining, jeering as they fidgeted and tried to get away through the wall of people. Finally they thrust their way out, stumbling behind the tarpaulin at the rear of the coconut shy, angry and publicly shamed.

VI

At age eight, it was the first year that Nid and Finch had been considered old enough to be allowed to wander around the Fair on their own, free to indulge their curiosity and spend their pocket money at will. They'd ridden on the roundabout and swings, looked at the animals, pushed and shoved their way through the crowds, pressing against legs and flowery skirts, watched the games, and played on the hoopla and duck stalls. Finch quickly used up his money but Nid, being more circumspect, had paid for them both afterwards, until his last coins were spent too.

The crowds, noise, amusements and gaiety were thrilling and intoxicating, creating a world so unfamiliar and exciting they'd wanted to hold onto it to the very last moment of the day. After tea, the boys pleaded with their parents to be allowed to stay up late, but were sent to bed at the usual time. Even the Moreton Steyning Fair would not be permitted to impinge on the calm order of their daily lives.

Home was a square, red-brick house facing onto The Green opposite Violet Ward's house and Morris's shop. The boys knelt up at their bedroom window, looking down on the early evening festivities as the sounds of music, talking and laughter drifted upwards. People were still wandering about, and teenagers huddled in their groups, or played those funfair stalls which stayed open into the evening. It was impossible to imagine The Green ever looking the same again, so magical and exciting did it seem, so transformed into a new world of colour and vitality. Finch wanted it to last for ever and ever. Indeed, he felt it would; it must, so intensely had its enchantment worked on him.

Eventually Nid began to nod off and he crawled away to bed, but Finch remained, watching as the sky faded and the coloured lights glowed ever more brightly. The youngsters had drifted away now, but people were still outside the Jug & Bottle; drinking, laughing and talking. His legs ached from holding himself up by the window and his eyes were tired and heavy, but he simply couldn't drag himself away. He just had to absorb every last moment of the Fair. Abruptly their front door opened below and he saw their father's balding head emerge and bob along their front path to The Green. He was smoking his pipe and walked up and down, noisily clearing his throat in the way that Nid and Finch had long come to recognise as the precursor to a stern directive.

However, the drinkers who'd spilled from the next-door pub's small bars carried on regardless, their conversations and outbursts of loud laughter continuing unabated. Frank Bird walked stiff-legged a few yards towards the pub, eyes down, smoking studiously, coughing his disapproval, but the patrons were either too happily engrossed in their conviviality, or too jovial to observe his reproach at their cheery noise.

Eventually, he marched back, swung the gate to with a crisp clang, and came back indoors. Finch heard the door below slam and the anxious murmur of their mother's voice, followed by the abrupt rumble of their father's, then a creak on the stairs. Exhausted, he gave way to the craving for sleep and slipped into bed. Within seconds, the sounds had drifted away, lost to conscious hearing.

***

The following day Finch woke to an unfamiliar clamour outdoors. The morning sun was shining brightly behind the closed curtains, but the unmoving mop of his brother's blond hair above the bedclothes showed that Nid was still asleep. Two bright balloon – red for himself; green for Nid – hung from the mantelpiece, and there was the toy dog he'd won on the bobbing plastic duck stall to remind him of yesterday's magic.

'Nid,' he called. 'You awake?'

'Uh.'

Finch slipped to the window and looked out. People were everywhere; dismantling the stalls and loading poles, canvas, funfair rides, boxes and crates into trucks and vans parked on all sides of The Green.

'They're taking it all down,' he said. 'Come and look.'

'Nnnn.'

'Come and look!'

'Nnng!' Now uttered with irritation.

Finch bounced onto his brother's bed, pulling the covers back and snatched at the pillow beneath his head; Nid wailed and growled, flailing with his hands, his eyes half-shut, and then flung himself back down, curling up, and pulling the covers over his face, puffy from sleep.

Their mother came into the room. 'Andrew, get dressed. Nigel! Aren't you getting up?' But Nid ignored her entreaty too. She sat on the bed, smoothing back his hair to feel his forehead. 'Don't you feel well?'

Three quarters of an hour later Nid was sitting wrapped in an eiderdown at the kitchen table, forlornly chewing on a slice of toast, face flushed and listless. Finch insisted that he felt alright, of course he felt alright; nothing would keep him inside, and so he was allowed out, provided that he come straight home if he felt at all poorly.

He hurried down the silent hallway; the narrow strip of dark carpet leading him to where the beam of light spilled through the fanlight above the front door. The door that separated him from the excitement beyond. Reaching up, he pulled the latch and slipped out into the vivid sunlight, letting the heavy door click firmly shut behind him, and then rushed through the front garden with its neat borders and square patches of lawn, leaving the gate to swing wildly as he ran back out into the exhilarating new world around The Green.

A large heavy truck was reversing away, piled high with canvas and poles. The marquees were still standing, but empty now of all their animals, stalls, tables, exhibits and food. The trestle tables and folding chairs were stacked high on the grass ready for loading, and the men, shouting to one another all the while, were pulling poles and stakes from the ground and flinging items onto the backs of trailers. Local retailers' vans with their smart liveries were parked on the far side, ready to carry away the remnants of various traders' stands. Across The Green, Morris's Greengrocers had reopened, and the smell of baking, and steady procession of women with shopping baskets, told Finch that the village Bakers near the Church was also open again as normal village life resumed.

He looked back towards their house, standing formal and quiet amidst all the clamour. Beside it, the Jug & Bottle was closed and silent too, but the tables of empty glasses and overflowing ashtrays told of last night's revelries.

'Wha'cha.' John stood, hands thrust in sagging shiny trouser pockets with his shirt already pulled free on one side. 'Good riot, eh?' he grinned.

'Magic. Did you win anything? I won a yellow dog.'

'Nah. Spent i' all on the rifle range, me.' He mimed firing into the sky and taking the recoil into his shoulder. Finch didn't stop to consider that John was too short and too young to have used the rifle range. 'I ough'a won, but I reckon they go' i' rigged. 'Ere, where's yer bruv?'

It felt strange for Finch to be without his twin, like looking with just one eye so that the full perspective was lacking, or of conversations only half-heard and not fully understood; Nid was always there, organising, understanding, making the decisions.

Suddenly, John squatted down and then sprang back up, beaming. Holding his hand out towards Finch, his fingers slowly unfurled to reveal a sixpence.

The two boys then roamed The Green, folding back the grass with the sides of their shoes, and in just twenty minutes had found and pocketed four pennies, a threepenny bit, another sixpence and a shilling. From the road, Robbie ran up to join them, puffing slightly.

'Wha'cha,' greeted John. 'See wha' we've go',' and he displayed their cache. 'Found 'em in the grass. Them idjits musta dropped 'em all. Finders keepers, eh?'

Robbie studied the handful of coins in John's grubby palm and sucked his breath in between his teeth to show admiration.

'Let's go down 'em tracks,' pronounced John in a manner that brooked no further discussion. 'Flatten 'em. C'mon, I'll show ya!' and he set off, dodging through the workers who were carrying away piles of trestles, leaving the others to follow in his wake.

From Main Street they took the Sheep Path to the point where it crossed the railway on a small brick bridge, and scrambled down into the shallow railway cutting, sending up clouds of small brown butterflies. It was here they wedged themselves into the steep grassy bank.

After a short time, a distant chugging told them that a train was approaching from town. John leapt up, pulled a strand of chewing gum from his mouth and, working it vigorously between finger and thumb, stuck a penny onto one of the rail lines furthest away. He retreated to the bank and the three of them stretched out onto their bellies, dizzyingly heads-down on the sloping bank, and lay in wait.

Away to their left came a deep rumbling from the approaching train which, in the confines of the narrow cutting, steadily increased in volume until the engine exploded from beneath the narrow bridge, swirling its choking steam and smuts about them. It thundered past them, massive and black, pistons working, wheels all a blur. Instinctively they ducked down, faces presses into their forearms, only rising to look once the final carriage had passed, hearing the first squealing of breaks as the train slowed into Moreton Steyning Station, in view away to their right.

John scampered down and pulled the penny from the rail, now hammered to a wafer-thin disc with a broken rim. With a thrill, Finch clutched it from him, turning it over and over, feeling its sharp edges, awed by their new friend's ingenuity. Robbie took it next, looking in silent admiration at the transformation.

'Wanna try?' chirruped John, pulling another coin deep from within his pocket and proffering it. Finch could barely wait; he wanted to make the magic happen too.

'You need to put it on the near track this time,' Robbie pointed out. 'The next train'll be from the station.'

Finch took some of the gum and chewed vigorously until he'd reduced it to a smooth workable putty, then drew out a long warm strand and used it to press the penny down onto the track nearest to them before they all settled once again to observe the spectacle. Coming from the station, the train this time approached slowly, clanking heavily past, waiting to build up speed.

Immediately after the last carriage had creaked and rumbled past, Finch jumped forwards and prised the coin from the rail. It was now a flimsy perforated metal disc, almost twice the diameter it had been.

He held it proudly until a thought struck. 'It's bigger now, it must be worth more. We can get more sweets with it, can't we? Let's go and get some!'

'No,' said Robbie. 'Don't be daft, it's still just a penny. My turn now. It's the up-express next,' and, taking some greying gum, he too pressed a penny to the near line.

By now they felt emboldened and eager, and crouched by the line to watch at close quarters, talking excitedly and in great anticipation.

Eventually a faint creaking in the tracks told them that the non-stopper was approaching. At first it was just a distant rumble, with a clicking and rattling of the metal lines. From far away in the distance the train's warning whistle split the air followed by a rising crescendo of noise and then, almost without warning, and with a thunderous boom, the engine rushed at them; one moment a toy train between the platforms, and the next massive and bearing down on them, a terrifying noise and fearsome presence and a great thump of air that flung them down onto their faces.

They clung to the juddering ground in fear of somehow falling off as the colossus thundered above, horrifying, monstrous, blotting out all the light. Finch and Robbie couldn't breathe for the roar and darkness, and the rushing air that sucked the breath from their lungs. They buried their heads and felt as if a cliff should be falling down about them. When finally the train had sped past, they raised their faces from the ground to see the rear carriage rapidly diminishing, returned once again to the size of a toy.

Beside them John was already on his feet, animated and energized, chortling and hopping from one foot to the other. His eyes were wide and wild with excitement. Finch and Robbie rose much more slowly and a little unsteadily. As he peeled the penny from the line, Robbie was still shaking inside. Another perfectly flattened disc.

With one each, they now began to amble beside the lines towards the station, but the newness and excitement of it all was burning inside Finch.

'How d'you know about that?' he just had to ask.

John shrugged. 'Do i' all the time at 'ome. There's lotsa bleedin' railways, 'undreds and 'undreds a miles. Go on 'em all the time. Sidin's 'n' shuntin' yards. Go down an' watch the trains, go in the sheds, 'elp 'em with the work an' stuff, you know. Sometimes I ride on 'em. I bin up with the drivers lots.'

'You haven't!'

They hadn't yet realised that kind of reaction only encouraged John to embellish.

'I know lots of 'em, don't I? Jack, Fred, Eric. Bin lots of places, me. Get a train to London and down the line to some other bleedin' place then back. I was in the cab helpin' the fireman. Hot work that, gets black as soot. Cooked us lunch on his shovel, 'e did, eggs 'n bacon 'n tha'. More 'n' you could eat. 'E sez I can go back anytime, 'im.'

Robbie and Finch, walking either side of John, looked towards him in wonder; this boy who so nonchalantly led such a thrilling city life, so very unlike their own.

'Doesn't your Mum mind you going off?' Robbie asked in surprise. He couldn't imagine his own mother sanctioning such excursions. There was hell to pay if he ever got home late. Besides, there was Jonathan to consider.

'Nah. Few weeks ago I went round all them marshallin' yards on an engine.'

'What's marshalling yards?' asked Finch, his head whirling with the imagined excitement of it all.

'Shuntin' an' stuff. Loadin'. Goes on all night, like. You can 'ear 'em, whistlin' 'n' stuff. Lotsa differen' engines, geezers makin' up trains an' shiftin' trucks abou'. Differen' loads 'n' stuff. Huge.' He waved his arms about. 'Goes on fa miles. I bin all round i'. Go there all the bleedin' time.'

'It must seem really quiet and sort of boring here?' suggested Robbie.

But John merely shrugged, 'Nah, not really.' By now they were approaching the station platform. 'I go' an idea!' he suddenly said.

Following his instructions, the other two hunkered down beneath the trackside hedge where they couldn't be seen from the station. Before long the Cullingham train arrived and, once it had halted alongside the platform, the two of them followed John across the tracks, leaping from rail to rail, bent down low so as not to be seen, and then climbed stealthily up onto the far platform. The carriage doors swung open and John sprang forwards and marched, soldier-like, arms swinging, to where several people were alighting. He surveyed them quickly, then confidently stepped up to a smart woman carrying a suitcase.

'Carry yer bag lady?' he chirped, reaching forwards to take the handle. She recoiled, partly in surprise, but John produced a surprisingly disarming smile, which she briefly returned, and then submitted her case to him. It was so large and John so small, it would have dragged on the floor had he not raised his elbows to haul it up, and even then he could only stagger behind her to the stairs where he disappeared from his companions' sight. He reappeared a few minutes later, grinning and tossing up a shiny coin.

"Orright, eh!' he pronounced.

Having invested their gains in sausage rolls from the Bakers, the boys returned to the station as Finch couldn't wait to have a go himself, fully confident of his ability to repeat the ploy. They'd missed two stopping trains while they were away, but had no trouble amusing themselves until the next service was due an hour later; pulling syrupy sweet plums from a tree near the tracks, dodging the soporific wasps that sent John into a panic; so that he flapped and wailed shrilly in alarm.

'Don't!' urged Robbie. 'You'll get stung if you flap.'

As soon as the train had pulled alongside, Finch ran to the nearest carriage. A door was flung open and a man with a briefcase got off. Seizing his opportunity, Finch darted forwards and clasped the handle.

'I'll carry it for you,' he gasped out as the man straightened, looking blankly back at him, trying to tug the briefcase from his grasp.

'Let go, boy,' the man said. 'What do you think you're doing?' Tall, he was already striding towards the stairs for the ticket office and Finch was being tugged along, unable to free his hand.

'Get off boy!' he snapped tersely, finally wrenching the case from Finch's eager grip. Finch could only watch with disappointment as the man marched briskly away along the platform, casting one brief disapproving look behind.

With few other passengers having disembarked, the train soon left the platform and, in doing so, revealed the service from Cullingham which had in the meantime pulled alongside the opposing platform.

Finch glanced across and saw through the carriage window opposite, a surprised look of recognition on his father's face. His stomach lurched. The other two ran up to surround him.

'What happened?' asked Robbie.

'Bugger wouldn't let 'im!' John was staring after the man, disgusted, his hands on hips.

'There's my Dad,' said Finch forlornly, watching his father depart for the ticket office, his face furious with intent and a stern expression.

***

Finch went straight home. He knew better than to prolong the situation, especially as there would be no Nid on this occasion to help him explain away his transgression. But then Nid wouldn't have gone on the railway in the first place; Nid was responsible and cautious, and in their parents' words 'sensible', not impetuous like him.

Hurrying up Station Road, he pictured the scene that would meet him at home: his father waiting to interrogate him, standing with his back to the fireplace, solemn and severe. He let himself in by the back garden gate and crept into the kitchen, where his mother glanced up from preparing food.

'Where have you been?'

'With Robbie and John.'

'Where?' she repeated, ignoring the deliberate evasion.

'On The Green, then we went down Sheep Path and then back round by Station Road.'

'Your father wants to see you.'

The windowless door from the kitchen to the hall separated Finch from the destiny that awaited him beyond. He knew he must face it, but tried to put off the actual moment by closing his fingers around the cool brass door knob and delaying the moment of opening the door for as long as he could.

'Go on,' she said, a touch of sympathy in her voice, but her tone permitting no backing out.

He took a deep breath, turned the knob which made its familiar squeak, and slipped into the empty hall. The house was silent, and Nid was nowhere to be seen. He was going to have to take this one on his own. Ahead, the sitting room door was open and his father's deep voice came from within.

'Andrew?'

'Yes...'

'Come here.'

Frank Bird held certain standards for himself and his family which he expected his sons to follow. He worked in a Bank, he had a position to uphold, and it was important that his sons should be recognised as such.

Finch edged round the door, as slowly as he could, the room falling into view bit by bit. The dining table and chairs by the wall, then the net-curtained window with its ornaments on the window sill, the bookcase in the corner, their mother's armchair, and back to the window, newspaper rack, coal bucket, tiled fireplace with the brown rug in front. Standing on it, with his back to the fireplace, legs set firmly apart, was their father, still in his dark work suit and laced black leather shoes.

***

For playing on the railway Finch was sent straight to bed with no food. It could have been worse, he reflected. In their room, Nid was in bed reading and looked up with surprise when his brother entered, their father sternly at his back, the door shut firmly behind him.

Nid listened with quiet curiosity as Finch recounted with mounting animation the day's adventures, re-living and embellishing his scrapes, despite the telling off he'd brought upon himself. Nid envied his twin's easy ability for fun and spontaneity, carefree and unhindered by any sense of constraint.

After a time Nid was called down for his tea and, left alone, Finch sat reflecting on the day and the empty hollow feeling now in his stomach, but decided that the fun had been worth missing supper for. After a bit he realised the bedroom door hadn't been latched and crept stealthily onto the landing from where he could peer down through the banisters.

The hem of Nid's tartan dressing gown was just visible where he sat at the dining table, swinging his feet back and forth as he ate. Finch could hear their parents talking in the kitchen, but with the door shut their conversation was inaudible. Feeling left out and rather sorry for himself he sat on the top step, aware of hunger gripping deeper into his stomach. After a while their mother emerged from the kitchen and walked into the sitting room.

'More toast, darling?' she said to Nid.

'Yes, please.'

'You must be feeling better. That's good.' She returned to the kitchen, but this time only pulled the door to. Their father started speaking again and now Finch could make out their conversation.

'I'm surprised at Robbie Bradbury, I really am. He's a responsible sort of lad. He really should know better.'

'Yes.'

'But that boy at Violet Ward's...'

'... John.'

'Yes, odd sort of boy. Looks a bit strange, don't you think?'

'I think there's a story there...'

The door opened again and both came out. For fear of discovery Finch retreated to the bedroom, but before long his brother returned and, with a flourish, produced a slice of toast, fluff from his dressing gown pocket still sticking to the butter. Good old Nid.

Finch sat at the window to eat. Down below The Green had returned to normal and people were criss-crossing on their way home. Only the small stage, still being dismantled, remained of the Fair's enchantments. After a few minutes he saw Robbie and John wander up from Main Street and pause outside Mrs Ward's house opposite. They were talking, Robbie with hands in pockets, a chubby fair-haired boy with a pleasing round face. John was kicking at the grass, rather forcefully. After a bit they stopped talking and looked a little awkward. Before long Robbie raised his hand in a parting wave and began to turn away. John said something and they both laughed, rocking back on their heels. They then talked on for several more minutes, slowly backing further apart. Robbie began to turn away again but John approached him, crossing the few yards that separated them and talking into his friend's ear, and then there was more laughter and some jocular shoving. Finally Robbie waved once more and they both turned away.

Robbie walked off down The Green towards home but John lingered, unmoving, watching Robbie until he'd rounded the corner by the sweet shop and out of sight, almost as if he wanted to preserve the moment, and only then did he turn away and go into Mrs Ward's.

VII

Robbie let on to no-one about their exploits on the railway and Finch, who always savoured an adventure, steadfastly kept their secret safe. Although he didn't know it then, it was also to be the last time Robbie would see John that summer. The following morning the Bradbury family went on holiday to the seaside, their first-ever such trip and, for the younger members, so exciting and different that for a week it eclipsed all else.

The boys shared a boarding house room with their father, Susan and their mother together in the other. From the windows, if the boys leaned right out and looked to one side, they could see the sea; a patch of intense blue between the red roofs, disappearing away into the equally cerulean horizon.

Each morning the five of them walked past the small harbour and fish market and down to the beach where they stayed all the endless day. It was sunny, golden and warm; the salt from the sea dried tight on their sunburned skin, and the sand was in their hair and between their toes. The glow from the sun lasted until they fell asleep, exhausted in strange beds, between their sand-roughened sheets.

They ate lunch on the beach and had tea trays from the beach café in the afternoon. They built sandcastles with shells and flags, made sculptures of whales and ships, and went crabbing in the rocks. Susan, in her pink ruched swimsuit learned to swim, while Jonathan floated effortlessly on his back, his eyes dreamily closed. Their father occasionally joined them in the water but their mother, despite her new swimsuit, merely paddled.

There are small square black and white photographs that show Tom and Sally seated in striped deckchairs, relaxed and smiling, bare foot and wearing unfamiliar shorts. Jonathan lies buried in the sand up to his neck and he's laughing, while Robbie is kneeling next to him in swimming trunks, holding a small metal beach spade. Susan had taken the picture and her shadow lies across the sand in front.

In another taken by Sally, Robbie sits astride his father's shoulders and Susan poses in her new swimsuit and pulls a cover-girl face. Jonathan crouches proudly in the sand car with lolly sticks and shells for dashboard controls, and they're all squinting into the dazzling sun so that their faces are creased up, smiling.

On their return, Moreton Steyning felt like another country; familiar yet alien, a place where they didn't quite belong or know the rules. Even the light was different; it was softer, flatter, and the colours more muted. They all felt they'd been away for weeks and expected much to have changed, but nothing had and life went on as normal, except in one respect.

Once they'd reinstalled themselves at Woodbine Cottage, Robbie was allowed to call round for John. He was looking forward to talking to his friend again after what had seemed such a long time. He was also in need of some good cheer at the ending of his first real holiday.

The house was as quiet and shut up as always but, after the usual lengthy silence, the door opened and Violet Ward stood looking blankly at Robbie. He wondered why she didn't admit him or tell him where John could be found and, after an empty pause, he eventually asked, 'Is John here, please?'

'No, holidays are over, Robbie' she replied. 'He's gone back home.'

VIII

With a conspiratorial wink as he passed through the kitchen on his way to the yard, Grandpa Rose pressed a shilling into Lizzie's hand. Standing at the sink, her mother saw and shook her head at him, chiding, 'You'll spoil that child.'

'Nonsense, Sarah. She's a good girl, aren't you, Lizzie?'

He was pulling on his heavy outdoor boots, while hanging awkwardly onto one end of the dresser. His pipe, as always, clenched between his tobacco-stained teeth. Widowed, and to all intents retired, having long since passed on the wheelwrights business to his two sons, Grandpa Rose now took cheerful refuge in his liberation from responsibility. Letting himself out, he clumped stiff-kneed across the yard.

It was several more minutes before Ron appeared, dragging on his jacket and lumbering through the kitchen ready to return to work, snatching at one of his sister's plaits as he passed.

'Shut the door!' his mother called with the weariness of one who knows their plea will yet again be ignored.

Lizzie was already pulling on her jumper and she bounded outside, taking care to close the kitchen door. It was Autumn half-term and a chill in the air showed that winter was nearer now than summer. On arriving at the Horse & Hounds she found a large delivery truck in the yard, blocking access to the door for the flat above the pub. At first she tried pressing herself against the wall and edging beside the lorry's massive tyres, which were nearly as tall as she was and smelled of hot rubber, but the chimney blocked her way through.

Beyond the truck, Maggie's father could be heard talking to someone. She could see by leaning forwards that it was the delivery driver, dressed in brown company overalls.

The two men stood between the cab and the rear wall of the pub. Rod Viney was in rolled-up shirtsleeves, with large forearms crossed over his broad chest. The driver stood opposite, a smaller man by comparison, pencil behind one ear and a cigarette on his lips. There wasn't much room and they were standing close to one another, eye to eye.

''Course, you've got to keep business going,' Viney was saying.

The other nodded. 'It all helps, that's for sure.'

The bigger man grunted, 'Those that don't help themselves...'

'Hard times...'

'There's always room. Anything, you know. You can always let me know.'

'I can sure do that, yes, I certainly can.'

'Just tip me the, you know, when you come. We can sort something. Usual arrangement, eh? Always helps, goes further, eh?'

'Oh yes.'

'Helps us both too, don't it?'

'It does that.' They nodded sagely at one another.

'Well, better get back. No peace as they say.' Viney unfolded his arms, 'What did we say then? Twenty do it?'

'Twenty five, mate.'

The bigger man pulled a roll of notes from a back pocket and counted them into the other's outstretched hand. 'Don't forget then,' he added with a nod, 'always welcome. Good for us both, eh?'

'Back in four weeks,' said the driver.

'Right you are, then.'

The lorry started up and rumbled noisily away through the yard. Not wanting to bump into Maggie's father, Lizzie shrank back behind the chimney and waited until she'd heard him walk away across the gravel in the other direction. He wasn't a man who had time for children, even his own. She knocked at the front door and after some time Maggie herself came down and stood on the bottom step, looking about, lean and barefooted.

'Hello,' she said, her expression blank.

'Coming out?'

'Can't, I'm looking after the little 'uns.'

Lizzie was disappointed, but not surprised. Compared to her own, this household seemed large and chaotic, controlled by a despotic father who, even the normally forceful and self-possessed Maggie, was subdued by.

Back out on The Square, she encountered Robbie and Jonathan emerging from their Uncle's shoe shop, and the three of them took the nearest path up onto Lullington Hill, where they roamed and larked about in easy companionship, having known one another all their lives.

Eventually they flopped down upon their favourite patch above the rabbit warren. It was getting late by then and the afternoon's autumn light was fading already. Way below in the vale, fields and hedges stretched to the horizon in shades of rusty brown where the low slanting sun met the recently-ploughed fields and the turning leaves of hedgerows. There were cows still in some of the meadows, not yet taken in for winter, while sheep grazed the upper slopes.

As the afternoon waned, the air became motionless, and sounds drifted up from far away; a tractor working its way slowly across a field in the distance, a cow coughing in a meadow. Like a chiffon scarf, a low coil of mist drifted across damp meadows beside the stream, and vertical plumes of smoke from leafy bonfires pierced the pale autumn sky as the approach of evening drained its colour. Soon the days would come when they would see their breath in white clouds, but for now they were happy, lounging in the cool grass, gazing up into the softening sky.

The unexpected sound of an engine close behind made all three start. It spluttered at first, but then roared, seeming to be just above their shoulders. The roaring increased and they sat up alarmed looking about them in vain, and then as if from nowhere an aeroplane suddenly swept so low over their heads that they all instinctively ducked. Lizzie cried out in alarm and the boys fell forwards to the ground. Jonathan was the first to his feet, gazing enrapt into the open sky as the plane circled some way above and then began to climb steeply, a small shape angled upwards with the engine roaring throatily.

It levelled off for a time and the sound faded, but then it suddenly plunged, swooping earthwards, engines now screaming in the downward surge. They stood astonished as it plummeted but then watched as with another roar, it pulled out of its dizzying descent and flew away on a level, far out over the vale, so that it was little more than a dark smudge in the pale sky.

Jonathan glanced back at the others, slack-jawed with amazement, and walked to the edge of the warren to get as clear a view as possible, his hands cupped over his eyes, shielding from the low sun.

For a time the plane flew on, then it banked steeply, heading back towards them before it once again lifted into a steep climb, its engines thundering as it accelerated high into the skies above so that they must strain to see it. Here it seemed to drift and hang for breathless seconds before once more tipping and hurtling down, this time directly towards them forcing Robbie and Lizzie to fall to the ground as the screaming roar increased. The aeroplane, a slender silhouette of wings, approached head-on, and Lizzie put her hands over her ears. Only Jonathan remained standing, gazing full into the approaching aircraft.

Abruptly, and with a deafening blast from its engines, the plane pulled out of its steep dive and screamed low over their heads, its chequer-patterned underwings seemingly just touching distance above. The three of them spun about to watch it fly away over the top of the hill, so low that they clearly saw the pilot wave to them from his cockpit.

Jonathan stood transfixed, face reddened with excitement.

'Robbie, I'm going to be a pilot when I grow up,' he gasped with fervour. 'I'm going to be a pilot.'

Chapter Two: 1958

It had become a regular pattern for the Bradbury brothers to stay with an elderly Aunt and Uncle during the school Easter holidays. At thirteen, Susan had long since considered herself too mature to associate with her younger brothers, and in any event she didn't want to be away from her own friends. She remained at home in Moreton Steyning, and this was not a matter of regret for the boys, who relished the prospect of any time spent away from family life and routine, and therefore didn't welcome the company of an older sister.

Although the distance was relatively short in miles, this annual journey felt like an escape to a different world. Even by the standards of Moreton Steyning in the late 1950s, their Aunt and her husband led an old-fashioned life. The eldest of their father's seven siblings, May, who was aged about sixty at that time, and Fred, seemed to inhabit a life from an earlier era. Home was an ancient rambling farm cottage in Aston Haddon, a large dispersed village some twelve miles distance across the vale.

Although their Grandmother had brought up eight children, only the boys' father Tom had produced living progeny, and Jonathan and Robbie alone represented the future of the Bradbury name; although only one would carry it forwards, but that would be later. Before that, there was Hugh.

The brothers were taken by their mother, each carrying a small bag, on the local bus to town where the three of them waited in the bus station café over tea and buns, watching the buses come and go until the service arrived that would take the boys to Aston Haddon. Sally Bradbury asked the conductor to see them safely off and paid their fares, and only then were they finally at liberty, taking up positions at the front of the bus to enjoy the long journey ahead. It was in fact a ride of barely more than an hour, but it always felt like a real expedition that would take them far away from all that was common place and routine.

The bus swayed out into the main road and soon turned off towards Aston Haddon and away from familiar places. A few people boarded but it was the middle of the day, too early or too late for the peak of travel. Before long they were following country lanes from village to village. Sometimes people got off, occasionally someone got on. A few people knew one another and a conversation would start up. The brothers were fully absorbed in gazing out of the front window at the ever-changing views and studying each new passenger as they got on. Occasionally the conductor walked down the aisle to check they were alright and make conversation, but presently a man boarded the bus and engaged him in talk about someone they both knew and the boys were left to their own devices.

After about half an hour the bus passed through a large village on a main road, where several people boarded. It was quite full for a time and someone swung into the double seats opposite the brothers, a young man of about twenty with dark wavy hair, smartly dressed, although casual. He nodded acknowledgement and, after several minutes spent gazing out of the side window, turned towards them and spoke.

'Going far?'

'Aston Haddon,' replied Robbie.

'Me too. But I haven't seen you two boys around. Is that where you live?'

Jonathan wriggled round, anxious to contribute. 'We're going to stay with our Auntie May and Uncle Fred,' he explained. 'Robbie and me. We're invited because it's Easter holidays.'

'That's nice. I used to like staying away at your age. Great fun. Always an adventure.' He smiled to himself, presumably at some recollection.

'Robbie and me are going to have adventures.'

'I'm sure you will. Where is it you're from then? I take it you're brothers?' By then the young man had turned to face them, one arm draped casually along the back of the vacant seat alongside him.

'Moreton Steyning,' said Robbie, indicating the direction where he thought it lay. 'This is my brother Jonathan.' Jonathan beamed back.

'And you're Robbie, right? Is that Robert?'

'Yes, Robert Bradbury. And we've got an older sister, Susan.'

They were well-schooled in this polite form of discourse. '...but she's not coming,' Jonathan quickly added, as if by the sheer mention of it, there might be a danger of it coming about.

'Quite right,' their new companion replied. 'Can't have an older sister around when there's adventures to be had.'

'Where do you live?' Jonathan asked with his customary lack of natural reserve.

'Oh, not that far.' And then leaning forwards, right hand extended, 'Hello, I'm Hugh Dollicot.'

The brothers solemnly shook hands with him.

'I've just dropped my car off,' Hugh explained, jabbing a thumb back in the direction they'd just come from. 'It's got some kind of problem with the starting. I'm not sure what, don't really understand these things, but it was making such a peculiar noise I've taken it to the garage back there. They're good fellows, they'll sort it out, and I'm getting the bus back. Hope it won't be out of action too long, it's all a bit of a nuisance really. Oh well... actually, planes are more my thing.'

'Aeroplanes!' Jonathan exclaimed, face radiant.

'Oh, you like planes too?' smiled Hugh.

'Jonathan loves planes,' Robbie explained as the moment had rendered his brother temporarily quite speechless. 'He can draw lots of them and knows all their names.'

'I've got a model of a Spitfire and a Lancaster bomber in my bedroom,' Jonathan was breathlessly saying.

'Ever seen a real one close-up?' Hugh asked.

Jonathan made his braying laugh. This was way outside of his world, so impossible as to be preposterous.

'No, really. Have you?' Hugh persisted.

The brothers simply laughed.

'Only in the sky!' chortled Jonathan.

'Well, come and see mine. It's at Aston Haddon. At the airfield.'

In response to their stupefied expressions, he added, 'Didn't you know there's an airstrip? It's out the back. Perhaps you don't if you've only ever visited. Actually, it hasn't been used much until the last couple of years. Quite an active flying club there now. Anyway, that's where I keep my plane and it's where I fly from. I go up whenever I can; at least once a week. A lot more often if I get the chance. What d'you think? Would you like to see it? Would your family let you come?'

They looked at one another open-mouthed.

'Tell you what,' he was saying. 'I'm going there on Friday. And that'll give you time to see if you can come. Just call into the office there and ask for me: Hugh Dollicot.'

***

Their Aunt May met her nephews off the bus, drawing each in turn into the soft marshmallow of her short round body, and obliging them to recount in detail everyone's health and activities.

They shared a long narrow room within the eaves of the old house, sleeping on hammock-type beds when they weren't being woken by the scratching of small creatures scuttling above their heads. They often rambled the surrounding lanes and fields and occasionally fell into halting conversation or impromptu games of football with a few of the local boys, although they kept a measured distance. Aston Haddon and Moreton Steyning were, after all, several miles apart.

Almost from the first day they saw small planes in the skies over the village, and Hugh's invitation to the airfield was rarely far from their minds. The Dollicot name having been checked out with their Aunt's WI associates and found to be perfectly respectable, the brothers were permitted to go.

The airfield was about a mile from the village edge, but shorter by the footpath which struck out across fields from behind the last houses. They could see it for some distance before they got there; a squat wartime control tower, concrete block buildings and a large hangar, their anticipation building the nearer they came.

Crossing a road after the last field stile, the brothers entered through large metal gates and stood anxiously, unable to decide what to do next. To one side stood one-storey buildings, and beyond, the tarmac apron and runway dissecting the grass field. Robbie pointed to the first building and led the way towards it. Several men were indoors in a kind of bar area. As they nervously pushed the door open a man lounging in a battered armchair looked up.

'Hello, boys. Can I help?'

'Is Hugh Dollicot here, please?' Robbie asked.

'Hugh? Yes, I think I've seen him. What day is it... Friday? Yes, he'll be here... down at the hangar. Know where you're going?'

They shook their heads mutely and the man came to the door, leaned out and pointed round the corner of the building. 'Follow it round, you can't miss it, and watch out for planes taxiing. Okay?'

Once past the building, the hangar was in sight and, more to the point, so were several aircraft. Robbie heard Jonathan's sharp intake of breath and his pace quickened so that his younger brother was forced to trot to keep up. They halted outside looking about until a voice hailed them from within.

'Hello! Over here!' Hugh, dressed in dark blue flying overalls, was beckoning from the entrance.

'You made it then. Excellent. Settled in with your folks?' he said over his shoulder, as he led them through the cavernous interior where several light aircraft were parked, and then over to a smart red and white plane.

'Just doing a few checks,' he explained. 'Here, have a look.'

For a time Jonathan forgot to breathe, and then his breath came out all of a sudden with a loud rush. He stepped silently forwards and gently placed one large palm on the plane's wing-top, running his hand softly along, stroking the smooth shiny surface, delicately measuring its every curve with his fingers. Robbie joined him, stretching up on tiptoe as he was considerably shorter, feeling the cold of the rounded fuselage with its glossy red and white paintwork.

'It's...' began Hugh.

'A Cessna,' Jonathan whispered.

Hugh, arms clasped about his chest, feet planted squarely on the floor, laughed. 'You do know your planes! What d'you think? Like it?'

'It's...' began Jonathan, eyes still roving about the plane, memorising every detail, but he failed to find any words to explain his feelings.

'I think it's very smart,' Robbie offered in place of his brother's mesmerised silence, watching as Jonathan began slowly to circle the Cessna, studying every surface and feature, hardly daring to touch, eyes shining. Hugh leaned back against the tail, arms still folded, legs crossed, watching them both, quietly bemused at their reactions.

'I've had it about two years,' he offered after a few minutes. 'No, about a year and a half, right after I'd learned to fly I bought it. I take her up at least twice a week, more often if I get time. You have to keep your hand in. I love it, soaring up there, everything laid out below you, seeing miles and miles to the horizon; the power of the aircraft and being able to do anything you want. There's nothing else like it.'

He looked back over his left shoulder to where Jonathan had reached the tail and was now reverently examining it. 'What do you think, Jonathan? Think you'd like to fly when you're older?'

'I'm going to be a pilot when I'm grown up,' Jonathan replied, matter of factly.

Hugh looked at him and paused for just a second. 'First class idea, that's excellent. Absolutely. Tell you what, boys – help me push her out and you can watch me take her up. How about it?'

It just couldn't get any better for the brothers. Out on the tarmac, in the sunlight, the Cessna looked even more magnificent. They watched as Hugh prepared the plane for flight then pulled open the cockpit door. He was just about to step up inside when he paused.

'Fancy a taxi along the runway?' he asked.

Robbie's spirits failed him, but Jonathan lunged forwards. 'Oh, yes. Please!'

'Up you come then. I can only take one at a time.'

He hauled Jonathan, who was ungainly at the best of times, up to the cockpit and Robbie watched his brother slump, glowing, into the passenger seat where Hugh strapped him in and pulled the door to. The engine burst into life and they both waved as the plane began to taxi across the tarmac towards the runway. Robbie could only imagine his older brother's feelings as his greatest dream came true.

A more reserved child, he stood a little awkwardly and nervously watched, happy to be merely an observer. Jonathan waved again from inside the cockpit as the plane picked up speed, the engine pitch rising as it purred along the runway before it slowed, turned and then accelerated back towards the hangar and Hugh pulled up some yards short and cut the engines. The passenger door swung open and Jonathan sat there radiating sheer joy.

Hugh jumped down from his side and then helped Jonathan clamber out.

'Did you see me, Robbie, did you see me!' he cried, hurrying over.

But Robbie had noticed something else. 'The pattern,' he said pointing to the underwing surface; it was chequered.

Jonathan's eyes followed his direction. 'It was you, Hugh!' he cried, jubilant.

Hugh looked puzzled.

'Over Lullington Hill. You were doing this,' and Jonathan mimicked with his hand the steep climb and rapid descent, followed by the sharp pull out of the plane they'd watched from the hilltop with Lizzie six months ago. 'You waved to us!'

'Near Moreton Steyning where we live,' Robbie offered. 'It was last Autumn, and we were on the top of Lullington Hill, and this plane with the black and white under the wings was doing loop-the-loops and things, and then it buzzed us and we all fell down, and then the pilot waved at us from really low.'

Hugh was standing between Jonathan and the Cessna, looking down on the boys, and then suddenly his face showed recognition.

'The chequer-pattern! Yes, that's got to have been me, mine's the only one. I do lots of aerial acrobatics, absolutely love it. Showing off probably. Yes, I remember... kids on the hilltop.' He laughed. 'So that was you! Well, well.'

***

Childhood instinct told the brothers not to let on to their family about Jonathan's plane ride, but henceforth they regularly scanned the skies over Moreton Steyning for the red and white plane with the chequer-patterned underwing. Twice they saw it; once from the school playground at lunch break, circling slowly high above them, and later from Lullington Hill again, climbing steeply and descending with a rush, but no more exciting aerobatics and it didn't fly over them although they'd stood on tiptoe and waved and waved.

II

Tom Bradbury had only ever worked at Netherington Hall. He was 14 when he'd started there as the pot boy, as his father had done before and, like him, had progressed to join the team of gardeners caring for the ornamental beds that surrounded the Hall, and its extensive kitchen garden and greenhouses.

His whole life was spent nurturing plants; tending the elaborate borders at the Hall, mowing and weeding the neat lawns, producing the vegetables, and fruit and cut flowers for the Harrison-Bates family from the secret and specialised world of their walled garden.

When he wasn't there he would be found in his own garden or allotment. He carried with him the wisdom and lore of generations past, his whole life was bound up in the soil. He wouldn't say he loved it; it was simply life. From childhood he'd watched his own father tending their plot, and had learned early that no one can exercise control over the vagaries of weather or season, and this had imparted in him a calm and accepting disposition. A reflective man, he was content in his own company and place in the world. With a steady patience, he moved through life, yielding to its currents and accepting the forces of nature that sometimes frustrated his efforts. One of those forces was his wife. The daughter of a small businessman, Sally was by contrast shrewd and acquisitive with money, restless, oftentimes dissatisfied, industrious and energetic. She was, nevertheless, the love of his life.

At that time, little had changed at Netherington Hall. Even the war was scarcely more than an interruption to the order that had prevailed for a century or more. After the army, Tom had returned to his job there and, together with the three other gardeners, all too mature in years to have served during the conflict, restored the gardens to their pre-war splendour. True, only two of those now remained, and one of them should have retired some years back; and there was no longer a pot boy to follow on, although that was partly compensated for by modern labour-saving methods. The pattern of service and life at the Hall nevertheless progressed very much as it had for decades past; quietly, formally, decently.

That year, summer had come suddenly, and almost without warning after weeks of the unsettled weather that had dogged June and much of July, providing the villagers with an endless source of conversation and complaints. The children had scarcely noticed the showers and grey skies which had often kept them indoors and away from the fields and hill, except that when they could get out the grass was always wet and the ground muddy. A few days before school ended however, the season changed abruptly, successive days dawning sunny and warm, so that a great sense of freedom foretold of summer weeks stretching ahead with all their limitless possibilities.

That morning was especially full of anticipation. As a thank you for all the extra work he'd put in getting the borders, lawns and cut flowers to a peak for their Silver Wedding Anniversary party, the Harrison-Bates had invited Tom's boys and 'a few friends' to the house for the day to help eat up left-over food from the party, and to play on the croquet lawn and tennis courts.

The lesser brother of a wealthy family in the county, the eldest son of which carried a minor title bestowed many generations ago for services rendered, Geoffrey Harrison-Bates was nevertheless a prominent local figure and his wife a regular hostess of parties and weekend gatherings at the Hall. For weeks leading up to the party, Tom had returned after his dinner to work on through the long summer evenings, creating the elaborate bedding out, tending, trimming and edging, only returning home for bed long after dusk.

The boys had been up there before, and somehow it always was 'up', and this was not merely a reference to the Hall's hilltop position, but that had only been for brief visits, such as when Tom had to call in and check on something, taking his sons along, plus Susan when she was younger, to keep the children out of their mother's way while she shopped or cooked. This, however, was the boys' first-ever proper, invited visit.

That morning they went with their father on his usual route to work, along the Sheep Path, taking turns to ride on the cross bar of his bike or trot alongside while he languidly pedalled. The old track crossed the railway line, then passed between fields and horse paddocks until it reached the outskirts of Netherington, a compact village of mainly red-brick houses on the main road to Cullingham and Tom Bradbury's home village. Leading off from the main road through ornate cast iron gates was the Hall's long curving drive that ascended between steep, laurel-topped banks.

They walked up, the boys only half-listening to their father's instructions to behave, not to take liberties, and always to say thank you. Tom would usually approach directly to the garden offices by a gate round the back, but for this occasion the children were to be delivered to the house. Frank Bird's car overtook them, bringing Nid and Finch sitting in the front, with Maggie, Ann and Lizzie in the back, wriggling round to wave through the oval rear window.

The Hall was an irregularly-shaped, somewhat austere but solid Victorian house; constructed of brick, with a conical turret to one corner and deep stone-mullioned bay windows. It seemed overwhelmingly large and grand to them all. The upper storey had decorative fretwork of ox blood coloured timbering and one entire wall was enveloped in a heavy creeper. To the side a broad, stone-flagged terrace with balustrades looked out over the expansive gardens that dropped gradually away and gave views over the tops of a distant belt of mature trees fringing the grounds to the countryside beyond.

Tom pulled the friends into an awkward huddle before him, controlling them from spilling out over the terrace with his hands on the outer children's shoulders, until Mrs Harrison-Bates emerged from the French doors with a well-practised smile.

'Not all yours surely, Mr Bradbury?'

***

What followed was, for the children, an almost unreal day; it was carefree, endless, a poignant point in time, suspended in its perfection, and that Robbie would remember for many years. They're long gone now but, at that time, below the terrace, sloping lawns led round to formal flower beds with neat, gaudy-coloured bedding and a rectangular fish pond, and from there it opened out on to a level area of grass where the croquet was set up. Beyond, against the walls of the kitchen garden, deep herbaceous borders were a distant blur of colours. None of them had any idea how to play croquet but, freed from any such restrictions, had huge fun belting the balls through the hoops and inventing rules and techniques that kept them entertained until the housekeeper brought out jugs of lemon barley water and a plate of sandwiches and biscuits for elevenses.

Tom came to check and invited them into the walled kitchen garden where he and Mr Higgins – and, just as it was always 'up', it was always 'Mr' Higgins – were tending the soft fruits while elderly Mr Frobisher pottered, a ghostly shape seen through the window whitening in the large greenhouse. To Robbie it was a magical world, unconnected to his own reality although he knew his father came there every working day of his life. Rows of pristine vegetables of every possible kind and vast beds of cutting blooms were separated by gravel paths, all enclosed by high brick walls to reflect the warmth, against which were trained fruit trees in fan-shapes and espaliers. Mr Higgins took them to see the impossibly neat tool and potting sheds and let them pick ripe strawberries before Tom returned them to the terrace.

Here they were amazed to find plates of sandwiches, slices of meat pies, biscuits and cakes and more squash set out on low tables. They piled their plates high as if the food might disappear if they turned their backs on it, and lounged about on the lawns below to eat. Emily Harrison-Bates wandered out again, stepping lightly down the curved stone steps from the terrace. She seemed so elegant and youthful in her neat, pale blue twin-set with pearls, hair neatly curled, bright red lipstick picking out her charming smile, born and bred to be a hostess as she was, and so unlike their own mothers.

'Are you all enjoying yourselves and have you had enough to eat?' she smiled, looking into each of their faces in turn. 'I'm sure we've got more if you would like it. No? All full? Well, that's good. Now, would you like to play tennis this afternoon? Yes? Then I'll ask Mrs Evans to bring out some racquets and tennis balls for you.'

She smiled again, then turned and tripped back in. Shortly afterwards the housekeeper emerged, arms full of an assortment of tennis racquets in their stretchers and a string bag of balls.

'Here you are, children. Mrs Harrison-Bates says you can use them, but please bring them back to the terrace when you've finished. The court's down there and, if you come back about three, I'll have some cold drinks for you before you go home.'

Their tennis was similar to their croquet but they somehow managed to all play one another on the one court, making wild swipes and running red-faced after the balls that almost always evaded their racquets no matter how much energy was put into playing. Only Maggie succeeded in hitting the ball over the net with any regularity, but the twins soon developed a variation on Rounders which the others quickly joined in with, dashing around the court trying to avoid being struck by wildly-thrown balls. Eventually, exhausted, hot and thirsty they gathered up the racquets and balls to return to the house for tea.

The direct route back up to the Hall took them across the dry, needle-strewn ground between the scaly pink trunks of a stand of larch trees, from where they could pick up a path that led from the perimeter walk. As they joined this, a young man and woman came into view, strolling towards them from the opposite direction.

Jonathan started. 'Robbie, look, it's Hugh!' he exclaimed. 'Hugh, Hugh!' and he ran forwards, waving madly and calling out.

The young man had been in conversation with the girl accompanying him but, hearing the shouts, looked up and across to where the group was emerging from the shadows beneath the larches.

'Well I never!' he said. 'It's... Robbie and Jonathan, isn't it?'

'Yes! Hello, Hugh,' cried Jonathan, lumbering forwards, and Hugh smilingly extended a hand in greeting.

'What are you two doing here?'

'We're invited,' Robbie felt bound to explain. 'Our Dad works for Mr and Mrs Harrison-Bates.'

But Hugh was simply laughing, bemused. 'Well, fancy that,' he said, turning to his companion. By now they were surrounded by the others, all jostling to observe this unexpected exchange.

'Perhaps you haven't met,' Hugh said. 'This is Caroline Harrison-Bates,' and the young woman smiled vaguely back at them. 'What are you all doing here then?' he asked.

'We're helping eat up the party food,' Robbie explained, which brought immediate laughter from Hugh and Caroline.

'We've been playing croakey and tennis,' Finch interrupted.

'Excellent,' Hugh replied. 'Hope you're better at them than me.'

'We saw you flying twice,' Jonathan beamed. 'Once from the playground and once from on the hill. We knew it was your plane straight away.'

'You did? That's marvellous.'

'We waved but you couldn't see us,' Robbie added, half apologetically.

'What a shame. Look, are you going back up to the house? Shall we go with them, Caroline?'

They turned and all walked together up the steep path to the terrace where jugs of iced lemon barley water and plates of biscuits were awaiting.

'Well! I don't get this treatment,' Caroline laughed. A younger version of her mother, she was fashionably-dressed in a full skirt, with wavy fair hair and she smelled of face powder and perfume.

The group was soon joined by Emily Harrison-Bates, fulfilling her role of hostess, and Tom Bradbury who stood a little distance apart, conscious of his working clothes and soil-grimed fingers that no amount of scrubbing ever fully cleaned.

'Mr Bradbury,' she cried. 'The children have been marvellous. They've had such fun and it's been wonderful having them here. Oh, and this is Hugh. His family's the Dollicots... you know, of Dollicot's the Brewers, and he says he's met your boys before. Isn't that simply wonderful?'

Tom looked over to where Hugh stood alongside Caroline; relaxed, smiling, casually dressed in open-necked shirt, and helping himself to biscuits.

'Mr Bradbury,' Hugh leaned across, proffering his hand, 'Robbie and Jonathan came to have a look at my plane at Aston Haddon. Excellent boys. They're a credit to you, and very knowledgeable about aircraft.'

Tom leaned stiffly forwards to take Hugh's hand while, beside him, Jonathan exuded pride.

'That's very good of you to show them. Much appreciated,' he replied, a slight gruffness in his voice revealing discomfort.

For the first time in his life Robbie felt a shaming disconnection from his father, who he could see did not belong in this company, and felt that he did not, although Robbie regarded Hugh as a friend.

'It was a pleasure. Any time,' Hugh was saying, with an airy wave of his hand to signify that it had been no trouble.

By then Frank Bird had arrived in his car and the others were being loaded in while Tom retrieved his pushbike. He rested his hands paternally on the back of his sons' necks.

'Well boys, time we were off too. What do you say?'

'How are you all getting back?' asked Hugh. 'You won't all get in there. Mr Bradbury, let me drop the boys back in the car, it won't take a minute.'

And so the brothers got to ride in Hugh's British racing green Austin Healey sports car, squeezed together into the single passenger seat where inevitably Robbie was crammed between Jonathan and the door. They sped effortlessly along the narrow lanes back to Moreton Steyning, the engine roaring and the wind in their faces, snatching at their hair. Hugh drove with casual self-assurance, turning the car nimbly into Main Street, where he pulled up outside the cottage with a final roar from the engine that brought surprised looks from passers-by.

Witnessing their dramatic arrival, Susan was beside herself with envy. At almost fourteen she could picture herself riding in an open-topped sports car with a handsome boyfriend like Hugh, and she watched as her brothers stiffly clambered out. Sally, a little bewildered by it all, accepted Hugh's smiling explanation until Tom arrived on his bike, a little breathless, having ridden home rather more quickly than usual; anxious to check on his sons safe arrival.

'The lad's walking out with Miss Caroline,' he told his wife once Hugh had gone. 'Seems he's one of the Dollicot Brewery family.'

'That's a good match,' Sally said.

***

For the rest of the day, the brothers enjoyed some degree of celebrity, and a begrudging and silent respect from Susan, who greedily took in her brothers' answers to their parents renewed questioning about Hugh, although they could provide little by way of real facts. After a while even Susan flounced off and Jonathan made his way upstairs to play with his planes.

Left to himself, Robbie wandered out to the garden, bouncing a tennis ball off the path which made a reverberating *thwang* as it ricocheted against the shed's brick wall and back into his hands. He was good at this, and could keep it going for some time, and so he didn't hear the side passage gate open until suddenly he became aware that someone was standing behind his shoulder. He caught the tennis ball on the rebound and turned.

'Wotcha.'

It was John Norbert, a little taller than when he'd last seen him a year ago, but every bit as untidy and skinny. His heart jumped with surprise and pleasure.

III

Ann knew that Maggie Viney was usually to be found in the pub's rear yard; a private, secluded and self-contained space, just like Maggie herself. Self-absorbed and self-reliant she'd be out there, engrossed in solitary games, seemingly oblivious to her isolation. By dint of their friendship, it had become Ann's playground too, a gravelly, dusty expanse, rutted by the tracks of delivery lorries which had exposed the gritty sandy soil beneath, and enclosed by a range of shambling tin-roofed sheds. It wasn't overlooked, except at the two entrances from The Square, one to either side of the pub, and was a perfect place for their play.

The Viney family had arrived in the village when both girls were five and Rod Viney had taken over as publican at the busy Horse & Hounds at the bottom corner of The Square. A thin, peaky-looking girl with sallow skin and lank dark hair, Maggie simply appeared at the village school one day. She was a self-possessed and knowing girl, and the other children thought her sly.

Ann never quite understood why it was that Maggie, who always seemed so confident, chose her to be her friend. Perhaps it was because Ann was less threatening than the other village children, but perhaps it was also because neither of them had attracted a large crowd of appreciative friends around themselves. Whatever the reason, Ann had little choice about it, and she had become a part of her more confident friend's world. Ann didn't mind, Maggie was fun to play with, even though their games tended to be on Maggie's terms, as indeed did most things.

That morning, entering the yard in search of Maggie, Ann's eyes were being dazzled by the harsh summer light as it flared off the gravel and white-washed walls of the pub. She felt dwarfed and oppressed by the yard's looming expanse and emptiness. From The Square behind, busy with its morning shoppers, the sounds of voices and vehicles drifted in, familiar and yet remote, accentuating her feelings of inhibition. A timid child, she clutched at her skirt, swinging it to and fro; a diminutive figure, humming quietly to comfort herself, with Maggie nowhere in sight.

Across the vivid and bleached-out yard, the sheds' interiors, so familiar as a setting for their games, now appeared dark and foreboding. She wanted to call out, but feared exposing her own voice, as if trespassing in this deserted space. Slowly she ventured to the nearest shed, stepping silently over the threshold to see if Maggie was inside, perhaps quietly absorbed in some game as she so often was, or playing house, arranging the broken chairs and stools to make a homely setting like they did together. It never occurred to Ann that Maggie was compensating for anything.

Inside, the air was cool and damp. Even though her rubber-soled sandals made no sound on the hard floor tiles, she stepped with soft and careful treads, fearful of disturbing the stillness. As her eyes adjusted to the gloom, chairs and clutter gradually emerged from the darkness, all familiar playthings, yet seeming alien without Maggie's confident, noisy company. A chipped ashtray full of pebbles and some old pub glasses were still on the floor from their last game, but gave no comfort. She whispered Maggie's name, fearing the sound of her own voice in this noiseless and airless place, but no answer came back.

Gingerly she edged through the linking door to the next shed, the one in which tools were stored. Dark, with only one small window and an earthen floor that made it inhospitably cold and clammy, the two girls rarely entered here, but Ann peered in all the same, just to be sure. Abruptly, from across the yard, the sound of brisk footsteps on the gravel came as the loud, rough tone of men's voices alerted her to Maggie's father approaching rapidly, in company with another person.

She slipped back into the darkness of the tool shed, praying they would go on past, but instead the footsteps paused and the two men entered the outer shed, temporarily blocking the bright sunlight that spilled through the open doorway, so that only the cool dimness remained. Recoiling in the gloom, Ann hardly dared breathe the musty air for fear of discovery.

'Warm one today, Fred,' Viney was saying.

'Yes, about time,' another voice replied. 'We've waited long enough, eh?'

'That's right. Good for trade, but kids round the place all day, under your feet. Now...'

Ann heard Viney grunt as if lifting something, then the rustle of paper and the chink of glass against glass. 'That should be right.'

'Yes... yes, just the ticket.' A chuckle. 'Warms the cockles, eh?'

'Yes. Missus alright?'

'Oh, not bad, you know. Yours? How's those kids?'

'Oh, you know, kids...'

'Yes, well... expect we were just as bad in our day. Reckon I was.'

More laughs.

'Probably, yes. What's it to be next time then? Same again? Something for your Edith?'

'Make it a Bells would you, Rod, and Jim says he wants two London Dry. I'll pick them up for him next time. And I'll have a box of Mackeson too. Same as usual today?'

'Right you are. Yes, usual amount.' There was the sound of paper notes being counted then a brisk 'thank you very much' from Viney.

'Well, best be off. Same day next month?'

'Yes. Well, must get ready to open up. Tell Will if he wants to order he'd best see me before the end of the week.'

'Right you are.'

The voices tailed off as they crunched back across the yard.

'Cheerio then. In tonight?'

'Should be.'

'Right-o.'

In relief, Ann's breath came out all in a rush and she found herself gasping to catch up, her heart beating so fast that she felt light-headed. She waited until she was sure she could hear no more sounds outside, and then crept through the sheds and stood in the open doorway, temporarily blinded by the intense brightness outside. Across the yard, Maggie was sitting on the doorstep to the flat.

'I was looking for you,' Ann said, somewhat pointlessly.

'Mum wanted me but I can go out now. What shall we do?'

'Your Dad was here.'

'I know. He went out with Foxy Fred.'

'Who?'

'Mr Slater... lives up by the garage.' She nodded in its direction. Maggie knew everyone, even though she'd only lived in Moreton Steyning for four years. That was a consequence of living in a pub. Sooner or later, and usually sooner, you got to see pretty much everyone in a village.

Ann sat down on the step beside her friend. Long-limbed, Maggie lounged with her brown legs flung out, hands cupped in the lap of the dress which she'd already outgrown. 'Anyone around?' she asked.

'Haven't seen them. We could go down Fresher's Field,' Ann suggested.

'Could do.'

'Or the pond. Maybe Lizzie's there with Robbie.'

'Let's go and see,' and Maggie jumped up, decision made.

Just then, scattering pebbles against the sheds with a noise like gunfire, Morris's greengrocery trade bike came skidding into the yard, gouging a long scar in the gravel as it slewed sideways before clattering to the ground. The rider, too small to reach the floor, leapt clear. They hadn't seen him for nearly a year but recognised him straight away. It was John Norbert.

'Woah! See that!' he roared, standing back to admire the scrape across the gravel, the bike abandoned on its side, with its wheels still spinning. 'Gotta be all a' ten feet!'

It wasn't, nothing like it, but John was proud as Punch, strutting up and down its length, hands stuffed in his trouser pockets, chortling throatily.

'Where've you been? When did you get back?' demanded Maggie.

'Coupl'a days. Here for the summer agen.' His small face crinkled into a broad smile. 'Back at me Aun'ie Violet's.'

'Where did you get the bike from?' asked Ann anxiously. She knew it was unlikely John would be working for Morris's – which in any event was Neville Potter's after-school job – and especially if he'd only just got back to the village.

'Borrowed i',' he laughed and, hauling the bike back up, he clambering on board. 'See ya!'

And with that, he sped off out of the yard, pedalling furiously, an absurdly small figure on the cumbersome trade bike.

Ann was troubled that she neither knew nor understood how John came to be in possession of the bike.

'D'you think Mr and Mrs Morris know?' she asked. Facts were a safe comfort blanket from the vagaries of life; a refuge from uncertainty. But Maggie merely shrugged, unconcerned.

By then they'd forgotten about finding Lizzie and had stayed in the yard until it was time for Ann to go home for her lunch. Maggie, as she so often did, elected to join her, uninvited. She liked going to her friend's house, so different from the overcrowded flat above the pub, which was noisy with the three younger children and the overbearing presence of her father. She ran halfway up the stairs, and casually called, 'I'm going to Ann's for lunch,' and bounded back down, without waiting for an answer.

The Dewberry's lived across The Square, in a white-washed timber and brick cottage, tucked out of sight behind the shops. It was reached by a narrow passage which led to a small cobbled yard, beyond which stood the cottage in its gardens.

'John Norbert's back, Mum. We saw him in the yard this morning,' Ann told her mother.

'Really. That lad from London? He was here all last summer wasn't he? He's back again, then?'

Her mother had accepted Maggie's unplanned attendance for lunch without comment. Usually it was just the two of them, mother and daughter together.

'Yup. He's staying for the summer again.'

'Is he staying with Mrs Ward?'

'Yup, with his Auntie Violet.'

'Don't say 'yup', it's 'yes'. Actually, she's his great Aunt.'

'What's a Great Aunt?' asked Maggie, mouth open, jaws working vigorously, food visibly churning.

'His mother's mother's sister.' Then, by way of further clarification, seeing Maggie's drawn brow, 'His Grandmother's sister. You've got Grandmothers haven't you, Maggie?'

'Mmm, but not here.'

The two girls spent the afternoon in Ann's garden, while Rags the Dewberry's whippet kept them company, stretched out on the lawn, lying on one lean flank, her tail thwacking the ground in happy accompaniment to her dreams.

Later the friends climbed the large cherry tree at the end of the garden, bracing themselves between the stone garden wall and the trunk until they could reach the first branches and swing themselves up into its crown and pull off the sweet dark fruits. They hung their treasure in dangling pairs over their ears, shaking their heads so that the cherries jiggled like earrings. Maggie, with her long limbs, could always get the furthest and sat astride a branch, high in the canopy, overhanging the footpath beyond the garden's end wall.

Hearing voices, they abruptly fell silent and peered down into the dark, sunken path beneath, to see who was approaching. Three lads were taking a shortcut to the outlying farms and they knew who it would be. Malcolm Draycott wasn't among them but Neville Potter was, and two of their pals. Maggie signalled to Ann to stay quiet. She had a pile of cherries in the lap of her dress and, as the youths passed below, flung the ripe fruits at their departing heads. They spun around, looking for the source of the attack, but the two girls had slipped hurriedly from the tree in a flurry of leaves and cherries.

IV

An entire year was a long time at the age of nine, but somehow, wordlessly and instinctively, John and Robbie had picked up their friendship from where they had left off at the end of the previous summer. It always surprised Robbie that his new friend hadn't associated himself with someone like Finch – boisterous, errant and impulsive like himself – but on most days John would come round to find Robbie and the two of them would go out; usually with the others, but often just on their own. Once again Lizzie, his usual playmate of choice, was supplanted by this curious incomer from London. Robbie was drawn to John; beguiled by him, along with his risk and danger.

One day early in August, not long after John had arrived back in the village, the two were sitting together on a low brick wall looking out over The Green, bored and generally undecided what to do, when Lizzie suddenly rushed past with Maggie and Ann in pursuit, yelling over her shoulder, 'We're meeting up at Swallow's!'

The boys watched in silence as the three small, determined figures disappeared from sight into Back Lane, then shrugged to one another and followed. If nothing else, it was something to do.

Glossy brown horses grazed the rough pasture in Church Piece, muscles twitching against the persistent flies. John studiously kept to the far side of Robbie, eyes darting, making sure to monitor their every move until he was safely through the squeaking metal gate and into the graveyard beyond. Robbie led the way beside the low stone perimeter wall and into a distant corner of the Churchyard where, beneath an ancient spreading yew, rested the chest tomb of Sir Hubert Swallow, Bart., *'Who toiled tirelessly for the good of his Country'*. Perched on the broad slab top, legs swinging over the edge, were Nid, Lizzie and Ann, while Finch and Maggie lounged against the cloth-draped urns and cherubs adorning the front. Old Hubert, whoever he was, whose name they somehow found so hilarious, had long provided the friends with a favoured meeting place.

'We're going up the hill,' said Maggie.

As this was a statement rather than a question, the two boys followed the others across the graveyard to the footpath that led past Snake Pond and up onto Lullington.

'Where's Jonathan?' Lizzie had asked Robbie as they'd begun to climb the steep fields towards its broad summit.

When he'd left home that morning, his parents and Jonathan had been preparing to go out. All smartly-dressed, noticeably so in fact, with Jonathan ill-at-ease in his school blazer, shirt, tie and best trousers. There had been an air about them that said this was adult business, and he felt he wasn't supposed to ask where they were going, and so hadn't. Lizzie had brought it back to his mind, but he shrugged and cast the recollection aside.

Lullington, where they all roamed and played, wasn't a hill at all, but a sinuous ridge of close-cropped, sheep-grazed grass. It extended for some two miles behind the village although, seen front-on and in profile from The Green, it had the deceptive appearance of a conical hill. Many paths climbed the slopes to the broad sward of its summit, which was crested by a gappy, overgrown hawthorn hedge. From here you could see for miles in all directions, out over the vale with its tight patterns of fields and dark patches of woodland and copses, to the distant line of hazy hills far beyond.

As they walked, the open fields soon opened up to the summit where the grass was springy and the ground pocked with rabbit holes. It was a breezy day, even more so with the cloud and sun quickly following one another, and pale vapour trails, like the vertebrae of fish, spreading across the expanse of sky. For a time they amused themselves chasing cloud shadows, and then one another.

After a while Robbie became aware of an aircraft noise and squinted up to see the characteristic chequer-pattern of Hugh's Cessna against the blue. They all waved frantically and called out 'Hugh, Hugh!' but he was too high. Nevertheless they ran about leaping, waving and yelling but the small plane was sweeping backwards and forwards, absorbed in its manoeuvres far too high above to see them.

'Let's make a message, you know, like SOS. In stones or something,' Nid suggested, but the hill had no rocks or walls to pillage.

It was Maggie who hit upon the idea of using their own bodies and she, of course, directed them. In two groups of three, they lay on the ground to form the two *H's* at either end, with cardigans and jumpers torn off to form the curving *U* and *G* between. That just left Robbie to stand alongside and madly wave Ann's red cardigan. They all watched in vain as the plane drifted level for several more minutes, and then it banked and climbed steeply before beginning one of its acrobatic dives. Finally, it pulled out of the descent, turned sharply and flew directly towards the hill.

At first it simply passed overhead without changing course, but then banked steeply and swept back over again, much lower this time and flew so close that they could clearly see every part. The rasp of the engines filled their ears, making the girls shriek with excitement and fear. When it roared upwards into a climb, they all yelled with delight and Hugh waggled its wings in acknowledgement, then performed a perfect roll.

***

For their ninth birthday in June, Nid and Finch had received brand new bicycles, and they emerged later that afternoon ostentatiously riding them; Nid's was a bright emerald green and Finch's a glowing ruby red. They sped in pursuit of one another around the triangle of The Green, two blond-haired boys, freewheeling downhill on one side and then pedalling vigorously back to the top on the other, weaving in and out of passers-by.

Ann arrived on her tricycle and for a while followed, but couldn't keep up until Maggie took over; her long legs splayed ludicrously so that she resembled a frog, furiously pedalling while Ann stood in the boot, holding onto her shoulders in charioteer style. Soon Lizzie returned to join in, riding her battered boys' bike. It had once belonged to her brother Ron, and she now rode it standing up on the pedals as the saddle was too high, swinging the frame from side to side in rhythm with her pumping legs.

Bikeless and excluded, nursing a cherished sense of injustice and envy, Robbie sat on the wall outside Mrs Ward's and watched. Beside him, John was silent, feigning indifference. Eventually the others grew tired and flung themselves down onto the grass, bikes scattered round about them.

'You can ride mine if you want, Robbie,' offered Lizzie.

'It's alright,' he said glumly and with rather bad grace, although she'd meant it kindly enough.

Generous of spirit, Lizzie was troubled if she thought someone was unhappy, but by now Robbie was wallowing in a fervour of grievance and wasn't to be solaced. A proper bike was something he cherished above all else.

'And John can ride Ann's!' laughed Maggie tartly.

Not even Robbie, however desperate, would have resorted to riding a girl's three-wheeled trike, but the image of John perched on the child's bike brought boisterous laughs from the others, as indeed it was intended to.

John lay back on his elbows at the edge of the group, gulped air and then belched loudly away towards the hill in a display of conspicuous indifference. In spite of her remarks, Maggie herself had no bike and, with five children in her family, was unlikely ever to get one. They all knew she had few toys and that mostly she shared Ann's who, being an only child, had more than enough and didn't seem to mind, or perhaps she simply went along with her more dominant playmate.

The day didn't regain the heights of that morning and the group eventually dispersed, Nid and Finch riding off round the village on their new bikes, while the three girls drifted away to Lizzie's. John and Robbie, now left to themselves, kept up their pretence to one another that they felt no resentment until eventually Robbie asked John if he had a bike at home.

'Nah,' he said, flinging a pebble. 'Ain't bovvered.'

Whenever Robbie tried to picture his friend's life in London, he felt it must be a place so big his mind couldn't comprehend its scope. He thought it must be somehow more exciting, utterly limitless in its possibilities, but also perhaps a little daunting.

'Have you got brothers or sisters?' he asked after a while. He'd never thought to enquire before. As he had two himself, he'd rather taken it for granted that everyone must have siblings.

'Me?' said John vaguely. 'Couple.'

Robbie inclined his head quizzically as John seemed disinclined to continue.

'One bruvva, one sister,' he finally replied and then, after a lengthy pause, 'not like yours.'

'Not like mine?'

'Nah, can't talk to 'em or play with 'em an' stuff.'

'No? Why?'

'Just stupid little kids, ain't they. Look, I got an idea. C'mon,' and he leaped up, beckoning.

Robbie had to run to follow him down the narrow shaded passageway in between two houses to Snail Path, and then along to the back yard of Morris's. With pantomime stealth to make his friend laugh, John crept in and emerged moments later pushing the large black trade bike, bearing *Morris's – purveyors of fresh fruit & vegetables* on the trade plate in florid red and gold script.

With a few hops and a skip to gain height he mounted, holding the bike upright, one leg buttressed against the yard wall as his legs were too short to reach the ground.

''Op on then!' he cried, standing up on the pedals for Robbie to take the saddle.

He knew he shouldn't, but the temptation was too great, and John's pranks simply too irresistible to forego. Before he could change his mind, Robbie had scrambled up and was holding grimly onto the frame behind his rear. John kicked off, and then they were away, bumping uncomfortably down the steep Snail Path.

They gathered speed quickly, lurching from side to side on the uneven and worn stones that sent the bike oscillating, while John wrestled with the over-sized handlebars. The old frame rattled and creaked alarmingly and Robbie could feel his cheeks wobbling with every judder and bump. He was barely able to hold himself in place on the saddle, with his legs flung out in an attempt at balance as they bounced, ever more wildly, the faster they hurtled.

''Ere we go!' yelled John, rump raised and crouching low, bracing himself like a skier approaching a jump, as they burst perilously from the bottom of the path and into Main Street.

To their left, the Cullingham bus suddenly came into view, bearing down on a direct collision-course. John flung the handlebars round, slewing the bike into a sideways spin that sent Robbie's arms and legs flying uncontrollably upwards. Unable to take his eyes from the advancing vehicle, he didn't see the obstacle that they were hurtling towards until he felt himself blindly pitched towards the ground, wincing in fearful expectation of painful grazes and bruising.

They landed heavily in a chaotic jumble of arms, legs, wheels and heavy bicycle, accompanied by a collection of strangled cries and yells, some of which at least Robbie knew must be his own. He'd felt himself bounce, yet didn't seem to be hurt. They lay in stunned speechlessness, the world about them momentarily stopped and silent, and then the road beneath them lurched and roared. For a few moments Robbie couldn't tell which way up he was and then felt himself tossed violently forwards, face down onto the hard tarmac.

'You bloody idiots!' yelled Malcolm Draycott.

Robbie hardly dared look.

The bus had pulled noisily to a halt and a few people hurried across to check the boys were alright and help disentangle them.

John had already bounded to his feet, ever indestructible, or so Robbie always thought. A man pulled the bike away and helped him up and, as he stood mumbling 'thank you's' and assurances that he was fine, he glanced nervously to where Malcolm stood. His nemesis glared back, red-faced with fury and humiliation, hand clamped to one bloodied knee.

'Nearly managed ta stop i',' John was saying to anyone who'd listen. 'Runaway bike. Just couldn't get i' ta stop. Really tried 'ard, ya know...'

Someone began to wheel the trade bike back to Morris's and, trying to conceal his pain, Malcolm hobbled off, casting back dark looks, mouthing, 'I'll get you, fat frog.'

***

Robbie was waiting in the garden late that afternoon when his parents returned, solicitous but subdued, despite knowing nothing of his earlier escapade.

'Alright, darling?' enquired his mother.

'Okay, son?' His father too was a little sombre.

'Yes, I'm fine,' he said, although his arm and shoulder were beginning to ache; an unwelcome reminder, as if he needed one, of Malcolm's threats.

Jonathan greeted him briefly, but shuffled off upstairs to discard his smart clothes, inviting no exchange on their respective activities. Robbie wanted to tell his brother about seeing Hugh's plane, but sensed this wasn't the time. Left to his own devices outside, he fed Digby and sat on the log seat, chin on hands, watching him enthusiastically demolish every scrap and felt sorry for himself; envying the old dog for his simple contentment.

After a time he could wait no longer and entered the dining room where he found his father had disappeared behind the newspaper, his nightly ritual. Robbie spoke through the kitchen door, left ajar, his voice pushing into the clamour of crockery and pans within.

'Mum... can I have a bike?' He heard the words in his head, as if they'd been spoken by a voice other than his own.

There was a silent pause from within. Behind him a slight rustle of the newspaper told Robbie that his father was looking at him over the top of the pages, but he ignored the temptation to turn around. From the kitchen he heard his mother's patient intake of breath. Something heavy was placed noisily on the cooker.

'Robbie, you know...'

'But Nid and Finch've both got bikes and they're younger than me,' he said plaintively.

'Only by a few months. And there's only two of them, and their father works in a Bank. You know that.'

'Ann's got a bike. And Lizzie.'

'Ann's is only a tricycle, and Lizzie's was her brother's. Anyway, that's not the point,' she said, coming to the kitchen door, cooking fork in hand. 'Look, you know we can't give you a bike at the moment. We've been through it before; many times. It wouldn't be fair.' And with that, she returned to the cooking.

'But Jonathan wouldn't mind,' he tried. He knew he was beginning to sound desperate. His voice had become a hard, peevish whine.

Behind him Tom laid the paper down. 'Come here, boy,' he said.

His tone was comforting but Robbie felt inured, unwilling now to be placated, despite his father's kindly manner. Digby pelted into their midst from the garden, panting and enthusiastic, tail wagging, but he ignored the dog. His father took hold of his arm, garden-worn hands rough on his skin, drawing him nearer. He stood there, beside the fireside chair, head sulkily drooping.

'We can't get you a bike yet, boy, not while Jonathan's at home. You know it wouldn't be safe for him.'

This was familiar territory, well-trodden, accepted, unquestionable. Something he'd grown up with: Jonathan's different-ness. Not less, just different. In his father's words, 'special'. He saw Tom glance up, Sally nodded back unseen, and Tom continued.

'Listen, we've got something to tell you. Jonathan's going to a new school in September.'

'A new school?' He repeated the words mechanically, trying to extract meaning from their bare bones, trying to picture what that might mean in their lives. 'Away from the village?'

'Yes, away from the village. It's for a trial, to see how it works out. He's twelve now, he needs to learn new things.'

'Is he going to the Seniors in Cullingham, then?'

'No, a school more suited to him. It'll be different because he'll be away during the week, but he'll come home at weekends, so you'll see him then. We went to see someone about it today and we think he'll get on well there. It looks very nice. Do you understand?'

'Mmm.'

'There's a good boy.' Tom ruffled his hair, coaxingly. 'If it all goes well we'll see about a bike. Alright? Good lad, now how about setting the table for your mother?'

***

They were a quieter family than usual over tea that evening. There was no further reference to their trip, or the reason for it, and Jonathan made no mention of the day at all. When the boys had eaten, the two of them wandered into the garden, as they usually did on summer evenings. It was cloudy and still, rather cool for early August, and it boded rain.

They sat together on the old bench beside the vegetable patch. Jonathan was impassive, gazing ahead, big hands drooping together between his broad, bare knees.

After a time Robbie spoke. 'Dad says you're going to a new school.'

Jonathan shifted his position, rocking slightly and leaning forwards, shoulders hunched. His voice was a little hoarse, like someone who hasn't spoken for some time.

'Yes.'

'Is that alright?'

His brother shrugged, seeming indifferent. 'Suppose so.'

'Is it nice?' Robbie was trying to introduce a cheery note.

'Lots of nice trees there.'

'Did you see any of the other boys?'

'Not really. Robbie?'

'Mmm?'

'I'm going to get you a bike. When I'm a pilot, I'm going to save up my money and, when I've got enough, I'll buy you a big bike. A red one.'

V

Maggie didn't have long to wait in The Square before they came out, the truck fully loaded with suitcases, and Ann sitting in the middle between her parents. Her father tooted and they all waved until the truck turned the corner by the pub, and Ann disappeared from her sight for two weeks.

The Dewberry's always went away in early August, staying in the same bed and breakfast at the seaside. Maggie could imagine it because Ann came back telling her of playing on the beach, catching crabs, making sand boats and learning to swim, but Ann was always afraid of the waves so she never did swim properly. Maggie knew that she would swim, given the chance; just like that, without having to learn, the cool deep water buoying her up, slipping through it like a silvery fish, floating and dreaming, the water rippling and gleaming off her body. She'd swim faster and better than anyone.

Ann had talked of little else for the last few days; the white-washed cottage called 'Seabreezes' in a lane of other little white cottages, her own room in the eaves from where she could see the blue sea from the window. The seagulls perching noisily on the roof and the harbour full of fishing boats, and the market where they landed and auctioned the boxes of slimy, slithery fish and the big pink crabs. There was a wide golden sandy crescent beach that was lapped by the deepest blue sea ever, with little white waves tipping over at the shore it was there that Ann would collect shells on the beach and watch the little grey crabs scuttling in the rock pools amongst the glossy, slippery green and brown seaweed.

Maggie put it from her mind and walked back towards the pub. Above her the window opened and her mother leaned out.

'Come up and look after the children, I've got to go out. Maggie, do hurry up!'

Her legs felt immobile. She couldn't will them to carry her back to the flat, up those steep, dark stairs to the mess, there was always a mess. She stood in the yard, eyes unfocussed and mind empty. Two weeks was such a long time. She'd been on a day trip to the seaside once from school, before she'd moved to Moreton Steyning, and they'd all run about on the sand and played Rounders. The teacher had bought them ice creams, but hers was nearly melted by the time she'd got it, and then it was time to get on the coach and come home again. Ann would come back from the seaside with a new doll or brightly coloured rubber ball and things they'd won on the pier; plastic animals, whistles, coloured hair grips, and sweets. Always lots of sweets.

A noise made her turn. Malcolm Draycott was cycling slowly past the yard entrance, so slowly she knew he'd been waiting for her to look around. She'd fallen for it and, as she turned, he spat into the gravel, a puff of dust rising from where the yellowy gob fell. On his left knee was a large sticking plaster. Anger burned inside her but she didn't feel like retaliating; not today.

Upstairs, she played with the baby while her mother went shopping, blowing rasping burps into the pink round belly, making Laura giggle and squirm. Even the younger kids were well-behaved, drawing with crayons and paper. She ignored the fact that she'd seen them scrawling on the wall. What did one bit more matter anyway? Who'd care? Only her father, and he needed no excuse to shout, the noisy louse that he was. When her mother came back she didn't feel like meeting up with her friends and instead slipped unseen into the storeroom, to her special treasures.

To avoid detection she didn't put on the light, so the room was gloomy. Ducking down she crawled as usual under the rusting metal racks, dragging herself on her elbows and belly, but something had changed. The light from the high passageway window no longer picked out her destination, instead, a square of darkness blocked her view. Stretching out one arm, she felt the cold surface of a large metal box. It was heavy and unyielding and she struggled and grunted to push it to one side sufficiently enough to squeeze past. Once she'd reached her secret place she crouched down again and, bit by bit, pulled the box from beneath the racks and out into the light by her feet. Sitting on her block of wood she prized off the lid with her finger nails. Inside were two large books with covers of a dull purple hue, like the ledgers her father used for his accounts which he kept by his bureau, on the other side of the storeroom.

Maggie pulled one onto her lap and opened it. It was full of his tight black writing. On one side were lists; drinks mostly, like gin, whisky and beers, but also cigarettes and cigars, and alongside were people's names: old Keach and Foxy Fred, Jim Bates, 'better-than-you' Frank Bird, Ted Collard and several more she knew from amongst the regulars. Down the right-hand side were columns of figures. It went on for pages and pages, although the book wasn't full. She pulled out the other ledger; it had 1954 to 1956 written on the front. She checked the incomplete book again, it started at the beginning of 1957. Flicking through, she found the latest entry was a week ago. The columns of numbers fascinated her; pounds and shillings and pence, one after the other, page after page. Maggie liked numbers and couldn't resist adding some up, checking column after column. She found two mistakes. He always thought he was smart, but he wasn't that clever, not by half.

Carefully, she placed the books back just as they'd been and pushed the box to where she'd found it. Above her head, Alice was looking serene and Maggie smiled back at her with satisfaction, a warm feeling in her stomach. Reaching up, she took down her new silver lighter and ran her fingers over its sleek shiny surface.

VI

'You don't go mixing with Neville Potter and his friends, do you hear?' his mother was saying over breakfast. 'You know I've told you not to. Mr Morris has had to speak to him yet again about leaving the delivery bike out, and he says he thinks Neville's been taking it out and larking about on it. He's had a good telling off and just as well. Mr Morris says he'll get one more warning and then he'll have to go if he doesn't pull his socks up. And he's careless, he simply dumps the deliveries down so the fruit gets bruised. I've a good mind to tell Morris.'

She looked up, 'Are you two finished then?'

'I can ride a bike,' Nid heard himself saying. 'I could do Morris's deliveries.'

He was picturing himself riding importantly on the big black trade bike, going from door to door, handing over bags and packages. 'Hello Nigel,' people would say as he took them their greengroceries, 'how are you today,' and, 'thank you Nigel, you deliver to us so efficiently'.

Her head jerked upwards from slicing the bread. 'You're too young,' she said shortly.

'I could do it!'

'Certainly not.'

'When I'm older, then. I can do it then.'

'No you can't. You'll have homework to do when you're older and you'll be studying.'

She vigorously buttered more bread and dropped a slice each onto Nid's plate and his brother's. Finch was silent, unusually so, observing the exchange from beneath his floppy fringe.

'When you're older you'll be going to the grammar school in Cullingham and there won't be time. And there will be homework to do. Besides.'

This 'besides' was delivered with such finality as to preclude any rejoinder.

'I could do it!' Finch chimed brightly from across the table.

A look from their mother, and her sharp exhalation of breath defeated even Finch, and the topic was closed. Finished. And that was the moment Nid knew his future was sealed; Grammar school awaited. There would be study, school uniform, College; working like his father, in a Bank. Sorted.

Once in the garden, Finch leapt onto the swing and energetically flung himself backwards and forwards to build up momentum, his shirt already having worked loose from his waistband.

'Good about old potty Potter, isn't it,' he was chortling, swinging high, his feet thrust forwards.

But it was John who'd been using the bike, Nid knew that. Maggie had been quick to impart her knowledge to all of them; knowledge being a powerful tool for reinforcing dominance. But for Nid, that knowledge was something of a dilemma, and it bothered him that he couldn't work out how he felt. He wanted to revel in Neville's downfall for the part he'd played in the attacks on all of them, and he'd got no doubt it was John who was behind much of the mischief with the bike. However, it was difficult to tell what was right and whether to feel glad or guilty for his own part in keeping the secret, although Finch clearly entertained no such worries, and rarely did. He could read his brother like a book.

'Yeah, what a laugh!' Finch was saying, getting to the point on the swing where the bumps started, and then he took a flying leap to land with a dramatic roll on the ground in front of Nid. 'See that?' he cried. 'Hey, I know! Let's make a swing boat.'

Nid had no idea how they were going to achieve that, but he was glad of the diversion and they soon set about lashing a plank across the swing's seat to sit astride, and then cast about for a long rope to throw over the frame to pull on. There was nothing suitable in the garden but then he remembered the bag of their father's old ties at the bottom of the wardrobe. They were going to the jumble, so he knew he wouldn't mind.

He ran in. Voices from the lounge and the chink of china told Nid his mother had a visitor, so he sprang lightly and silently up the stairs, two at a time and pushed open the door to their parents' bedroom, somewhat apprehensively as this wasn't a room they were supposed to go in, and it had a stillness and mystery that set it aside from the rest of the house.

Quietly, he pulled open the heavy mahogany wardrobe door and pushed the clothes apart, breathing in the stale smell of bodies which clung still to their fabric, feeling in the darkness for the bag amongst his father's immaculately shiny black shoes, but it wasn't there. He slid open the sock drawers, peering in, sliding his hand to the back of each to check, and then groped along the topmost shelf, high above his head, amongst the woollens. Still nothing. Finally, despite it being obviously too small, he pulled open the little drawer where his father kept his cuff links and watch and reached to the back, just to be sure. His fingers felt objects and, fumbling, closed around a metal form, something he didn't recognise. He pulled it out into the light to look.

Sinking back onto his heels, he gazed at a photograph in an ornate silver frame, beginning to tarnish black. Two people held a baby. They were shoulder to shoulder, smiling proudly, almost shyly, their heads slightly inclined to one another. It was his parents but they looked different, much younger, his mother's hair longer, softer, his father smooth-faced. They gazed out with fresh young faces, not unlike in their wedding photograph on the dressing table under the window. The baby could have been him or Finch, but where was the other? As twins they were always photographed together.

He reached into the drawer again and drew out a small leather-bound case which clicked open to reveal two more pictures. On the left a blond toddler in dungarees, smiling up at the camera, and on the right, the same little boy riding a big wooden train. He's clearly trying to propel it along with his feet, face all studied concentration, chubby legs protruding from baggy dungarees. Although the photograph is black and white, Nid can tell that the dungarees are blue and they have a little embroidered donkey on the bib.

He could feel his face frowning with perplexity. Finch and he had never had a wooden steam engine like that. He turned the case over. On the front, embossed in faded gold lettering, was the name 'James'.

Carefully he returned both to the drawer and slipped back downstairs and out into the garden.

'What?' said Finch.

'Nothing. Couldn't find it.'

'What?'

'Dad's old ties.'

'What for?'

'The swing boat, stupid.'

'I'm not stupid. What shall we do now?'

'Did we ever have a wooden steam train?'

'No.'

'Did anyone we know? One of the cousins?'

'Nope. Are we going to get one?'

Nid didn't bother answering, but the mystery of the unidentified child troubled him all day, hanging about, unwelcome but persistent. Unable to rationalise what he'd seen he didn't share it with Finch until much later on. When he did, in their bedroom after tea that evening, Finch was keen to rush into their parents' room to see the pictures for himself but his brother held him back by the shirtsleeve. There was something secret about it and he didn't want to be discovered in there.

'Do we know anyone called James?' he asked.

'I don't.'

'Are you sure?'

''Course I'm sure.'

'It's definitely Mum and Dad in the photos. Maybe it's a friend's baby,' Nid mused, casting about for explanations.

Finch shrugged, 'Let's ask.'

'No! Look, it's a secret. Otherwise why would they be hidden like that, and why've they never shown us?'

'Maybe they forgot. Let's ask.'

'No!'

'Maybe there're more. Why don't we go and look?'

Their parents were eating downstairs, the sound of their voices drifting up the staircase from the dining room below.

Nid was hesitant, but the idea was too tempting.

'No... well, alright. But quickly, and I'll show you the ones I found but be really quiet.' He felt the need to share it with Finch, for a twin's special empathy.

The boys slipped across the landing, and Nid gently drew the frame and album from their drawer and handed both to Finch, who squatted on the floor poring silently over the photographs lying in his lap. Then he looked across at his brother.

'It looks like us,' he observed.

Nid took the leather wallet from him. The round face with blond curls spilling over the forehead gazed, smiling, back at him, the boy's expression innocent and open.

'Not completely. His hair's wavy, ours is straight. You can't see where they're taken either, there's not enough in the background.'

'There's grass here, where he's on the toy train,' whispered Finch, pointing. 'It could be our garden.'

'There's grass in all gardens!' Nid hissed back.

'Is it a boy?'

'It must be. 'James', see?' and he pointed to the wallet cover.

Just then, the creak of the landing floorboards heralded the appearance of their father. Frozen and dumbstruck, they were like startled rabbits caught in his stern gaze. Both stared back, wide-eyed awaiting their fate, but their father didn't speak. His eyes took in the photographs in their hands, the earnest looks on their faces, but his expression didn't alter.

'Put those back where you found them and come downstairs,' he said, and turned away. They heard his firm departing tread on the stairs.

VII

It was Fair day and Lizzie sat perched on the corner of her mother's dressing table, watching as Sarah put on her face. Lizzie's bare feet were on the paisley-covered dressing table stool, her toes tucked reassuringly under her mother's warm legs. It was part of their ritual, this time together; it was calming and comforting, however impatient Lizzie was to go out. All the familiar little gestures and actions, the faces her mother pulled as she put on her make-up, and the sweet scent of her face powder and lipstick.

Sarah Rose studied herself in the mirror; a country woman in her late thirties, smooth-faced but with the first lines spreading out from her light blue eyes, her hair wiry and unkempt, too busy for more than a hairbrush dragged through it each morning. Laid out before her, duplicated in the mirror, were her manicure set in a pink faux-leather case, the pale green dressing table set of hairbrush, mirror and comb her father had bought her just after she married, the favourite gilt powder compact, a tarnished silver ring tree, and two lace mats made by her own mother shortly before she died.

Behind Lizzie's legs was the drawer where Sarah kept her smalls and, on the opposite side, that containing her lipsticks, scent bottles, jewellery and oddments. Lizzie knew every item; she loved to play with them all, taking everything out and sorting it and then faithfully arranging each one, before pulling on her mother's colourful necklaces and bangles. Sometimes she tried out her make-up and, however gaudily she'd plastered on the bright red lipstick and patted on clouds of her face powder, her mother would laugh and say she looked pretty.

Sarah was getting ready now to go to the Fair, wanting to look nice by briskly brushing out her stubbornly wavy hair. She held the compact open in front of her face, dabbed on the germoline-coloured pink face powder, pulling down her top lip to smooth her cheeks and turning her head from side to side as she pressed the fluffy pad to her face. She glanced at Lizzie and snapped the compact shut before taking out her eyebrow pencil. She feathered a brown line along her brows, smoothing first one then the other with a finger, and then selected a lipstick from the drawer, twisting up its bright red finger of colour before carefully applying it, pursing her lips like a blown kiss, then folding them in to finish.

She turned. 'Will I do?' Lizzie pressed her face to her mother's cheek, breathing in the sweet smell of her make-up.

'Come on then, let's do you,' she said and her daughter clambered onto the dressing table stool and watched in the mirror as Sarah firmly brushed out the long, pale blonde hair with her own hairbrush and swiftly plaited it with practised fingers, tying the ends with red ribbons to match her daughter's new striped dress.

Behind them the bedroom door banged open, revealing in the dressing table mirror Ron standing on the narrow landing. He wore smart black trousers, fashionably narrow.

'Where's my blue shirt?' His reflection looked past them into nothingness.

'Where's my blue shirt, *please*,' Sarah replied over her shoulder. 'I ironed it for you yesterday. It's hanging inside the airing cupboard door.'

There was the sound of the back bedroom door being flung open.

'A thank you would be too much to expect, I suppose,' she breathed.

Where Ron was concerned, it certainly was. The world existed to deny Ron his wishes, to restrict or frustrate his every move, a force that could only be countered with truculence and the burning desire to be somewhere – anywhere – else.

'Can I go to the Fair now?' Lizzie eagerly asked.

'Yes. Did Grandpa give you some spending money?'

'Yes.'

'I thought he might have. Off you go then.'

The minute she stepped out from the front gate, Lizzie was in that special world that was Fair day, happily swept along in the animated crowds that were moving towards The Green, from where the sounds of lively music and an excited hubbub drifted towards her.

At the corner by Mrs Patterson's sweet shop she was confronted by the usual magical transformation of the village centre into a crazy, noisy, colourful mêlée, buzzing with people and movement. The sun was shining and it was already warm. The loud music from the fairground rides filled the air and the sticky sweet smell of candyfloss wafted across, mingling with that of hot pies, even at that hour.

Robbie, Jonathan and John were sitting on the wall outside Mrs Ward's, watching the goings on.

'Budge up,' Lizzie said and they made room. Robbie handed round a bag of floral gums, hard and chewy and perfumed. She was bursting to tell her news.

'Guess what!'

They all leaned forwards, eagerly and conspiratorially.

'Sharon Soames is opening the Fair,' she gushed, and looked around excitedly for their reactions, but their three faces simply stared back blankly at her.

Lizzie was deflated. 'Sharon Soames – you know! You do,' she pleaded. 'The film star. She's ever so famous, and she's really pretty. Oh you do know her, you must!'

Robbie and John still looked blank, then Jonathan suddenly remembered.

'Yes, she comes from round here. Robbie, you do know her. She's in Mum's magazine. Are we really going to see a film star?'

By lunchtime the Fair was thronging with people under a blazing mid-August sun. They'd already been on most of the rides, eaten their fill of sweets, candyfloss and sausage rolls and were now hanging around the small stage for the celebrity opening, elbowing their way between the adults to get a clear view. To their right, the Vicar was in a permanent state of agitation, glancing first this way, then that. Colonel Benbow had come out from the Manor and stood at some distance beyond the stage, pacing impatiently with his hands behind his back, restlessly slapping the fingers of one hand into the palm of the other. After several tense minutes, a silver grey Daimler finally emerged from the upper road and drew alongside the Colonel. He stepped smartly forwards and, with military precision, pulled the door open with a flourish.

There was a communal murmur from the crowd and heads craned. Lizzie pressed forwards, desperate to see as Sharon Soames, in her narrow sky-blue satin dress, matching high-heel shoes and white gloves, and with her golden hair falling in a soft curve to her shoulders, stepped elegantly out. She smiled, lips a perfect Cupid's bow of red, revealing pearls of glistening white teeth. She was like a little drop of golden Hollywood sprinkled on the dowdiness that was Moreton Steyning.

'She's beautiful,' Lizzie gasped, face pressed in the crush against Robbie's shoulder.

The Colonel gestured towards the stage and the lovely creature stepped lightly across the grass towards the Vicar who bobbed and shuffled from foot to foot with uncontrolled anxiety, his face even more florid than was usual. Pausing, she extended one slender white-gloved hand and the Vicar, with finger tips together as if he were about to preach a sermon, bowed and then lightly took her fingers as if she were royalty. The clamour of excitement and approval from the crowd was reaching a crescendo when, with practised flourish, Colonel Benbow directed the Vicar to take the stage.

Round-faced and perspiring, as much from his fluster as from the heat, the Vicar mounted the steps, with microphone in hand, and steadied himself for his customary words of welcome.

'Ladies and gentlemen,' he began, to gently ironic cheers from the crowd. 'Ladies and gentlemen, welcome to the one hundred and fifty-sixth Moreton Steyning Fair, and for the one hundred and fifty-sixth time the sun's shining!'

This brought louder cheers and a round of applause. It was even close to the truth, at least as far as living memory was concerned.

'I want to welcome each and every one of you to our village Fair and especially our visitors from outside Moreton Steyning. You're all most welcome and we hope you have a wonderful day... and spend lots of money!'

More laughter from the increasingly high-spirited audience.

'It's been my very great privilege as Chair of the Fair Committee to present the Moreton Steyning Fair to you for the past seventeen years and, I have to say, it just gets better every year. My very great thanks to all those involved for their very hard work, and long may it continue!

'Now, something a little different this year and, if I may say so, an excellent development that I think we would all like to continue. As many of you will know we have been graced today by a very special guest to formally open our Fair.'

He paused to allow the ripple of applause to die down.

'Which, I'm sure, will make the day go with a real swing. If I may, I'd like to ask Colonel Benbow to take the stage and make the announcement. Colonel...'

The Vicar shuffled back and the Colonel briskly mounted the steps and strode to the front of the stage.

'Ladies and gentlemen, good day to you all and it gives me very great pleasure to present to you our very famous guest who has done us the great honour of formally opening our little Fair here today; a lovely young lady who hails from not very far away and whose presence here today is every bit as glorious as the lovely sunshine we're enjoying yet again. A young actress who's already making her name in film and on the stage... Ladies and gentlemen, may I please present to you... Miss Sharon Soames.'

As the Colonel stepped back, his arm theatrically extended to invite the celebrity guest onto the stage, the crowd applauded, cheering enthusiastically.

Smiling, Sharon Soames stepped elegantly up and sashayed to the front of the stage where she paused to drink in the universal admiration, one foot turned lightly so that her leg curved deliciously beneath her satin pencil skirt.

Taking the microphone from the Colonel and holding it to her lips she lowered her head, gazing out from beneath the coil of blonde hair that caressed one side of her pretty face, and spoke softly.

'Hello everyone!' she purred.

The large crowd erupted into cheers and clapping and ribald hoots. She smiled lusciously, microphone swinging loosely from one slender hand, simpering for their delight as she held a coquettish pose.

'Oooooh, she's lovely,' Lizzie squealed, pinching and kneading Robbie's arm in her excitement. It was several minutes before the crowd fell silent again.

'I'd like to thank you most sincerely for inviting me here today to Moreton Steyning Fair,' the lovely creature was saying when, without warning, a rasping voice rang out from nearby.

'Trollop!'

There was a shocked gasp from the crowd which fell immediately deathly silent and the Vicar, even more beetroot, whether from embarrassment or from the heat no one could say, seemed frozen to the spot in horror.

A crowd of older boys near the front began to snigger and elbow one another to the calls of disapproval from those close by. Near the steps, Lizzie saw Malcolm Draycott collapse forwards in mirth. The Colonel, old soldier that he was, leapt to attention as another cry pierced the air.

'Leave 'er alone ya dirty ol' man!'

With three quick strides and grim-faced with fury, Colonel Benbow strode forwards to Malcolm and slapped him so hard on the back of the head that he was flung forwards, staggering like a drunk, and then, grabbing him roughly by the arm, he marched him away from the stage and angrily thrust him from the Fair to the accompaniment of loud cheers from the excited crowd.

Lizzie elbowed Robbie in the ribs. 'That was John's voice,' she hissed.

'I know!'

They crouched down and there was John, below the steps, sniggering so helplessly he was rolling on the ground holding onto his ribs.

***

Much, much later, when the crowds had drifted away from the village and the locals had drifted into the pubs, Robbie and Jonathan, John and Lizzie made their way to Snake Pond. It was still very warm, one of those golden summer evenings that linger in the memory. Slipping off her sandals, Lizzie clambered onto the half-submerged log, leaving the boys lounging at the pond's edge as she made her way along its fissured surface, stepping carefully over the stumps of branches to the very end where the bark was worn away to reveal a surface silvery-grey and polished smooth with age.

She sat and let her feet dip into the cool water, swilling them about in opposing circles that sent lazy ripples to the shallows. The boys looked up and Jonathan waved, then stripped off his sandals and socks and followed her out, wobbling awkwardly. The log dipped as he dropped down beside her and he let his feet slip into the water.

'It's lovely, isn't it?' she said.

'It's been very hot.' Perspiration still clung to his forehead and neck, darkening his hairline.

They nodded sagely together, then Jonathan turned towards her, eyes squinting against the low sun.

'John was a naughty boy today,' he reflected.

'And Malcolm got the blame!' They shared a laugh and their movements made the log gently rock.

'Lizzie.'

'Mmm?'

'Did Robbie say?'

He was frowning, but Lizzie couldn't tell if it was from the sun in his eyes or from what he was about to say.

'Did Robbie say what?'

'About school?'

'About school? No...'

'About the new school I'm going away to next term?'

His gaze was out over the water which pooled, tranquilly about their ankles, and then he glanced back to her, his expression uncertain.

'A new school?' she said, turning to face him, but he was looking down now, into the depths of the pond, where the shafts of sunlight illuminated the swirling particles of silt. 'What new school?' she asked.

'Mum and Dad took me there. I'm going to stay there during the week and come home at weekends. They say I'll like it and it'll be better for me.' And with that said, Jonathan kicked his feet in the water, sending up sparkling sprays.

From across the pond, Robbie looked back at them, eyes also squinting into the sun so that he too was frowning. He waved. Beside him John was chatting, paying no attention.

'Is it far?' Lizzie asked, her voice dropping to a whisper. Jonathan had always been with them, a comforting, imperturbable presence; ever smiling and always considerate. Lizzie simply couldn't imagine him no longer there every day, but there was no mistaking his seriousness now.

He shrugged his shoulders. 'Quite far, I think.'

They sat in companionable silence, watching the pond skaters racing to and fro on little dimples of water, while huge dragonflies quartered low over the pond's surface, their shimmering wings noisily whirring and rattling. Lizzie could hear the other two talking, their voices drifting over the still water.

'Woz tha' then?' John had said. He was pointing away, through the mature trees behind them.

'Stubbin's Mill,' Robbie replied.

'Woz tha'?'

'It's just an old windmill. It's lost its top and hasn't got any sails anymore.'

John was looking mystified.

'A windmill, for grinding flour, like in Holland. You know, the wind blows the sails round and it makes flour. It hasn't been used for years and years, it's all shut up now. Anyway it's at the back of Mr Perkins' garden now you can't get to it.'

Even from where Lizzie sat she could see the light in John's eyes.

'Let's 'ave a look,' he urged.

'You can't get in, it's private. It's in someone's garden.'

'Bet ya bleedin' can. We can find a way, eh?' and he made a punch at Robbie's arm. 'C'mon. Let's 'ave a look!'

'Robbie, we're not supposed to go in there. You know... Mum said,' Jonathan was calling from next to Lizzie, but Robbie was on his feet already, looking over towards the mill. None of them had been in there and, like most village children, had always wanted to despite, or perhaps because of, being warned away by the adults.

'They're all gettin' bleedin' drunk in the pub anyway,' John was saying, 'No one abou' ta see us.'

Robbie glanced at John, then across to Lizzie and Jonathan. 'Shall we?' he called.

It was just too irresistible. They made their way into the belt of trees that bordered Perkins' land. The broken old windmill stood way behind the cottage at the top of The Green, and even Ray Perkins scarcely used this once-industrious area. Left now more or less to nature with its fencing in poor condition it was simple enough to squeeze through. Once inside, the tall grass made it easy for them to creep unseen towards the dark brick hulk of the old mill. They all slunk with their heads bent low, slightly breathless from the excitement and intrigue.

Even in its unused and abandoned state the mill was a large and imposing structure, extending upwards to three storeys at least, above which the brickwork was crumbling and the sails had long since fallen to the ground. Piles of bricks and the remains of one complete sail lay strewn amongst the brambles and undergrowth. Away to their left, beyond the big fruit trees of an ancient orchard, were the lawns of Perkins' cottage, but that was much too far away for any risk of their being seen, although there was little likelihood of anyone being at home on Fair evening.

The four of them stood below the curving walls and gazed up. The mill was easily the tallest building in Moreton Steyning and felt overpowering, casting a long, dark shadow across them. One rotting wooden door hung ajar on its rusted hinges.

John yanked it open before anyone could object, releasing from within the musty, acrid smell of dust and old grain mingled with that of the damp earth, even on this balmy evening. They stood on the threshold, peering into the gloom until their eyes adjusted and large pale shapes slowly emerged; wooden bins, abandoned sacks, age-bleached timbers. One by one they stepped slowly in, stumbling and picking their way through the debris strewn about their feet. Lizzie tripped, but Jonathan grabbed her arm. They were all silent, feeling their way in to the breathless gloom.

From one corner, narrow wooden steps led upwards. They exchanged apprehensive glances but John darted forwards and began to mount them, hauling himself up the steep open treads by the handrail, stretching up to reach from one to the next.

'C'mon!' he chirpily urged, and Robbie began to follow, neck craning upwards.

Cautiously Lizzie joined them but Jonathan, unsure, held back until finally he too began to mount. A small window let some light onto this next floor and, by the time Lizzie had got to the top of the stairs, John and Robbie were already exploring. Pale and almost ghost-like in the dimness, a grey millstone filled the centre of this circular room, and its massive timbers extended vertically through to the floors both above and below. More sacks and rubbish were abandoned on the dusty floor, and on a wooden bench against one wall was an old china mug, perhaps the last sign of the miller at work. John picked it up and peered in, pulling a face. Robbie ran his hands over the rough surface of the millstone, as Jonathan reached up to trace the cogs of the wooden wheel above.

None of them spoke, not even John. Massive, dark and empty the old windmill felt alien. That and the knowledge that they were trespassing made them all tread hesitantly, fearful of disturbing its silent neglect. Clammy and cold, the musty air and dampness hung so heavy that even breathing felt difficult. For reassurance Lizzie stayed close to Robbie, her back pressed against the cold millstones, uneasily looking about the room, when suddenly an inhuman voice rent the chill air, making them all freeze in horror. Open-mouthed and wide-eyed they stared at one another in shock, holding their breath to try and discern more sound, but equally in fear lest they should.

And then it came again, but more drawn out this time, a kind of wail emanating from above. Their eyes flicked from one to the other. Lizzie felt the hairs on her forearms rise and sweat prickle on the back of her neck; she struggled to breathe in against the tightness that bound her chest. Beside her she could sense Robbie rigid with fright. None of them moved, but their eyes slowly lifted to stare at the ceiling of dusty, worm-eaten beams and planks. Lizzie shuddered at the thought that these alone separated them from whatever had made those unearthly sounds.

As they waited, too afraid to move or make a sound, there was a scraping noise above, followed by a creaking as if something heavy was moving on the boards. John crept forwards, eyes aloft, until he was beneath the source of the sound. Lizzie gripped Robbie's shirt for reassurance and could feel the tension in his muscles beneath the warm, damp fabric. Next, there was another wail, softer this time, almost breathy, followed by a kind of grunt and then a sudden loud thud on the floor that made them all leap in fright. The sounds came more frequently now, a kind of mewing noise followed by a series of fierce grunts.

Lizzie looked into Robbie's face, mouthing imploringly, 'What is it?' trying to hold back tears of foreboding and stop herself from shaking uncontrollably.

When she looked round again, John had moved and was creeping towards the stairs that led up.

'Don't!' she hissed in terror, but he merely waved his hand dismissively and began to mount the ladder-like treads towards the square of darkness that opened into the room above and whatever horror was there.

The wailing became more shrill now, almost a shriek, accompanied by rhythmic groans as if something were in an agony of torture. Terrible images of monsters and unspeakable things swam in Lizzie's head as they watched, in mounting dread, as John slowly pulled himself up the near-vertical steps, his head inching towards the threshold. As he reached the final step the banging on the floor increased, the awful sound filling and echoing in her head so that Lizzie had to clasp her hands over her ears and close her eyes. When she peered through them again John was clambering back down and, to her shock, he was laughing.

'He's a' i' up there! Your bruvva. It's her bruvva! He's givin' 'er one!' and he mimed, jerking his hips rapidly backwards and forwards, cackling with coarse laughter.

Robbie and Lizzie looked at one another. Behind them Jonathan spoke, his voice cracking with anxiety.

'What is it Robbie? What's happening up there?'

'It's 'er bruvva,' chirped John, jubilantly. "E's bleedin' a' i', the dir'y bugger!'

Robbie hesitated. 'It's just Ron. He's playing tricks on us. Come on, let's go,' and he turned and led the way back down the stairs.

As he followed them, John was still chortling with vulgar delight.

VIII

It was Monday; red as a pillar box and hot like late August should be.

Mondays were always red; vivid and intense, a day when things happened. While Tuesdays, well, they were brash and orange. Wednesdays, were green, calm and quiet, and Fridays were pale blue. Saturday's were also green, but darker than Wednesdays, more spruce-coloured, and Sundays? They were yellow and bright, but Thursdays... Thursday was Ann's favourite, it was a deep luscious indigo; a magic colour, so purple it wasn't blue, and so blue it wasn't purple; shiny and lustrous, a hue that simply gleamed back at you. Eight was Ann's favourite perfect number, all curves and twists, with a rich deep blue too, blue like the depths of the sea or the sky at dusk; unfathomable and endless.

She'd told Maggie once, but Maggie had just looked at her as if she were peculiar. Maggie didn't know about the colour of things. After that Ann didn't tell anyone.

Few people were about in The Square although the shops had opened and a bus stood waiting, its engine thrumming; just one person on board, a man reading a newspaper. It was hot already, hot and still, with the harsh sun bouncing off every light and reflective surface, hard and cruel. The summer weather had been settled since early August, when the family had gone to the seaside, and Ann's skin was now deep brown, like a piccaninny her Grannie said, and her fair hair bleached straw-yellow, sticking out obstinately, all stiff and dry from the sand and salt. As she walked slowly across The Square, swinging from her right hand was her new prize possession from her holiday, a bright yellow hula hoop which she was keen to show off to Maggie, although Ann already knew her friend would instantly commandeer it.

She soon found her, flinging pebbles from the pub yard up onto the tin roofs of the sheds, where they clattered and rattled before tumbling down about her. Maggie saw Ann approach, but carried on.

'Won't your Dad be cross?' Ann asked. Dominant and authoritarian, Rod Viney was everything Ann feared in an adult.

Maggie gave a diffident shrug and glanced round.

'What's that? A hula hoop. Hey, let me try!' and she grabbed it from Ann, jumping into its centre and with arms aloft, threw herself into a wild oscillating gyration. The hoop spun unsteadily for a few turns, then fell wobbling to the floor like a spun penny.

'Let me.'

Ann demonstrated, but in truth she was little better than her friend. For a while they took turns, and even tried doing it together before falling onto the gravel in a tangled heap, laughing shrilly. An upstairs window banged open and Rod Viney's dark head appeared. He shouted down, voice brusque.

'You girls! Keep it down or clear off.'

They fell momentarily silent and then Lizzie appeared at the yard entrance. They were all brown as berries that summer; Maggie, loose-limbed and lithe like a boy, while Lizzie had golden-bronzed skin that seemed to glow, although today she was more serious as she approached, watching the two of them disentangle themselves from one another, smothering their giggles.

Her eyes alighted on the brightly-coloured hoop and they watched as she wiggled furiously, plaits flying backwards and forwards, the full skirt of her red and white striped dress twirling back and forth above her knees.

'I can do it!' she cried, 'look!' and it swirled about her, rising up to her chest then down to her hips, but staying in perfect motion. The other two clapped and laughed until a noise behind them foretold of Viney's arrival from the flat.

'Clear off, delivery's on its way,' he rapped out, marching across the gravel towards the sheds, his notebook under one arm, counting through a wad of notes. A heavily built man with a large head, thick dark wavy hair and strangely beautiful eyes, his mere physical presence was as overbearing as his manner was domineering.

They left and made their way round to Wheelwright's. The men were out working somewhere, so they had the yard to themselves and found a cool place to sit on the cobbles, in the welcome deep shade cast by the carpentry workshop.

'Guess where we went on Fair day,' Lizzie said, after they'd sat in silence for a few moments soaking up the delicious coolness from the stones beneath them.

'Swallow's?' Ann suggested.

'Nope.'

'That's not special,' Maggie derided. 'Up the Church Tower?'

'No, but close,' said Lizzie.

'Church crypts.'

'No, getting colder.'

'Vicar's garden?'

'Malcolm Draycott's?'

'No! Cold! Give in?'

'Go on then,' shrugged Maggie who, not liking to be defeated, now affected disinterest.

'Up the windmill.'

'You didn't!'

'Who?'

'Me and Robbie, and John and Jonathan.'

'What was it like, was it creepy?' asked Ann. The place had always seemed foreboding to her with its dark ruined cap just visible above the tall trees.

'Very,' Lizzie replied, a slight tremor to her voice revealing the anxiety she still felt. 'We heard all sorts of sounds and it was...'

'Ghosts?'

'No, I don't know, but it felt...' and she shuddered.

Maggie was leaning forwards eagerly. 'Did you see anything?'

Lizzie shook her head vigorously, arms rigid between raised knees. 'No, just... horrible noises. Robbie didn't like it either, you can ask him.'

'Was John scared?'

'A bit, maybe.'

'You must've disturbed the demon,' Maggie said, with a look of satisfaction.

Lizzie turned sharply. 'What demon?'

'The Demon of The Windmill,' Maggie intoned. 'He lives inside and haunts the mill after the last miller died a horrible death. He was crushed and ground to a pulp between the millstones, so that the flour was all red and the blood dripped all the way down from the top and soaked all the flour sacks in blood and gore. There was a terrible thunderstorm afterwards and the top of the mill blew off in the gales; its sails were shattered and fell off just after a terrifying shriek. After that, no one would go in there because it was haunted by the Demon ghost of the mill.'

She paused to observe their reactions while Lizzie and Ann sat silent and astonished.

'How d'you know?' Ann whispered, desperately seeking some sort of reassuring clarity. There was safety in facts. Facts were her refuge; they couldn't lie or change. They simply were what they were, protection from uncertainty, a comfort blanket to draw around herself.

'People in the village know but they won't talk about it, but sometimes in the pub... people drink and then they talk. That's why everyone says to stay away from it. Anyway, if you anger the Demon by going into the windmill he takes a terrible revenge and releases a great thunderbolt that can strike you down dead!' And her expression and stance reflected the awesome power of it all.

'What does he look like?' asked Lizzie, her face now taut with alarm.

'Awful.' Maggie rose, squatting on her haunches before the others. 'He's got horns and scaly skin that's covered in green blotches, he stinks something rotten and there's a foul stench when he makes a noise, and he roars like this,' and she demonstrated, with her head thrown back. 'And he holds a big sword and when he pokes it at the sky,' and here she leapt to her feet, both hands clasping a huge imaginary sword above her head, 'there's a great thunderbolt that strikes people dead.'

She stood stock still for dramatic effect, arms still raised, while they stared back, slack-jawed.

Lizzie looked to Ann, 'D'you think...?'

'I don't know,' she mumbled back. 'If people say...'

'They do,' Maggie retorted, returning to her position between the other two, her assured presence settling the matter.

As they sat reflecting on all this, Neville Potter turned into the yard on Morris's trade bike, basket loaded with green-groceries. He hadn't seen them, obscured as they were by the heavy shade cast by the workshop building, until Maggie, unable to hold back, yelled out, 'Stinky Potter!'

He stopped in frozen animation astride the bike, one foot on the floor, eyes dazzled by the harsh sunlight, until he picked them out from the shadows. At this he pedalled forwards, reaching into the big wicker basket and lobbed potatoes at them rapidly, one after the other, so that they bounced off the workshop walls behind them, each with a loud thud. Shrieking, they threw ourselves to the floor to try and avoid the stinging, bruising blows, but he circled again before making another charge and flung several more.

Absorbed in the attack, he'd failed to see Ron enter the yard from the road behind. Implacable, Ron assessed the situation in an instant, swept up the yard bucket and in one seamless movement, scooped it full of water from the trough and flung the contents over Neville who was turning for his third approach.

By the time Neville was taking his second shocked gasp of breath, the kitchen door had slammed on Ron's departing back, the metal bucket still clattering noisily where it had been flung, juddering onto the cobbles.

IX

From the day they'd discovered the photographs, the twins had subjected their parents to meticulous scrutiny, watchful for any signs that might reveal the mystery of the boy James, but neither gave anything away, continuing with the normal events of day-to-day life in their sons' presence.

Nid and Finch discussed many possibilities, whispering in their room or down the garden, away from the house lest they be overheard. Perhaps the child was a long-lost relative, or maybe the son of relatives from abroad. Perhaps he'd been adopted and then given back, or maybe he was nothing to do with them at all, just someone their parents had met. But everything pointed to a link, the boy even looked like them, but they couldn't understand why it was a secret and that was what intrigued them so.

They hung over the banisters, hoping to catch a word or mention, rushed abruptly into rooms even though they were regularly chided for doing so, and generally hung about around their parents, but they heard nothing that would throw any light on their discovery. Once Finch even crept down to the closed living room door after the two of them had been sent up to bed. From within, he could hear the low rumble of his father's voice and pick out just a few words, something about work, followed by the lighter, higher tones of their mother's voice, but nothing to reveal what lay behind the photographs.

A few days later Nid came up with a plan.

'We'll have to be Detectives,' he said. 'We've got to follow Dad, it's the only way. We'll find out what he says and where he goes, only we've got to make sure he doesn't spot us.'

'Like real Detectives!'

'Yes.'

They began by following Frank Bird to work, ensuring they were up and out extra early and hid themselves in the side passageway, watching round the front garden wall until their father emerged, smartly dressed in his dark suit, striding purposefully, briefcase in hand, across The Green to the Bank's small branch on The Square. Of course they knew all this, but it didn't detract from the excitement of being undercover agents, and they slipped their hiding place and darted across The Green before pressing themselves flat against Mrs Patterson's sweet shop to watch his diminishing figure as he marched away along Main Street. Once they judged it safe they moved forwards, a few cottages at a time, crouched low behind hedges and walls, keeping a safe distance behind him.

Frank rounded the corner at the Horse & Hounds and strode across The Square to the small half-shop that was the premises for the local branch. Being a Tuesday, he was opening up for the day rather than working at the main Cullingham office. With an ease born of habit, he propped his briefcase up against the window sill, clicked it open, pulled a key from a pocket in the lid and used it to open up the door before disappearing inside. As they watched, the lights came on, the blinds at the windows flicked open and they could see the dark shape of their father moving about. After a few minutes all was still inside and ready for business.

Their vantage point now was the corner of the pub yard, opposite the branch. Nid, ever-prepared, had brought a notebook and pencil and they busied themselves keeping a log of all the comings and goings in The Square. Lizzie's mother arrived and boarded the waiting Cullingham bus, various people went in and out of the newsagents and butchers and at 9.45am the Bank had its first customer; Malcolm Draycott's mother, of all people. The twins sauntered across The Square in their best nonchalant fashion and strolled past the window, peering intently in to see her leaning against the counter and talking, shopping basket beside her. Their father's hands were visible, counting out coins onto a small pile of one pound notes before her.

'She's getting money!' Finch gasped once they were past. 'Maybe it's a bribe.'

'That's what Banks are for, numbskull,' Nid replied. 'What d'you expect?'

Finch ignored the chide. Blessed with great equanimity, he barely noticed his brother's criticisms and instead pointed to the ancient stone cross nearby.

'We could sit there. We'll get a much better view and no one'll think it's odd.'

Nid accepted the idea, even though it wasn't his, and they took up a position on the stone steps. Around them people came and went. Several boarded or arrived on the Cullingham bus and eight entered the Bank through the course of the morning, but nothing seemed out of the ordinary. After a while they began to get bored, wearying of the tedium of surveillance, then Maggie idled over from the pub.

'What're you doing?' she demanded, curiosity aroused.

'We're spying,' Finch said as Nid made a loud 'shhh' beside him, 'but it's supposed to be secret.'

'Who're you spying on?'

'Our Dad.'

'Your Dad! Why?'

'It's a game,' Nid butted in. 'We're being Detectives.'

But Maggie's curiosity was stirred and she settled herself down on the steps alongside.

'Is he up to something?' she asked. 'I bet my Dad is.'

'No. Why?'

'Oh, I dunno. Reasons,' and she tailed off, pensive, then brightened. 'Let me help. What do I do?'

'You can keep a watch on everyone getting on and off the bus,' Nid directed, 'and tell us if there's anyone unusual.'

Three strangers arrived on the 11.15am which kept them interested for a while, and then Maggie went off to tail them around the few shops they had before returning to report nothing untoward, except for one man that had gone into Robbie's Uncle's shoe shop to collect a pair of repaired shoes and come out with the wrong ones. As she stood relating this back to them, she abruptly stiffened and then ducked down behind the cross.

'It's my Dad!' she hissed. 'He'll be going to the Bank.'

They spun round and there was Rod Viney, walking briskly across to the branch, a white canvas bag swinging from one large hand.

'Quick!' she hissed, taking control, although it wasn't clear exactly what they had to be quick doing, but they followed her across The Square anyway, maintaining a safe distance from Viney, and crouched down behind a parked car to watch him go into the Bank. The day being warm, the door was wide open and, from their vantage point, they could hear their father's greeting of 'Hello, Rod' from within.

'Morning. Good one again,' Viney replied.

'In the eighties according to the paper. It was eighty-eight yesterday they say.'

'That so? Must get a bit warm in the Bank.'

'It certainly does. Not so bad here with the door open, but it's stifling in town. Still, must be good for your business.'

'Oh yes! Brings on a good thirst, it does.'

'Paying in are you?'

Viney plonked the canvas sack onto the counter with the heavy sound of many coins.

'If you will, Frank.'

The three of them darted forwards to press themselves against the branch's outside wall for a better look. Being nearest to the open door, Finch could just see in by leaning slightly forwards. Their father was counting out and weighing money while Viney propped his forearms on the counter, leaning forwards, large shoulders hunched up under his ears.

'Yes, been a good one again,' he repeated, swinging one leg forwards, loose from the hip.

'Seen Will?'

'Yes, several times.'

'Better is he?'

'He says so. Here, got some good offers at the moment if you're interested.'

'What's that?'

'Spirits, excellent price whenever you're interested. Can't better it, you know.' Viney shifted position, leaning sideways on one elbow now, head turned to talk through the hatch on a level with their father.

'No?' came the voice from within, tone casually enquiring.

'You like a Scotch, don't you? Spot of G&T?'

'Certainly.'

'Can let you have a bottle or two. You know, special offer. Can't beat it.'

'Well...'

'Overstocks, that sort of thing.' He gave an encouraging nod. 'Just for regulars, you know. Special customers.'

'We like a G&T now and again, Norma and I.'

"Course you do, very nice. Gordon's is yours, isn't it?'

'Yes, actually.'

'Coming in lunchtime for a Shandy?'

'Yes, I'll need something to cool me down.'

'Well, I'll have something for you. Nice surprise for your Norma, eh?' Viney was standing back now, taking the receipt. 'See you lunchtime.'

Finch shoved Nid in the back and they marched quickly away as Rod Viney emerged, casting a quick sideways glance that took in Maggie beside them, but said nothing as he strode back across The Square to the Horse & Hounds. They drew into a huddle to discuss matters, but nothing they'd overheard seemed of interest to the boys, and Maggie soon wandered off having apparently lost interest in their sleuthing.

***

It was late afternoon when Frank Bird came walking back across the parched grass of The Green where the twins had spent the afternoon playing cricket. By then they were hot and thirsty and, remembering their strategy of sleuthing, waved to their playmates and followed their father, at a safe distance, towards the back garden gate. As Frank swung the gate open, it briefly revealed their mother, reclining in a flowery dress in a deckchair on the lawn under the shade of the apple tree, open book on her lap. She heard the gate and looked up with a half-smile.

'Is it that time already?'

'Gone five.'

'I hadn't realised. Good day?'

'Another hot one.'

'Isn't it. I haven't got the energy to do anything.'

The gate closed behind him and the boys crouched, jostling one another to peer between the slats.

'Here, I got this off Rod Viney,' he was saying, drawing up his briefcase and clicking it open. He placed a green bottle on the wooden table beside her and she looked up questioningly.

'It was a good price. Offer from the brewery. Good of old Rod really, he didn't have to. He's just offering a few regular customers. It's because I pop in there most branch days for a sandwich and a Shandy.'

She was still looking at the bottle and turned it about so that the label faced her, but she didn't pick it up.

'Think I could fancy a long, cold G&T. How about you? Think we could treat ourselves? Sun's over the yardarm and all that,' he said.

'I suppose so.'

'Well, you don't have to. I thought you'd be pleased.'

'No, it's not that. It's a nice idea...'

'What then?'

'Oh, I don't know. It's him, I suppose.'

'Rod?'

'Mmm.'

'What about him?' Frank's voice sounded quieter now; he was in the kitchen preparing the drinks.

'I'm never that sure about him.'

'Bit of a rough diamond I grant you, but he's a good landlord. Runs a tight ship, won't take any nonsense. Ice?'

'He runs a tight ship with those kids and that poor wife of his all right,' she called from the garden.

'Well, he's got a lot of children. Can't be easy.'

'Five of them. Yes, ice please.'

'He's got a business to run, he has to keep them in order.'

'Is that what you call it? Thank you.'

He'd returned and handed her a long glass which chinked with the sound of ice cubes.

'Cheers then.'

'Cheers.'

There was silence as they both drank deeply, which reminded Nid and Finch of how thirsty they both were, so Nid lifted the latch and they went in.

'Hello, you two,' she smiled, resting her glass on one knee. 'Do you want a cold drink? You both look really warm. Get yourselves some squash.'

After the harsh sunlight, the kitchen was cool and dark. They poured long drinks in imitation of their parents and sank down onto the cool lino floor, leaning back against the cupboards with legs flung out, draining their first glasses in seconds, then refilled and let the chill liquid slowly quench them. The burr of their parents' voices drifted in on the heavy air as they slumped, too weary from the heat to move from the delicious coolness of the kitchen floor and shade.

'School next week then,' their father was saying. He'd pulled out the other deck chair and was sitting opposite Norma under the apple tree.

'It comes round so fast.'

'They've had nearly six weeks! They'll have forgotten everything.'

'Oh, I don't think so.'

'These are important years now; they build the foundation. It's only another two until Secondary School. They need to study.'

'Even so, they're only nine.'

'You can't have too much learning, Norma. They won't make the grade if they don't work hard. I expect Nigel to go to the Grammar.'

'Well, I hope so too,' she replied.

'I know, of course I do. He's a sensible and a bright boy. We want him to fulfil his potential, don't we?'

Beside him, Finch felt Nid stiffen. Outside there was a pause, perhaps they were sipping their drinks, then their father spoke again.

'I'm not so sure about Andrew, I'm afraid. Too impulsive, he doesn't concentrate. I just wish he'd apply himself better.'

'You can't separate them, they're twins.'

'But you can't have one holding the other back, can you? I don't think it would be fair on Nigel. There's a bright future there, you know. We have to make sure he fulfils his true potential, don't we? We promised ourselves, after all.?'

Finch sensed a movement and looked round. Nid had got to his feet, body turned away. He placed his glass firmly on the table, then retreated down the hall and upstairs without a word.

X

Jonathan was standing at the back door staring out, his eyes unfocussed.

'I wish I could stay with you, Robbie,' he was saying mournfully.

Their mother, forever bustling, pushed him from the lean-to and out into the garden. 'Get a move on or we'll miss the bus,' she urged, exasperation creeping into her voice.

'Can't I stay with Robbie?' he persisted, beginning to plead. 'I want to go to the pond too.'

'No!'

'Dad..?'

Tom emerged, locking the lean-to behind him and turned to look back over his shoulder at Jonathan. 'We can't buy a uniform without you there, now can we?'

'The sooner we get there, the sooner we'll be back,' Sally intoned, already moving to the side passage.

Tom put a hand on his older son's shoulder.

'You're going to look really smart you know. We'll be so proud of you, your Mum and I. And you'll have all the girls chasing you in no time!'

This bribery partly worked and Jonathan, looking abashed, allowed himself, albeit reluctantly, to be steered out through the back gate.

'Bye Robbie,' he called plaintively, as they hurried down the road to catch the bus, propelled along by Sally.

Robbie watched them for a bit, a half-perceived sense of sadness weighing down inside him. Something told him this was the day everything changed for his brother. He'd no longer be one of them, a child-boy playing with the younger kids. Now he'd leave the familiar and safe world of Moreton Steyning and enter a bigger world where everything was strange and different, where people didn't know him. And where he simply didn't want to go.

Hearing a familiar whistle he saw Lizzie outside Wheelwright's, standing high on tiptoe, smiling and waving.

'Mum's-got-our-sandwiches-what-shall-we do?' she gushed.

'I thought we were going to the pond.'

'Okay,' she said, happy to concur. 'Shall we get John?'

They didn't need to look far; he was on The Green, kicking stones about, bored and predisposed to fall in with any plans they made for the day. It was warm already and they first piled into Mrs Patterson's, emporium of all things sweet. She pulled three ice cream blocks from the chest freezer and placed them in cornets.

Leaning forwards, John sneered disparagingly, ''Ere missus, ain't ya got bigger ones?'

'That's enough from you. This is how they come and you can have them or not.' She was used to cheek and pressed the cones into their hands.

'Lend us, I'll pay ya,' John hissed, predictably enough.

They emerged from the shop with the sticky ice cream already running down onto their palms.

"Ere ya are then,' said John and presented them, in outstretched grubby hand, an assortment of sweets pilfered from the counter-top display.

***

The three of them spent the day at Snake Pond. It was hot; so hot it sapped all their energy, the weight of the air bearing down on their bodies, the sun burning red onto their eyelids, all in a final flourish to late summer. They lounged, talking and laughing, retreating to the shade from time to time to catch their breath in the heavy languid air; their sandwiches already eaten and all the lemon squash drunk by late morning.

Lizzie had on shorts and waded with Robbie thigh-deep into the pond, warm as bath water, while John looked on.

'Come on,' she called imploring, but John merely shook his head.

'It'll cool you down,' Robbie tried.

'Nah.'

'Oh, come on!'

He diffidently waved an arm and lay back on the browned grass, hands folded behind his head, but Lizzie wasn't to be deterred and swished her way back through the shallows.

'John! Oh, come on in. You'll like it, you will!'

'Nah, s'alright,' and he rolled onto his front in a display of casualness, presenting his back to them both.

'Oh, go on!' she pleaded. 'Look, it's nice, you'll like it,' and she splashed out sending up sprays of brown water with each step, and padded over to him, grabbing hold of one arm. 'Come on, or I'll pull you in!' and, giggling, she began to tug.

An inch or two taller than John and a fit and active girl, Lizzie had little difficulty in spinning him round on his front until he faced the pond and then began to heave him, face-first, towards the water's edge.

'Gerroff!' he yelled, but she was laughing wildly and enjoying the fun.

Robbie stood thigh-deep in the warm, brown-as-tea water, watching their cavorting.

With feet planted solidly and both hands gripping one wrist, she began to drag John towards the pond, ignoring his helpless struggles and hoarse cries.

'Leggo! Gerroff!' he bellowed, but she continued to haul as if in a tug-of-war, backing into the shallows, yanking him nearer and nearer to the edge.

'Aagh! No, leggo, leggo!' A tone of panic had entered John's voice.

Breathless with exertion, she paused and bowed forwards with hands on knees to catch her breath, then braced herself to complete the task.

Shrill now, he cried out. 'No! Snakes! Help! Snakes!'

Astonished, she dropped his outstretched arm which splashed into the water. Immediately he recoiled, flinging himself away, legs drawn up to his chest to avoid any further contact with the pond.

Lizzie stood plaintively in the shallows, quiet now. 'They won't hurt you, John,' she said softly. 'They're only grass snakes.'

***

Later, hot and weary, the three were lounging. A few people had passed the pond on their way to or from the hill, but it was now quiet and still in the torpid heat of a late summer's mid-afternoon.

Robbie lay on his front, chin on arms, gazing through the dried-up grass stalks, watching the insects, although even they scarcely moved. No one spoke and the very air seemed heavy with inertia. His eyes focussed dully on an ant which was hauling a dead bee up a grass stalk and he wondered where it would go when it got to the top. It all seemed rather pointless, so much effort for a carcass.

The air itself drowsed, leaning heavy with the heat as it pressed his body into the ground, drowning him in its soporific lull. He could feel his eyelids drooping and his consciousness sliding into a low drone inside his ears. After some minutes the droning gathered momentum, and soon seemed to fill the air. He forced himself back to wakefulness and, rolling over, saw the familiar chequered underwings of Hugh Dollicot's plane as it passed low overhead.

Lizzie had roused too and, jumping to her feet, began to wave, 'Hugh, hello, Hugh, Hugh!' But flying low, the plane quickly disappeared behind the tall trees and was soon lost from sight. They didn't see it again and Robbie wondered if Jonathan, wherever he was that afternoon, had seen it too.

'It's Friday,' Lizzie remarked by way of explanation to no one in particular, then lay back staring into the distance, once more overcome by tiredness.

Lost in their own thoughts and slumber, they didn't notice the changing colour of the sky as it faded imperceptibly from bold brassy hues through shades of blue and grey to slatey lilac. A light breeze lifted the leaves and twitched at the grass stems and then a warm drop of water fell on Robbie's forearm. He stirred and looked about, sensing the change in the light. Above them, the sky hung heavy and low.

'Look at the pond,' said Lizzie.

Ripples were welling and intermingling and, as they watched, the surface started to leap and jump to the sound of loud plops and splashes and then large droplets began to fall onto their hot bare skin.

'It's bleedin' rainin'!' John exclaimed, leaping to his feet.

In an instant the pond was covered with spitting, boiling water and the sound of huge raindrops splattering on leaves quickly filled the air. They were all on their feet by now, leaping about in the deliciously cool rain that in just a few seconds was streaming off their bare skin.

'Singing in the rain,' Lizzie was chanting, prancing up and down, her arms outstretched, her glistening face held up to the quenching raindrops. John followed her, aping her movements, but he didn't attempt to sing.

Robbie snatched up their things, hurriedly stuffing them into Lizzie's bag. 'It's getting heavier,' he warned.

'It's so lovely!' she cried, her hair now plastered to her head.

Their clothes were already showing large dark patches of wet when a low rumble of thunder brought the carefree dancing to an abrupt stop.

'We'd better go back,' Robbie urged and began to lead the way, hurrying down the path, back towards the village. Scarcely had they reached the lane when the rain gathered its forces, and in moments had turned its surface into a torrent, and a mist of grey streaks blotted out all view of the cottages opposite.

There was no time to run the length of The Green to home, so the three of them darted across the lane to the Church, hauling the doors open to the stone porch and then the huge creaking oak door and practically fell into the nave, breathless and drenched. As they closed the heavy latch behind another roll of thunder rumbled, louder this time.

John strode in ahead. 'Jeezus, big innit.'

'It's just a Church,' said Robbie.

'Look 'ow 'igh tha' is.' John craned his neck up to the dark wooden roof timbers, reverberating now to the drumming of rain.

'Don't you have Churches like this?'

'Dunno.'

'Haven't you been in one?'

'Nah, wha' for?'

Robbie really didn't know how to answer this and looked round for Lizzie, who was standing anxiously by the Font and also peering upwards. 'What is it?' he asked.

'Nothing,' she said, her face small and wan.

Making his way along the aisle, John paused to look at one of the marble memorial statues. 'Who's tha'? Ugly geezer, in' 'e?'

As the boys gazed up at the powerful features of the recumbent Lord of the Manor, the window before them suddenly flashed, followed a few seconds later by a great roar of thunder. Behind them they heard Lizzie shriek and she grabbed their arms, pale with terror.

'It's only thunder,' Robbie said, 'Don't be silly.'

'You don't know!' she wailed.

'Don't know what?' but she was shaking and looking about in distress, and wouldn't answer.

'Won' hur' ya,' John tried. 'Not if ya don't get hi' by lightnin'.'

This didn't seem a helpful point to make but made little difference anyway as she began to pace, wringing her hands and casting woeful upward glances.

'Come and sit down,' Robbie urged, settling into one of the pews. 'It'll pass soon and then we can go out again. Come on.'

'Yeah, c'mon,' said John, 'Don't be a bleedin' idiot. Yer actin' like a girl.'

'You don't understand,' she whimpered, just as a blinding flash illuminated the Church, accompanied by a massive clap of thunder that seemed to rock the building's very foundations. She shrieked and dived under the pew behind Robbie's legs, grabbing at his ankles in blind terror. They could hear her whimpering beneath them and her small hands trembled against Robbie's legs.

'What is it?'

'Aw get up, for gawd's sake!'

'I can't, I can't!' She was almost sobbing by now as another loud rumble echoed about the building.

'It won't fall down,' Robbie reassured. 'It's withstood many thunderstorms. We're quite safe, you know.'

''Ere, 'ave a sweet,' John tried, offering down a Black Jack. A small hand emerged and she slowly crept out and crouched on the floor between their feet, head drooped, silently absorbed in unwrapping it.

She chewed for a while then whispered, 'It's the Demon.'

'The Demon! What demon?'

'The Demon of the Mill.'

There was a pause during which another loud roll of thunder made her flinch and cry out, but more quietly now. 'Maggie said.'

'Maggie said what?'

'Maggie said if you go into the windmill there's a Demon because of the dead miller and he gets angry and releases a thunderbolt that'll strike you dead,' and she looked plaintively up, her sodden plaits dripping small pools of water onto the floor either side of her. They stared blankly back.

'Well, we went into the windmill, didn't we? And we heard those awful noises.'

'That weren't no devil,' retorted John.

'It was, it must have been,' she wailed.

''Course it bleedin' weren't! That was your bruvva!'

'How do you know?' she persisted.

'Because I saw 'im, didn't I? I went up them steps.'

'But the terrible noises, like a great horrid beast.'

'That was 'im an' 'er.'

'But Ron doesn't sound like that. I should know, he's my brother.' She was recovering herself a little now.

'He does when e's doin' i'!'

'Doing what?'

'I told ya! Doin' i'. Shaggin' 'er, the dir'y devil!' and he mimed, laughing, his movements rocking the pew backwards and forwards.

'How d'you know?'

'I told ya, I bleedin' saw 'im. An' it's the noise *they* make.'

'Who makes?'

'Me ol' lady 'n' 'im.'

'Who?'

'Me ol' lady, me muvva, an' 'im.'

'Who's him?' asked Robbie, perplexed also.

''im! Paddy.'

'Is that your Dad?' Lizzie was distracted now from her terrors.

John let out a rasping noise, not quite a laugh. 'Nah, 'course 'e ain't.'

'Where's your Dad then?' she persisted.

'Dunno. Buggered off.'

'Don't you see him?' asked Robbie.

'When I was young. Don't remember, but don't matta' do i'?'

This unexpected information was more than he'd ever revealed before and Lizzie and Robbie fell silent, absorbing the picture of John's life away from the brief summers spent at Moreton Steyning. After a few moments they became aware that the pounding on the roof had dwindled and the light through the windows was now brighter.

'The storm's passing,' Robbie said, getting up. 'We can go back out now.'

They followed him to the studded oak door. John helped lift the heavy latch and they heaved it open to check that the rain had indeed finally ceased, but lined up on the seats on either side of the porch were Malcolm Draycott, Neville Potter and the rest of the gang, also sheltering from the sudden storm.

As one, they rose. John slammed the door closed and the three of them pressed their backs against it until they could get the latch down again to hold it safely shut. From outside, they could hear the others whooping with glee and calling out mockingly.

'What do we do now?' Robbie asked, as the gang began to drum on the door, calling and taunting them to open up.

John was peering through the keyhole. 'There's six of 'em bustads,' he reported, then yelled, 'Get knotted, ya fartin' bustads! Stinkin' shitty farm pigs!' This provoked further yells from outside with bouts of door kicking and attempts to yank it open.

'We're trapped,' whispered Lizzie. 'They won't let us out now they know we're in here.'

'There's another door, let's try it,' and Robbie led the way at a sprint to the north door, but it was locked and there was no key to be found.

'There's a door in the tower,' Lizzie suggested, 'and maybe we can find a key in the vicar's room.'

They hurried down the nave and pulled aside the curtain that screened the base of the tower, and the outer tower doors that were never used. They too were locked. To one side was the small room used by the vicar which was at least open. They scouted around inside but there were no keys to be found.

Meanwhile, the Draycott gang had started up a chant and were banging on the door to intimidate them which, as far as Lizzie and Robbie were concerned, was working. Sooner or later, they felt they were going to have to run the gauntlet past them. It was either that or stay in the Church until the gang got bored and went home.

'How long d'you think they'll stay?' Robbie asked.

'Ages,' said Lizzie, gloomily.

John was looking about. 'Woz up there?'

'The Bell Tower.'

He pulled open the small corner door and began to mount the steep spiral tower steps, two at a time. The others followed, unsure where all this would lead, and all shortly emerged onto the bell-ringing floor. John was gazing about, looking for inspiration. Robbie pointed to the ropes.

'They're for ringing the bells. You pull on them,' he explained, and could already see John's mind working. 'We can't ring the bells,' he anticipated.

'Why bleedin' not?'

John took hold of one of the ropes, tentatively fingering the thick candy-striped handgrip and looking up to the high ceiling where the heavy rope dropped through from the Belfry.

'I don't think we should,' Robbie implored. 'We'd get into awful trouble.'

Gripping the rope John pulled but he was too small and light and nothing happened. Robbie stepped forwards anxiously, his hand outstretched to deter him but, just as he did, John took a run and a leap and clung monkey-like to the rope using all his weight to bear down on it. High above they heard the big bell wheel rotate and then the clapper struck the metal.

A great reverberation sounded through the tower.

Lizzie clasped her hands to her ears, her mouth open with astonishment, just as John was swept rapidly upwards, still clinging and chuckling with delight. A few moments later, as the rope dipped back down, he used all his weight and momentum to haul on it again, and another peal rang out before he disappeared once more towards the ceiling. He repeated this two more times before leaping to the floor, rubbing his hands with satisfaction, pugnacious grin about his face, and the ringing resonating throughout the tower.

Lizzie was looking worried. 'Someone'll come,' she cried.

'Quick, we'd better go down,' urged Robbie and they clattered back down the stone tower stairs but now they noticed something they couldn't have seen on the way up; a large black key hanging on the wall on the inside of the tower door. John rushed with it to the outer doors. They hadn't been opened for years but he rattled and shoved the key with force and a few moments later the lock gave a satisfying clunk and turned. The three of them put their shoulders to the doors and pushed them open, emerging into the dripping shrubbery without.

From the direction of the lane came the sound of loud shouts. Robbie and Lizzie peered round the corner of the tower towards the porch where Malcolm and the gang stood puzzled and the Vicar now came puffing up the Church path, arms waving and his mouth working. He was pointing upwards, red-faced with outrage, breathing hard. The gang was gesturing and shrugging, exaggeratedly innocent expressions on their faces.

'Quick, we'd better go,' said Robbie. Behind them John locked the tower door from the outside and pocketed the key.

They were well beyond the graveyard wall before they felt it was safe to stop and John abruptly doubled up with laughter. Trilling and strutting, he wheezed, 'Them bastuds is gonna get the blame!'

'No they won't,' Lizzie said. 'We locked the main door from the inside. How could they have been in there to ring the bell.'

'No it ain't!' he crowed. 'I done an' bleedin' unlocked it, didn't I, whiles you woz watchin' that fella shoutin'.'

***

The two boys paused outside Mrs Ward's. Lizzie had gone home already and Robbie had to leave too, but John seemed reluctant to go in and repeatedly recounted the afternoon's events, laughing more wildly at the outcome each time he relayed it. Eventually Robbie made to move but his friend delayed him, imitating and ridiculing the gang's expressions and the Vicar's accusations, cock-a-hoop because they had no way to prove their innocence.

'I'm off tomorra',' he suddenly said, hands in pockets, drilling a stone at the wall again.

'You're going?'

'Yep, goin' 'ome.'

This took Robbie by surprise, but he tried to hide his disappointment. 'We start school next week,' he said dully. 'D'you?'

'Dunno,' John shrugged. ''Spose so. Not if I can bleedin' 'elp i', eh!' and he chuckled, but seemed to be laughing more to cheer himself up than from genuine mirth.

'Coming again next summer?'

'Mebbe. Dunno. If she wants ta get rid of me agen. 'Spect she will.'

'Going on the train?'

'Yep.'

'Okay, then... I'll see you.'

'Yep. See ya.'

'Bye then.'

'Ta-ra.'

Walking home, Robbie wondered if he'd ever see John again. The next summer holidays were so unimaginably far off.

XI

A thick, heavy mist draped the garden. Against its enfolding greyness the old fruit trees were but mere sketches against the blank sky and the fields and hill lost from view altogether, swallowed into the emptiness. A damp chill seeped into Ann's bedroom and she slammed the casement to and then hurried downstairs, curious to explore this changed world.

Slowly she drew open the front door. Beyond, nothing stirred and sounds were stifled by the eerie pallor. A deathly half-light had settled over the village and all that was familiar was now absent or changed. She stepped hesitantly along the front garden path, beneath the old medlar tree and round to the damp footpath behind their garden. Here, myriads of silvery droplets picked out the cobwebs that laced the mossy stone walls, and water pattered softly and incessantly from overhanging trees onto the fallen leaves beneath her feet. The world had become a silent, dripping place; closed in, still and secret.

It was an ancient path, sunk deep behind the gardens of the old cottages. Each of these cottages was approached from its own cobbled yard, all of them tucked behind the shops fronting The Square. In one direction the old footpath led up towards Rushbrook End and the hill, but Ann didn't take that route today, instead she turned left and followed it down towards Main Street. She walked slowly and aimlessly, pulling off gloves to brush her fingers against the cool, dripping leaves and grass stalks. She saw no one. Even after the path had emerged into the road by Luff's hardware shop, there were few people about, just an occasional dark shape hurrying through the obliterating silver-grey mist.

It was the Autumn half-term week but, after the excitements of Bonfire Night, the school holiday was already nearing its end. Dispirited, she resolved to find Maggie and wandered towards the pub but there was no one to be seen in the yard. She approached the front door, cautiously reaching upwards to knock, and jumped back in alarm as it was hauled open to reveal Rod Viney. He stopped abruptly, discomforted and surprised to see her, but he only hesitated for a moment, calling over his shoulder, 'Margaret!' before continuing on his way out and across the yard.

At the top of the dark stairs the flat door banged and Maggie came slowly down, bending low at the half-way point to peer past

Ann and out through the opened yard door, pulling a face at the weather beyond.

'I said I'd come round and play,' Ann explained, adding half-apologetically as her friend seemed disinclined to speak, 'Mum's going out.'

'Mmm, okay.'

'What shall we do?'

At that moment Viney returned, bags in hand, and pushed brusquely past, his broad frame briefly filling the passageway. He disappeared through the latch-door and into the bar, where the smell of beer and cigarettes wafted, until the door was closed crisply behind him.

Maggie, with a blank expression watched him go and then, after a short pause, came down into the passage and, inclining her head said, 'In here.'

With no further explanation, she pushed open the battered door beside them and Ann found herself standing at the top of a short flight of stone steps, looking down into a gloomy semi-basement storeroom closely-filled with racks which held bottles and boxes. Maggie led the way between the tall shelving and then, without warning, suddenly pressed herself to the damp, clammy floor and began to wriggle porpoise-like beneath them.

Ann hesitated, but Maggie called to her to follow. It was dark and claustrophobic and there was barely enough height beneath the racks for her to push herself along on elbows and knees, but she followed Maggie's jiggling feet towards a faint well of light. Here they both emerged into a tight cornered area which was concealed beyond a broad brick pillar and dimly-lit from above by a small high window.

'There,' said Maggie, indicating the block of wood for her friend to sit on while she herself squatted opposite. Above their heads Ann noticed three narrow shelves and, arranged upon them, various items. She could feel Maggie scrutinising her face as she studied them; a pretty doll, a toy dog, coloured pencils and ribbons, a box covered in pictures, some cards, a hairbrush, a whistle, something of tarnished silver and a metal toy cow. She glanced at Maggie who gazed steadfastly back, her look questioning.

'Well?' was all she said.

'What are they?' Ann whispered, feeling she must somehow keep her voice hushed.

'They're mine, my toys. I found them. They're secret, understand?'

Ann looked again at this curious collection, so carefully placed. 'Can I?' she asked. Maggie nodded and she picked up the little brown dog.

'Jumbo,' said Maggie by way of explanation as Ann turned the small toy dog over in her hands and stroked its coarse fur, bare in patches. It had tiny glass beads for eyes and black wool threads for a mouth, now coming unstitched.

'This is my den,' Maggie suddenly announced, her voice betraying no emotion. 'It's my Dad's storeroom.'

'Doesn't he know?'

'Nope. He can't get through here, see, and you can't see it from anywhere. That's why I chose it. Anyway, I'd know if anyone came in and moved anything,' and with that she took the toy dog and placed it proprietorialy back on the top shelf, beside the doll. As she did so the door from the passage opened and both froze at the sound of footfall on the stone steps. Maggie urgently signed for Ann to be silent and they held their breath. Men's voices, deep and heavy, reverberated in the dead air.

'Come on down, Frank. Now... yes, here we are. Johnnie Walker Black Label, very nice; to go with the usual Gordon's, eh? There you are. I thought you'd like this too, a very good Bordeaux... one to put aside for Christmas, eh? Happy with that?'

'Well...'

'I think you'll like that. Here you are. Oh... and some pipe tobacco? This is your brand isn't it, what d'you say?'

'Yes, very nice.'

'I think I've got a small box for them... yes, here you are. Wife well?'

'Very well, thanks.'

'The boys?'

'Yes.'

'Doing well are they?'

'Not too bad. Andrew's a bit of a dreamer. We have to apply a bit of pressure there but Nigel's a bright lad you know, real potential there, one for the Grammar. Norma and I hope he'll go on to College.'

'Chip off the old block!'

This was followed by some embarrassed laughter.

'Settle up next time I see you. Might have another little something for the Christmas stocks too. Port or something, what about it?'

'Well, perhaps, yes.'

Ann mouthed 'Who's that?' to Maggie who, leaning forwards, cupped a hand to her friend's ear and breathed,

'Frank-better-than-you-Bird.'

'The twins' father?' Ann mouthed back and her friend nodded. They listened to the footsteps ascend the steps and then the door closed, leaving only silence. Ann released her breath with relief and looked across to Maggie. Her friend's brows were furrowed and she was gazing away, eyes unfocussed.

'What is it?'

Maggie didn't answer for some moments and then abruptly dived back under the racks. There was the sound of scraping and Maggie grunting with effort before she re-emerged, flailing legs first and then her torso, yanking a heavy metal box behind her. She squatted and with strong fingers prised off the lid and pulled out first one and then another large book, both with dusky purple covers, dropping the first onto Ann's lap so that its weight made her legs sag.

Purple, thought Ann, the colour of a bruise. 'What are they?' she asked as quietly as possible.

'Ledgers.'

'What's ledgers?'

'Account books, stupid.'

Ann felt belittled by the rebuke but realised she was being let into some privileged secret and so thumbed blankly through page after page of columns containing figures and names. It meant nothing to her although she knew she was supposed to understand something significant.

'They're my Dad's ledgers,' Maggie persisted. 'Only they're not. He keeps his ledgers on the shelf out there,' and she pointed back towards the passage between the racks, 'with all the pub order books and stuff, on his desk. He keeps these hidden.'

'I don't understand.'

She sighed heavily. 'Don't you see? These are the real ledgers. The others are just pretend. This is where he writes it all down, all the business he does, like just now with Better-than-you-Bird, all the extra money he gets. No one else knows.'

'Does it matter?'

'Of course it does! He hides it from the brewery and everyone. It's his secret, people aren't supposed to know. But I know.'

'What if they found out?'

'There'd be real trouble. But it's a secret, d'you understand?'

Ann nodded solemnly.

'Cross your heart and hope to die?'

'Yes.'

'Swear,' she demanded.

'I cross my heart and hope to die,' Ann intoned and solemnly crossed her arms in front of her chest.

XII

Autumn had passed slowly and without incident to hasten the weeks, and their summer escapades with John now seemed distant, just a faint memory, almost unreal. Life was different now that Jonathan was away at his new school during the week, and Robbie missed his brother's familiar and assuring presence in the bed opposite. The routines of school days filled the hours, although at weekends when Jonathan came home, the two of them could rediscover their easy companionship, albeit briefly.

They were together for the Christmas holidays and, as was usual, the Bradbury family spent Boxing Day at nearby Netherington, crammed into the small stuffy front room of the boys' Grandmother's cottage.

Stretched out on the floor in front of the fire, its head impossibly close to the heat, was Grandma's dog, Sprout. Bloated and blissfully content she slept and dreamed, legs dancing and whiskers twitching while she softly yelped, blowing bubbles through her curled lips. Occasionally her tail thwacked the floor in dreamy pleasure.

So overweight, she could only waddle, her fat white belly slung between stumpy legs, Sprout was something of a Jack Russell, but old age and obesity had long since obscured any pretence she may have had to an actual breed. She was called Trixie but known to the family as Brussels Sprout, a reference to her malevolent digestion which could, and frequently did, clear a room of people within minutes.

One by one the adults fell asleep, their heads lolling onto each other's shoulders, with hands folded over full bellies in the pleasing stupor that followed a large Boxing Day lunch, aided by the stifling warmth of the fire that filled the room with an ever-deepening glow against the fading light outside. No one bothered to get up and switch on the lamp. Susan, stretched languidly on the floor, was reading the new book that was a Christmas present, while the brothers played with their new train set on the lino behind the armchairs, and the sharp needles shed by the Christmas tree dug into their bare knees.

They worked together in quiet absorption, assembling a station and railway huts from the magazine rack, some books, their Grandmother's wooden sewing box and the slippers that Sally had slipped off in the warmth. For nearly an hour the only other sound was the occasional crackle and gentle settling of cinders and burned-out logs from the fire, accompanied by the burring of their Grandmother's and father's slow regular snoring, until a creaking of chair springs and general yawning told them the adults were stirring. Tom leaned out over the side of his armchair, peering around the chair wing to inspect their efforts.

'Where's that then, Clapham Junction?' he joked, and the skin furrowed above his cheekbone as he smiled. He clasped the arms of the chair decisively. 'Better check up at the big house before it gets dark,' he said to the others, pushing himself to his feet.

The brothers jumped at the chance to go out and gratefully breathed in the sharp, chill air outside. Along the silent High Street not a soul stirred. With dusk approaching, the glow from festive lights spilled from every cottage onto the darkening gardens and hedges as they passed, and they peered into bright living rooms strung with curled paper chains, each one over-filled with families sitting around their fires.

Gloomy laurel and rhododendrons made a dark tunnel of the steep drive up to the Hall but, once at the top, the wide expanse of purple-hued winter sky with a sliver of new moon, cast a half-light once again, enhancing that magic hour before dark when the birds sing, even in winter.

The house was closed-up and in darkness. With the family abroad, Tom and Reg Higgins were taking it in turns to check around and ensure that all was well. Tom left the boys wandering on the terrace while first he walked around the outside of the house and then went into the walled gardens to check the greenhouses and the heaters against any frosts. The brothers gazed out over the tall trees, skeletal against the winter sky's last light.

'Remember when we were here in July?' Robbie said. 'Good wasn't it? Shall we go and look at the tennis courts again?'

They walked down the sloping lawns towards the distant courts. In the cold, grey light they seemed bare and dismal, such a contrast from the chaotic fun of that day, a portend perhaps of what would come.

'We saw Hugh here,' proffered Jonathan who hadn't said much. 'I haven't seen his plane since Summer.'

‘I haven’t seen it much either.’ Robbie knew how much it meant to his brother to see the Cessna swooping over the hill. Now that he was away at his new school on weekdays, he missed any chance to spot it.

They walked through the belt of trees beyond the courts and followed the perimeter gravel path around the base of the hill while they waited for Tom to finish. The day was fading fast and, by the time they returned across the lawns to the terrace, a dreary gloom had descended. There was no sign of their father who was still checking the greenhouses, but as they passed the fish pond Robbie became aware of a movement away to their right, back down by the courts.

He nudged Jonathan. ‘Look,’ he whispered, pointing.

A dark figure opened the gate and crossed to one of the courts where he bent for a few moments over the net support, then straightened and walked back out, pulling the gate to behind him with a loud clang. For a few seconds he disappeared from view amongst the larch trees and then re-emerged on the lawns above them, striding back up to the terrace. As he neared the top he was briefly silhouetted against the last light in the darkening sky.

‘It’s Hugh,’ Jonathan breathed.

‘Yes,’ replied Robbie.

By then the figure had disappeared from view, slipping away between the shrubbery at the top of the drive. At that moment Tom reappeared on the terrace.

‘Okay, all done. Ready you two?’

Without looking at one another, they murmured ‘Yes’ and followed their father to the drive and back to Grandma’s cottage for tea.

***

The news came two days later, in the dead, grey half-light of a winter’s morning when the curtains were still closed against the cold, although everyone was up. The dining room fire was newly-lit but the crackling, spitting logs had barely taken the chill off the room and Tom was standing before it warming his hands. The sound of the side gate's bang had scarcely registered before the lean-to door was flung open and Reg Higgins burst into the room, bringing with him a rush of chill air.

'There's been a break-in, Tom. You'd best come up the house.'

He stood, a little breathless, his head lowered, one arm outstretched to steady himself against the corner of the mantelpiece, the smell of frost still clinging to his heavy overcoat.

'What!' Tom straightened sharply.

'Checked this morning, first thing, before we go over to Bea's mother's for the day; it'd be too late when we get back, already dark.' He paused for breath. 'Went round the back, all looked normal, then when I got to the rear hallway window, I saw it; glass on the floor, hole neat as you like, just so you can get a hand through. They must've got the window open and squeezed in. There was no sign yesterday.'

'Anything taken?' Tom was already pulling at his coat from the hook by the back door.

'Don't know, haven't been in. I ran back home and rang the Police then cycled up here, quick as you like. They're on their way.'

Sally stood in the kitchen doorway, tea towel in hand, frozen in the act of drying a cup. 'That's terrible, Reg.'

'Bad business.' He sagely shook his head.

Tom pulled open the lean-to door, car keys in hand, for they'd acquired their first car that autumn, and briskly led the way out. 'Take a slice of bread!' Sally called, but he was already hurrying past the lean-to windows.

'Isn't that awful?' she said turning to the boys. 'And at Christmas too. The family's going to be terribly upset. Nothing too valuable's been taken, I hope. Big house like that, standing empty these dark nights and not overlooked up there on the hill, anyone could go creeping about and they wouldn't be seen. You can see how worried Reg Higgins is. He feels responsible, no doubt.'

To the boys it sounded tremendously exciting, and it was only the anxiety of their parents that stopped them regarding the incident as the highlight of the holidays so far. It was very nearly lunchtime before Tom got back, but the boys hadn't strayed from the house all morning, determined to be there when he returned in order to hear all the latest news first-hand. He seemed weary when he came in, head down.

'Darling, you must be famished.'

'Not particularly.'

'What happened?'

'Break-in all right. It must have happened late yesterday. Reg had checked after lunch and there was nothing wrong then.'

'Anything taken?'

'I should think so.'

'Oh dear. Have they made an awful mess?'

'No, pretty professional job the Police say. Looks like the culprits knew what they were after and how to get in. Very neat in fact.'

'How awful.'

'Yes. They'll send a team in on Monday, fingerprints and all that. We've locked it all up and I've boarded up the broken window.'

'Oh, goodness. What about the family?'

'Reg's had to call them. They're pretty shocked of course.'

'They must be, it's dreadful.'

'They're going to cut their holiday short and come back in a few days. Police need them to identify what's been stolen.'

'Of course.'

After that, updates on the great crime mystery were eagerly awaited on a daily basis. Tom and Reg Higgins doubled their checks on the house, one visiting in the morning, the other just before dark. Both were in attendance to let the Police investigators in after the weekend and to guide them round, and all the staff were at the Hall for the family's early return from their Christmas holiday two days later.

It was Jonathan who changed things. The brothers were making their way to Swallow's to look for their friends but he'd been lagging behind, rather to Robbie's irritation. He called to Jonathan to catch up but his brother had stopped and was now standing stock still, staring away into the distance.

'What is it? Jonathan what is it! Come on, hurry up!'

'Robbie?'

'What!'

'You know the burglars?'

'Yes... what about them?'

'At the Hall. You know they go at night, in the dark don't they?'

'I suppose so.'

'Well, you know when we were there, with Dad, on Boxing Day? It was getting dark. We saw Hugh...'

All the drama and excitement of the break-in had put the oddness of their sighting of Hugh out of Robbie's mind. 'What d' you mean?' he said, rather more harshly than he meant to.

'Well, what d'you think he was doing? At the tennis courts?'

'I don't know.' Robbie walked back and now stood in front of Jonathan. They stared at one another, faces taut.

'What d'you think he was doing?' Jonathan whispered again.

'I don't know,' Robbie said, annoyance forgotten. 'It was odd, wasn't it?'

Jonathan gazed away, thoughtful. 'You don't think...?' The question hung in the air between them and there was an anxious, almost pleading look on his face.

'I don't know... no, I don't think so. Surely not?'

'Hugh's our friend, isn't he?'

'Yes, I think so...'

'He is, I'm sure he is. He can't be a burglar, can he? He's our friend, isn't he?' Jonathan looked forlorn.

Robbie punched him reassuringly on the arm. ''Course! And he's friends with the family too. He was with Miss Caroline when we were there last summer, wasn't he? She likes him.'

They brightened at this and pretended to one another that they'd put the whole matter out of their minds, but it tugged away at Robbie throughout that day and it was clear from his reserve that

Jonathan too was anguished by it, although they'd played rowdy games with Nid, Finch and Lizzie for several hours until dusk.

Tom was already home when they got in, standing with his back to the dining room fire, rubbing the warmth into the seat of his trousers, and talking to Sally as she laid the tea table. Susan was perched on the edge of the fireside chair to catch every word of their exchange.

'So, what did they say?' Sally was asking.

'Not much. What could they say? I should think they're pretty upset, although they've put a brave face on it.'

'Some of it must have been in the family for years.'

'No doubt.'

'Pictures and silver, all that sort of thing...'

'That's right.'

'It's not always the value.'

'No. Worth a few bob though, what's gone. Some of it handed down through the General.'

'Did they give any idea?'

'No, they wouldn't, but the Police'll know, no doubt.'

'Terrible business... is anywhere safe? What do the Police know?'

'I don't know, Sally. We'll have to wait and see. They spent about two hours with the family going round the house, checking the inventory and said they'd be in touch in a day or so. That's all I know. I suppose we'll have to wait and see. Hello you two, what've you been up to?'

'Have they caught the burglars yet, Dad?' asked Jonathan, joining his father by the fire and tucking himself under the arm that was extended around his shoulders.

'Bit soon, lad, I'm afraid.'

'Do they know who did it?' he asked, but Tom just laughed.

'Not yet, boy. They don't work that fast!'

'I expect it's a big international gang of jewel thieves,' offered Susan.

'You've been reading too many comics,' Sally retorted.

***

The turn of the new year brought a spell of hard frosts that dug deep into the earth and held a grip all day-long. Not the welcome kind that fringes every leaf and blade of grass with crisp white shards accompanied by clear sunny skies, but cold, leaden days with a black frost that locked all water into hard grey sheets.

Up near the school the village children had worked for hours on a large frozen puddle on the lane, burnishing it to a smooth pewter-like surface. They took it in turns, queuing at one end before taking a rapid sprint and, legs locked into a skating pose, launched themselves onto its polished surface. Robbie was uncoordinated on the ice but it was Maggie who reigned supreme, utterly fearless, and out-distancing even most of the boys. Everyone was there, Nid and Finch in opposing blue and green scarves, Lizzie, her pink-cheeks glowing in the new jumper knitted by her mother, and Ann, scarcely visible under her duffle coat and red bobble hat.

There was jostling and pushing in the queue but, all in all, everyone got a go, more or less fairly. Anyone not queuing stood along the sides cheering on the sliders if they were a friend, or jeering and trying to put off anyone who wasn't. A kind of truce prevailed between the various factions and even Malcolm, Neville and the others all joined in without too much incident. With a great deal of shouting and whistling, there was an informal competition to see who could slide the best and the furthest. Without doubt, it was Maggie who was the winning girl.

Dressed in a fraying jumper far too small for her, with wrists and legs mottled blue and mauve from the cold, she pounded along the approach and then flung herself onto the ice, arms outstretched to balance, face set and resolute. Her friends stood alongside whooping and cheering as she flew past, damp dark hair thrown back, gliding right to the very end of the slide until she stumbled and cart-wheeled to keep her balance on the gravel beyond, yelling with triumph. Lizzie and Ann applauded, eyes bright from the excitement and cold.

With the gauntlet thrown down the older boys took over, noisily and boisterously competing to challenge. It grew ever more rowdy and the friends were beginning to wander away when Susan appeared, accompanied by three friends, parading together in matching head scarves. Although she normally ignored her brothers in public, on this occasion she came over to them, all agitation with the thrill of momentous news to impart.

'Hey, you two! Guess what?' Satisfied with her advantage and, having paused to observe the effect, she blurted out before they could respond, 'They've found the burglar!'

'Who?'

'Don't know, but he was seen. The people in the house at the bottom of the drive saw this man creeping about, just like a cat burglar or something, and now the Police're looking for him.'

'How d'you know?'

'Dad said, of course, stupid!' She turned to grimace derisively to her friends. 'The Police've been doing house-to-house, questioning people in Netherington to see who saw what, and that's what they said,' she added in a sing-song voice that told the boys she was doing them an undeserved favour by imparting this information.

'When?'

'I don't know! You'll have to ask Dad. C'mon,' and with that she flounced off, exchanging smirks with the others. The four of them departed like a gaggle of geese, multi-legged and heads together, giggling.

Robbie didn't need to look at Jonathan to know what he was thinking. At home they found their father getting ready to go to a local league football match in the village. Tom looked up, surprised at their early return.

'Alright you two? What's up?'

'Nothing,' said Jonathan, sounding as suspicious as it was possible to be.

'We just came back to get something,' Robbie interrupted, lying. 'Susan said there's some news,' he added, in what he hoped were casual tones.

'Well, hopefully, yes. The Police came to talk to me up at the Hall this morning, all official like. It seems Mr Birch, you know, he lives by the Hall gates, apparently he'd seen a chap in dark clothes going up the drive and was pretty sure it was late on Boxing Day. I told them, "well that would have been me with the boys going up to check the place", but according to the Police it was a much younger chap and he didn't have lads with him. They wanted to know what I'd done up there and what I'd seen, so I said we were there after four and walked all round and checked the greenhouses and sheds as usual and there was nothing amiss then. Fellow must have slipped up after, they think.

'Anyway, there you are. Looks like they could have their thief. The Police're talking to other folk in Netherington and eliminating anyone else who may have been around, but nobody was about much on Boxing Day evening; it all sounds pretty suspicious, anyone going up the drive at a time like that. I hope they get him. Mr and Mrs H-B and Miss Caroline are most upset.

'Right, I'm off to the match. It starts in two minutes.' And with that, he'd pulled on his jacket and cap and was soon gone.

Jonathan stood by the mantelpiece pensively fingering the Christmas cards. 'That was Hugh,' he said, without looking up.

'I know. We ought to tell them.'

'But he wasn't doing anything wrong.'

'We don't really know, do we?'

Jonathan looked up. 'He couldn't've been. Why would he?'

'No, it doesn't make sense,' Robbie agreed. 'I don't know what we should do.'

'We've got to tell Hugh,' Jonathan replied with resolve. 'He'll know what to do.'

'But how?'

'I don't know. Maybe if we go to Aston Haddon he might be at the airfield next Friday.'

'But we can't, we'll both be back at school next week. Anyway, it's such a long shot. I don't suppose he flies much in the winter. We haven't seen him, have we?'

Jonathan had to agree with that and they fell into silence.

Eventually, as there was no point in moping about the house on their own, they went out again. Jonathan was sullen and broody, and no one proved to be around. At the Horse & Hounds the pavement was blocked by the brewer's dray unloading beer barrels into the cellar. With nothing else to divert them they stood and watched as the two delivery men handed the metal kegs down from the lorry and rolled them one by one through the open hatch. From within they could hear Viney's voice: 'Another two...'

He didn't know at what point he became aware of it, but suddenly the letters jumped off the side of the barrels and into Robbie's conscious mind.

'Jonathan, look! 'Dollicot's Brewers'. That's what Mrs Harrison-Bates and Mum said. Hugh's from a brewery family. That must be the one.'

He saw a pink flush of excitement spread into his brother's cheeks and they hurried across The Square to the telephone box. The two of them squeezed in and began to thumb through the heavy phone books, their fingers too cold and numb to separate the pages quickly enough to satisfy their eagerness.

'Look, here we are.' Robbie ran his finger down the list: 'Dobbs, Dodwell, Doley. Here... 'Dollicot's Brewers, Fringleton, and then there's three other Dollicots, all private numbers.'

'Let me see.' Jonathan pulled the book towards him, but none of the entries had the initial 'H' and the brothers didn't even know where Fringleton was.

Chapter Three: 1959

The baby was poorly, her round face flushed and scrunched up as she cried and struggled on her mother's lap, wriggling round to pull fretfully at the bib of Lois's pinny. The two younger children were sick too, confined to bed in the room they shared with Maggie. Lois was sitting at the kitchen table, her cheeks also burning, flushed pink against the greyish pallor of her tense face. She placed a wrist against her forehead, wiping it from side to side and breathed out deeply and softly, her eyes closed.

Behind her, Maggie leaned against one of the kitchen chairs, anxious, unnoticed. 'Mum?'

'Mmm?'

'You sick?'

'Tired... Probably got a touch off the kids.' Lois's listless gaze was cast across the kitchen, unfocussed, her lean arms holding onto Laura, and her unbrushed hair hanging bedraggled across her shoulders. She heaved the baby up to prevent her from sliding forwards and turned round. 'Your father wants you; go and help him, Maggie.'

'Don't you want anything?'

'No, I'm alright. Go and help your father.' Her voice was flat, without emotion.

Leaving the flat's unaccustomed quiet, Maggie took the dark and steep inner stairs and found Rod Viney behind the bar, stacking glasses and bottles on the shelves. He noticed her but didn't look up, continuing to polish and arrange the glasses in front of the mirrors.

'Mum's not well,' she said, as he didn't speak or show any sign of setting her to work. She wasn't going to offer, was she?

'You been disturbing her?'

'No!'

He ignored the riposte. 'Where's Stephen?'

'How should I know?'

This time he turned sharply about. 'Watch your tongue, young lady!'

'I don't know where Stephen is. He doesn't tell me.'

'Well go and find him. I want you both for errands.'

Resentfully she stomped from the bar and into the street, where immediately she heard a ball being kicked about in the yard behind. Maggie took the longest route, a slow deliberate circuit of the building, and found her older brother playing with his Christmas present, drilling the football against the rear wall of the pub.

'Dad'll tell you off,' she declared.

'No he won't.' He carried on kicking, her presence flatly ignored.

'He will too! Anyway, he wants you.'

Stephen caught the ball on the rebound. 'What's he want?'

She yelled, 'I dunno!' and dashed back into the pub, where even the company of her father was acceptable if it had involved successfully baiting Stephen. He arrived a few moments later, football under one arm, and stood in the middle of the room looking questioningly at their father who ignored both of them until he'd stacked the last of the bottles under the counter.

'Come with me,' he said, and strode along the dark passage and out to the yard sheds from where he produced two brown paper-wrapped packages. He gave the larger one to Stephen which chinked and clearly contained bottles and the smaller, a rectangular box, to Maggie. 'You,' pointing at Stephen, 'take that to Ted Willis. Margaret, take this to Len Potter.'

'Nodder!'

'Mind your manners,' he snapped, taking a slap at her, but missed.

'Do I have to go to the farm?'

'Listen here, you two. Go straight where you're going, no messing about and give the parcels direct to Ted and Len. They'll give you an envelope and you bring them right back to me. Got that? Right, go on and straight back to me or there'll be trouble. Now!'

They left the shed together, exchanging hostile stares. It was an unspoken feature of their childhood, a silent understanding that they were in competition; the oldest boy and the oldest girl. Stephen, then eleven and a half, was almost two years older than

Maggie, but no taller, and had their father's thick, curly black hair, which was cause enough for her to despise him. With a cold, burning anger she wholeheartedly resented her elder brother; hating him for all the times he'd slipped out to play with his mates, carefree, while she had to help with the kids and household chores.

Stephen took the lower exit from the yard while Maggie left from the other and crossed The Square to Rushwood End lane. Under her arm the parcel felt light and, once she'd turned the corner and was out of sight of the pub, she pulled at the sellotape and teased open the wrapping to reveal the familiar labels of cigarette packets. Nodder Potter was never seen without a fag hanging from his lips, she mused.

The dead cold of the last few days had lifted and the lane to the farms was now muddy. The Potters lived in one of the farm workers' cottages near the top, between the Draycott's at Lee Farm and Rushwood End Farm itself. As she passed the Draycott place, Maggie heard the animals and voices further away in the farmyard, but there was no sign of people and she passed no one as she trudged up the gloomy lane.

The Potters' cottage was a square, brick-built place, approached along a crumbling brick path through the now bare front garden where the only feature was a small vegetable patch and the gaunt stalks of Brussels sprouts. The smell of a Sunday roast wafted as she reached the front door and knocked. Mrs Potter answered and called to her husband. He emerged, all lizard-like and shifty eyed. He's a sly one, Maggie reflected.

'Hello Maggie?'

She gestured with the package and he took it with a slight smile, his thin lips folded in on the cigarette in his mouth. Turning away, he placed the packet on a small side table in the hall behind him and reached deep into his jacket pocket, elbows moving. There was the sound of notes and the chink of coins. He pulled an envelope from the table drawer, his hand slid inside it and then he licked the flap and sealed it shut.

'Take that to your Dad, Maggie. Off you go.'

She took the envelope wordlessly, the coins jingling noisily inside. Maggie took a moment to measure the thickness of paper money within it before stuffing the envelope into her cardigan pocket.

She'd gone just a short distance back down the lane when she heard the whistles accompanied by the loud bleating of sheep. Rounding the bend she saw a flock of sheep approaching with two youths and a sheepdog bringing up the rear. The shorter of the two she recognised as Malcolm Draycott, someone she really didn't want to meet in such narrow confines, the other his older brother.

The ewes were approaching quickly, filling the width of the lane with their jostling and bleating, while the Draycott's snappy sheepdog Ned was active at their heels. Maggie was hoping the demands of shepherding would distract Malcolm, but he was already looking up and she could see that he'd recognised her and was smirking, remarking something to his brother.

When the leading ewes were a few yards away, Maggie moved over towards the hedge to avoid them. She picked her way carefully onto the grass verge, muddy and boggy from the winter rains and the constant passage of farm animals, taking care to avoid the ditch which was brim-full of dark water. The flock was large and moving briskly, at least seventy or eighty ewes pressed on by the boys who were now talking animatedly to one another.

'Louse! You couldn't even slide as good as me!' she heard herself yelling before she even knew why. The brothers merely laughed, watching her all the while.

Then, in response to a sharp whistle from Malcolm, Ned darted along the far side of the flock, abruptly deflecting the startled ewes towards her. Maggie stepped back smartly to avoid them, but instead sunk down into the deeply-churned mud of the verge, until she could feel the cold goo squelch over the tops of her shoes. The ewes kept pushing and jostling, their rough greasy fleeces pressing against her legs, their heads lowered and bleating loudly, yellow slit-eyes wide with alarm. She tried to move but her feet were held fast by the mud and there was nowhere left to escape to.

The brothers were laughing heartily and there came another whistle, and then yet more ewes crowded forwards until she was forced even further backwards, stumbling up to her knees in the chill, muddy waters of the ditch, her hair entangled in the thorny twigs of the blackthorn hedge behind.

Anger and humiliation burned her cheeks and she couldn't bring herself to look up as she heard the departing roar of their coarse laughter. Pulling herself free she hurried home, calves numb with cold, mud squelching between her toes, furious with herself for having allowed the Draycotts to get the better of her.

She'd hoped to sneak in, but her father was by the sheds, moving crates. He took the envelope without a word, but was looking down at her feet.

'Get those filthy things off and wash them under the yard tap. Don't you dare go inside in that state! What're you thinking of, as if there's not enough to do with your mother ill.'

She sat on the cobbles by the yard tap, pulled off her sodden muddy shoes and socks and washed them under the numbingly cold water before hobbling on her heels, wincing at the pain of the sharp gravel, to the outer door where she took small revenge by drying her feet on her father's scarf which hung on a hook inside. Seated on the bottom stair, she pulled her wet shoes on again and left her socks outside to dry. Behind her, the inner door to the bar was open and she could hear her father now moving around inside; it would soon be opening time. She edged along the passage and peered in.

The lights weren't on yet, but he stood in the centre of the room, silhouetted against the front window. Behind him, on the wall, was the photograph with an engraved metal plaque on its wooden frame:

'Presented to Mr Roderick Viney, publican of the Horse & Hounds, Moreton Steyning, in grateful recognition of his generous support. September 1956. Moreton Steyning Parish Council'.

Looking fresher-faced and slimmer, he was standing sideways-on, his right arm outstretched, presenting a donation to Parish Councillor Robert Anstiss, who smiled appreciatively towards the camera.

Today, in unconscious mimicry, Viney stood, his opened envelopes tucked under his arm, counting notes and coins between his extended fleshy palms.

II

It was a bleak first week back at school for the Bradbury brothers, following the Christmas holidays. The house felt empty, colourless and bare; the paper chains, cards and tree having been taken down, and each decoration carefully re-wrapped in tissue and returned to the loft for another year. The skeletal tree was consigned to the garden for burning, and the presents put away, now no longer new or novel. The only signs that remained of their Christmas-gone were the sharp tree needles, discovered for weeks ahead on the floor, in Digby's fur and down the backs of chairs.

That Friday evening Robbie was the first home, and was immediately sent outside to fill the scuttles with coal for the fires. Susan followed, arriving off the Cullingham bus, flinging her satchel down before dashing upstairs to change from her school uniform. Tom was next, rubbing his hands together.

'Alright, boy? Cold out there, Sally. We'll be having snow, I think.'

'Any news at the Hall?'

'The robbery? No, nothing.'

'They haven't found that fellow?'

'Not as I've heard.'

A vehicle pulling up outside heralded Jonathan's imminent arrival. A few moments later the back gate banged for the third time and he bounded in, specks of white on his dark school uniform.

'Hello, boy. Is that snow?'

'Yes. Hello Robbie,' and Jonathan gave his brother a friendly nudge. Robbie noticed an exaggerated cheeriness which seemed a little out of place. There was still the matter of Hugh to deal with, and they'd had no chance to talk about it for a week while Jonathan had been away at his boarding school.

'Had a good week, darling?' Sally dusted the snow from Jonathan's shoulders and affectionately flicked it from his hair.

'What've you done this week, then lad?' Tom was now sitting by the fire polishing his shoes.

'Numbers, spelling, drama, football...'

'Good, keeping you busy then?'

'Yes. Mum, can I get changed?' He paused at the door to the stairs, his head inclined and an expectant look on his face, silently urging Robbie to follow him up. In the bedroom he pulled off his school blazer and carefully hung it up in the wardrobe, slipped off his school tie, rolled it neatly and set it in the tallboy drawer, placed his shoes beneath the wardrobe and worked his feet into his tartan slippers, and then finally pulled on a thick maroon woolly before sinking down onto his bed. Robbie watched this fastidious routine, knowing it was pointless to interrupt before it was completed.

'I've got something to tell you,' Jonathan announced, his face radiant with suppressed excitement.

Standing at the window, Robbie saw the tiny flakes of snow falling outside sparkle in the light of the street lamp opposite. 'What?'

'We're going to see Hugh.'

'Hugh! How?'

'I've written to him and he's going to meet us at the Church at ten tomorrow, so we've got to make sure we get there in good time.'

'You've written to him! What d'you mean?'

Jonathan's feet were firmly planted on the floor, his weight pressing down into the sagging mattress of his divan. 'I wrote a letter from school,' he replied, unconscious of the astonished and doubting expression on his brother's face.

Robbie sank down onto his own divan and the two sat opposite one another, eye to eye.

'Where did you get the address, and the writing paper and the stamp?' Robbie quizzed.

'In the phone book. Robbie, I got the address in the phone book. Don't you remember we looked it up?'

Jonathan looked pityingly back at him and Robbie recovered himself. 'Yes, of course.'

'Well, I wrote to them.'

'Who? Where?'

'Dollicot's Brewers at Fringleton.'

'But we don't know where that is.'

'It doesn't matter,' Jonathan replied, and Robbie, for a second time, was stung by his brother's common sense. 'We learned letter writing last term and Mum gave me writing paper and stamps and things so I can write home. You know I do, we write letters every Tuesday. I write to you too.'

Robbie felt foolish. 'But what did you say?' he asked.

'That we've got something very important to tell him and to meet us in the Church porch at ten o'clock tomorrow morning. That's alright, isn't it Robbie? I did right, didn't I?'

After food that evening, Tom rose from the table and pulled back the curtain. 'Settling now,' he proclaimed.

Susan, Jonathan and Robbie raced to the front window and peered out. The lane was already white and snow now fell thickly and heavily, both soft and heavy at once. 'You'll be tobogganing on the hill tomorrow,' Tom remarked.

They gazed out, transfixed by the flakes, floating and falling, drifting, spiralling in the street lamp's glow.

At regular intervals they looked out, each time measuring with their eyes the depth of the accumulating snow. By mid-evening the kerbs had softened and snow lay along the hedges, fences and on every cottage roof. They hurried upstairs to look out of the bedroom windows and down into the back garden below. Every twig and branch was now covered and a strange pale light reflected back into the room. Susan threw the casement window open and they all hung their heads out, breathing in the fresh, tangy smell of snow. Down in the garden, the sheds were as white as igloos and the vegetable and flower beds had disappeared beneath great eiderdowns of white. The sky above was the colour of bruised lilac.

Abruptly the lean-to door opened, sending a stream of sparkling electric light across the pristine snow, and then Digby emerged, a small black shape, pussy-footing its way across the snowfield, nose extended to sniff as large snowflakes fell onto his coarse dark fur. He suddenly sneezed, briskly shook himself off and then bolted down the garden, performing great loops where the lawn used to be, scattering snow in all directions. Even old dogs love snow.

'Let's look out the front!' cried Susan, all claims to seniority put temporarily to one side. Even older sisters love snow.

They pulled open the front door, ignoring their mother's entreaties about the cold, and gazed out onto the transformed scene; silent, muffled, empty and beautiful. The lying snow was perfect, not a soul having passed. Large flakes fell and spiralled in dizzying patterns and, in the pool of light from the street lamp, hung suspended for breathless seconds.

There was an exquisite silence as Robbie lay in bed that night, an eerie icy light from behind the curtains seeping through. He didn't know whether to be the more excited about the snow or about meeting Hugh the following morning.

***

The snowfall had continued well into the early hours and now lay thick along the lane, blanketing everything. Beyond the roofs of the houses opposite, Lullington Hill rose white against the grey sky and only the tracks of a fox marked the still-untouched snow in the street outside.

Tom had already pulled the sledge out from the shed and stood it ready, propped up in the lean-to, by the time the brothers came down. They breakfasted quickly then pulled on their warmest clothes and set out, pulling the sledge behind them.

'We can't come up the hill yet,' Robbie called to the other children, already out playing as the two of them laboured up The

Green and along the top lane towards St Mary's Church. The snow came halfway up their calves and Robbie couldn't see how Hugh was going to make it, but he said nothing to Jonathan. They got to the Church porch in good time and settled onto the wooden benches opposite one another. They didn't talk much at first, but just gazed out through the huge Churchyard trees at the transformed landscape beyond.

After about a quarter of an hour the Church clock struck ten. Robbie saw Jonathan look up and fidget.

'He might be late,' Robbie offered. 'The snow.'

'What if he doesn't come, Robbie.'

'I'm sure he will.'

'What if he didn't get the letter? Or he can't get through the snow?'

'He'll try, I know he will.'

They settled back in silence once again, rubbing at hands and legs as the cold began to work its way into their immobile limbs.

'I'm going to walk around the Church and make sure he's not round the other side,' Robbie said, and set off. The snow was deep, very deep. On the hill slopes above children were tobogganing, their shouts and shrieks of excitement carrying through the cold, still air. Robbie wanted to be up there too but he wanted even more for Hugh to come. He hadn't expected him to be round the back of the Church, but he'd just had to walk off the tension and anxiety of waiting. As he rounded the corner of the tower Robbie prayed he'd see Hugh's green sports car in the lane, but there was no one and nothing. Only their footsteps marked the snow; no vehicle had passed that way all morning.

Jonathan looked up as Robbie returned and then slumped back down again, but he said nothing for some while. Eventually, through frost-numbed lips he mumbled, 'I don't think Hugh's coming.'

'Let's wait just a few more minutes,' Robbie said, more for his brother's benefit than for his own. In his heart he'd given up and now felt numb with cold.

After some while the Church bell sounded once. 'Half-past,' Jonathan whispered. He'd shrunk down inside his overcoat so that only his nose appeared above the collar, a glistening drip on the end of it.

'Perhaps we'd better go then,' Robbie suggested, but his brother remained immobile.

'Five more minutes.'

'Alright then.'

'He'll come if he can, I know he will.'

They sank back into silence once more, too cold even to talk. Suddenly Jonathan sprang to his feet and dashed from the porch, waving. Robbie rose too and looked out to observe him lumbering clumsily through the snow towards the lane, calling 'Hugh, Hugh!'

A dark figure had come through the lych gate and was picking his way along the snow-covered path towards the porch. Jonathan was running towards him and only then could Robbie see that it was indeed Hugh Dollicot. The pair shook hands and Hugh clapped a gloved hand on Jonathan's shoulder and then they walked towards him side-by-side, Jonathan beaming his relief and contentment. At the porch Hugh stepped forwards and extended a hand.

'Robbie, it's good to see you again, but you look frozen.'

'I'm alright,' Robbie said. Everything was alright now, he could see it on his brother's face.

'Shall we go inside the Church?' Hugh suggested. 'It might be a little bit warmer in there.'

They stepped in, all three noisily stamping snow from their shoes and trouser bottoms, sending a ringing echo through the cold, empty building. Hugh looked a little older, but with the same boyishly wavy dark hair and youthful, open expression. He wore a heavy black overcoat with the collar turned up and a thick woollen scarf around his neck, but no hat. Pulling off leather gloves, he stuffed them into his pockets and rubbed his fingers together to warm them.

'I'm sorry I'm late boys, it's really thick snow up here,' he said. 'I thought I wasn't going to get through. I just made it into

Netherington on the main road but I had to walk from there.' His breath hung in the air as white clouds.

'What do you think? Shall we sit down?' He indicated the front pews, so they sat as they stood, with Hugh nearest to the door and Jonathan in the middle, between the other two.

There was a pause. They were all unsure how to begin, and then Hugh spoke. 'You wanted to talk to me boys,' he said. 'What's the matter, what's happened?'

Jonathan glanced to Robbie, then turned back to Hugh. 'It's about the robbery at Netherington Hall. Mr Birch saw you there.'

'Robbery!' Hugh exclaimed, 'I didn't know anything about a robbery. My goodness, when was that, what happened?'

'At Christmas,' Robbie chipped in. 'On Boxing Day night.'

'It was Mr Birch,' said Jonathan.

'Mr Birch did it...?'

'No. On the drive... he saw someone, but it wasn't the burglar.' Jonathan was getting flustered now, unable to get his words out in order.

'No...?'

'We were at Grandma's for lunch...'

Hugh was looking confounded.

'Hugh,' Robbie interrupted. 'Dad took us with him up to the Hall on Boxing Day afternoon when he went to check round because the family were away. We walked down to the tennis courts while we were waiting for him, Jonathan and me.' He saw a look of enlightenment on Hugh's face.

'And you saw me there, right?'

'Yes!' said Jonathan. 'We didn't know it was you, but then we saw you and it was you.'

'Mr Higgins, he works with Dad at the Hall, he went up there to check everything and he discovered it. The break-in,' Robbie continued. 'He called the Police and they interviewed everyone and took fingerprints and everything, the Detectives did, and Dad went up there too. Anyway, he told us that Mr Birch, who lives in The Lodge by the gates, he told the Police he'd seen a young man in black on the drive on Boxing Day.' Robbie paused for breath. He could see Hugh looking at him with a serious expression on his face.

'So the Police are looking for me?'

'Yes.'

'We didn't know what to do,' said Jonathan. 'We knew it was you up there, but when Dad told us we didn't say anything because we didn't want to get you in trouble with the Police. It wasn't you, was it Hugh? I know you're not the thief.'

Hugh smiled, abashed, and shook his head gently. 'No, definitely not, but you mustn't get yourselves into trouble, you two.

'It's Caroline... we always played tennis a lot and spent a lot of time around the courts; you saw us up there last summer, didn't you? I used to leave notes for her up there, hidden in one of the net posts, there's a slot where the net cable comes out. Just silly stuff, little notes, messages, where to meet up, that sort of thing. Sometimes she'd leave one for me and I'd slip up and find them between our meetings and leave a reply.'

'Secret messages?' asked Jonathan.

'Yes, that's right, secret messages, just between the two of us. I think she rather liked it, her parents being very formal and that sort of thing. Anyway, I'm afraid we've had rather a falling out. She sort of gave me my marching orders just before Christmas, before they went off to Corfu. I was a bit out of sorts, I only remembered over Christmas that I'd left a message up there just before we split up and... well, I would have looked a bit foolish if she'd found it after what had been said.

'So... I was going near there on Boxing Day, on the way to see friends for the evening, so I called in and retrieved it.'

He looked up at them both. 'I feel rather foolish now, I must say.'

'Why did Miss Caroline tell you to go?' asked Jonathan dolefully.

Hugh gave a small, quiet laugh, 'Oh, Jonathan, she was sort of a bit cross with me, thought I was being irresponsible by spending too much time on fun; flying, going out, cars, that sort of thing. She'd been on about it for weeks and then, finally, that was it. Finished. I suppose I had it coming.'

There was silence for a short while, then Hugh pulled an envelope from his pocket and turned towards the two of them. 'But how on earth did you find me?'

Jonathan brightened, pulling himself up straight.

'Well, Robbie and me remembered Mum and Mrs Harrison-Bates said you were from a brewery family, and Robbie saw the name on the barrels at the Horse & Hounds. Then we looked it up in the phone book and it said Dollicot's Brewers at Fringleton and some other Dollicots, but none of them were 'H's', so then we went back to school and I did a letter and sent it from school. We do an hour on Tuesdays after arithmetic lessons to do letters home, but I wrote to you instead. I'm sure Mum won't mind.'

Robbie could see the crumpled envelope still clasped in Hugh's hand. In Jonathan's large scrawl, it read: *Dollicots Brewers, Fringleton* and across the top, in large capitals: *FOR HUH DOLICOT*. Then, in red and underlined: *ERGENT, PRIVAET.*

For a brief moment, Hugh's eyes met Robbie's, and they exchanged a fleeting glance of shared admiration.

'Is that where you live, Hugh?' asked Jonathan. 'At the brewery?'

'No, but nearby, at Little Stansford. My family's got the Manor there.'

'Do you run the brewery?'

Hugh laughed. 'No! My father owns it, and my great Grandfather established it, so it's been our family business for over sixty years. I work there, but not enough according to Caroline; or my father for that matter.'

'What will you do now?' Jonathan asked rather plaintively, following a pause to take in all this information.

Hugh looked about him for a few seconds, thinking to himself. 'I think I'll go up to the house,' he said. 'I'll see Mr and Mrs H-B and tell them I've heard about the robbery and offer my sympathies. I'm sure they're terribly upset. And I'll mention I went up there Boxing Day afternoon to collect a note I'd left for Caroline. That way they'll put two and two together and we don't have to let on that anyone else knows I was up there. How about that?'

'Sounds perfect,' Robbie said while, between the two of them, Jonathan beamed with satisfaction.

'I don't know how to thank you both,' Hugh added. 'You took quite a risk and I feel very humbled. It was very thoughtful of you both. You must let me repay you somehow.'

'Will you come sledging with us?' asked Jonathan with eagerness.

'Can you?' Robbie asked, but rather more tentatively. 'Have you got time?'

To his credit, Hugh barely paused. Or perhaps he was as keen to go sledging as they were. Anyway, he smiled. 'Well... why not? That'll be fun. Shall we?'

So they collected the sledge from the porch and took Hugh through the deep snow past Snake Pond and up onto the slopes of Lullington Hill. The windmill and village were spread out way below, amongst the white fields. Most children were further round, on the other side of the hill where the slopes were longer and steeper, but it suited the brothers to have an area pretty much to themselves and the three of them cavorted and larked about, taking turns to sledge, two at a time, falling off almost as often as they stayed on board all the way to the bottom, before being pitched laughing into the deep snow.

Time and again they toiled, red-cheeked from the effort and cold, hauling the sledge back up the increasingly slippery run to the top, frequently falling and slipping. Finally, Hugh flopped to the ground at the top, after a particularly long sledge run with Jonathan.

'Boys, I'm famished!' he said.

They agreed they both were too. 'I think we have to go home for dinner,' Robbie reluctantly admitted.

'What will you do, Hugh?' asked Jonathan.

'Oh, I'll be alright. I'll pop into the pub for a bite and then I'd better set off and pick the car up.' He looked up at the sky. 'I think we'll have more snow and I don't want to get stranded.'

'Will you call in at the Hall?' Robbie asked.

'Yes, long as I don't get there too late. If not, in the next day or so. And look, I'm not going to say a thing about you telling me, or you seeing me up there, and not letting on to your parents or anyone else. It's our secret, right?'

'Right,' they chimed.

III

It was one of those beguiling days which February often brings, when for a few benign hours it felt more like spring than winter.

Robbie and Lizzie were cycling along the old track. Ahead, the still-uncut blackthorn hedge stretched dusky purple, looking like smoke against the fair sky. The first dog violets of spring bloomed amongst the leaf litter on the sunny bank where piles of freshly-dug soil spilled over from a badgers' sett. The track's surface was uneven and Robbie rode his new bicycle with toes frequently touching the ground, veering uncertainly from side-to-side.

Two days before, Lizzie had been woken by the sound of excited voices down in the street. She'd looked out of her bedroom window to see Tom holding the saddle of a shiny blue Raleigh two-wheeler. Robbie sat astride it, gripping the handlebars in studied concentration, both feet on the peddles and wobbling nervously forwards. Jonathan stood frozen, with arms outstretched as if in readiness to catch his brother if he fell off. She'd leaned out and called, but Robbie had glanced up only momentarily, too fearful of losing his concentration and falling off. Tom had waved up to her.

'Birthday present,' he'd called out.

Today was their first trip together on their bikes. She, as usual, rode Ron's old bike which was heavy and battered and far too big for her, but she was well used to it.

'Race you,' she'd called, pedalling energetically ahead, but he wasn't confident yet and made no attempt to catch her up. Above their heads the jackdaws were clattering in the tall trees and took off, wheeling noisily away, filling the air with their strange fluting cries. Both turned to see what had disturbed their roosting and saw the twins pedalling furiously towards them.

Twisting about in her saddle, Lizzie called, 'Robbie's got a new bike!'

Nid and Finch came alongside, panting from their exertions.

'For my birthday on Thursday,' explained Robbie, brimful with pride.

'We'll be getting a big Hornby 00 Gauge layout for ours,' said Nid.

Finch was vigorously gouging his front tyre into the rutted track. 'Dad said we have to do well at school first,' he interrupted.

'Well, I will,' and Nid wheeled away, pressing down hard on his pedals as he slowly encircled their little group, like a watchful sheepdog.

They played at cops 'n' robbers, a popular game following the big news of the Netherington Hall robbery arrests. Three men had been chased across the fields by Police with dogs after a tip-off about strangers at a remote farm cottage. Several farm workers had joined in, leaping ditches and farm gates, grabbing stakes and shovels as impromptu weapons, everybody yelling like mad and the Police dogs barking until eventually the robbers were cornered by a field barn and arrested.

Tom told the boys the Police had found some of the family's missing paintings and silver in the cottage, although by no means all of it.

***

Much later, the twins having gone home, Robbie and Lizzie returned to Wheelwrights for lunch. By the time they got in, hollow with hunger, the family had already eaten so they sat alone at the large kitchen table.

A commanding rap at the window interrupted their food and Lizzie perceived three indistinct figures through the frosted glass, one tall and two shorter. Her parents and Grandpa were relaxing in the family sitting room beyond the hallway, from where she could hear the Saturday afternoon football on television. No one stirred so she rose and pulled open the yard door herself.

Ern Taylor and his wife stood before her; behind them their daughter, Grace.

'Is your Dad in?' said Ern, peremptorily.

From the sitting room, Lizzie's mother looked up from a magazine, an expectant half-smile on her face, the men too absorbed in the match to notice the callers.

'Mr Taylor's at the door, Mum, with Mrs Taylor and Grace. They want to speak to Dad.'

Joe turned. 'What does he want?'

'I don't know, he says he wants you.'

Sarah and Joe exchanged puzzled glances and Joe reluctantly rose and walked through to the kitchen while, behind, Grandpa urged on his team.

'Afternoon, Joe. I think we'd better come in and talk, there's a few things must be said.' It was Ern Taylor speaking.

Lizzie was conscious of an uncomfortable silence as the four of them passed through the kitchen and inner hallway, ignoring Sarah's enquiring look. Joe didn't take the visitors into the sitting room, instead opening the door to the front room reserved for 'best', closing the door behind them. Through the still-open kitchen door Lizzie saw, across the hall, the questioning look on her mother's face. There was a low mumble of something from Grandpa and then the two of them fell silent, but her mother's eyes were turned to the wall behind. After a moment Sarah got up and shut the kitchen door and Lizzie and Robbie could see nothing further.

'What d'you think that's about?' Lizzie whispered, as she served bowls of jelly and evaporated milk for them both, straining to hear for sounds.

He shrugged, equally baffled, and watched as she took her bowl to the kitchen door, pressing an ear against the wooden panel, where she ate as quietly as possible, avoiding slurping the slithery jelly so as not to be discovered. From beyond the door they could discern a low mumble of speech in the sitting room, suggesting that the television had been turned down. Lizzie's mother and Grandpa were trying to eavesdrop as well.

The voices from the front room rose and fell at intervals. Lizzie could hear the hard, flat tones of Ern Taylor's who seemed to be doing most of the speaking, followed by something from her father, and then Mrs Taylor spoke, her shrill, bird-like voice in little staccato gobbets of sound. After a few minutes the front room door opened and the draught dislodged the kitchen door latch so that the door bounced open slightly. Peering silently though the crack she saw her father's back just inches away from her, so close she could smell on his jumper the oil he used at work. Beyond him, at the sitting room doorway, stood her mother; expectant, a tense uneasy expression on her face.

The door from the front room had been left open. Within was gloomy, in stark contrast to the warm glow from the welcoming family sitting room. Ern Taylor stood before the empty fireplace, feet firmly planted, hands clasped behind him and with his face set. In the centre of the room Mrs Taylor agitatedly worked her handbag, resolutely studying the ornaments on the bureau. Grace was silhouetted against the window, her fair hair haloed in the light, shoulders tense but slumped. Mr Taylor cleared his throat several times. Joe Rose guided Sarah in, hand held against the small of her back, and then firmly closed the door behind them both.

Lizzie slipped out of the kitchen and ran to her Grandpa, climbing onto his knee.

'What's going on?' she asked.

'Nothing, pet. Grown-ups business, nothing for you to mind about. Why don't you two go upstairs and play and let Grandpa rest his eyes.'

This was code for Grandpa Rose's afternoon nap so they left, passing the front room door as slowly as possible on their way to the stairs, but could hear no more than the burr of conversation inside, although the voices seemed louder and sharper than was normal. Lizzie paused at the top of the stairs and then motioned Robbie into Ron's room which was above the best room. They knelt stealthily, ears pressed to the floorboards, and Lizzie forced her breathing to be as slow and quiet as possible.

Mrs Taylor was talking quickly and then Ern Taylor said, 'Well, it needs to be sorted.' She heard her mother speaking more loudly and quickly than was usual and then her father, slowly but firmly, followed by Mrs Taylor's voice, raised and urgent. The door opened and someone came out. Grandpa answered, 'Yes, as soon as I see him,' and then the door closed again. After a while there was a new voice, higher, softer, and Lizzie realised it was Grace. It was the first time she'd spoken.

Suddenly Robbie scrambled to his feet, hand clamped to his mouth. He was gasping and struggling not to cough. She grabbed his arm and quickly steered him to the back landing where he sucked in a great lungful of air and coughed loudly, doubling up. Through the rear landing window overlooking the yard they could see Ron approaching. The back door them slammed, followed by the rattle of the kitchen door latch as he came into the hallway below. Looking down over the banisters they saw Grandpa emerge from the sitting room, the sporting pages scattered from his lap onto the floor.

'Hold on, boy,' he said. 'Your folks want you – in there,' and he motioned to the front room.

'What for?'

'That's for you to find out, I reckon,' and Grandpa returned, bending stiffly to retrieve the newspaper.

They were looking right down at Ron's head, onto his fashionable greased-back hair, co-conspirators in their eavesdropping. Ron hesitated, then clasped the door handle with one hand, the other tucked nonchalantly into his jacket pocket, and with an intake of breath he wrenched the front room door open. Once more it revealed the dark interior, no one having switched on the light. Joe and Sarah stood in the centre of the room, facing Ern and Mrs Taylor who were by the fireplace, with Grace a few feet away, silently absorbed in studying her fingers.

At the door Ron stiffened, then slicked his palm over his hair. They all turned and looked towards him. Ern stared steadfastly and

Mrs Taylor coughed. Grace turned away and gazed emptily out of the front window. Joe beckoned him in and Ron stepped forwards, his bearing surly. This time the door was left open.

'Reckon you know what this is about,' Ern Taylor said.

'Of course he does!' Mrs Taylor snapped.

Ron spoke gruffly. 'What's this?' he turned to his father, hostility in his voice. 'What'm I supposed to've done?'

'What's he done!' snorted Mrs Taylor.

'That attitude won't help, you know,' Joe Rose said quietly.

'What?'

'You know what,' Taylor interjected.

'Just a minute please, Ern,' replied Joe. 'Let me talk to the boy.'

They all fell silent and looked at him. Grace still stared out of the front windows, her gaze remote, yet picking violently at her fingernails.

'It's about Grace, as I think you know,' Taylor said. At the sound of her name, she glanced across and then returned to studying her hands, mouth full and sullen.

'She's expecting.'

'What's that got to do with me!' Ron exclaimed, voice rising.

At this everyone began to speak – or shout – apart from Grace who fidgeted even more as if by sheer restlessness alone she could conjure herself from the room. Ern Taylor strode up to Ron and began to shout in his face.

This brought Grandpa to the door. 'What's all this! Can't we discuss this like adults? I never heard such a commotion. Ern, what's the matter with you?'

They all fell silent, then Mrs Taylor spoke again. 'He denies it,' she cried, pointing accusingly at Ron. 'Even now.'

'I didn't,' Ron replied, belligerently.

'You did!'

'I think we all need to calm down,' said Joe, pressing his big palms down upon the air as if to suppress the waves of hostile energy. 'Ron, Grace is expecting and she's told her folks that you're the father. Now, what've you got to say?'

Ron shuffled and swayed. Grandpa put a hand on his shoulder. 'Stand up to it lad if you're man enough,' he said.

There was another silence as Ron stood, swaying slightly, head hanging loose from his shoulders.

'What if I am?' he finally said. There was a collective release of breath and a small distressed sound from Sarah. The tension in the room relaxed.

Beside Lizzie, Robbie spluttered again, having tried to control another cough for several minutes. Grandpa stepped back and closed the front room door with a firm clunk.

IV

'If it's a boy, they're going to call it James.'

These quietly-spoken words of his mother's drilled into Nid's consciousness. Ahead, Finch was marching behind their parents, taking long strides and swinging his arms in exaggerated imitation of their father's brisk military walk. Many people from the village were returning from the Church, but most were in their own groups, talking, laughing and commenting on the wedding.

'Pretty ostentatious under the circumstances,' their father was saying.

'She wanted an apple blossom wedding.'

'Really, such a show!'

'The Rose's are very upset, underneath it all.'

'That boy's always been difficult.'

'And she's no better than she should be.'

'As has been proved...'

They turned the corner to The Green and Finch fell back to join Nid.

'They said something about James,' Nid whispered to his brother.

'What?'

'I don't know! Listen.'

It had been a particularly well-attended ceremony, owing much to curiosity; a chance to see if Grace was 'showing'. Frank and

Norma stopped to speak to another couple also walking home from the service and the twins hung about around their little group. After a few minutes' talk the other pair drifted away. It was a dazzlingly bright and blowy late April day and Frank and Norma paused on The Green looking about them, smartly dressed for the wedding, a handsome couple enjoying the early spring sunshine. About their feet orbs of dandelion seed heads were like bubbles floating above the grass. Excited noise and chatter drew their attention and they all turned to watch as the bride and groom and their respective families passed along the top of The Green en route to the Methodist Hall for the reception.

'I gather she's hoping for a boy.'

'Hmm.'

'It's due in July.'

'None too soon then.'

Norma frowned and the two of them exchanged a knowing glance, but said nothing further, then they walked towards home, the boys following.

'Who's James?' Nid suddenly heard himself saying. He was skipping along beside his parents, conscious that he was desperately trying to look and sound casual. Such artifice was unnatural to him; it was more Finch's area.

Frank and Norma turned to him, slightly startled, and he felt his nonchalance begin to crumble under their collective gaze.

'What do you mean?' his father said.

'Well, you said 'James',' Nid replied. 'Who's he?' The very sound of these words, spoken in his own voice, surprised him. Close by, Finch had his head down but was peering up at them all through lowered eyelashes.

'No one,' said Norma.

'It can't be no one,' Nid persisted, despite himself.

'Well, no. It's what Grace wants to call her little boy if they have one.'

'Why?'

'I suppose they like the name.'

'Maybe they're calling him after someone,' piped up Finch, brightly.

'I don't think so,' she said, and pushed open the front gate, topic closed.

Indoors Norma and Frank dropped into armchairs and took up newspapers and magazines. Also wanting to read, Nid sat with them but Finch, ever restless, went out into the garden. Indoors no one spoke for some time and then Nid heard his mother again.

'I've such a headache.'

'Hmm.'

'It's so bright today, it's positively boring right into my eyes. Nigel...'

Absorbed in reading, he responded reluctantly.

'Get me my headache pills, will you? They're in the dressing table drawer with my hair pins. Go on now! And a glass of water, please.'

Upstairs, a bright light filled the silent bedroom, gleaming through the net curtains and falling as a pool of warmth on the shiny elastoplast-pink eiderdown. This normally out-of-bounds room felt strange and unfamiliar to Nid, filled as it was with such intense stillness; a place of mystery and privacy.

Dust shimmered in the shafts of sunlight as he approached the dark shape of the dressing table, silhouetted in front of the window. He slipped open one of the drawers but it was full of underwear. Trying the one to the other side, it rattled open to reveal rows of hair rollers and boxes of pins. At the back he could see the Aspirin. He paused with his fingers still around the drawer handle and allowed his head to raise to the mirror, his eyes drifting up over the smart white shirt, now tie-less and opened at the neck, and the chin, small mouth, rounded upturned nose, blue eyes and blonde fringe. The image stared back at him, reflective, eyes narrowing a little in thought. They studied one another for a few moments and then Nid pulled his mouth tight and they looked away from each other.

His fingers released the drawer handle and silently sought a small drawer beneath the mirror. It slid open softly and smoothly, revealing wads of small envelopes tied with ribbon, along with several small boxes. Nid took a box out and peered inside. It contained a St Christopher on a silver chain. The next held a broad gold wedding ring. Picking up the envelopes he saw his father's firm handwriting on the top one and quickly replaced them. No time to read anything. Then he took out a small gold envelope, the flap undone, and peered inside. It contained a small card with the picture of a stork carrying a blue bundle in its beak. Nid opened it and read:

Congratulations Norma and Frank on baby James. With love Auntie Ellen & Uncle Jack.

Coiled within was a lock of curly blonde hair, fine as silk.

From downstairs he heard his mother call again, now with agitation. 'Have you got them? Right hand drawer!'

He was barely breathing now and began to see stars in front of his eyes. Hurriedly he pushed the contents back into the envelope, replaced it and closed the little drawer, then took out the pack of Aspirin and bounded conspicuously back downstairs.

***

'Go and play outside,' she'd said. 'I want to rest.'

She'd said it in a way that brooked no arguing, but Nid was relieved to go out into the garden and join Finch who was happily absorbed in kicking the football, self-content and carefree as he always was. How Nid envied him.

It was one of those days; so bright he had to screw up his eyes, and with a gentle warmth that suggested the early summer yet to come, despite the nagging breeze. They began to kick the ball about under the apple trees, pretending to be their favourite players, flinging themselves to make spectacular saves, scoring hat tricks, imagining being carried from the pitch on the shoulders of their team mates to the worshipping cheers of the home supporters. Finch had just dived to deflect Nid's latest goal, slapping the ball away with palms outstretched. Now Nid set the football down for a corner kick and dashed forwards to take a perfect ballooning shot at the goal mouth. The ball curved wide, seeming to hang suspended for moments in the air and then descended towards the back of the goal. Finch leapt forwards, leg wildly swinging and booted it far away with a loud cry of 'Yes!' The ball soared high and cleared the fence into the Baker's garden next door where they heard it bounce onto the path.

'What a save!' cried Finch, arms aloft, head thrown back in triumph.

'You ninny! Look what you've done.'

'It's alright, I'll climb over and get it.' Finch was already hauling himself up onto the fence when there was a low growl. The Bakers' terrier-cross lay basking on the lawn and close by her feet was their football. They knew from previous experience she wasn't to be messed with.

'We can use the old one. I'll get it,' and Nid ran back to the house, recollections of earlier events welling again in his mind.

Something made him open the back door stealthily. After the dazzling brightness of the sunny garden the house was dark and he straight away heard his parents talking, their voices drifting along the hall from the front sitting room.

'...brings it all back,' Norma was saying.

'I know...'

'You think you've got over the worst, and then...'

'It's the same for me!'

'He would have been thirteen, you know.'

'You think I don't?'

'Imagine, thirteen. At secondary school, in his uniform. I can just see him, so smart, so clever.'

'Leave it can't you, Norma?'

'It's alright for you.'

'Alright for me!'

'Yes...'

'How?'

'It's different for a mother.'

'How can you say that?'

'...never seeing him grow up.'

'You think I don't!'

'Realising his potential...'

'I think about him every day. Every day, Norma! Every single day. What he'd look like, what he'd sound like. How well he'd do at school, what he'd be interested in, what subjects he'd be studying, what he'd want to be when he grew up. What sort of man he would have been. Grandchildren...'

There was the sound of a stifled sob from their mother.

Frank cleared his throat. 'If you think I don't think about him, you're mistaken. Very mistaken.' He sounded disturbingly unfamiliar; gruff, even husky.

'It doesn't get easier. Somehow it just gets harder. Every year they grow up and I think; is that how he'd have looked? Is that how he'd have sounded? Would he smile like that too, give that look, have that laugh in his eye?'

'Stop tormenting yourself, Norma.'

'I can't help it. It's the anniversary... it's the same every year. Thirteen, and he was such a lovely little boy with those chubby legs and curly blond locks. So cuddly... You never forget, as a mother you never do.'

'Leave it Norma, will you.'

'Just two, Frank. Just two years old.'

'Leave it will you!'

There was silence, not a sound, nothing, then all of a sudden his father strode from the sitting room and marched brusquely upstairs. Nid heard his mother sob loudly. He turned and walked back out into the garden.

'Can't find it,' he said to his brother.

V

It was Easter before the brothers saw Hugh again. They went, as usual, to stay at Aston Haddon and, just as before, had walked across the fields to the airfield and watched as the Cessna came into land. They found Hugh pushing the plane back into the hangar and he'd called out and waved, cheery and amiable as usual, and then he took them into the small airfield bar for lemonades, relating how he'd gone to the Harrison-Bates to commiserate about the Boxing Day robbery.

'I think they were a little surprised when I told them I'd walked through the grounds because I'd realised I might have left my watch; well, that's what I said about why I was there. Anyway, they said the Police might want to speak to me to "eliminate me from their enquiries", that sort of thing. They came out to the brewery in fact. Didn't hear any more after that until I read it in the paper. They got the three of them it seems, just like that. Sounded pretty exciting, wouldn't you say, pursuing them across the fields? Real cops and robbers stuff,' and he drained his half of beer.

'They got quite a lot back,' Robbie had said.

'So I believe. I don't know the details, I don't really see the family now I'm afraid. Awful shame though, some irreplaceable stuff lost. I did feel very sorry for them.'

***

Now it was summer once more and the following week the school holidays would begin. That was the day Robbie had come home and his mother had said, 'Violet Ward's great nephew's coming for the school holidays again.'

'That brat?' Susan had disdainfully remarked as she stood before the over-mantel mirror brushing her hair, admiring her young reflection.

'He's arriving on Saturday, on the first train in the afternoon she said, so you can meet him if you want.'

It was almost a year since Robbie had seen John and he found himself eagerly anticipating the arrival of his strange friend of two summers, counting off the days until the weekend. At the right hour he was waiting in the lane outside the station.

He supposed he shouldn't have expected John to look the same at ten and a half as he had a year ago. He imagined he himself had changed somewhat and they were, after all, exactly the same age, but for a moment he scarcely recognised John. He was taller now, although still short for his age, at least four inches shorter than Robbie who himself wasn't tall, and he was leaner too, somehow more rangy. Yet his face had become thinner and that accentuated its crumpled and lined appearance.

He'd emerged from the station dressed in a conspicuously dusty and over-sized school blazer, crumpled shirt partly unbuttoned, short trousers that were too long in the leg, sagging grey socks and scuffed sandals. Hanging from one hand was the same small and worn suitcase. Robbie had called, 'John!' and his friend had looked up, face creasing in the sunlight. Robbie had waved and John had paused, looking about in his general direction and had then grinned and walked over.

'Watcha!' That familiar greeting, the same scratched, hoarse voice. 'Nice bike.'

'For my tenth birthday. What d'you think?'

'Not bad.'

'Hop on.'

John clambered up behind, shoving the suitcase against the small of Robbie's back. 'Back agen then,' he announced.

'All summer?'

'Yep.'

Shortly after, they stood outside Violet Ward's, both smiling with approval at their reunion, not sure what else to say, awkward still with one another. Robbie could see John close-up now, the tangle of dark, rough-textured curly hair, grey shadows under his eyes, a large bruise on one temple. He was a markedly odd figure, under-sized yet somehow aged.

'What're we doin' then?' John eagerly asked. 'Who's about?'

'Oh, everyone.'

'Ol' Draycott? I'm gonna bleedin' get 'im, I am! Ol' Finch, Nid? Maggie, all of 'em?'

'Yes, everyone.'

He jerked his case up from the ground and, yanking it open, pulled a paper bag from amongst the tangle of none-too-clean clothing and held it out to Robbie. It was a bag of sherbet lemons. Robbie doubted his friend had paid for them, but they each took one and sucked hard on them. They were acid sharp and soapy-sweet.

***

John was round the next day, straight after breakfast. Sally looked up as he swaggered in from the lean-to.

'Well, here you are again, John. And you've grown this last year.' As the boys went out she called after them, 'Behave yourselves. No mischief.' It wasn't something she normally felt the need to say to her youngest son.

Before long they were at ease with one another once more, laughing and fooling about in the garden. Robbie showed John the inside of the greenhouse and picked two ripe tomatoes but he wouldn't try one, distrustful of its shiny redness, although he seemed fascinated by all the gardening paraphernalia, pulling out tools and other items. He pointed to the shelf.

'What's them fireworks?'

'My Dad's sulphur cones.'

'Wha's tha'?'

'You know, you light them and they send out smoke and it kills all the pests in the greenhouse.' But, of course, he couldn't know.

Eventually they went in search of their other friends. Talking and joshing one another as they ambled along to The Square. Robbie was dismayed to see the familiar shock of Malcolm Draycott's red hair disappearing into the Newsagents, leaving a bike propped against a post, outside. Robbie ducked out of sight behind a vehicle – he really wasn't ready for any kind of confrontation this early in the holidays. Turning to look for John he realised his friend hadn't followed and earnestly hoped he wasn't going to get entangled with Malcolm.

Emerging shortly after, Malcolm thrust his purchases into one trouser pocket, raised his bike and stood hard on the pedal. He was about to swing his right leg over when Jack Duckett turned the corner nearby. A stocky boy of about twelve, he was well-known for enjoying a scrap and was a mate of both Malcolm and Neville's. They greeted one another and began to cross The Square, with Malcolm wheeling his bike alongside. Robbie watched in silent astonishment as a slow, licking coil of something grey began to emerge from Malcolm's saddle bag. Pressing back against the car so as not to be seen by the two older boys, he turned to stare at the apparition which now curled and swelled like a genie from the back of the bike. Soon it was looming menacingly over the two lads who continued to walk on, absorbed in conversation, still entirely unaware.

As the two crossed towards the pub, the grey spectre billowed high above them and other people now noticed and were beginning to point and comment. Malcolm at first ignored the staring, but then realised with discomfit that it was he who was the focus of all this amusement. By now the vapour was being ejected like a volcano as a great spume of dark smoke spewed out. Malcolm and Jack turned to look back to see what everyone was staring at and both momentarily buckled at the knees in shock. Malcolm flung the bike away in alarm so that it clattered onto the cobbles and Jack stumbled backwards, emitting a low screech.

In the warm, still air the smoke quickly began to sink and was soon wafting thickly about them as they coughed and staggered, flapping wildly, as the locals looked on and chuckled.

John was in his familiar pose; bent double, racked with throaty laughter, a box of matches clutched in his hand.

VI

It wasn't only Maggie who had a secret. Ann had a secret too; a big one – only it was one she didn't know about. Nevertheless, it was a secret that pretty much everyone else knew. The neighbours knew, the shopkeepers, probably her teachers knew too. Even

Maggie knew. Ann's mother certainly did, but she wasn't going to tell, was she? Not to Ann, her daughter, her only child.

Ann felt her home life to be a normal, quiet family life, just the three of them in their cottage, sandwiched between the old path and the shops which fronted The Square. Her father, Sid Dewberry, was a Carpenter. He worked away a fair bit, his boxes of tools and wooden saw horse always in the back of the cream-coloured truck which he parked in their cobbled front yard. They rattled as he drove out, bumping along the passage between the Newsagents and Drapers, tools and boxes clattering against the metal truck's sides, heralding his arrival and departure.

They grew to measure their lives by that clattering, Ann and her mother; his going out, coming back in, out again, in, and finally out once more.

Nellie had been pretty; she still was, but her face had lost its bloom and her once-fashionably narrow cheeks now seemed rather pinched and hollowed. She wore her baby-fine brown hair curled in the same style as when she'd married Sid and was still trim with soft, evasive hazel eyes. She was quiet, what some people called 'a home body', but yet there was a brittle edge about her.

Nellie and Ann had breakfasted alone, as they regularly did. They'd eaten their dinner that way the night before too; cold cuts from the weekend family roast. It was a quiet house but they were used to it that way, company to one another in their solitude; an only child and her mother, quiet observers to their bond.

Ann made her way outside. The front garden was a riotous tumble of July growth, uncontrolled and wild, scented of white clover and the alpine strawberries that trailed everywhere. She didn't go into the yard and take the passage directly out to The Square, but instead turned back from the front gate and followed the narrow path that led behind the shops, an indirect way that dipped down to the old sunken track at the rear of their cottage. This was her regular route out; not boldly, straight out across the yard and passage, but this discrete and indirect path tucked behind the old walls. Deep in its silence, it was damp and fecund in winter, and overgrown with weeds and wildflowers in summer, as it was now. She loved its sense of timelessness and permanence, how her silent tread on its ancient worn stones and mossy turf made no impact. It never even knew she was there.

On reaching Main Street, at the lower end of the old track, her transport from the world of home would be accomplished. She would emerge from her world of silence beside Luff's and the Greengrocers, amongst the houses and the first of the farms on the village outskirts, with all the activity of people and shops and the regular passage of cars, into a world transformed.

But Ann didn't get that far today. The narrow side-path was a tangle of tall weeds, with ivy and honeysuckle spilling unrestrained from the walls on either side, so that she must press her way through, tipping her face against the sway of tall stems that brushed her cheeks. To her right was the stone wall bordering her own garden while, high up and on the left, a red brick wall enclosed the yards behind the shops. As she squeezed her way through, Ann became aware of voices ahead and above her. She stopped, lest she be heard rather than from a wish to eavesdrop, but couldn't avoid hearing since the voices came from immediately beyond the brick wall, from the Bank's small rear yard. She stopped, breathing softly and silently for fear of discovery.

'...Good reputation, no doubt about that. That's right, isn't it?'

'Well...'

'No doubt about it. Regulars – lots of regulars. Good turnover, good position, excellent, anyone can see that.'

'Yes.'

'It's just... here.' There was the strike of a match and her nostrils strained for the sweet sulphurous smell which soon drifted from beyond the wall.

'Thanks.'

'Anyway, ticking along well. Built it up, good clientele – as you know. Plenty of regulars. They can't argue with that.'

'No...'

'That's right, isn't it?'

'Yes.'

'And you know how it is, don't you?'

'Mmm.'

'Growing family. It never ends. First they grow out of this, then they grow out of that. They wear stuff out before you can say knife and they're always hungry. Well, you must know how it is, with your two, two at once, eh! And then that little one came along.' There was a gruff laugh. 'Bit of a surprise that, we could have done without it, as if four's not enough. Now there's the school uniform and all for the older boy, it never ends, eh? How's yours? Getting on all right?'

'Oh, pretty good. Eleven Plus next year, of course. We're hoping...'

'Yes, good future, certainly.'

'Norma and I are hoping... well, Nigel's very bright; very conscientious. Applies himself well.'

'Always a future in the Bank, eh! Look then, Frank. Just for a bit, keep things on an even keel, you know. Brewery... you know how it is, they get on your back. Don't give a fellow room to breathe. I need to keep the business going, build it up. Don't want to let things slip, eh?'

'Mmm.'

'Keep it going along well. Won't be for that long, year at most, I reckon. Maybe even six months. Make sure things don't slip back. Got to keep the regulars satisfied, eh!

'I'm sure, with a good word from you... that's all it needs, bit of endorsement, eh? After all, I've been in this business fifteen years; there isn't much I don't know about keeping a pub – three of 'em. I built that White Hart up from nothing, you know. It was nothing before I took it on, complete failure. A good word from you to the top brass, that would see it right, I reckon. They take note of you, Frank, up in Cullingham. Good company man, you are.'

'Yes, well, I...'

'I've always seen you right, eh? A few choice bottles of this and that, and the baccy. I think you've enjoyed them. Just a good word in for me. Won't harm, eh? Ease the cogs!'

'Rod, I'll do my best. I can't promise, you know. It won't be up to me.'

'Yes, yes. You're a company man, Frank. Top brass respects you. Your word counts.'

'Well, maybe. I'll do my best. Look, I must go in and open up; I'm running late already.'

'Right you are, Frank, see you lunchtime. Yours'll be on the counter waiting.'

There was no answer to this last remark, which was delivered not with a tone suggestive of generosity, but sounding somehow expectant and conditional. Ann heard their departing footsteps across the yard; one solid and measured, the other brisk and heavy and then she turned and walked directly out onto The Square. Rod Viney was striding purposefully through the Pub's main entrance and disappeared quickly from view

She made her way along the top lane towards the swings where she expected to find the others, feeling ready now for some company and diversion. This route passed the school, its gates locked for the summer, the playground silent and empty. For a few weeks at least, no longer the haunt for casual torments from other children. As Ann drew near, she sensed a movement beyond the large elm which shaded the entrance, and she could just make out a dark figure on top of one of the stone gate pillars. This figure crouched momentarily before dropping down into the school playground, whereupon he ran, for clearly it was a boy, stooping low, and away towards the buildings. A second figure, also a boy, ably scaled the pillar and followed the first.

She cautiously approached, pressed herself to the nearest pillar and peered through the gate railings. Beyond the blank expanse of the playground, looking back towards her from the nearest corner of the school building, were three faces: Malcolm Draycott, Neville Potter and Squinter Brazell. Ann caught her breath but the deep shade cast by the elm's heavy canopy had rendered her invisible to them. One by one the faces withdrew and then they were gone.

With a sense of shock, every bit as pleasurable as it was startling, she dashed to the swings to tell the others of her discovery.

Robbie, the twins and John were all engaged in rough horse play while Lizzie looked on from one of the swings, languidly pushing herself backwards and forwards with one foot scuffing the floor. She waved and Ann ran over and blurted out what she'd witnessed, her breath snatching in her throat as the words came tumbling out. Nid was the first to disentangle himself from the boys' scrum.

'What were they doing?'

'I don't know,' she said. 'But they didn't want to be seen, and they shouldn't have been in there anyway, should they?

'Let's go and find out!' cried Finch.

'What if there were more than three of them? You know what they're like.'

Indeed they did.

'And we might get into trouble ourselves,' Ann pointed out. 'We're not allowed in school in the holidays when it's all shut up. Mrs Henderson says.'

'Yeh, well she won't be able to see nuffin', will she?' said John. 'She ain't there.'

'If they're up to no good we can find out and then they'll get caught, won't they?'

Lizzie's remark sounded sensible enough and, quite honestly, they were all dying to know what was going on and needed little impetus to convince themselves to investigate. At the school entrance the tall metal gates hung between the two stone pillars, padlocked together. This was no obstacle to John, who simply placed one foot on the gate hinge and nimbly swung himself onto the pillar. From there he sprang softly to the ground beyond. Lizzie, equally light and agile, quickly followed and then Finch and Nid. Finally, Robbie scrambled rather awkwardly to the top before reaching back to haul Ann up, who scraped her knees against the rough grainy stone. The two of them briefly teetered on the top, dizzied by the height, then Robbie grasped the top of the gates and jumped heavily to the ground.

'Come on, Ann!' called Lizzie, encouragingly.

Below her, five faces peered up, willing her and expectant. Beyond were the school buildings, seemingly so far away that they were dwarfed, and the hard grey asphalt of the playground appeared as a very long drop below. Suddenly there was a noise from beyond the school.

'Quick!' urged John. 'Bleedin' 'urry up, or they'll see us.'

'Just hold onto the gate,' Lizzie whispered up. 'Like I did.'

With limbs trembling, Ann crouched and grasped the gate's top rail and then flung herself from the pillar with such an arc that she landed some feet beyond the others, wobbling slightly and astonished at the achievement, but also rather excited.

'Quick now,' hissed John. 'All a ya, keep low.'

They fell in behind and, running silently, bent low like fugitives in the night, followed him across the empty playground to the front of the school building where, pressing their backs against the rough stone wall, they edged towards the corner where Ann had seen the three faces.

John, who had assumed command, looked round and pronounced the way ahead clear so they advanced, one by one, creeping stealthily. At first they passed beneath the windows of their classroom, normally such a familiar and often noisy scene, but now not one of them spoke. Ann snatched at the back of Lizzie's skirt for reassurance so Lizzie reached back and took Ann's slender hand into hers, the small fingers digging into her palm.

At the rear corner of the building, John repeated the procedure before advancing into the smaller back yard that led across to the boys' and girls' toilet blocks and the Caretaker's stores.

Still there was no one to be seen. A high perimeter wall encircled the school grounds and enclosed the rear yard, leaving between the school building and boundary wall, only a narrow access from the main playground. John walked cautiously to the centre of the rear yard, looking all about him; a small lone, wiry figure. He adopted a crouching, furtive stance, then silently summoned the others to join him. Still there was no sign or sound of anyone.

They gathered in a huddle, gazing silently about, their eyes roaming every corner and entrance, ears straining for any sound.

'They must've gone,' whispered Finch. 'Maybe they climbed out over the back wall.'

'We didn't hear them.' Robbie's voice was hushed and uncertain. 'I think we would have done.'

They paused again, senses once more probing for the least sound or movement, standing close by one another, edgy and anxious.

John was silent, eyes darting uneasily.

An animal-like roar came without warning. Lizzie and Ann leaped apart in astonishment, Robbie spun round and blundered into John, and the twins had time only to turn before the others rushed at them, hollering and bellowing. At first Ann thought the sheer noise had thrown her from her feet. The ground seemed to be instantly swept away from under her so that she was flung onto the tarmac, the backs of her legs stinging with white pain. About her the others lay sprawled, the boys yelling and groaning while Lizzie stared ahead, shocked. Ann whimpered as a tear brimmed in one eye.

Like a demon-force released from Hell, now whooping and laughing, Malcolm and the others raced away, through the narrow gap towards the main playground and were lost to sight.

Slowly the group picked themselves up, rubbing at the red burns that had begun to well painfully at the backs of their legs.

'Them bastuds!' yelled John, making two-finger gestures towards their line of exit. 'I'll get them bleedin', wankin' bastuds!' And he leaped to his feet, strutting and angrily punching the air, the backs of his knees an angry deep red. 'Fuckers!'

'What do we do now?' said Robbie. 'They might be lying in wait for us.'

Lizzie rubbed her legs vigorously. 'I think we should just go,' she said, her voice small. 'Anyway, what did they get us with?'

'A rope,' said Nid. 'From the stores.'

'Let's just go,' Robbie urged. 'We'll walk briskly back to the gates. One of us can keep a look-out while the others climb over.'

John started to walk back towards the front playground. There was nowhere to hide, the area being open right the way across to the outer wall so they stole slowly forwards into the open playground, once more alert and watchful, anxiously scanning the area, but there was no one to be seen and, once again, not a sound. Ann rubbed plaintively at the painful welts on her legs and wished she hadn't seen the boys climbing in so all this would never have happened.

They edged towards the gates in a protective huddle and were no more than a few yards away when, from the shade below the elm, the gang broke cover and once again rushed, whooping and shouting at them. Squinter raced around behind, Malcolm straight towards them, arms raised, Neville darted to the other side. Between them they held the rope again.

Squinter encircled them while the others pulled it tight, drawing them all into a tight knot, arms pinned to their sides, trapped, humiliated and helpless. Ann's face was pressed into Finch's back, behind her John wriggled and squirmed, bellowing with fury. On the edge Nid and Robbie kicked out wildly but it was futile; the older boys kept a safe distance, taunting them while laughing and chanting.

Finally Malcolm and the others ran off. Speedily they scaled the gates, kicked off from the top and tore off down the lane, still whooping with triumphant delight.

Ann didn't tell her mother about the ambush, but there were angry red marks on her legs so she said she'd slipped on the swings. It was her secret.

VII

Maggie knew something was up, she knew it the minute she got out of bed. There was an atmosphere in the flat, an air that said 'take care, go easy'. It was like a threat that's withheld, but no less a threat for that. Even the children had fallen quiet; no squabbling or arguing, nothing flung across the floor in a pique. She sat on her bed, or rather on her side of the narrow bed she shared with Shirley, and gazed towards the closed door of their bedroom.

Loud footsteps on the stairs, that's what had alerted her. Now they came up again, thudding on the carpet-less treads. He flung the front door closed and marched heavily along the hallway outside. The kitchen door creaked, it always did, and a chair scraped sharply across the lino. It had been drawn back vigorously and with force.

'What did I say...? What did I say? What am I always saying? How do you do it? How can you possibly have got through all of it? How can you, Lois, how can you? Other women manage.' His tone was abrupt and harsh.

'I...'

'Why can't you manage, what's the matter with you? Are you a bloody half-wit or something? Christ, it's bloody hopeless! What d'you think I am? Working all hours; I'm down there working fucking all hours and what do you do with it all? You've got nothing else to see to, have you?'

'I can't...'

'It's always been like this... you've always been like this. It's not good enough, Lois!'

'That's not fair!'

'Not fair! It's not like you've anything else to take care of. God knows you've had enough practice having brats. Christ, you ought to be a bloody expert by now. You've even got the girl to help, and still you're bloody hopeless. You always were. Hopeless, even when we were in Dunborough. Fucking useless.'

There was a hollow silence.

'Christ, I've had enough of this!'

The chair clattered and the door slammed shut, the glass panel rattling as his heavy footsteps pounded back along the hall and then thundered down the stairs, still audible behind the bang of the front door. Her mother's stifled sob was inaudible but Maggie still heard it. She heard it in her head and in her stomach.

A few minutes later Lois called out, 'I'm going to the shops; watch the little 'uns, Maggie. Maggie...!'

'Yes,' she called, and strained to hear her mother on the stairs. She watched from the window as Lois turned the corner away from the yard. In the flat the kids began to whine.

'Pack it in you two!' There was only Shirley and Alan; the baby was asleep on the settee, oblivious ,and hadn't even cried. Stephen was out, but then he was always out. In that, at least he'd had some sense, Maggie thought. He'd got one up on her, but only in that.

She retrieved the chair in the kitchen from where it had been flung onto its back, and began to carry the partly-cleared remains of breakfast to the draining board. Half-hidden beneath a plate was where she discovered the letter. It was type-written and addressed to him.

It was rare to see anything of his; he kept it all so close, so hidden. Maggie opened it out – it was crumpled as if screwed up in anger – and began to read. It was a letter from the Inland Revenue, written in dense official language and with columns of figures. She smoothed the page out onto the table, pulled up a chair and, sitting on her folded legs with chin supported on her fists, set to fathoming it out. She'd never seen anything like this before and it took a time but the outcome was clear: he owed money, quite a lot of money, in overdue income tax.

She'd just turned it over to read through the second page when the front door was wrenched open once again and heavy steps marched along the hall. Sliding the plate back over the letter Maggie darted to the sink, noisily loading crockery into the washing up bowl then, sensing a presence, looked round. Her father stood at the door, glowering.

'What're you doing?' he barked.

'Washing up.'

'Where's your mother?'

'Shopping.' Two could play at this.

He rummaged on the table. 'Shouldn't you have cleared this up!'

She glowered back, the sort of look that would normally earn her a clout round the head, but he merely snatched up the letter and strode back out. She heard him descend again, and then the cellar storeroom door opened and closed. He'd gone down to his office.

***

She was lounging on the lumpy settee when her mother came back, walking soundlessly along the hallway, past the open door. Maggie followed Lois to the kitchen where she'd placed the shopping basket on the table and was silently unloading bread and some tins.

'What's up with him?'

'Who?' Lois didn't look up.

'You know.'

'Your father?'

'Mmm.'

'He's your father, not 'him'.' They exchanged a glance, then Lois looked away. 'Nothing,' she said.

'What was he shouting about then?'

'Oh... business stuff.'

'What sort of business stuff?'

'You wouldn't understand.'

'I would too!'

'Don't be cheeky, Maggie.' But neither her tone nor her look supported the reprimand. She seemed exhausted.

'What is it then?' Maggie persisted.

'Nothing, just money things,' Lois sighed.

'Is it trouble? Is something wrong?'

'It's nothing for you...'

'I want to know!'

'Leave it will you. It'll be fine; just leave it. Now go out.'

'What's going to happen?'

'Nothing's going to happen.'

'Do we owe money?'

'Maggie!'

'Do we...?'

'Yes, a bit.'

'Will we have to leave the pub?'

'No, of course not.' Lois paused at the cupboard, in the act of placing the tins on the shelf. 'Your father will sort it.'

'How?'

'Mind your own business, Maggie. Go out and play!' She turned sharply to look at her daughter and Maggie gazed steadily back at her, seeing only her sad, resigned face.

'It'll be all right, your father'll see to it. Now go on out, Maggie, please,' Lois said softly.

VIII

Since the playground ambush John had burned with unresolved revenge, but the ensuing days provided scant opportunity for settling old scores and so he simply seethed; all pugnacious fury and futile scheming. Robbie tried to interest him in games and activities but John was too agitated for simple pastimes, and stood kicking malevolently at anything in his path, or wreaking destruction on whatever came into his hands. Today it was Robbie's football. He blasted it against the outhouse and then punched it away on the volley so that it soared high into the apple tree branches, sending down a shower of ripening fruit that thudded onto the lawn.

Robbie flung his arms upwards in despair; his friend was impossible in such a mood. Sally, arriving through the side gate, frowned as her eyes took in the scatter of bruised fruit.

'Robbie!'

'Sorry...'

But she knew it wasn't her son that was responsible and grimaced, holding his look with raised eyebrows, head indicating back over her shoulder towards John who continued to wreak vengeance on the outhouse wall.

'Sorry...'

'Take your Dad his lunch; he's down at the allotment,' and she gave Robbie a hard stare that said 'and stay out of trouble'.

They found Tom working, shirt sleeves rolled to above the elbow, silently absorbed in the ceaseless cycle of the seasons and its needs: summer, autumn, winter, spring, meant harvesting, storing, sowing, tending; the predestined order of things. The Bradburys had worked the same plot for more than a century; a hundred years or more of patiently improving and cultivating, generations of skill and nurture, sanguine in the face of nature's harshness. His fingers were cracked and grimed with soil that never washed off. It filled his life and he knew little else. Sally sometimes thought her husband was married to the soil; he was certainly rooted in it. He had little time for much else, only family.

John and Robbie threaded their way amongst the plots, some neat and productive like the Bradbury's, and others a shaming tangle of weeds and caterpillar-shredded brassicas. Ahead Tom hoed in easy rhythm, stooping now and then to pull something from the ground, eyes on the soil amongst the ordered rows. He glanced up and then straightened, hoe held like a staff.

'Hello, you two!'

'Got your lunch,' Robbie said as his father planted the hoe against the small makeshift shed, stepping forwards to take the package. John wandered away, disinclined to speak. Plants weren't his cup of tea. He distrusted them, and had no use for such things.

Embarrassed by his friend's unsociability and conspicuous show of boredom, Robbie sat down to chat to his father. 'What're you doing?' he asked, hoping to deflect attention from John's surliness.

'Oh, bit of hoeing and weeding. Summer cabbages're coming on and there's a good picking of runners and some raspberries too,' Tom said, pointing and then looked back over his shoulder, observing the other boy. 'Well, young John, what d'you know?' and, slowly unwrapping his lunch, held out a sandwich. 'Fancy a bite, boy?'

They took one to share, it little occurring to them that Tom would be foregoing half his lunch, and the three settled onto the plank bench and leaned their backs against the sun-warmed shed, looking out over the burgeoning plot.

'Where's Jonathan?' asked Tom, after a period of silent eating.

'He's drawing, at home.'

'He must have drawn the entire British air fleet by now.' Then, after a pause, 'mind you include him...'

'I do, Dad.'

'I know.'

John, restlessly swinging his legs back and forth, was juddering and rocking the bench beneath them so that it bumped irregularly against the shed. Tom looked askance at him, brown skin about his eyes furrowing as he squinted against the sun's glare. 'The lad's right fidgety today,' he remarked.

John gazed away, disregarding the attention he'd drawn, feigning indifference. He'd no use for adults either.

'Reckon there's some good strawberries in there.' Tom nodded towards the plot. 'What d'you think, John? Think you can find them? Have a look, we'll have a few, shall we? For dessert.'

John's head sharply turned in surprise at being addressed directly but then he stepped forward to the allotment, disturbing a flock of dust-bathing sparrows as he went, sending them spiralling upwards, singing themselves into an ecstasy. Soon only his rump was visible as he foraged amongst the rows, emerging with red-stained handfuls of squashy fruit. He returned several more times for further pickings before the arrival of neighbouring plot-holder Arthur interrupted, and saved the remainder of the strawberry crop from devastation. Tom and Arthur had been at school together and fell easily into conversation.

'He's back again, I see,' Arthur began, jabbing a thumb over his shoulder as he parked his wheelbarrow, rattling-full with tools.

'Who's that?'

'Sid... Dewberry.'

There was an exchange of glances.

'Just drove by as I was walking over. He weren't coming from home.'

'Ah.'

'He'll have been in Marsh Nethering.'

'No doubt,' said Tom.

'Poor woman, that wife of his. Regular as you like and barefaced as they come. It ain't right, it certainly ain't.'

The adult-speak went, literally, over Robbie's head but there was no mistaking the name of Ann's father, or of their tone. John was watchful, motionless for once. The two men studied their plots, reflectively.

'Well, it's the same thing, wherever you get it,' Tom observed.

'Right shame it is. Nice woman, too. And that little girl – what is it, Ann? You'd think he'd have more thought for the lass whatever else he's tired of.'

'Arthur, the boys...'

'Ah, right you are.'

The conversation moved then to gardening matters and John and Robbie drifted off with a parting wave. They collecting the bike from beside the gate, John hopped on the back and they swept out into the road.

'Who's tha' Dewberry?' asked John, leaning back, taking in the swish of air upon his face as Robbie pedalled them rapidly along the lane.

'Ann's Dad.'

'Tha' Ann, wot we know?'

'Yep.'

Robbie took them up through The Square and leaned hard into the far corner, swinging them nimbly round into the top lane. He was confident now on the bike. Behind him, effortless, leaning back with his legs splayed for stability, John sat relaxed and casual, ever balanced to perfection. They always rode like this; completely at one with the movement of the bike, every slight shift or sway anticipated and compensated for as if by intuition. For years to come, this is how Robbie would always remember John.

'Where we goin' then? Up on the 'ill?'

'Could do. Let's get Nid and Finch, we can-'

But Robbie's words were drowned by a yell from behind and his bike lurched abruptly as John flung himself to one side, sending them into a wild swerve towards the middle of the lane. Glancing back over his shoulder, Robbie spied Squinter Brazell accelerating faster on his larger bicycle, his elbows out and head low, face twisted into a sneer as he swung his front wheel on a collision course towards them. John lashed out again but Squinter evaded, veering away and gave a vicious kick at Robbie's front wheel that sent them wobbling uncontrollably for several yards ahead.

He then dropped back but, before Robbie could regain proper control, Squinter had sprinted forwards once more and this time took a hefty swing with his foot at their rear wheel. John was flailing, kicking and roaring his fury, ferociously punching out with bony arms but Squinter, a strong thickly-set lad, dropped his head below bulky shoulders and put up an elbow to deflect the frantic blows which rained now to little effect.

They rode this way, side-by-side, like duelling charioteers, John furiously punching and kicking while Squinter lunged at them with his far larger bike, dispensing well-aimed kicks from sturdy legs that jolted Robbie's bike frame and sent painful judders all the way up his arms.

'Squinty pig-eyed bastud!' roared John. 'Ya muvva's a slag, you shaggin', fuckin' bastud!'

Struggling to maintain control, as much from John's wild movements as from Squinter's attacks, Robbie was looking over his shoulder trying to anticipate where the next blow or deflection would come from that would send them oscillating, wildly off balance. The only way to outrun the attack and maintain enough momentum for the bike to stay upright was to pedal faster, but Squinter was suddenly alongside once again and, leaning over, grasped the crossbar with one large hand, vigorously rocking their frame from side to side. John grabbed at Squinter's sleeve, trying to prise him off and, with the other hand, gouged fingernails into his knuckles, the pair of them bellowing at each other like bulls. With the added weight of Squinter and his bike, Robbie finally lost control and veered wildly away, mounted the kerb with a jolt and crashed into the front hedge of Harris's cottage. His rear mudguard caught against their front gate post and his precious bike only came to an abrupt halt in their neat front hedge, pitching himself onto the lawn while John came to rest comically sprawled in the privet.

Lying stunned and disorientated, Robbie waited for pain to replace the shock. From somewhere beyond he heard further shouting; a man's voice this time, followed by a blow and a hoarse yell which he recognised as Squinter. Slowly he and John began to extricate themselves. Indestructible as always, John bounded up, vigorously rubbing at the cuts and scratches sustained from the hedge, talking maniacally to counteract the pain that he gave no indication of feeling. Robbie raised himself far more slowly, casting guilty glances back towards the cottage windows but neither Mr nor Mrs Harris appeared to be in, for which he was grateful as he would surely have been marched round to his mother for a severe telling off, and it would indeed be his mother and not his father who would have administered it.

Back in the road there was no sign of Squinter, or of his bike, or of the man who'd chastised him. They hauled Robbie's bike from where it languished, still entangled in the now-misshapen hedge, rear wheel and mudguard horribly jammed against the concrete gate post. Robbie carefully lifted the frame free of the foliage while John vigorously yanked at the rear wheel producing, as the mudguard scraped clear, a sickening grinding noise. They rested the Raleigh down on the pavement and stood silently to survey it. Robbie's cherished blue bicycle lay at his feet with leaves and bits of twig still attached. A feeling of despond welled deep in his stomach.

'Yeah, s'orright, see,' chirruped John, squatting to strip the foliage away. 'It's fine. Good as new. Ol' Brazzell's a wanker, can't do nuffin'. Look, get all them leaves off, it's orright. Eh, d'ya see that? 'E got a right thump, 'im. Serve 'im right, eh, he weren't expectin' that, the bastud.'

Robbie crouched and brushed away the last of the leaves before lifting the bicycle gently onto its wheels, steadying it like a new-born calf. Holding the saddle he looked the frame over, brushing the dust and hedge fragments from the metal with his fingers so that it shone once more, but he still couldn't bring himself to look at the rear wheel. John was on his feet, still chattering machine-gun fast, but something gnawed at Robbie's spirits and caught in his throat. He let his hand glide down the frame to the rear mudguard, cupping the curve of the metal in his palm until it reached the buckled and twisted damage.

John had stopped talking and now hunkered down beside him.

'Eh, that'll be orright,' he said. 'Easily pull that out, bit a paint...'

Robbie's throat was tightening and he could feel himself beginning to choke on the emotions that welled upwards. Wheeling the bike, he led the way down Snail Path to home, avoiding The Green where he might be seen. He didn't want anyone to see the damage, and he certainly didn't want to have to talk about it. Back home he gingerly pushed open the side gate, praying he'd find the garden empty. His luck was in and they took the bike straight into the shed and propped it against the old chest of drawers before surveying it again.

''S'only the mudguard,' said John breezily. 'Wheel's orright. That's the main thing. If ya wheel's buckled, yer buggered. Soon fix this.' And immediately he began to wrench at the mudguard.

Robbie froze, fearing further disfigurement, but John was bent over the wheel, hands grappling for a hold. Then he was leaning back, feet braced against the chest of drawers, face deep red with the effort, sinews in his thin arms straining. The metal creaked and then eased out, still a little crumpled but no longer dented. Robbie had no idea he was so strong, he looked so insubstantial.

'There,' John confirmed to himself, dusting off his hands with satisfaction. 'All it needs now is a bit a paint. I'll bring i' along tomorra'.' And he was round again the next morning, only a little later than usual, bearing a tin of deep purple modelling kit enamel paint.

'They didn't 'ave dark blue,' he explained.

Couldn't find one to nick more likely, thought Robbie.

They found a small brush amongst his father's things and John carefully applied the paint to the scratch. It wasn't the right colour and it wasn't the neatest paint job, but it covered the damage and remained there until the day Robbie outgrew the bike and passed it on, ever a reminder of John.

IX

There was a lot to be said for having a broken arm, Finch reflected. All that attention and sympathy to start with, and then there was the business of everyone writing on the plaster; all the names and jokes and drawings, but he'd quickly discovered what a useful instrument it could be. A sturdy weapon, a shield, a prop to lean on, a tool for rubbing or scraping or, when it suited, a sympathy dodge for avoiding the things he didn't want to do. It even had its uses at school. He'd found he could conceal his books behind it and the teachers couldn't see if he was doodling. Before the spelling test he'd written the answers on it and come third; to everyone's surprise, including his own. That was smart, he thought to himself. Not even Nid would think of that.

It was the first time he'd broken a bone, although it wasn't to be his last, not by any means. It was to become something of a habit over the next few years, but this occasion was the first and still something of a novelty. They'd been up on the hill, playing cowboys and Indians, a favourite game of that year, emulating the Westerns they watched endlessly on television. They'd all raced up there, through the fields of implacable, self-absorbed cows.

'Bags I'm sheriff!' Finch had said.

'You were last time, it's my turn now,' Nid had insisted. 'And anyway, I've got the badge,' and he'd prodded at his chest to make the point.

Maggie pushed in. She wasn't going to be left out of any allocation of plum roles. 'I'm going to be the Indian Chief,' she declared.

A general bartering ensued, eventually settled by several rounds of '*one potato, two potato*', but she still managed to be the Indian Chief. Maggie always knew how to make it come out in her favour.

They'd spent most of the afternoon charging about the slopes, forging rivers, withstanding sandstorms, fighting off gun-slingers and generally working their way through the set-pieces of traditional Westerns. Finally they set up a camp, encircled it with wagons and took up their positions to await the inevitable Apache raid. Maggie led the attack, riding bareback down the hillside leading her Indian braves; Robbie and Ann.

From his defensive position behind the wagon's water barrel, rifle butt at his shoulder to take the recoil, there suddenly came into Finch's head the irresistible image of the Cavalry galloping to the rescue, all smart uniforms and brave resolute faces, their horses pounding across the prairie at full gallop, nostrils flared, manes streaming; the platoon sweeping down the hillside with flags flying, pistols at the ready, bugles sounding their approach: *doodle oodle doo dah dah!*

He slipped away and quickly made his way, unseen by the others, behind a low rise and up to the hilltop above. Way below the Redskins were encircling and closing in, tomahawks in hand, firing their arrows at the dogged settlers who kept up a steadfast defence, determinedly shooting from beneath the wagons. The air was thick with the cries of the Apaches and the sounds of desperate gunfire.

Bugle in hand, Finch gathered in his mount, a black stallion which pranced beneath him with pent up power then reared on its hind legs, its front legs flailing the air, glossy flanks gleaming, and it whinnied its battle-cry before carrying him on thundering hooves, down the sweep of the hillside towards the camp far below. Down they galloped, the bugle calling , to effect the dramatic rescue. Finch pulled his Springfield from its holster and held it to his shoulder, taking accurate aim, while his horse galloped true and straight, impelled ever-onwards by his spurs which glinted in the burning sun. In his rifle sights was the Apache Chief for he knew that without their leader, the Redskins would surely take flight.

Suddenly the ground flipped up to meet him and Finch landed with an ugly thud. His horse had fallen and he lay sprawled, head facing downhill with a tussock of cool grass in his face, his left arm trapped awkwardly beneath him. It was some minutes before the others noticed and slowly made their way up to see what he was up to.

'What're you doing?' said Nid. 'Get up.' He sounded gruff, but there was an anxious edge to his voice.

'Are you hurt?' Lizzie asked, crouching solicitously. 'Are you alright?'

A dull tingling throbbed in his arm and, as he rolled out onto his back, the pain made him wail out loud. They all crowded round, six anxious faces peering down.

They made a make-shift stretcher from branches pushed through the sleeves of their cardigans and carried him down the hillside to home. It was a fair walk under such circumstances and they took turns to bear his weight and heave him through gateways and along narrow paths. Once they'd reached The Green Lizzie ran on ahead to tell his mother while the others, tired now, bumped and jostled him down the slope towards the house.

Norma dashed out, face white and drawn with an expression Finch had never seen before, and ran, actually ran, to where they were lugging him, all of them flagging now from the effort.

'What happened?' she demanded, her face tense and voice somewhere between stern and panic. She spun round to face Nid who stood with one hand steadying the sagging stretcher and he froze, shocked and alarmed by her wild look.

'Mrs Bird, Finch fell over,' said Lizzie kindly.

'He's alright,' Jonathan reassured. He was holding the stretcher at Finch's head. 'I know he'll be alright. Please don't worry Mrs Bird. We've brought him back very carefully. We made a stretcher specially.'

She turned impatiently away. 'Quick!' she ordered, 'Bring him indoors. Be careful. Nigel, fetch your father. He's gone down to the Newsagent's. Quickly. Go now!'

There was panic in her voice, and the sound frightened them. Nid pelted away, followed by Lizzie who just wanted to help. The others carried Finch into the house and Norma lifted him gently and laid him on the settee and then peremptorily dismissed them all. She stroked his hair, but didn't speak. There were lines in her face he hadn't seen before and she was leaning over him, the softness of her summer dress brushing against his face and he breathed in the sweet smell of her face powder.

Before long Frank burst in and he and Norma spoke brief, grim words, hurried and urgent, while Nid, his face small with fright, stood in the background, for the time being, ignored and forgotten.

An ambulance took Finch to Cullingham General where he received the plaster cast which swiftly became his Badge of Honour, and the dramatic events of that Saturday soon passed into ordinariness.

***

'I'll be glad when they take that thing off,' mused Norma across the breakfast table. 'Look at it, it's filthy. Andrew, how *do* you do it?'

It looked fine to him and, frankly, he was going to miss it. By now it had several layers of signatures, rude drawings and jottings, grass and mud stains, red paint and ink marks and some ground-in bubble gum fragments. It felt like an old friend; something that marked him out as different from the others, a bit special. He liked that.

Today was different too. Propped up against the sugar bowl was a large pink envelope with 'Norma' written on it in their father's small, tight script. She kept eyeing it and glanced over her shoulder to the hall, smiling in a self-absorbed way when his footsteps sounded on the stairs. He came into the kitchen, bent over her neck and kissed the cheek she presented, eyes briefly turned to his.

'Happy anniversary, darling,' he said, patting her on the shoulder before taking his seat at the other end of the table. In front of his place, propped against his tea cup, was another large envelope with 'Frank' written in her smooth elegant curves.

'Happy fifteenth, darling,' and she drew a parcel from the drawer beside her and held it out to him, a warm contented look on her face.

Frank reached into his trouser pocket and presented her with a small package. The brothers exchanged looks, then silently observed their parents' shared performance of present-opening; eager smiles, surprised gasps and appreciative noises. Hers was a necklace. She unwrapped it first, under his benign gaze, and then immediately clasped it around her throat, turning to face the three of them for their admiration, palm held flat against her chest, smile about her lips.

'Now you,' she encouraged, watching his every move.

He carefully pulled away the wrapping paper and slipped a shining item from the narrow box within, before holding her gift aloft to admire.

'Oh, darling,' he said.

'I know.' She spoke softly, 'I thought it was time.'

They both looked upon the silver cigarette lighter that he held between them.

'It's engraved too,' she said.

He read silently and they exchanged looks.

'Are you pleased?' she asked.

'Of course.'

'I spent a long time choosing it. I wanted you to be pleased.'

'It's marvellous.' He weighed it in his hand and flicked the cap. A slender flame emerged. 'It's a lovely choice, Norma. Absolutely splendid.'

'I was so sad about the other one...'

Frank gave a sigh. 'Me too.'

'Especially as, well, you know...'

He took a deep breath. 'Yes...' There was silence for a few moments. 'It's a mystery, but Rod looked everywhere. He reckons someone must've had it.'

'But it had your initials on and everything. There could be no mistaking.'

'I know...'

'You'll have to take good care.'

He slapped his jacket pocket. 'Safe in here,' he said, and they surveyed one another.

'What's an anniversary?' Finch asked brightly.

'It's when you've been married, of course,' said Nid, who reckoned he knew everything.

'How long have you been married then?' Finch asked his mother, paying no heed to the insult. This was something he'd never thought of before. Parents just 'were' married, as if they'd been born to that state.

'Fifteen years, darling,' she said, her tone altered to that adopted by adults when explaining things to children.

'Did you give Dad a lighter when you got married then?' he asked.

'No,' she replied. 'Not then. A couple of years later.'

'For your anniversary?'

'No, something else. Now take your cast off the table, Andrew, it's dirty.'

'Speaking of Rod, I've recommended him for a loan,' their father interjected.

'Oh, darling, is that wise?'

'Well, he says he wants some readies, bit of a cash-flow issue with the business apparently. He came round to ask the other day. Anyway, he's been pretty decent old Rod, one way and another and I didn't feel I could let him down. That was an excellent Claret at Christmas, you said so yourself.'

'I wish you wouldn't be so close.'

'Oh, he's alright.'

'His poor wife...'

'He's a man's man, I grant you.'

'Nellie Dewberry hasn't got a good word to say about him.'

'Mmm, well she should know about that sort of thing.' He took up the newspaper and began to turn the pages. 'It's only for a few months anyway.'

She stood and leaned across him to pour more tea.

'Suits you, Norma.'

She put her hand to her neck again and smiled girlishly, flushing slightly.

'I can wear it to the dance,' she said.

***

The music drilled straight into Finch's head, connecting directly to his nerves and muscles so that he jumped and bounced in helpless excitement. He was like a jiggling string puppet, tweaked by some external force, unable to stop or control his wild movements. Opposite him, Nid was leaping too. Finch could see his brother was helplessly giggling, face scrunched in hilarity, and realised that he too was laughing uncontrollably.

Now the adults were on the floor too, the first bars of music drawing them from their tables, and they were beginning to turn about the dance area, some awkward and stilted in the unaccustomed public intimacy of dance, and others like their parents, waltzing with cool practised ease, their faces serene. To one side the younger couples swung one another back and forth, excitedly throwing themselves into jive steps, while their parents maintained the slow and steady rhythm of the dance steps from their youth.

'Johnnie Venus and The Stargazers' were performing on the stage above their heads, sharp-suited with guitars and drums, thrillingly close and alive and loud. Lizzie was trying to coax a reluctant and embarrassed Robbie into an attempted jive while Jonathan looked on indulgently from the side. Two girls swung one another giddily around, bumping into passing dancers in the convivial crush. About them, most of the other village kids also leapt and jiggled and shrieked.

The 350th anniversary of Moreton Steyning Fair was a landmark event that was being celebrated with a formal dinner and dance in a marquee, specially erected for the occasion on Church Piece. After several up-beat songs that kept the audience animated and on their feet, the music moved to a quieter interlude and most people drifted back to their seats. Frank and Norma were seated alongside the Bradbury's, with whom they were distantly friendly, largely on account of the boys' friendship. They looked happy, eyes bright and held wide, still marking their wedding anniversary.

'A present?' Robbie's mother asked, pointing to Norma's neck.

She put a hand to her throat again, as she had earlier. 'Yes,' she said. 'From Frank – our wedding anniversary.' There was an exchange of understanding smiles between the two women while the men looked about them, into the crowd. 'Fifteen years,' she added.

'Ours will be eighteen next year,' Sally Bradbury replied. 'And Susan will be sixteen, just imagine.' And then she paused, uncomfortable, as if she'd said something wrong.

'Yes,' said Norma. 'They grow so fast.'

Just then there was a commotion. Robbie and Jonathan, who'd been sitting drinking lemonade, had both risen abruptly from their chairs which they now pulled away from the marquee's sides before bobbing down towards the floor. As they straightened, they held between them, each with one arm beneath an armpit, an enraged John, struggling up from beneath the canvas.

'Them bastuds wouldn't let me in,' he blustered.

'You have to buy a ticket,' explained Jonathan carefully, 'And then you can have the dinner, but that's finished, and now there's the dance.'

John glanced dismissively at him before pushing out past the chairs, ignoring the looks and comments that his arrival had drawn from families further along the row of tables. They were all dressed in their best, but John stood amongst them in his familiar scuffed sandals with grubby short trousers and crumpled once-white shirt, hair a dusty, wiry shock about his small, lined face.

Fortunately his arrival was overshadowed by Johnnie Venus's announcement of a popular up-tempo song and there was a general scraping back of chairs as most people returned to the dance floor amidst a contented murmuring of approval and anticipation. John's eyes swept the now-empty table and he helped himself to the remaining contents of several glasses of alcohol and a bowl of salted peanuts before following the others, who were pushing their way between the poised couples, towards the front of the stage.

As The Stargazers launched into the number with clanging guitar chords and thudding drum beat John jumped visibly and then stood rigid as if in shock, staring up at the group.

The loud, fast music was again thrilling and they all threw ourselves into more leaping and running. Even Jonathan, normally awkward and lumpen, stepped out and bounced heavily, grinning joyfully as he swung his arms about, never in time with the music. Lizzie grabbed him and he swung and dragged her backwards and forwards, and she was laughing, her skirt swinging wide, while Nid and Robbie clapped and sang along with the chorus and bounded from leg to leg. Even the adults gyrated in dignified attempts at modern dance styles, laughing pleasurably.

In the midst of all this animation and joyful energy John was motionless, still staring up at the group who were bouncing about on stage to their driving beat, heads nodding, feet tapping. The two guitarists stepped together in time and Johnnie Venus encouraged the audience to clap during the chorus.

Abruptly John leapt from the spot and launched himself into a gyrating fervour, his wiry frame flung back and forth, arms spinning and legs bouncing, head frantically bobbing along to the tune. The others clapped more vigorously, taking a step back to make room and watch him. He jerked and thrashed, flinging himself about so that, from time to time, he collided with several dancers who tutted or smiled amusement, depending on their disposition or mood.

The song received rousing applause and was followed by one of equal vigour to close the first half of the evening's entertainment, keeping nearly everyone on the dance floor, glowing pink with exertion and the warmth that now filled the packed marquee. The friends took up their positions, literally so for Robbie and Finch who poised themselves like readying sprinters. As the music began, they launched once again into their dancing, jostling one another and bumping into other dancing couples. This song was familiar too, with a well-known chorus line that many sung along to, their combined voices filling the crowded marquee.

As the refrain died away with the guitars and drum taking up the beat again, another layer of noise became apparent: discordant and unmusical. At first it continued as an undercurrent, but presently a wave of awareness swept through the dancers and those at the rear of the dance floor, near to the entrance, began to fall silent and motionless. Gradually this wave passed through the marquee towards the stage, so that eventually all the dancers drifted to a stop, as if in slow-motion, and then stood looking back towards the entrance, puzzled and mildly concerned. The Stargazers faltered and, as the noise became more evident above their playing, the song drifted to a lame close with no applause to mark its ending. With silence now in the marquee, the raised voices and ugly shouting were all too clear.

The friends strained but could see nothing through the audience who themselves craned or moved forwards, a loud murmuring now rippling through the crowd, directed towards the entrance. Rough shouts came to their ears.

'Get out of it, go home!'

'Clear off...'

'Here, you!'

'What's it to you? Get out of his way!'

'Push him away! Push past!'

'Get away! Get out of it!'

'You old git, leggo! You can't bloody stop us.'

'Not past me you're not!'

'You old fucker!'

'Watch it, you! We'll have none of that filth You're not wanted here. Get out of it! Get lost. You've got no tickets, none of you. Get out of here. Go on, clear off!'

There were grunts and cries. Several women cried out anxiously and a number of men pushed forwards amidst a clamour of angry voices. John shoved at the legs in front of him and elbowed between the full skirts and stiffened petticoats. From the entrance there was the discordant noise of scraping furniture and further shouts, followed by an abrupt movement amongst those at the front who suddenly parted, revealing Lizzie's Uncle Ted and several other local men, struggling with a group of youths.

People were shouting now from behind and several more men pushed forwards to help eject the gate-crashers who, being younger, fitter and prepared to scrap, had thrust their way in and were grappling with Ted Rose and the others, throwing wild punches in all directions. To one side, as the brawl threatened to spill out onto the dance floor, Jack Stebbings was struggling to prevent the ticket desk and takings from being overturned, a look of wild anxiety on his face.

John darted forwards and seized the takings table from one side. "Ere, I'll 'elp ya, guvna',' he said, backing up with it, propelling a bewildered Jack, who still clung grimly to the other side, towards a corner of the marquee. Finch dived forwards and, taking hold of another side, helped manoeuvre the table to safety behind the coat racks.

'Thanks,' wheezed Jack, positioning himself out of harm's way and wiping his glistening brow with the flat of one hand which he then draped across the coat rail to support his sagging frame.

A woman was shouting, 'Hit him, Harry! Let 'em have it!' and the crowd was surging to and fro with the thrust and swagger of the tussle. From between the hanging coats, Finch could see back down the marquee to where his mother sat, returned now to the table, her strained, anxious face peering to and fro, any view of the brawl obscured to her by the range of backs in front. At her side Sally Bradbury was talking, leaning to speak to her above the shouting, but Norma wasn't listening. He couldn't see his father.

A loud noise from the direction of the entrance marked the arrival of several more village men from outside to help with the affray and drew Finch's attention. John's hand, quicksilver swift, slipped from the cashbox, clutching a fistful of notes which he thrust into his pocket, his face all the while maintaining a detached lack of expression.

''Andy fer a rainy day,' he quietly muttered.

X

'Complete and absolute yobs,' was Sally's assessment, delivered back home over a pot of tea to restore the proper order of things. Having poured she slumped heavily back into the armchair, full evening skirt ballooning up. 'I never saw such a thing!'

'New times we live in, Sally,' remarked Tom, shirt sleeves now rolled comfortably to above the elbows and neck tie discarded. He was a man of few words and avoided discord.

'Well, they're poor times. If my father...' but she gave up, unable to express his imagined outrage, save to slap her outstretched fingers against the arm of the chair. 'Well, the birch would've been too good for them and that's for sure... and the language! I never heard the like.' She spoke as if the others hadn't actually been there and witnessed the events, reworking it in her mind, firm and resolute in her evaluation. 'You were never like that.'

Tom glanced up with a brief, mirthful snort. 'I would've had my hide tanned. He only had to go to his belt buckle...'

'I hope someone's giving names to the Police.'

'Probably.'

'And we were having such a lovely time.' She shook her head and poured more tea. 'Someone just has to spoil it. I'd have thrashed them if they were mine. They're not too big to take a broom to.' At this point Jonathan let out a chuckle. 'You two! Bed!' she said. 'Just look at the time.'

The tumult of the evening's excitements, and the sharing of their recollections as they lay in their beds kept them both awake for hours. As a result Robbie was tired and crabby the next day and Jonathan stayed in their bedroom all day long, quietly absorbed in drawing. It was after Sunday lunch when John finally appeared, strutting into the garden, hands thrust deep into his sagging pockets.

'Reckon I'll be a train driver,' he breezed as he jauntily approached across the lawn.

'Yes?' Robbie wasn't sure he was in the mood for this swagger.

'Yep. I'll buy me own engine,' and he paused, eyeing Robbie who ignored this invitation to banter.

'I'll buy one, me. Big 'un. Lotsa steam and go really fast, eh? Wha'd'ya think?' He was gesticulating excitedly, shaping the bulk of the engine with his outstretched arms.

'Maybe.'

'Reckon I could.'

Robbie shrugged.

'Eh? Reckon I could?'

Robbie pulled the corners of his mouth down.

''Ow much d'ya think one of 'em'd cost?'

'Don't know.'

'A good 'un mind? 'Ow much?'

'Quite a lot.'

'Fifty nicker?'

'Could be.'

'Fifty nicker ya reckon?'

'I really don't know. Anyway, where're you going to get all that?'

He just grinned, smug, holding Robbie's gaze, and then held up a great wad of crumpled bank notes. The shock made Robbie look around in alarm but there was no one observing them. 'Where'd you get all that money? Put it away!' he hissed.

But John merely chuckled and casually thrust the cache deep back into his trouser pocket. 'Found i',' he said.

'You found it! Where?'

'At the Fair.' And he eyed Robbie pityingly, for his dumbfoundedness.

'Where at the Fair?' Robbie's mind was racing. Had John pulled it from someone's pocket? Surely not? Not that much. Not even John could be that reckless, could he?

'Takin's box. In the fight.'

The takings box? You took it from the takings box!'

'Yep.' And he chortled throatily, face crumpled, small dark eyes dense as distant stars. 'When they was all fightin' an' stuff.' He mimed a few punches, head ducked low as if to evade return blows. ‘I ’elped ’im rescue i’.’

‘Who?’

‘Tha’ old fella.’

‘Jack Stebbings?’

John shrugged vaguely. ‘’Im with the cash box. I ’elped ’im rescue i’ from the fight. When ’e wasn’t lookin’, I ’ad some of i’. ’S’only right, I’d ’elped ’im.’

Robbie looked on helplessly, thoughts reeling. ‘What’re you going to do with it?’

‘I told ya!’

‘But where are you going to keep it? It’ll be missed, won’t it?’

‘Nah. Bet ’e don’t even know ’ow much ’e ’ad, ’e was really old, ’im. I’ll ’ide i’ til I see an engine wot I fancy, back ’ome like. There’s lots of ’em there.’

Robbie was speechless, partly because his sleeplessness hadn’t equipped him to deal with this outcome, but also because he simply didn’t know how to respond. Meanwhile, John sat beside him on the old bench, energised, legs swinging cheerily, hands in pockets, peering brightly about, brimful of happiness. Robbie sat in silent shock, and yet John looked so contented, so uncharacteristically optimistic that he couldn’t bring himself to say what he was feeling, even if he could have known how to express it. He realised for the first time that hope wasn’t an emotion he’d ever seen in John. His best mate for three summers; irrepressible, belligerent, swaggering, resourceful, defiant. He’d seen all those sides of John, but never before had he seen such buoyant contentment.

Robbie was relieved when he was finally called in to tea, and he made no move to ask if he could invite John to join them. Undeterred, John sauntered off, whistling chirpily, and Robbie was ashamed to realise that he felt no regret at seeing him depart.

Later, curled in an armchair, pretending to read a book, grateful for the pretext for a rest ahead of bed time, he was interrupted by an urgent rapping on the lean-to which startled them all. Sally looked up and tut-tutted before nodding to him. Robbie rose and saw John's tousled head bobbing agitatedly outside the door, making no attempt to come in. Then he rapped noisily again and Sally glared so hard that finally Robbie roused himself and opened it.

John's demeanour was at once in contrast to the afternoon's and he was, if possible, even more dishevelled than usual. 'Come out!' he hissed urgently.

'Why?'

'Come out. 'T's important! Quick!'

Heaving a sigh, Robbie pulled on a coat as the evening was fresh and followed him into the garden. 'What is it?' he wearily asked.

'Gotta go.'

'What?'

'I gotta go. The ol' girl, she's 'urt 'erself, broke 'er leg or sommat...'

'Mrs Ward?'

'Yeah, me Auntie... Look, I gotta go back 'ome. Amb'lance is comin' or sommat an' I'm off from Cullin'ham, cos of 'er leg or 'ip, or wha'ever i' is.'

Robbie struggled to grasp this turn of events. 'You're going?'

'I'm tryin' a tell ya! Ya ain't listenin'. The old dear's goin' ta the 'ospital an' I gotta go. We've gotta hide i'.'

'We? What?'

'The dosh!'

'We?' Robbie felt the horror gripping him again but John pressed on, urgent and insistent, brushing his anxiety and unwillingness aside.

''Course. Now c'mon. I gotta go in the amb'lance in ten minutes.'

'What!'

'To the 'ospital. Then I gets the train 'ome from there, okay? Look, I thought about i'. In the shed. No one goes round them things at the back; them's all covered in cobwebs 'n ' stuff. No one'll go there an' if they does, you can move i'.'

'No!'

'C'mon, you gotta. What sort of a mate are ya?'

'It's stolen.'

'It ain't stolen. It was gonna get nicked anyway.'

This didn't seem clear logic but Robbie's thoughts were tumbling over themselves, and John had by now led them to the shed.

'Look, in 'ere,' he said, frantically rummaging beneath the bench amongst the clutter. In moments he'd pulled out an old tobacco tin containing carpet tacks. 'It's goin' in 'ere, look,' he said, snapping the lid shut and then tucking the tin deep beneath the old chest of drawers with outstretched fingers. 'Safe there,' and he looked cheerfully back to where Robbie stood at the door, resigned and appalled.

How could he refuse the bright and hopeful look on John's face.

''S'alright,' he chirped reassuringly. 'Be alright.'

'But what if someone finds it? My Dad...'

''E won't.'

'You don't know!'

''E won't!'

'You don't know! What if he does? John!'

'I gotta go now...' He was already walking briskly back across the lawn.

'John..!'

He paused at the gate, glancing back, hand already on the latch.

'You can't leave it there. Look, you can't!'

'Gotta.' He shrugged helplessly, innocently.

'When are you going to get it?' Robbie wailed, desperate now, numb with tiredness and horror.

'When I'm back.'

'Yes, but when's that? You might not come back.' Robbie was following John down the side passage, plaintively calling to his departing back.

'Dunno.'

'But why can't you take it with you?'

'Kids about... too many people... nowhere safe to 'ide i'. I'll see ya, right!'

And with that he was off, pounding along the lane and rounding the corner to The Green without a backwards glance, suddenly out of sight.

Robbie stood for some time after John had disappeared, staring in empty disbelief towards the silent, empty corner before turning disconsolately back for home. Approaching from the other direction along the lane was Lizzie, pale blond hair neatly braided and tied with conspicuous yellow ribbons and a puzzled frown on her brow. She'd been skipping gaily towards him but, sensing his disquiet, now approached as if in slow-motion and paused a few feet away, regarding him solemnly, but with quiet anxiety in her eyes.

'What're you looking at, what's happened?' she asked, softly and sympathetically.

He looked over his shoulder, towards the corner as if searching for some explanation from the buildings that had witnessed their separation. When he turned back to her she was still gazing at him, eyebrows drawn together in consternation. 'What is it?' she asked concerned.

He could tell from her expression that she'd read something in his face that she couldn't fathom, and which now worried her.

He shook his head, 'Oh... it's John, he's got to go. Mrs Ward's fallen and broken her leg. The ambulance is taking them to Cullingham.' He met her gaze directly and she looked past and over his shoulder towards the sweet shop corner and then, head tilted quizzically to one side, turned back to his face.

'Is she alright? Poor Mrs Ward. What's John doing then?'

'He's got to go back right away. That's all he said; it all happened really fast and he's just run back and said he's got to go and get the train back home from town.' Robbie shrugged. 'I don't know any more,' he said in a tone of helplessness.

Lizzie shook her plaits back over her shoulders, folding her arms neatly over her chest. 'Is he coming back?'

'I don't know ,' he said forlornly. He was wondering if he should tell her the full story; about hiding the money, about how much it was, about what John had done. The knowledge of it burned hard in his chest, like molten rock. He knew his voice sounded tight and odd.

'I expect he'll be back next summer,' she reassured. 'Even if he doesn't come back before the end of the holidays.' And she smiled at him, kindly and encouragingly.

A small groan escaped Robbie and he shifted restlessly, anxiously feeling sorry for himself. He didn't know what to say or do.

'He's only gone back a week or so early after all,' she coaxed. 'It'll be term again next week.'

'I know,' he whined, 'but...'

Lizzie raised her arms questioningly, eyes wide. 'It's not very nice for Mrs Ward if she's hurt herself, but John'll come back again next Summer holidays. I'm sure he will, he always does.'

What could he say, she was right; but then so much was wrong. He turned away from her and stared back down the lane once again, wondering if the ambulance would pass by, but none came. Her voice called him back.

'It's not that bad, John going. We're still here, all of us.'

'Oh, I know. It's not that.'

Her look was tense now, mouth drawn tight. 'What is it then?' she almost whispered, although they stood alone, close together in the empty lane.

He shuffled uncomfortably under her pleading gaze. 'Nothing, no... nothing.' Again he shrugged. 'It's just, well... he's fun to be with, isn't he?'

Lizzie turned her mouth down but said nothing.

'It's good when John's here. We all have such a lot of fun and there's good adventures and stuff.' Robbie waved his arms about airily, beseeching her agreement. She stood picking at the ends of one plait, head tilted down. 'That's right, isn't it?' he encouraged, but she only shrugged, wordlessly.

Now it was his turn to try and fathom what was wrong, but Lizzie simply sighed lightly, and when she spoke again her voice was small.

'It doesn't always have to be like that.'

'What d'you mean?'

'John. Why does it always have to be that way?' she said.

Robbie looked at her, searchingly. They stood quite close but her eyes were evading his, looking about the street, soft and grey, pensive. 'You're always with John when he's here but you're my best friend, and you've been my best friend since we were little, but when he comes here you're just with him and you don't bother to see me until he goes home.'

She gazed away, forlornly silent now, her voice faded to nothingness, and he stood in noiseless, awkward shock. Lizzie never complained and they'd never had angry words together; trusting, sweet-natured Lizzie.

'I'm glad he's gone,' she suddenly said and, turning, walked stiffly back along the road to Wheelwrights. He watched her go; a small tense figure, the brightness of her hair ribbons shining out in the gloom.

Twice today he'd felt betrayed by his two closest friends. Or had it been him, he wondered, who'd done the betraying?

XI

Ann's head rose and fell slowly and rhythmically with the rise and fall of the dog's sleeping breaths; the colour of smouldering coals burned inside her closed eyelids. Something hummed – the obsessive droning of bees somewhere in the garden? Soporific warmth clung at her drowsing senses and her sun-warmed limbs turned liquid, seeping into the fetid earth beneath her down-turned palms. She curled her fingertips to stroke the grass and the cool unmown blades slid between her fingers, juicy and squeaking. Rags thwacked her tail on the ground and snorted abruptly, bobbing Ann's head which had lain reassured on the dog's warm, lean flank.

But it hadn't been this way yesterday. The garden had felt strange, not as they'd left it when they'd gone away on holiday, but as if a segment of living time had been snatched from its heart; something they would now never live through, simply stolen away. In their absence its living growth seemed to have crept forwards, stealing up towards the house from the safe enclosing walls of the garden. It was a smaller, but not a safer place. Familiar petals lay scattered, browning and wilted, replaced by brash impostors whose colours leapt from the dark advancing foliage.

'Oh, the philadelphus,' her mother had said, scooping up a handful of withered white petals and cupping them forlornly to her nose.

But it was the house that was truly alien, its very familiarity now jarring, smelling oddly of brick and warm fabric; altered, yet the same. The cases they'd brought in from the car and wedged into the hall, their shapes wrongly filling its tight space, everything out of kilter.

Nellie had stopped to retrieve the post from the mat, shuffling the envelopes, a frown on her forehead framed by her fine hair, frizzy from the salt air.

'Anything?' Sid had asked as he dropped the first bags in the hallway.

'No, just the usual, looks like.'

They'd revived themselves with tea while Ann had crept quietly out into the garden, through the back door, thrown wide to let the air in, or was it to suck out the strangeness? She'd stepped onto the path, dwarfed by the smothering foliage. Even Rags padded slowly, one paw raised, sniffing at the heavy air. The lowering sun had sent splashes of gold onto the overgrown lawn.

Now she lay as if she were falling, slipping down through the soft air, drifting and floating into the warm embracing earth while her thoughts rose, inchoate, to catch her. She reached out for them, fingers groping amongst the glossy-stemmed lawn, caressing the soft-scented orbs of clover. But that morning he'd gone off to work; gone out and her new tennis set was upstairs waiting, still sandy from their beach games. He wouldn't be back that night to play with her, not back to teach her how to play on the garden lawn, patting the ball backwards and forwards, throwing it softly onto her outstretched racquet so she couldn't miss, and retrieving her ineptly-struck shots from wherever they fell, laughing, encouraging,

'Good shot! Here, try again. Oh... bad luck.' On the beach, she'd flung herself into the softly caressing sand, racquet outstretched, clumsy and uncoordinated and he'd laughed kindly. His real daughter.

Her eyes had flashed.

Rags yawned and stretched, then rolled onto her back inviting a tummy-rub so that Ann had to sit up. 'Good girl,' she crooned, stroking the short soft hair and baby-smooth pink skin of the dog's warm belly. Rags snorted again with a snatch of her muzzle, wriggled back and forth and thwacked her tail resoundingly against the ground, then crept away to a patch of cool shade.

Her eyes had flashed and then died.

The tennis racquets and box of new balls were upstairs. She could take them over to Maggie and play with her instead, but Maggie would assume control. Ann didn't want to play with them now.

She pulled her sandals back on, matching the straps to the pale patches on her sun-browned feet, and let herself out of the garden. She found Maggie in the pub yard, impassively seated on an old kitchen chair by the sheds, the two younger children playing in the gravel about her. She squinted towards Ann but showed no inclination to speak.

'We got back yesterday,' Ann said after a few moments' silence, and then offered somewhat pointlessly, 'It was late,' to choke off a rising sense of guilt that impelled her to defend herself for not having been to see her friend already. But Maggie didn't respond; merely lounged on the chair, legs hanging limp.

'I learned breast stroke...'

It was an achievement she was truly proud of. The swelling waves that threatened to engulf or sweep her from her feet while the surf foamed suffocatingly about her face, drawing tight breaths from her gasping lungs, had brought a thrilling fear. 'Go on,' her father had said, 'I've got you. Keep going,' gripping the back of her costume and holding her up while she made desperate clawing moves in the water, laughing lightly. 'See, you've done it!' The sea-water ballooned his swimming trunks and Nellie had stood safely in the shallows, smiling and waving encouragement, the incessant suck and slew of the waves on the shingle swirling about her ankles.

Any but the tamest paddle in glass-smooth waters brought apprehension for Ann. She sought reassuring praise from Maggie, or at least some acknowledgement of her hard-won triumph. Things were easy for Maggie.

'Yeah?'

'Like this,' and Ann mimed into the emptiness between them.

Maggie scrutinised her in silence. 'Seen the others?' she asked.

'No, we only got back last night.'

Maggie made a murmur and gazed off-handedly at the kids who flung battered toy cars about in the dirt. The dull metal revealed by the missing paint was the same colour as the dusty earth beneath the thinning gravel.

'I brought you something. Here,' and Ann held out a knobbly flint with a hole through it.

Maggie leaned forwards, lifting it from her friend's outstretched palm and held the hole to one eye.

'We missed the dance at the Fair,' Ann said. 'Was it good?'

'Didn't go.' Maggie was surveying the yard through the stone which she then turned about in her palm.

It was foolish to have asked her, of course; the Vineys never went anywhere together. Maggie was looking at Ann now, paying attention, but then the boy slapped the girl, who wailed and lashed out at him with a vindictive kick.

'Pack it in!' Maggie yelled. The boy furtively shoved at his sibling but neither ignored their older sister's scolding. No one ignored Maggie. 'I can swim,' she said brightly.

'Can you?'

'Yeah, crawl.'

'Where'd you learn?'

'Ages ago – at the seaside.' And she rose from the chair, walking through the middle of the toy car game. But then she stopped and watched the heavy brewer's wagon which was pulling into the yard. It drew to a halt behind the pub and the motor shuddered to a stop, the door swung open and a lean ferret-like man dropped to the ground, cigarette on his lower lip.

'Yer Dad about?' he rasped, and the cigarette wobbled.

Maggie marched wordlessly to the front door and rapped loudly on the knocker, then stood back observing.

'Alright?' he winked, first at one then the other of them. Ann gave a small, awkward smile, but Maggie merely regarded him. She seemed mildly bemused, Ann thought.

Rod Viney's heavy frame swung from the door, a look of bonhomie about his countenance which froze at the moment of recognition.

'Where's Jack?' he remarked abruptly, one foot poised.

'Sacked,' the other man shot back with matching brusqueness.

Viney halted on the top step. 'Sacked?'

'Stuff gone missing.' The cigarette ceased its jiggling and came to a halt, stuck to his drooping lower lip. Ann couldn't take her eyes off it.

Viney stared. The hand that clutched the door latch now drifted slowly downwards to his side where it hung, uncertain.

'Gone missing! What?'

The drayman was implacable. 'Drink.'

'Drink?'

'Bottles. And fags.'

'Bottles and fags? Where? When?'

The ferret-looking man shrugged, but perhaps he smirked. 'Search me.' He pulled a folder deep from his overall pocket. 'Here's yer delivery,' and he ran a finger down the list.

Rod Viney recovered himself. 'Clear off you two!' he barked, gesticulating with one large hand. 'Delivery's here. Go on, and keep those kids out the way.'

The two friends sidled behind the lorry but Maggie was looking back, appraising with a curious look about her face.

'What is it?' Ann whispered.

'Nothing. Wait,' and she clutched at her friend's skirt to hold her close.

Ann watched Maggie watching.

Crates of bottles and various boxes were stowed down into the storeroom before the lorry moved round the front, the cellar flaps there open ready to unload the beer barrels from Dollicot's Brewery down into the cellar.

'What is it?'

But Maggie just looked distant, thoughtful. 'Bet you don't know, do you?' she said, and then looked about cautiously before gesturing Ann to follow her into one of the sheds. Once inside Maggie stuck her head out of the open doorway, scanning the yard. Only then would she speak.

'What?' whispered Ann, as Maggie motioned her to the dark corner where they squatted on upturned logs.

'You don't know about the robbery.'

Ann drew in a sharp breath, whilst making a suitably eager face to draw Maggie out, but her friend was determined to hold her position of command for as long as possible; first by settling herself with her back against the work bench, and then checking once more over her shoulder that no one was about. 'It's John.'

Why wasn't she surprised. 'What?'

'At the Fair. He stole the takings.'

'What! How?'

'Shhh. Now listen, and cross your heart you won't tell.'

'Cross my heart,' and they drew closer together while Maggie whispered the story into Ann's ear. When finally she leaned back, satisfied with the drama of the relayed events and their effects. Ann was left in astonished silence, her thoughts whirling with a mix of amazement, shock and disquiet. 'What's he going to do with it?' she breathed.

Maggie pulled the kind of face she'd seen adults employ; the kind that says "what can you expect, but no good will come of it".

'Where's he hidden it all?'

'It's buried in a box, up on the hill, like ancient treasure, and he's got a map – but no one knows.'

Ann gasped again with silent astonishment, eyes wide like saucers. 'But doesn't that make him a criminal?'

'Finders keepers,' was all Maggie replied.

XII

Grandpa Rose was asleep on the settee, snoring softly, his mouth lax and arms flung wide with palms uppermost in a perpetual gesture of innocence. Responsibilities now relinquished, he drifted, peaceable and guileless. His life tracked a course through their daily lives, merely brushing against each of them as he passed by on his day-to-day activities, pottering about the yard, workshops and house, forever finding unimportant things to do.

Lizzie had longed for his cheerful, nonsensical chatter when she'd arrived home the night John had left in the ambulance, but Grandpa merely breathed deep and low, a somnolent burr ruffling his grey-stubbled cheeks and, although she'd rattled the door latch deliberately, he'd slept on, oblivious. From the best lounge came the quiet rustle of newspapers where her parents sat reading away their Sunday evening. Lizzie slipped upstairs to her bedroom and climbed onto the window seat to peer down onto the street where, earlier, Robbie had stood with her, forlorn. It was empty now. He'd gone indoors, but some minutes later his bedroom light came on to illuminate the gloomy evening.

Nursing her resentfulness and hurt, she curled into the cushion, angry at John for his power over her best friend, and aggrieved with Robbie for favouring him; John with his skinny legs and strange monkey face, and his rough-sounding voice that seemed to scrape in your ears. He knew things they didn't know, saw things they didn't see. He knew things they weren't supposed to know.

Eventually Jonathan's shape appeared at the window, arms spread as if in supplication, and then the curtains snapped shut, their pink colour dully illuminated by the single ceiling light until, not long after, the light was extinguished and the room fell dark behind the curtains.

***

Lizzie had scarcely finished her breakfast the next morning when Robbie slipped in from the yard, greeting her with an uncertain look, and took a seat opposite her at the big kitchen table.

'Mum's gone into town,' she said, opening the conversation and he smiled, grateful that the cross words of the last evening were set aside. 'She's going to see Mrs Ward in hospital, if she can, while she's there. Did you tell your Mum?'

'About what?' He looked blankly back, suppressing a sense of guilt.

'Mrs Ward, and John going home.'

'Yes, of course.'

'I think it'll all be all right, you know. I think Mrs Ward will get better soon and be home again quickly. And I think John will go back to school in London, and then I'm sure he'll be back here again next summer. Just like he always is.'

He gave a half-smile. 'I expect so.'

'Really, you're not to worry. My Mum'll look after her and I expect yours will too, won't she?'

'Yes...'

'Anyway, we've still got the rest of this week before school starts, haven't we? What shall we do?' and she smiled winsomely, the falling-out forgotten.

He scarcely had time to answer before a loud rap at the kitchen window, followed by the yard door being pushed open, revealed the twins. They were both in a state of restless excitement.

'Guess what!' Finch began, clambering eagerly onto a kitchen chair. 'You know the dance?'

'Yes...'

'After the Fair?'

'Yes...'

'You know the fight?'

'Yes!' cried Lizzie, bursting with impatience for the tantalising story.

Finch leaned forwards, arms flung across the table, pausing to take a firm hold on their attention and to heighten the drama of what he was about to impart.

'You know the boys who broke into the marquee and stole money?'

She looked on astonished and her mouth fell agape. Unobserved, opposite her, Robbie was grimly silent.

'They didn't take it?'

'Well, not all of it,' interrupted Nid.

'John had it!' cried Finch, playing his trump card.

Lizzie's hands sprang to her shocked face.

'The box was open and he had the notes in his hand. I saw him!'

'Whose money?' she said.

'Just money, lots.'

'But John didn't say anything. Robbie?' and she turned to look at him, her expression startled and questioning.

But Robbie merely stared back at the three of them, nonplussed and expressionless.

'John's had to go back,' she explained to the twins as Robbie still hadn't spoken. 'He told Robbie,' she said. 'John went round there last night.'

And they all looked across the table to Robbie, who took up his cup of milk and drank lengthily, although it was empty.

'What did he say?' Finch cried.

'Nothing really.'

'But what did he say about the money?'

Robbie spoke slowly, hesitatingly. 'Oh, I don't know. It was all very garbled. Something about hiding it, I think.'

They all lunged forwards. 'Where!'

'On the hill?' He sounded more questioning than certain.

Nid was impatient. 'Where on the hill?' he demanded.

'He must've buried the money,' cried Finch. He was clambering up onto the table top now in his eagerness. 'Did he hide it?'

'Yes,' said Robbie, sounding more certain now.

'He hid it? Whereabouts?'

'I...' But Robbie was vague, twisting in the chair, his eyes gazing blankly into the room beyond them. But the twins persisted. Lizzie frowned, puzzled and once again hurt, having discovered he'd kept the story from her last night.

'What did he say? Where did he hide it? He must have told you!' Nid was inquisitorial.

Finch lurched excitedly. 'I bet he made a map! There's always a map when you bury treasure.'

'How about it, was there a map?' persisted Nid.

'Maybe...'

Finch had one knee on the table by now. 'Did he leave it with you? X marks the spot. You know, dig here?' He was marking out an imaginary map on the wooden surface. 'Or did he take the map away with him? He's going to come back next year and dig it up, I bet!'

'Did he take it with him, the map?'

'I... suppose he must have.' Robbie shrugged, feigning indifference. Lizzie was looking at him, but he was staring down at the table surface; his eyes unfocussed, avoiding them all.

'Who else knows?' demanded Nid, who was at the head of the table.

'I haven't told anyone,' Robbie said.

'Not even Jonathan?' asked Lizzie, in surprise.

'No.'

'Maggie knows. We told her,' Finch said and dropped back into his seat, excitement spent for the moment.

'Then Ann'll know too,' Lizzie said. 'She got back from holiday yesterday.'

'Right then, said Nid. 'We all get together and then we've got to work out a plan. Okay?'

'Yeah!' Finch cried.

'Yes,' said Lizzie, enthusiastically.

Robbie nodded, but wordlessly, and he cursed John for the terrible trust his friend had placed in him.

XIII

He was still thumping about on the other side of the cellar wall, stowing the beer barrels, his heavy feet scuffing the quarry-tiled floor, grunting with the effort.

Grunting with resentment more like, thought Maggie.

She'd squeezed her way between the newly-delivered boxes and crates that were piled on the storeroom floor, and had then slid under the racks, swimming across the cool floor with a swish, gulp, swish, and then come up in her secret corner where she settled herself onto the wood-block seat. It was good having Ann back from her holiday, Maggie reflected. Her friend had gone home for her tea now; just Ann and her mother, the two of them alone.

He's like mine, her Dad, thought Maggie; no damned good, only she doesn't know it. But sometimes, like today, her eyes said it. One day she'd know, but she couldn't be the one to tell her. The two friends were the same age, but Ann was too young to understand a thing like that. Maggie knew about those things, though; she knew.

The storeroom door banged open and her lousy good-for-nothing father bustled down the steps, breathing heavily. He could move fast for all his bulk. He snapped on the light with one flash of his big hand and then fell heavily into the chair by the desk. It creaked its complaint, but almost immediately he rose again, sending the chair scraping back until it banged against the shelves behind him. He grunted as he moved several of the boxes stacked on the floor and slit one or two open using the thick outside of his broad palm, pulling out several bottles to check them before clanking each back into place. Briskly he counted the bottles and the boxes of cigarettes before booting the lighter cigarette boxes across the floor, out of the way. Only then did he fall heavily back into the sagging chair. All this she knew from the sounds and the play of shadow on the thin cast of light fanning out towards her beneath the racks.

The chair creaked again as he reached upwards, and then the thud of a heavy ledger as it slammed onto the desk. The pages flicked as he scanned through, muttering to himself, and he scratched something down in his cramped scrawl, the noise of the pencil soft on the paper. Then he sent the chair scudding back across the tiles so that it clattered once more against the racking behind.

A large shadow abruptly blocked the grey light that pooled about her ankles, and there was a heavy grunt and rasping outlet of breath, accompanied by a scuffing which was not far behind her. With alarm she realised he was groping beneath the racks and quickly raised her feet from the floor, out of his sight. A loud scraping told her he was drawing the box of hidden ledgers out from under the racks. She breathed quiet and shallow for fear he should sense her presence.

***

Later, as the lowering sun broke clear of the building, a shaft of golden light poured through the small, high window and a flash of platinum shimmered off the cigarette lighter. The storeroom was empty and silent now; it belonged to Maggie alone. A warm, comforting glow spread through her belly and she gazed upwards at her silver lighter which gleamed in the late afternoon sunlight.

Stretching upwards she took it down from the shelf and turned it about in her palm. It was smooth, cool, hard and bright, although small patches of tarnish now tainted its perfection. She scratched at the blemishes with her fingernail, drawing the surface close to her face and gazed closely at the delicately engraved pattern around the base, clearly visible now in the stream of unfamiliar brightness from the low sun.

A few weeks ago, it would have meant no more to her than on the day she'd found the lighter. But now she knew, from lessons at the end of term, that the little shapes on it were musical notes. She fingered them softly, puzzled at such an unexpected decoration, and then went in search of a scrap of cardboard, which she tore from a delivery box, and carefully copied down the notation, taking care to reproduce the fine horizontal lines and positions of the notes upon them, like so many stiff little tadpoles.

Maggie knew just where to go with it. For the last year the twins had been taking piano lessons and she tucked the copy in her dress pocket and hastened round to their house on The Green. Ignoring the brothers' surprised looks at her unannounced visit, she produced the music.

'Can you play this?' she said.

''Course,' said Nid taking it. 'It's music, isn't it?'

He was always a show-off, that one, she thought.

'Anyway, what is it?'

'Dunno,' Maggie shrugged. 'Found it in the pub. I just wondered.'

She stood alongside the large, dark upright piano as Nid carefully balanced the cardboard scrap on the music stand above the keys, then settled himself on a cushion placed on the piano stool. His brother lounged against one end of the keyboard, forehead cupped in fingers which threaded their way through his blonde fringe. There was never any dispute as to who would be the one to actually do the playing.

The notes sounded soft and hesitant at first, then gathered momentum as Nid grew comfortable with the snatch of tune. The halting but ringing piano notes now filled the empty room as he moved his small hands over the keys, frowning slightly beneath his own blond fringe as he peered at the notation before him. It was only a short section of tune, a gentle and rather mournful melody, and with gathering confidence he could soon play it through, and then he repeated it several more times, looking round questioningly to Maggie.

'I know it!' Finch declared. 'It goes,' and he sang, *'There was a boy, a very strange enchanted boy...'*

Nid played it through again, two or three more times, while his brother sang along.

A movement at the lounge door drew their eyes.

'What are you doing?'

The tone was peremptory; unexpectedly and perplexingly harsh and demanding, but that wasn't what startled them. It was the look of haunted alarm. Norma stood framed in the doorway, her hand still resting on the doorknob, face anxious and taut as if she held herself in readiness to avert a tragedy, but one that had already occurred.

Nid froze, his expression shocked, almost fearful. His fingers were suspended above the keys, while Finch peered silently back at her, frozen in the act of singing, sober now.

'Nothing...' said Nid, voice wavering.

'What are you playing?' Norma tried again, now controlling the alarm in her voice, making an effort not to sound angry or frightening.

'I don't know.' Nid's voice was constrained under her inquisitorial look. He withdrew his hands from the keys and dropped them by his sides as if to hide his guilt.

Sensing his discomfort, she composed herself quickly, drawing her distress back around herself, like the brightly-hued satin lining of a cloak glimpsed only briefly. 'Darling, I just wondered,' she said stepping fully into the room, her gaze now softened so that only a pale ghost of her fear remained. 'I heard you from the garden. I hadn't heard you play that before. Is it new?'

The twins relaxed a little, but still regarded her with distant suspicion, their voices and faces tense but clinging for support.

'It's Maggie's,' said Finch, at which his mother turned her full gaze on him. Her mouth smiled with reassurance, but her eyes still held their look.

'Maggie,' she said. 'How nice, what a pretty tune. What is it?'

Maggie shrugged sulkily, 'Dunno.'

'Oh, what a shame,' Norma replied. 'I wondered where you'd got it.'

'Found it,' said Maggie and snatched the card from the music stand and scrunched it into nothingness in her hand. 'I've got to go back now,' she lied, and pushed past Norma into the hall, letting herself out of the front door and into the still-warm sunlight of early evening.

XIV

Finch drove the spade into the turf, legs splayed, his weight thrown forwards over one braced knee, shoulders and head held low. His face was obscured by the blond hair that fell from the crown of his head, flopping with each vigorous thrust of the blade into the earth. He was grunting with the effort, jabbing fiercely with right fist upturned, spade handle gripped rigidly as he dug with determined effort, tossing the spoil wildly over his shoulder so that it scattered all about.

'Oi!' yelled Maggie, jumping back.

Within minutes a jagged hole, several inches deep, had been gouged from the dry, flinty earth. He parked the spade into the ground with one sharp thrust then straightened, looking about him, puffing, his face flushed with the effort. Nid peered into the hole. Beside him Ann leaned over the edge, gazing down into the emptiness.

'Not deep enough yet,' Finch said, wiping away sweat with the back of one dusty arm so that streaks of grey appeared on his brow and cheek. 'It's gonna be well hidden, at least two feet down.'

'That's not been dug before,' said Nid, poking a sandal-shod foot into the hole and scraping at the sides with his toes. 'It's still hard and unworked.'

Ann dropped to her knees and drew some loose soil crumb from the base of the hole, letting it drop back through her fingers. Behind them Maggie turned away, eyes roaming the hillside. 'What about over there?' She was pointing away and upwards, beyond where a breeze now feathered the seeding grass, silvering its surface.

They all turned to look. At about fifty yards distance, a small dark area suggested a possible disturbance. They hurried over, even Robbie, although he alone knew how futile this exercise was, how pointless all this effort and excitement; the surreptitious borrowing of spades from their fathers' sheds, the debates and arguments over where to look and why, and yet somehow he was caught up in the quest. They gathered raggedly around a scrape of disturbed soil.

'Rabbits,' Nid diagnosed flatly.

Finch started to dig again, but the soil beneath was hard and dry and clearly untouched. Maggie, impatient, had already wandered in search of more promising hiding places but it was Jonathan who this time called their attention. Taller than the rest, he could see further and was indicating a patch of rough ground beneath the hedge some considerable distance above them on the hillside. It had been obscured by the dark shade beneath the trees in the overgrown hedge but, as a cloud passed over the sun, the softer light had revealed a patch of disturbed ground. He led the way rapidly up the steep slope where, once again, the friends clustered around, hopeful and expectant. Robbie followed behind, hindered by their father's heavy digging spade which weighed almost as heavily as the knowledge that lumped in his gut.

A patch of bare ground, about a yard across, confronted them, its surface broken and tumbled.

'Brilliant! Well done Jonathan!' exclaimed Finch, springing forwards and beginning to scrape away at the jumbled soil with the edge of his spade. This time Robbie joined him and both dug into the earth with energy and purpose, tossing the tumbling spoil onto the grass while the others jostled forwards, watching and pointing as the others' efforts uncovered the layers beneath.

'Here Robbie, let me,' and Jonathan gently lifted the heavy spade from his brother's grasp. Standing Colossus-like astride the hole, he gouged into the earth, hefting immense shovel-loads of soil without effort and settling each neatly into a pile to one side of the deepening hole.

They pressed close to watch his automaton-like movements, steady and rhythmical, each massive thrust with the spade accompanied by a slight grunt before, impassively, he carefully placed the spoil in its tidy heap. In no time he had excavated a sizeable crater. He paused, straightening himself up, barely even breathing hard, one large hand resting on the spade handle which was propped at his hip, while they all surveyed the results.

'I can't see anything yet.' Lizzie was leaning forwards, holding her plaits against her chest, peering into the gaping crater beside Jonathan's large feet.

Maggie, lying on her front beside her, pointed. 'What's that?'

'Just a bit of wood,' said Nid. He too came forwards and began to poke about, but produced nothing.

'Are we sure it's the right place?' Finch asked.

'We don't know, do we?' said Maggie. 'He's taken the map away, he must've.'

That there was a map was, by common consent, an incontrovertible fact, although no one had actually seen it, or spoken to John about it. Nevertheless it was common knowledge; known and believed by all. All except Robbie. He knew there was no map and never had been. He alone knew where the money was.

He cursed John for his terrible trust in him.

'It's nowhere to be found,' Robbie confirmed, shrugging and trying to sound and look convincing. No one demurred.

'We've just got to keep looking,' pressed Maggie. 'Dig deeper. You can see the ground's been disturbed here and it's a likely place up under this hedge.'

'Yeah, you wouldn't be seen from here.' Confident now, Finch was helping to dig again, jabbing fiercely into the stony ground.

'Let me,' said his brother, roughly seizing the spade, and soon he and Jonathan together were digging and throwing, digging and throwing, mirror images of one other's movements while complete opposites in appearance. In no time Nid was obscured from the knees downwards, standing in the base of the hole, tearing into the stony earth with grim-faced determination.

'What's that?' cried Maggie again, dropping to her knees at the rim, reaching down into the depths. 'Look,' and she pointed to a pale flat surface just visible to one side.

Jonathan stepped in again, working with the big heavy spade to clear the area of loose soil. There was a loud *chunk* and the spade juddered as it bounced off something hard.

'It's a rock,' breathed Ann to his right, but no one else heard or responded. Perhaps they didn't want to.

Jonathan kept pounding away, helped or hindered by Nid who determinedly poked and gouged at one edge of the solid object until finally, between them, they could raise one end, levering it clear of the ground like a tooth wrenched from its socket.

'It's a rock,' Jonathan confirmed and turned to Robbie for affirmation, disappointment settled deep into his face.

'Maybe it's been put there to cover the treasure,' Lizzie suggested hopefully. 'You know, to hide it. Perhaps the box is underneath.' She looked around, seeking support.

Finch, jumping in beside his brother, fell to his knees, rump in the air, and scraped away at the earth below the up-ended rock. 'There's nothing,' he confirmed forlornly. Nid tossed the spade aside, stepped from the hole and flung himself down on the grass. 'We'll never find it,' he moaned. 'Are you sure it exists?' and he turned to Finch who stood in the hole, hands disconsolately on hips.

'I saw him take it! Of course I'm sure. It's got to be here somewhere,' and Finch looked vainly about as if by sheer effort of will he'd spot the hiding place.

'We can't dig up the whole hill,' Nid complained. 'It'll take forever.'

'Are you sure he didn't say something?' Lizzie turned her grey eyes on Robbie, wide with hope.

He shifted uncomfortably. 'No, nothing.'

'Nothing at all?' Maggie pressed. 'He must've said something.'

'Yeah, he's got to have said something! You gotta think hard,' Finch urged. 'C'mon, what exactly happened?'

'Tell us exactly,' Nid said, sitting up now, scrutinising him. They were all scrutinising him.

'Just think about it, Robbie.' Jonathan was trying to be helpful. 'When he came round the next day after the Fair. You know, we were tired and he came round when you were in the garden, and then he came back in the evening didn't he? You went out to see him.'

All eyes were surveying Robbie. He swayed slightly and shrugged, diffidently he hoped. 'It's just like I keep telling you,' he tried, as casually as possible. 'He came round and said he'd found some money and he was hiding it. Then later, he said he'd put it in a box and it was in a hole up on the hill and he had a map. Maybe he was joking, or telling a lie... I don't know.' And he raised his arms entreatingly, helpless. They all just looked.

'He got it because I saw him take it,' Finch said firmly, 'with my own eyes. A big handful of notes. Lots of money. At least...'

'How much?' asked Ann.

'Ten pounds...'

'Twenty at least,' said Nid.

'You didn't see it!'

'No, but ten pound's not a big handful. Not with all the money they'd have taken from the tickets, nitwit!'

Maggie intervened, turning to Robbie. 'Didn't he show you the money?' she demanded.

'Well... sort of. He held it up quickly, but mostly it was in his pocket. It was quite a lot, I think.'

'Twenty at least,' said Nid resolutely. 'At least.'

'But whose was it?' Ann asked.

'It was the takings,' Maggie brusquely replied, brushing aside the question as an irrelevance.

'I know but...'

'Why don't we write to John and ask him?' Finch cried, triumphant with the idea. A wave of ridicule and laughter drowned him out.

'We don't know where he lives!'

'Mrs Ward will know,' he persisted, but was ignored.

'Look, here's what we do,' said Maggie. 'We split up, and each of us will go to a different part of the hill and search for anywhere that's been dug. You've got to look for the ground being disturbed; that might mean grass or weeds dug up or dying, piles of earth, fresh soil that looks like it's been turned over. All that. Anything that doesn't look right or seems suspicious.'

'And there's likely to be footprints nearby,' Finch interjected, newly enthused.

'We'll meet back here tomorrow at ten,' she continued. 'That way there'll be plenty of time and we can be really thorough. And no one's to tell anyone. On pain of death. Right?'

'Robbie, didn't John say anything at all?' Lizzie was looking at him again. She was the same height and her eyes were level with his. 'You know, when he left on Sunday evening. When he had to run off and go in the ambulance with Mrs Ward. Didn't he say anything?' and she smiled reassuringly, her steady guileless gaze searching his face. 'Not anything?'

He tried to think of what to say to her, to sound convincing, to answer the unanswerable, but before he could speak Jonathan had interrupted. 'Whose are the takings, Robbie?'

'They're the ticket money. And money from the bar at the dance,' Nid stated authoritatively. He was smart and liked to show it.

'They're not really John's then,' suggested Lizzie, uncertainty creeping into her voice also.

Maggie pulled a face and shrugged. 'Don't see why not. He found the money.'

'Well, he stole it, didn't he?'

'Yes, it must belong to someone,' Ann persisted, grateful that the conversation had returned to her.

'We should tell the Police then,' said Lizzie. 'If it's stolen. Shouldn't we?'

'But then John'll get into trouble. He'll go to prison!' said Finch. 'For forty years.'

'I think we should tell the Police; if it's stolen from someone.' Ann looked anxious, but not as anxious as Robbie now felt.

'Yes, let's tell the Police,' Nid agreed. 'We tell them we know the money's been stolen, but we don't say who by. If you don't come with us Finch then we can say no one saw, because none of us will have been the one who did, right?'

'But I want to come...'

'Then we tell the Police we heard that someone's hidden the money up on the hill.'

'Maybe there's a reward,' Maggie suggested.

'We might get our picture in the paper if they find it,' Finch beamed. 'Like after the robbery at the Hall.'

And they carried on like this, and all the while anxious thoughts were whirling about in Robbie's head, his stomach knotting and clenching so that he had to breathe deeply through an open mouth to prevent light-headedness. How guilty was he, and what exactly was he guilty of? Certainly of assisting a criminal, and definitely of not reporting a crime to the Police. Then what would happen to John if the money was found? Or to himself for that matter? He shuddered inside, feeling desolate, willing it all to end.

Finally, after much debate and as much argument, they wandered off to go home, the matter still scarcely settled, any entertainment from the possibility of hidden treasure exhausted for the moment. Jonathan, who'd been watching his brother, rose to follow the others but Robbie hung back, fretful and despairing. He hadn't the will to rouse himself.

'What is it?' Jonathan asked when his brother didn't move, morose and still rooted to the spot by the anxiety that gripped him inside.

He didn't speak for a few moments, but knew he must tell his brother. He needed his help.

'Come and sit here,' he said. 'I've got to tell you something.' Jonathan slumped heavily onto the grass beside him, his big face at once open and puzzled. Robbie took a deep breath. 'I know where the money is,' he confided.

Jonathan's features steadily registered astonishment. 'Where, Robbie? But how? Why didn't you tell?' and he looked both perplexed and sorrowful. 'Did John tell you, then?'

'It's at home,' confessed Robbie, 'hidden in the shed.' He waited while Jonathan absorbed this information and its implications, feeling sickened with John for getting him in this situation, but mostly with himself.

'He hid it there that afternoon,' he continued. 'It's in a tin pushed underneath the chest of drawers.'

Jonathan turned to him with a gathering frown and a look of kindly pity.

'I didn't know what to do! He just left it there and ran off. Then with Mrs Ward hurting herself and him going off like that. It's just... left there!'

They exchanged looks.

'I didn't know what to do.' He was almost wailing now, plaintive and fearful, needing a big brother's support.

Jonathan was looking down between his knees. 'Don't worry, Robbie,' he said. 'We'll work out what to do.'

'But what?' he persisted. 'I've been trying to think, but if I tell anyone I'll have to tell on John and he'll get into all sorts of trouble. He'll be sent to an approved school or something, and he probably won't be able to come here again. And if I just leave it, well... it's stolen isn't it? It belongs to someone else. I should hand it over, but I can't without telling. What am I to do?'

Jonathan clapped him on the shoulder, large hand and arm so hefty it pushed him sideways. Robbie smiled grimly and Jonathan smiled back, repeating the reassuring slap, stingingly. After that they made their way back down the hill to home, each silent in their own thoughts. Robbie could see his brother's jaw working, a sure sign that he was thinking, mouthing thoughts as he turned the problem over and over in his mind.

Down at The Green the ice cream van was parked outside the Jug & Bottle and a small crowd was gathered around for cornets and lollies. By the time the two of them had passed, most people had drifted away and the area was empty save for a few stragglers buying bricks of ice cream for family teatime; all on that quiet late afternoon in those last days of August when little happens, after the long active weeks of summer.

They were passing Mrs Ward's, which was empty too, when without warning the van began to lean and then to sway back and forth as if alive. Several figures ran to the side nearest them and, clutching the roof, assisted in vigorously rocking it, all the while yelling, 'give us a free one, Antonio!' The brothers paused to watch for a moment as the hapless ice cream seller unsteadily handed out free cornets while Malcolm, Neville and the others laughed, taunted and rocked.

Round in Main Street, a dark figure on the far side of the road, whistling softly to himself, almost stopped Robbie in his tracks from fear. The local bobby was approaching, deep strides bringing him ever closer until he drew opposite and nodded a greeting. Jonathan had hesitated as well.

Without warning Robbie heard himself calling across, 'There's boys making trouble on The Green.'

PC Burgess broke into a trot, whistle blowing shrilly.

XV

Their father was coaxing, but stern. Beneath his intense gaze, Nid squirmed anxiously. He'd begun to squirm a lot lately. Finch was simply impatient.

'You know the difference, don't you,' Frank Bird was saying, 'between telling the truth and lies? The difference is important. What you say matters; the truth matters. I expect you always to tell the truth. You understand that, don't you?'

'Dad, Dad...' Finch was pleading. He was fidgeting, eager to get going, to run outside and play.

'Covering something up, whatever the reason is, and you might believe it's a good reason at the time, there's never an excuse or a good motive for not telling the truth. Whoever you think you might be helping, whatever the grounds, there can never be a good reason.'

'Dad...'

'Andrew! Please, I'm talking.'

'But Dad...'

'Do you understand? Both of you?'

'Yes.' Nid spoke glumly and quietly.

'Andrew?'

'Yes, Dad, but can we borrow the spade?'

'The spade? Whatever do you want the spade for?'

'Playing pirates,' said Nid, quick as a flash.

'What?'

'We've got to bury Long John's Silver's treasure.'

When Frank had arrived home from work the twins had been practising their piano exercises. It was a rule: three times a week, half an hour each, one turning the pages for the other. Scales, exercises, arpeggios, and simple tunes. Norma had sent them into the front room, brooking no excuses; it was practise time.

They'd lifted the heavy, highly polished piano lid and sat together on the stool, childish fingers spread across the smooth ivory keys, the uncertain notes ringing out, disturbing the still air of the 'best room'. Nid completed his practise efficiently, then watched while Finch worked his way unevenly through the same set of exercises. Norma was in the kitchen but they soon heard the kettle boil, the chink of crockery and the back door close as she took a tray and book into the garden. Before long they'd lapsed into game-playing and foolery, distracting one another, playing Chopsticks and silly ditties. Nid began to finger the notes that Maggie had brought round, inaccurately at first, but he soon recalled them and then Finch copied until he too could play the lilting snatch of tune and they hammered it out together, laughing. They didn't hear the front door.

Frank had stood at the open doorway; watching, unspeaking, unobserved.

'Where did you learn that?' he'd said.

Nid had jumped off the stool as if stung. 'We were just doing our practise.'

'I know.'

Finch swivelled slowly round on the stool. In the centre of the room Nid stood stiffly. Their father strode forwards, his presence immediately filling the lounge. He was in his work suit, a tall, formal figure rising up towards the ceiling, a neat moustache about his stern mouth, looking down on them both.

'Where did you learn that?' he'd repeated, and then waited.

'Someone at school,' said Nid uncomfortably.

'Really? Who?'

Nid didn't answer but Finch leapt from the stool, taking that piercing look onto himself.

'Friends; dunno. Someone found it,' he'd shrugged.

'Who was that then?' persisted Frank.

'Dunno.'

'I expect you to say if you know; to answer questions truthfully.'

But he'd accepted their plea to borrow the garden spade to go digging on the hill. 'Don't lose it. Don't lend it to anyone else and don't damage it. And I expect you to clean and oil it and put it back just as you found it. Do I make myself clear? Very well. And mind you behave yourselves.'

Nid and Finch looked at one another silently, co-conspirators.

XVI

Geoffrey Harrison-Bates was an accomplished host. He worked his guests like a conductor presiding over an orchestra, bringing in each one when required to contribute to the success of the whole, all of which he held in an effortless grasp. His wife drifted seamlessly about the principal reception room, smiling, charming, ever at ease, demonstrating a pleasing interest that she conveyed to each and every guest. Erect, impeccable and precise, and displaying a certainty born of permanence, Geoffrey moved his guests from group to group, playing them like instruments to his will.

At their midst was Caroline, in a pink-flowered chiffon dress with a full-skirt that floated about her pretty calves. It had a fitted bodice with dainty cap-sleeves and a modest neckline that accentuated her neat figure. She wore a discreet pearl necklace about her delicate throat and on her left hand a bright diamond sparkled. She proudly displayed it for admiration.

The reception room, larger than the entirety of the Bradburys' cottage, felt overwhelmingly grand to the two brothers. Twice as long as it was wide, it was illuminated by two large bay windows, each with a different aspect; one looking out towards the drive, the other, in the longer wall, overlooked the terrace and lawns. The walls were hung with paintings of glum-faced ancestors. By a vast carved stone fireplace at the mid-point of the longer wall, Geoffrey Harrison-Bates now stood with one hand resting lightly upon the mantelpiece, which was adorned with green and blue ceramic birds and family photographs held in silver frames. Glass in hand, he was entertaining a group of people Robbie didn't know.

The room was filled with people they didn't know; at least a hundred and fifty, all gathered in small groups, quietly talking and greeting one another, smiling and nodding while their hosts worked the room with practised ease.

As if clinging to one another for reassurance the Bradbury's stood in a slightly awkward huddle, and it was one of those rare occasions when Tom wore a jacket and tie in which he felt both conspicuous and uncomfortable. They were all in their best; Jonathan in his school uniform, hair slicked back despite a tendency for the front to spring unbidden into a wave; Susan in the fashionable shift dress that she'd persuaded her reluctant mother to buy and which she now wore with a combination of blossoming self-awareness and girlish self-consciousness. Robbie had been cajoled into a short-trousered suit, while Sally stood at the edge of their little ensemble, facing out into the throng in her best coat, the one bought for a family wedding, with a neat little hat pressed onto her firm, wavy hair. She smiled vaguely, displaying a mix of gratification and politeness to any observer, but with a hint of unease.

A sharp, rapid clinking silenced the burr of conversation as Geoffrey chinked a silver paper knife against his glass of punch. It was only in the silence that Robbie became aware of the level of noise that had been there before. From all directions, faces turned to Geoffrey, politely half-smiling and expectant. His wife drifted to his side and looked up at him as he welcomed their guests with a brief speech.

'Ladies and gentlemen,' he opened. 'I ask you to raise a glass and toast the future happiness of Caroline and Edward. To Caroline and Edward...'

Everyone turned to the smiling couple, intoning their names. Tom and Sally, not trusting the unfamiliar punch, raised glasses of sweet sherry. Even Susan had a small glass of punch, but Jonathan and Robbie were restricted to lemon barley water with which they both stiffly raised in salute.

In an anteroom, a long table had been laid with a lavish buffet. The Bradbury family edged towards it but hung back, Tom was anxious not to appear presumptuous. All of the garden and household staff were there with their families, while the other guests were friends of the extended family of the Harrison-Bates and their prospective son-in-law, along with a few locals from Netherington. In the evening there was to be a more informal dinner and dance for the young couple with their own friends, and the immediate and younger members of both families, but this afternoon's celebration was a more general proclamation of their match.

Tom found himself beside a Netherington family he'd known for years and he and Sally stood talking to them, more relaxed now that the unaccustomed sherry had taken effect. A male cousin of the family's had meanwhile engaged Susan in conversation and she glowed with the pleasure at being treated as an adult. She stood shoulder height to him beneath the family portraits, smiling charmingly and trying out an adult persona that she might perhaps adopt when older, if it fitted her.

Jonathan and Robbie, their plates heaped with the kind of tempting food they would normally only be offered at Christmas, stood in one corner, silently eating and observing. Reg Higgins, the senior gardener, stepped over and indulgently conversed for a while, asking the brothers about school and plans for future careers.

Jonathan knew that he wanted to be a pilot, Robbie was less sure what his course in life should be.

'Plenty of time,' Reg assured him, and moved smilingly on.

The Vicar drifted past, his plate also piled high. 'Enjoying yourselves, boys?' he beamed at them, pink-cheeked from the punch, before joining a group who stood chattering nearby, the atmosphere now informal and everyone more animated and relaxed.

'Do you want some more lemon barley water?' asked Jonathan, who'd drained his glass and polished off his plate of food. He was always the first to finish.

'I don't know. Do you think we can?' Robbie looked uncertainly about, not knowing what was correct. Before he could say more Jonathan had set off in search, leaving him standing awkwardly alone beside a large bronze bust set upon a pedestal. All around, groups of people were happily eating and talking, so that a convivial hubbub filled the air. Despite the constant movement of individuals, bodies formed a screen that cut him off from the main portion of the room, drifting to and from the food and between groups, ever in flux, trapping him in the alcove with the brooding bust.

A burst of loud laughter and gaiety to his right, suddenly broke through the general noise of conversation, and several people stepped back in amusement, their hands raised to faces and heads tilted back in merriment, turning to one another to reinforce their general jollity. As they broke apart, the view towards the bay window opened up revealing a figure standing before the heavy burgundy-coloured brocade curtains. He had a glass raised to his lips obscuring his face but, in lowering it his silhouette was exposed against the sunlit window, highlighting a tumble of dark curls against a broad forehead.

The people nearest to him were regrouping, concealing Robbie's clear view once more. He leaned to one side then raised himself on his toes, one hand pressed upon the aquiline nose of the bronze bust for support, but it was no good; his view was closed again. Then

Jonathan was at his shoulder carrying two glasses of lemon barley water.

'What're you doing, Robbie? What're you looking for?'

'I think I saw Hugh.'

'Hugh! Where?'

'There by the window. Can you see, you're taller?'

Jonathan stretched up and there was no mistaking his smile of recognition. 'C'mon, Robbie,' he said, and immediately began to thrust his way between people who were now energetically conversing again. They turned in surprise as Jonathan pressed through their midst, leaving Robbie to trail helplessly in his wake, mumbling apologies.

'Hugh!' Jonathan gasped, bounding up so vigorously that his drink spilled out over his hand.

Hugh, standing alone, was at first startled and puzzled, but then recognition dawned.

'Goodness, I didn't know you were here! How are you both? How nice to see you.'

'We're fine,' Robbie said.

'I must say it's good to see a familiar face, I scarcely know a soul. I'm not really sure why they asked me. Politeness I suppose. Look, it really is good to see you. What've you both been doing? It must be ages since I last saw you. How long is it, at least six months I should think? Was it at Aston Haddon?'

'Easter,' replied Jonathan. 'It was at the airfield. Have you been flying, Hugh? We haven't really seen you. Have you still got the same plane?'

'Oh, a bit, when I'm not kept too busy at work. Not as often as I'd like, frankly. And yes, I've still got the Cessna. You must come and see it again when you're next over there. Why don't you?'

'Yes, thank you,' he said, as he'd been taught to do.

'Excellent. I'm sure you can tell me a thing or two about the plane, can't you Jonathan?'

But, for once, Jonathan had other things on his mind. 'We've got to speak to you, Hugh,' he burst out loudly.

Wondering what his brother was going to say, Robbie couldn't help noticing that Jonathan was now nearly as tall as Hugh, who merely inclined his head slightly to look quizzically back. 'Certainly...'

'There's been another robbery!'

Robbie spun round in fear that they should be overheard, but the other guests were all too absorbed in their socialising.

'I hope the Police aren't looking for me again,' Hugh lightly joked.

'No, it's really important!'

Hugh suppressed a smile. 'What is it and how can I help?' He led the brothers a few steps to one side, further into the bay and away from the nearest people, and leaned back onto the window sill so that Robbie was nearer to his height and Jonathan had now to look down. Hugh took a drink, then settled the base of his glass into upturned palms rested on his lap and looked up at them both in anticipation.

Jonathan shuffled, collecting his thoughts, then mouthed a few words in silence as he tried them out, finally whispering down to Hugh.

'John took some money at the dance and he hid it under the chest, it's in Dad's shed, and it's not his, the money that is. He stole it so it's got to be given back because it isn't ours. And Robbie, well, it's not Robbie's fault. John wants a steam engine but he can't because it's not his money. And it's not ours. Dad doesn't know either. You'll know what to do Hugh, I know you will.'

'Who's John?' Hugh asked, baffled.

'He's my friend,' said Robbie.

'Let me get this right: John took some money that wasn't his?' He looked to them in turn for affirmation and both nodded. 'And then what? He hid it? In your father's shed?'

'Under the old chest of drawers, in a tobacco tin,' said Jonathan, who liked to be precise.

'Okay, and what happened then?'

'Nothing, because Mrs Ward broke her hip and had to go to hospital and John had to go in the ambulance too and then go home.

And that meant Robbie had the money and it's not his. But no one knows.'

'Right, I think I'm getting it. So you're left with this stolen money and you don't know what to do with it. Is that right? How much is it?'

'Sixteen pounds, three shillings and four pence,' said Jonathan. They'd counted it out together one day after carefully ensuring their parents were safely busy elsewhere.

'Right...' said Hugh, shifting his position and draining his glass before placing it beside him on the window sill. 'And what about John?' He turned to look directly at Robbie.

'He had to go back home to London,' Robbie explained. 'He only spends the summer holidays in Moreton Steyning and he won't be back again until next summer. In fact he might not even be back at all. He stays with his Great Aunt and she broke her hip, so he had to go home without warning and he hid the money and left me looking after it.'

Hugh breathed deeply, regarding Robbie solemnly, then gazed down into his lap, not speaking. This was a different Hugh to usual. 'What do you think you should do?' he said.

Robbie felt he was being tested.

'Give it back. But I don't know how. If I do, then they'll know I had it and they'll want to know how I came by it and I'll have to tell on John.'

'You don't want to get John into trouble?'

'No...'

'He's your friend? Is he a good friend?'

'Yes, he's sort of my best friend when he's here. I see him every day.'

'Okay. And what kind of friend is he? He's put you in a very difficult position after all.'

'We...' But how could he explain John's craziness and impetuosity, his ferocity and loyalty?

Hugh could never have had a childhood like that. He exuded good manners and propriety. To his relief, Jonathan interrupted his struggle so that Hugh turned from looking into Robbie's face to tilt his head upwards to Jonathan, who now leaned forwards familiarly, with one hand against the stone mullion above Hugh's head.

'Actually, I don't really think John's been looked after properly,' he said, to Robbie's utter surprise.

'What do you mean?' asked Hugh.

'John's a naughty boy sometimes. Well, quite a lot of the time actually, but I don't think he knows what he's doing is really wrong. I think his Mum and Dad haven't told him properly, so he doesn't really know what's right and wrong.'

He'd put it more clearly than Robbie had ever understood.

Hugh turned back to him again. He was frowning, but smiling. 'Is that right?' he asked.

Robbie nodded.

'It sounds as if John needs help too. So... we must find a way of returning the money without incriminating either you, or your family, or John, mustn't we? Tricky.' He stood up. 'I'm going for another drink. Hold my place here while I have a think about this.' And he stepped away and was soon swallowed up by the throng.

'Hugh will know what to do,' said Jonathan, beaming with unshakeable confidence in his own best friend.

Chapter Four: 1960

Maggie noticed Neville's breath before she even knew of his approach; it was the thin ghosts of vapour that rose above the curve of the hedge, shortly followed by the crisp sound of brisk footsteps on the old track ahead. She hesitated from the encounter, just lingering before the corner and gazing out over the corrugated fields where each furrow crest was thinly crusted with icy snow. The slight overnight fall had turned the distant meadows the colour of peppermint ice.

He rounded the corner, whistling softly to himself, swinging one leg wildly to kick at a rock, his arms flung high in celebration until his eyes suddenly alighted on Maggie, then both arms fell limp to his sides in self-consciousness. Neville's movements were loose and limber but on seeing her he stiffened, his walk now slowing, turned heavy and awkward as he approached her. She stood her ground on the grassy verge, the ice-crisp snow on the grass tips cold against her ankles. Even the air was crisp, searing cold in her nostrils and scented of snow.

Maggie turned her head, watching as Neville Potter passed, slowed now to a trudge, rotating on his heels so that he remained turned towards her.

'My Dad says yours ain't done his delivery.' He edged slowly away, walking backwards now.

'What's that?'

'Whatever he gets.'

'Yeah, what's that?'

'Stuff he gets, drink an' cigs. You stupid or something! He ain't had his stuff, my Dad says. What's happened; he ain't heard?'

'Nothing to do with me.'

'Well, tell him.'

She shrugged.

'Tell him! My Dad wants to know. He hasn't heard.'

'He can ask.'

'Yeah, well I'm asking you. Tell your Dad.' And he turned abruptly about and strode away, falling into an easy stride, arms swinging loose now.

The track dropped quickly as it approached the village and Maggie was soon home, legs and hands mottled and numbed from the cold. At the pub, lunchtime service was drawing to a close and the regulars were emerging from the bars, coat collars pulled up, breath instantly fogging in the chill air. She wasn't allowed in during opening hours, so made her way round to the yard and up into the flat where the younger kids were spilled out across the living room floor and her mother was at the kitchen sink, her back towards her.

Maggie could tell Lois's indifference by the way she stood; the droop of her shoulders as she dropped the plates, one by one into the rack, bubbles slithering down.

'There's bread on the table,' Lois said, without turning.

Maggie helped herself from the unevenly cut loaf, scraping on butter, pressing two rough slices together.

'Don't spill crumbs.'

As if anyone would notice, or bother to clear them up, thought Maggie.

'I've got enough to do. Maggie!'

'Yes!'

She slipped the latch and crept softly down the inner stairs towards the bar. The sour smell of beer rose up into her nostrils with the thick fire-warmth, and the sting of tobacco smoke hung ghost-like in the air. Silently she settled on her favourite step; it was the one where, sitting sideways, she was invisible in the gloom of the unlit staircase to anyone in the bar below, but which gave her a clear view beneath the slope of the stairway ceiling down into the lounge bar, provided that the door at the bottom had been left open. Today it had been.

Time had been called a while back and the bar was almost empty now. The fire had burned down and the last cinders settled with a soft noise and a puff of smoke from the ash that remained in the grate. On the table a lone pewter tankard showed where Gramps

Norris had spent his usual lunchtime. Nearby a pair of outstretched legs, crossed at the ankles, indicated a customer lingering in the corner. The man rose, uttered a gruff cheerio which was answered from behind the bar, out of sight, by her father. The smoke in the room billowed in the draught from the firmly-closed street door and the figure walked briskly past the front window, bent forwards into the chill.

After that there was silence for a while, only disturbed and indeed intensified, by the steady ticking of the wall clock. Then his legs appeared, loose trousers sagging at the knees, moving swiftly across the bar to the tables and, chink, chink he collected up the glasses, stepping nimbly from table to table; straightening the chairs, kicking a stool back, turning at the hip for a backwards glance at the fire. No point in making it up now, was there?

The snug door opening, the sound of firm footsteps.

'You're in late today, Frank.' That bonhomie.

'Yes, busy morning.' The other's legs were in sight now, paused in momentum; neatly-pressed trousers, long overcoat, a black briefcase hanging by the left ankle, leather shoes. A cough. 'Wasn't sure I'd make it.'

'Business must be good. Money's always in fashion, eh!'

These legs turned towards the door, swivelled at the ankle, a stride to one side, right foot rested on the toe, one hand on the door knob no doubt.

'Er... Frank, got a minute? It's just that...'

The briefcase jerked up, checking his watch. Pub time's never right.

'Won't keep you a minute... Just a quick word. Been meaning to have a quick chat. All right is it? Here, have a seat.'

His legs came into view again and one thick forearm drew back a chair from the table by the fire. He chuckled humourlessly, one finger pointing to the grate. 'Must make it up! Look at that, nearly out. Always lots to do. We're all busy, eh? Business always keeps you at it.'

Frank Bird sank slowly into the chair presented to him, his body up to his chest dropping into her view. A bottle-green scarf was wrapped about his neck even though the Bank was only across The Square. If he leaned forwards, she saw his chin working as he spoke. Her father moved across in front, briefly obscuring her view with his broad back and knitted waistcoat over his shirt. He pulled out a stool onto which he perched, and inclined forwards from the waist, one large forearm along the table's edge, hand softly drooping. His other rested on one thigh, fingers agitatedly stroking at the fabric of his trousers. Frank Bird clutched at the briefcase on his lap as if unwilling to relinquish any readiness to depart.

'Yes, sorry to hold you up. Just haven't found a moment, you know how it is.'

Bird raised his fingers from the briefcase handle in vague acknowledgement.

'Yes, a word then... Good of you to wait like this. Know you're busy.'

'What is it, Rod?'

The fingers scratched at an imaginary itch above his knee. 'Bit tricky, Frank. The loan...'

'Yes?'

'Well... thing is... turnover's a bit low... time of year... one thing and another... growing family, you know...'

There was no response, just silence.

'Wanted a quiet word, just the two of us, like. Know you'll understand, one businessman to another; both involved in business and money matters, eh? Cash flow and all that.' He raised the hand from his thigh and rubbed the fingers and thumb together.

Silence still.

'Fact is, I could do with an extension. Well, perhaps not an extension, sort of reduced repayment? Tricky at the moment, you see. For the time being. I know you'll understand. You know, local chap...'

'Really, we should be discussing this in the branch, Rod.'

'Well, no need for that, is there? We know one another. There's lots of ways to get business done, eh?'

The hands on the briefcase drew together.

'Better like this, man-to-man,' and his big hand gestured. 'Now, what I was thinking, Frank... reduce it... say, a third? That would be alright, would it?'

'Rod...'

'Don't want to fall behind... keep the payments up.'

He was leaning further forwards, tone inveigling.

'Rod, I can't....'

'You can see my point. Good business this. Well, you know that, you're in regular, aren't you? Things a bit slow at the moment, that's all, and I've got commitments, of course; I'm a family man. We both are. Say a third, what d'you think? Third be alright?' And he slapped his thigh as if in settlement of a deal.

'Rod... It doesn't work like that. Really, we should be having this conversation properly, in the Bank. Officially.'

Viney chuckled, a hollow sort of sound as if attempting to laugh off an absurdity.

'Really, we should...' Bird clasped at his briefcase handle. 'It's a contract.'

'Certainly, but...'

'I can't just...'

'You know me, local business, good manager. Look, just a third off – for now. Just for the time being.'

Bird heaved a sigh, so deep she saw his chest rise and fall. He placed the briefcase firmly on the floor by his feet and released the fold of scarf about his throat.

'Look, Rod. These things are fixed. They don't work that way. It's a contract, you signed it. You knew what you were committing to.'

Silence now from her father and he sat back, drawing both hands between his knees, rubbing the palms together. She could hear the noise they made, it was sandpaper-like. The stool beneath him creaked. He breathed deeply, head dropped low, then he clapped his hands back onto his broad thighs, pulling up straight from the waist.

'Frank, it's all business. Look, I'm a good Bank customer, you know that, and you're a good customer of mine. I look after my customers, don't I? I've seen you all right, haven't I? Bottles and baccy, Christmas-time extras, something for Norma... eh? I've looked after you, haven't I?'

Bird was immobile and silent for a time.

'I treat my clientele well, it's important, good for business too. That's right, isn't it? Glad to do it; bottle or two here and there, something a bit special, not the regular like. Something for the wife, special occasions and all that. Reckon you were pleased. That's right isn't it? That's how it works.'

Maggie could hear the altered tone in his voice, coercing now. Bird resettled himself in the chair, elbows braced on the wooden arms, hands firmly clasped in front of his chest, thumbs working restlessly over the backs of his hands.

'You've been generous, Rod.'

'That was a good claret, wasn't it? Knew you'd like it, and a good price, eh? So...?'

'Rod, you put me in a difficult position.'

'Just between us... just the two of us...'

'It's not that;. I mean, I recommended you to the Bank.'

'No one need know. Just a little business between us. You know, like the extras I get you. Just a little something... to oil the wheels, like.'

There was a silence, then Bird firmly clasped the ends of the chair arms and pushed himself to standing. As he bent down to retrieve his case Maggie briefly saw his face, his jaw held rigid and expression blank.

'I'd better get back.'

'It's all okay then?' Her father rose from his stool, hitching up his trousers as he straightened. 'Good to sort things between two pals, eh? We know how to get things done. Best way.'

Bird had already turned and was walking away towards the door, the part of him that was visible from the stairs diminishing with each step.

'I'll see you, then.' Her father's tone was bright, imposing. She could tell that he was standing by the door, holding it open, the chill air from the street sucked inwards. Bird went through without further comment and the door closed behind him. She heard her father make a noise in the back of his throat, the kind that says, 'so that's that, then'; self-satisfied and mocking.

In the silence that was left she held herself still, although her back, which was pressed hard against the terracotta-coloured Lincrusta wall, was sore and she longed to stretch out her numbed legs. A loud click behind and above, and a shaft of light that obliquely filtered down onto the stairs, told her that the latch-and-brace door from the family's lounge above had been opened and there was no time to pretend she was simply on her way down. Briefly silhouetted and bending forwards, her mother stood at the top, vacuum cleaner in hand.

'Maggie, what are you doing there?' she called, stepping down, crab-like, one step at a time towards her.

The grey light from the bar was abruptly blocked; he was standing in the open doorway below.

'What're you doing?' he growled. 'What're you up to! When did you get there?'

'I was just coming down,' and Maggie scrambled to her feet, bounding down the remaining treads. Viney stood, hands on hips, assured now. He looked up at Lois as she too emerged from the dingy stairway.

'What's she up to?'

Lois placed the vacuum cleaner on the floor. 'Nothing, I'm sure.' And she bent down to the socket in the skirting.

'Margaret, what were you doing there? Were you spying again?'

'No!'

He slapped her stingingly across one cheek with the thick spongy palm of his hand. The shock silenced her, sending a weakness rippling through her stomach and down into her legs.

'You better not be, young lady. I've had more than enough of your insolence, more than enough! D'you hear? Get upstairs and get them kids some tea.'

He pushed past and began his heavy ascent, voice resonant from within the confines of the stairwell.

'I'm going up to sleep so get that hoovering finished quickly, I don't want to be disturbed. Margaret, I'd better not hear you or the kids. You got that?'

Tears of anger and humiliation pricked in Maggie's eyes but she suppressed them, even from her mother who was now wiping the ash from one of the tables. Lois glanced sideways to her daughter, rubbing vigorously at the table's sticky, beery surface. 'You shouldn't rile him, Maggie.'

Her throat was too tight to answer.

'What were you doing down there anyway? You know you shouldn't be eavesdropping.'

'I wasn't,' she breathed. She didn't want her mother to know she was upset, but of course she knew.

'And you shouldn't be down in the pub in opening hours either. You bring it on yourself, you know.' Lois paused, leaning heavily on the table, the damp cloth crumpled in one hand, looking round at Maggie over one shoulder. Her expression was both kindly and reproachful, but what could she do, thought Maggie? However sympathetic, she couldn't even look after herself.

II

Hugh's letter had arrived some weeks after the party. So long afterwards in fact, that it was already the new year and Robbie and Jonathan had begun to let the matter of the stolen money slip from their minds, both now absorbed in the new school term and reassuring routines of their daily life. Occasionally, when his eyes had alighted in the garden upon his father's shed, Robbie would visualise the money contained in the tobacco tin; how it was pushed deep under the wooden chest of drawers amongst the dust and debris, but he would quickly banish it from his mind. Even John was a mere memory, albeit one that tugged at him, nagging into his thoughts, claiming his attention although John's actual presence was remote now.

He'd begun to lose faith in Hugh's help, giving way to a reluctant belief that other issues had supplanted their problem in Hugh's mind, even though Jonathan remained confident their friend would provide a solution, reassuring his brother that they must simply wait.

Eventually Hugh's letter arrived, and by great good fortune, on a day when Robbie himself retrieved the post from the mat before it was observed by anyone else. It came in a firm, cream-coloured envelope, addressed in Hugh's hand, and enclosed two sheets of matching hammered vellum writing paper. Hugh wrote in a large well-formed script, regular but with a flourish, with a broad nib in black ink.

Dear Jonathan and Robbie,

I am sorry not to have written earlier about your difficulty that we talked about at Caroline's party, but I have been giving it serious thought. Meanwhile a busy period at work, and of course Christmas, has kept me fully occupied. I trust you have both enjoyed the holidays and that you and your family are well?

After some reflection, I believe that the issue is straightforward. It came from the villagers and so should be returned there. As far as I can see, the simplest way is by means of the Church which collects money from the Parish. Perhaps the collection box? I'm sure there is one, most Churches seem to. Certainly ours here does. That way it will not be possible to trace its source but you can be sure that it will be spent in such a way as to benefit the villagers to whom it belonged.

I know you are sensible and resourceful and will find a way.

Whenever you are at Aston Haddon visiting your relations, as I believe you do on occasions, I would be pleased to see you both again at the airfield. In the event that your parents are concerned that you have received an unexpected letter, you can tell them that I have written to make you this offer. As you know I am often there on a Friday, whenever my work permits.

Well, I must get on, but I hope that this suggestion is helpful in your dilemma. I know you will act for the best.
Be assured of my best wishes to you both,
Kind Regards

Hugh

They'd acted swiftly, seizing a moment while their father was at work, their mother at the shops and their sister visiting friends. The brothers walked briskly but unobtrusively across The Green, passed quickly along Church Lane, unnoticed by those bustling in and out of the Bakers' shop, and then passed silently through the lych gate to traverse the empty Churchyard before slipping into St Mary's Church.

III

Nid was crouched over the small desk in the bedroom he shared with Finch, fingers coiled in his hair, a small frown betraying deep concentration.

'Oh, c'mon,' wailed Finch who lay upon his bed, hands alternately behind his head and then thrown down upon the eiderdown with a thwack. 'I'm bored!' He drew the word out to its longest extent to emphasise the point. 'I want to go...!' Another thwack, and this one made the bedsprings ring.

Nid grunted and pressed his pencil ever deeper into the paper but did not look up. His brother let out a low wail through clenched teeth and Nid hunched his shoulders to his ears, resisting the entreaties, blocking out the intrusion.

‘I’ll go on my own, then.’ Finch had raised himself and was sitting on the side of his bed now, staring at the back of his brother’s head, watching those twirling fingers, the soft blond hair wrapped and then unwrapped, pulled taught and then springing back. ‘I'm going then.’

Nid let out a sigh.

‘Right, I’m going!’

Finch paused for a reaction, but there was none. He rose slowly from the bed, continuing to stare at his brother’s back, hearing the scratch and swish of the pencil on paper until, reaching the door, he pulled it open and silently left the room. Only then did Nid look round into the empty space that was left.

Norma insisted that Finch wear his hat and gloves and she fully fastened the toggles of his duffle coat, even though he was ten and a half, and well past that kind of cosseting. Immediately he reached The Green he pulled them open again and ran towards the top, for no reason other than to gain the view out over the lower part of the village. It was already mid-morning, and anyone who was intending to be out would already have left home, so he took the path onto the hill near the Baker’s shop, up towards Snake Pond and went in search of the Bradbury brothers. A chill wind buffeted the bare branches of the trees, and chased small ripples across the pond’s blank surface which reflected back the grey sky. He sent a few stones skidding across the water and cheered himself noisily for his efforts, but it all felt rather meaningless without his brother’s presence. Nid would always insist his own throw was the best; he always reckoned he was the best, did Nid, even though he appeared to take little pleasure in it when he was. Finch wasn’t like that, he’d brag to everyone.

Today there was no one to see and not a soul to tell. A strong gust clattered the tall branches of the encircling trees and scattered the reflections on the pond’s surface.

All of a sudden Finch felt he wasn’t having fun here anymore and returned by the path to Church Lane. As he stepped out into the street, far away to his left, he caught sight of Robbie and Jonathan.

Delighted, he hurried after them but they were walking uncharacteristically fast and he could barely keep pace. It reminded him of the day he and Nid had spent being Detectives, following their father and spying on him at work. He'd got bored that day and they'd discovered nothing; it had all been Nid's idea anyhow. Something to do with the old photograph of the boy James that his brother had found, but now he felt he could make a proper go of sleuthing. He'd show them.

He hugged the garden walls of the cottages, stooping down low, and observed Robbie and Jonathan as they went through the lych gate into the Churchyard and along the path to the main entrance. Crouched inside a garden gateway Finch watched as the brothers disappeared into the Church porch. With no time to waste, he sped along the lane, through the lych gate and round to the back of the Church to the unused door where, by standing with one foot on a projecting stone in the old walls, he could peer through the large, rusted keyhole.

By luck, the brothers, were now inside the Church, standing close together by the main door which was opposite, and deep in conversation. Robbie unbuttoned his coat and drew something from his inside pocket, and then the two stood facing one another with something held between them. They were both looking down, speaking in earnest, and too quietly for Finch to make out a single word. Robbie looked Jonathan in the face and the older brother spoke and then they both looked across to the wall at one side of the main door. Robbie was holding a small package and Finch scrabbled on the stone for a better foothold, pressing his face against the old timber door, focussing his eye through the unused keyhole that was furred up with dust and debris. It was a small packet, or perhaps an envelope, in any event it was white and seemed quite light, and was clearly held easily in Robbie's hand.

They looked at one another again and drew together, peering down at the package which Robbie held, narrow edge uppermost. He unfolded the top and they both looked inside. Robbie riffled softly with his fingers within and then looked Jonathan in the face again. The older brother nodded and Robbie decisively folded the top over once more and then walked smartly to the wall. He paused a moment, looked back at Jonathan, one arm raised, and then his arm fell to his side. There was no longer a package in his hand.

Jonathan led the way out and the two brothers left the Church without speaking further, closing the main door behind them.

It couldn't have been better, Finch felt. He'd wanted something exciting to happen and now there was no doubting he'd found it. He hurried to the corner of the building and looked round to watch his friends departing but, instead of returning by the same route, they were now walking towards him. He flung himself to the ground and rolled soldier-like towards the nearest gravestone. He must have made it in sufficient time to be out of their sight, or else the brothers were too absorbed in their own matters as neither noticed him, although they frequently cast their eyes about, and once or twice looked back over their shoulders as if to check that they were not being observed.

'But when will it be?' Jonathan was saying.

'I don't know,' his brother replied, looking down at the path and shaking his head.

'When do they look? How often? Is it only Sundays?'

'I don't know...'

'I wonder if...' But after that Finch could hear no more. He lay outstretched on his stomach watching their departing backs.

For a time he was unsure of what to do next. He could try and follow them again, catching up with them across Church Piece, but doubted he'd get near enough, unseen, to hear anything further. Or he could go into the Church and see if there were any clues in there. He decided that's what a Detective would do, and so he encircled the building in the other direction, just to ensure he wouldn't be observed from the brothers' route and then, checking about thoroughly to satisfy himself that no one was around, slipped into the porch and hauled open the heavy Church door.

He stepped down into the chill, gloomy interior and looked about, unsure why he'd thought he'd be able to find any clues. He replayed the brothers' actions in his mind and followed Robbie's movement to the wall alongside the main door. He mimicked the way Robbie had walked and he raised his arm in the same way. Beyond his own fingertips he saw the letter-box opening of the Church donations wall box.

'Geronimo!' he breathed.

The box was quite high in the wall. He found he could push his fingers in through the opening, but couldn't reach downwards inside and so he pulled a chair across and clambered up. Now he was able to squeeze three fingers in. At first he felt nothing but then, by waggling his fingers about, his fingertips brushed against stiff paper that felt like the edge of an envelope.

A table displaying Parish Newsletters, leaflets on the Church's history and other community and parish matters, lay beyond the Church door. He hurried to it, frantically running his hand over the various items spread upon it, pushing piles to one side, searching for something that might reach into the box. Hanging from a string, and attached to a pin which was pressed into the side of a wooden cupboard alongside, he found it: a pair of scissors.

He wrenched out the pin and dashed back. By juggling with one blade of the scissors, which he was able to thrust downwards though the opening, he was able to grip a corner of the envelope and, holding his breath, drew it to the top just enough to seize it with his fingertips and pull it out. It looked exactly the right size and thickness to be whatever Robbie had put in there. Now that he held it in his hands, Finch felt both deep satisfaction and curiosity, but also some uncertainty.

He slumped down onto the chair and turned the envelope about, feeling its thickness, weighing it in his hand, and finally tossing it from one to the other, ruminating. He hummed to himself. He felt pleased. Not even his brother had had a hand in this discovery, it was his alone.

The envelope had been sealed but, as Finch ran his finger along the flap, he realised the glue had not yet fully dried. He used one fingernail to ease under the edge and then, almost without thinking, began to tease at the edges, drawing them slowly apart. The paper tore slightly but mostly he was able to pull the flap free without much damage, sufficient to open one corner and peer inside at the contents. He caught his breath as he recognised the crisp edges of paper money; at least a dozen notes. Finch whistled to himself, running the fat of his thumb across their edges, recognising their distinctive dry smell.

Suddenly he became aware of his surroundings. He was sitting he realised, in the village Church where anyone might enter at any time, holding in his hand a small fortune in paper money. Hurriedly, he folded the envelope over so that it was small enough to stuff into his duffle coat pocket and then he carefully replaced the chair and scissors. The pin that had held the scissors was nowhere to be found so he pushed them discretely below a pile of Parish Newsletters. He looked anxiously around him once more to check that all was as he had found it, and realised he'd walked mud from the pond path across the stone floor, so he grabbed a footstall and used its tapestry top – which read 'St Mary's Church, Moreton Steyning', along with a motif of ivy – to remove the worst of it. He felt pleased with himself; that's something he felt only a proper Detective would have thought of.

With a final pat on his pocket to ensure the envelope was safely stashed, he stealthily pulled open the Church door, checking carefully from the porch that no one was in view, and hurried away, remembering to take the quiet route homewards across Church Piece, just as the Bradbury brothers had done.

He'd scarcely begun to wonder what he'd do with his new-found knowledge and wealth. Perhaps relate his adventures to Nid, or maybe challenge the Bradburys, or even secrete the money where only he knew, in order to one day spend it. Now he began to turn these things over in his mind as he toiled along the muddy path. What would Nid say, he wondered, and tried to picture his brother's astonished expression, miming to himself how he'd relate the discovery and skilful retrieval of the hoard.

A final stile from the fields led into Back Lane, a short narrow street of cottages and former agricultural buildings. Off the lane to the right lay the entrance to a long, irregularly-shaped yard which extended behind some of the houses fronting The Green, and led eventually to the rear of the Baker's shop and its flour warehouse. Beside the lane were the former stables and now-unused premises of a Saddler and harness-maker which formed part of a ramshackle arch over the yard entrance. The village youngsters often wandered in for games, although more often than not, they'd be ushered out again by the Baker if they were ever found in there.

Today Finch wasn't tempted, he had more pressing business. He passed by on that side of the lane, alongside the tumbledown Saddlers' workshop with its greyed wooden doors and broken windows. Suddenly, and without warning, he was yanked backwards by the hood of his duffle coat so that his heels scraped along the ground, and then he was spun around like a puppet twirling on its strings. With arms pulled helplessly upwards by his dislodged coat which now covered his face, he could see nothing and was thoroughly disorientated. Raucous laughter and shouts resounded in his ears. Struggling, he kicked out but that only made the laughing all the louder and the shouting more ugly.

Someone said, 'Look what I've found!' and he felt himself lifted from his feet and manhandled some distance before being flung backwards against a brick wall with a force that knocked the air from his lungs.

Malcolm Draycott's older brother held him there by the neck of his coat, his broad blotchy-red face leering scathingly into his own, before turning to enjoy the amusement of his associates. Finch wriggled and tried again to kick out, but someone grabbed at his wrist and, turning, he saw Squinter Brazell lunge forwards and begin to pull at his coat pocket.

IV

Nid settled himself on the piano stool and lightly lay his outstretched fingers upon the keys. He paused and then, with a slight movement of his upper body, began to play from the music before him, a long practice piece set by Mrs Sim, who taught pianoforte to children and visited weekly to school the Bird brothers. He knew the piece well. He'd worked on it since New Year and solidly and accurately began to play it through. It had three distinct sections: a lyrical introduction, slow and fluid (Mrs Sim called it *flowing* and *full of expression*), followed by a stirring, rhythmical central passage (*powerful, feel the strength, Nigel*), and finally a sequence that Mrs Sim termed *redemptive* (about *finding yourself*, she said), which returned to some of the themes of the introduction and then worked them to a moving and satisfying finale.

It took Nid some ten minutes to play the music all the way through and he performed it with scarcely a mistake, correctly registering the changes of tempo and 'feel' of the music that Mrs Sim was so fond of. As he'd reached the rousing central theme, the piano notes ringing out in the empty living room, his mother had come to the door and peered round, encouraging smile upon her face.

He finished, sitting back on the stool with palms resting upon his thighs and looked down onto the backs of his hands, breathing softly. He liked the piece, well he supposed he liked it, and Mrs Sim had praised him: 'Very good, Nigel. It's a challenging piece and you've mastered it well.' His mother came into the room, dropping a newspaper onto the seat of his father's armchair in readiness for Frank's return that evening.

'That was very good, darling,' she said. 'What a lovely tune,' and she smiled at him again, encouragingly, 'Keep it up,' this added briskly as she left the room, her skirt swishing against the door frame. Nid heard her mules clip-clopping along the hall, back to the kitchen.

He sat there for a time and then mechanically executed a few scales and fingering exercises. From the kitchen she called again, ‘Practise makes perfect!’

His hands came to a rest on the smooth, pale keys. He stared down at his small, clean fingers with their tightly-chewed nails. Then he turned the pages of the music on the stand in front of him to a new piece, specially picked for him by Mrs Sim. It was to prepare him for his piano exams. ‘Very good, Nigel,’ she’d said, ‘You’re making excellent progress, you’re already well ahead of the other children. Make sure you keep up with your practise.’

He began to play again. ‘Is that a new piece?’ called Norma. This was a song with a melodic refrain and Mrs Sim often sang along when it came to that part, softly forming the words, swaying slightly, turning the page for him at the appropriate part. ‘Lovely piece, that,’ she often said.

It was known that Nid was ‘good at music’, a capable boy who was studious at his lessons, who applied himself, who worked hard, who had talent. Even his father, who was never known to play music himself (his mother sometimes picked out a tune, one handed), or to select music to listen to as a pastime, ‘knew’ that his son, his half-twin was ‘good at music’ and a ‘good scholar’. Nid had heard it said often. His teachers remarked that he achieved well, that he was ‘promising’, whatever that meant. What was it that he promised? Promised to go to Grammar School, promised to pass his piano exams. Promised to work, to apply himself, to study, to achieve; his success all planned for him.

He played the refrain of the song that his teacher called ‘lovely’. It was he felt, a collection of notes, one after the other, and he faithfully rendered the dots and lines on the sheet music into pressure upon the white and black keys beneath his fingers. He heard the sounds that his teacher called ‘lovely’, ‘flowing’, ‘stirring’, ‘redemptive’ (what did that mean?). He knew by the way Mrs Sim swayed and sang, by the way his mother smiled and his father nodded approvingly – which in other circumstances was rare – that they felt something; that the notes, inflections and rhythms conveyed something to them which moved or pleased them. But it all meant nothing to him, it swirled about him, but at its core was a blank hole.

Almost daily he went through the motions of representing emotions, of conveying deep feelings and meanings through music, but he felt nothing at all himself. He was, he felt, a complete phoney; a faker, discontent and restless, cheating them all.

***

The back door banged and Nid heard his mother call, 'Feet!' A few seconds later Finch burst into the living room, breathless and flushed.

'Quick! I've got to show you something,' he hissed, gesticulating frantically as he rushed away upstairs.

By the time Nid had reached their bedroom, Finch had discarded his duffle coat and flung himself down onto the bed, clearly agitated.

'What is it?' demanded Nid, but the answer was in front of him: Finch held out a crumpled envelope, stuffed with paper money.

The two brothers stared at one another. 'What's that?' demanded Nid.

'It's money.'

'I know that! Where did you get it?'

'I found it.'

'Found it!'

Finch sat up sharply, 'Shhh! Mum'll hear.'

'What're you doing with it? Give it here,' and Nid snatched the envelope away, fingering the tops of the notes, roughly calculating the value. He stared, shocked and accusing at Finch who gazed back, all excitement spent. 'Where'd you get it?' Nid repeated. He knew he sounded like their father.

'I reckon it's the treasure.'

'What treasure?' Nid snapped back brusquely, impatient and alarmed in equal measure.

'John's treasure. You know, that he buried.'

'Why?'

'Because Robbie and Jonathan had it. I saw them. I saw them put it in the money box in the Church.'

'How did you get it?'

'I pulled it out again,' and Finch sat back, arms folded across his chest, with a look of achievement.

'Why?'

'Because they were trying not to be seen and I wanted to know!' It was Finch's turn now to be shushed by Nid. 'I could see they were up to something and I followed them,' he continued in a loud whisper. 'It's the dance money, isn't it? That John stole. It is, isn't it? I reckon it is.'

'But why didn't you leave it there? It's nothing to do with you.'

'Because I wanted to know what it was, stupid! Anyway, I didn't know what they were doing until I got it out. They must have found it up on the hill and kept it quiet, or else they knew all along. What d'you think?'

Nid flung his arms upwards, theatrically.

'We can't leave it lying around here, Mum or Dad might find it.' He looked anxiously about, then turned on his brother. 'You've got to take it back.'

'I can't! Anyway, I want to ask Robbie about it... Hey, it's a big secret, right? We've got a right to know about it. I'm gonna ask him; he'll have to tell us now.'

'It's dangerous. You idiot! You can't hang onto all that money. Suppose someone sees it?'

Finch paused, when his brother was like this he was almost as bad as their father. He took a deep breath.

'The Draycotts and all them, they nearly got it.'

'What! How?' Nid rushed at him and stood leaning over so that Finch instinctively recoiled back onto the bed, bringing his legs up.

'They jumped on me at the Mill Yard,' he said.

'Did they see it?' Nid was kneeling alongside the bed, impeaching. 'What happened?'

'They pulled me into the yard. Look!' Finch pulled up his cuff to show the red marks on one wrist. He spat onto his hand and rubbed vigorously at them. 'Derek Draycott dragged me and pushed me against the wall.'

'What did you do?'

'I kicked him!'

'Yeah, and I bet he kicked you back. Who else was there?'

'Both Draycotts, Squinter and Jack Duckett.'

Nid sat back onto his heels, reflecting. Being caught alone by them was risky under any circumstances. With a pocket full of stolen money, the consequences could have been bad; very bad.

'Anyway, they didn't get it, did they? They shoved me about though. Brazell put his hand in my other pocket but I got away from him. Duckett gave me a thump too...'

'They could've got the money, don't you realise? As easy as anything.'

'I know!'

'What then? You could've been in real trouble.'

'Anyway, they didn't.' Finch knew the reality of this. He'd been reflecting on it all the way home, abruptly sobered by the narrow escape after his triumph of retrieving the stash.

V

Grandpa Rose had taken to searching. Endlessly he peered into cupboards, chasing the thought that had taken him there and which had now slipped beyond reach, leaving him bewildered, held in a moment of purpose forever lost. At such times he would pause from his restless searches and stand with a look of puzzlement, baffled by his own confusion and disorientation.

Lizzie saw these episodes and sought to help by offering to retrieve whatever was lost; perhaps some matches or tobacco for his pipe, or the newspaper, a pencil, or some sweets or biscuits (he had a sweet tooth), but Grandpa couldn't tell her what it was he sought and would shrug mutely, or laugh, or merely grimace with agitation, uncertain what it was that now unsettled him. His eyes would roam and then he would turn and soundlessly shuffle from the room only to resume his quest elsewhere.

She watched him go, wanting to chat with him like they used to, talking nonsense and laughing together conspiratorially. Grandpa was always her friend and ally, but his gaze now told her that he wouldn't respond, wouldn't give her sweets from his pockets or slip spending money into her palm or recite silly rhymes from his own childhood. So she went in search of friends for company and amusement. Robbie was away that day, visiting family, so she went to find Maggie who, while not offering Robbie's easy companionship, could be relied on for diversion and entertainment.

The Horse & Hounds yard was empty but the door to the upstairs flat hung open and, hearing muffled noises from above, Lizzie entered and began to ascend. Only greyish light from the opaque glass panel in the door at the top illuminated the steep staircase but the door was slightly ajar. She pushed softly so that it swung slowly to reveal the hallway within, and was taken aback by the sight of Maggie standing stiffly against the opposite wall. Her head was turned away and she was gazing watchfully to her left, along the hall. She must have heard the slight creak of the hinge, or else she perceived movement for, although she was clearly deeply absorbed in whatever she was observing, she glanced sharply towards the door. As she did, Lizzie caught upon her face a look of haunted tension.

Maggie snatched her face away and then immediately looked back to Lizzie, her expression now angry and bearing a deep frown.

'What d'you want?'

She hadn't expected this form of welcome, not even from the forthright Maggie.

'I was looking for you...'

There was a pause, during which Maggie showed no reaction but continued her vigil, her gaze hard and focussed, looking down the long dark corridor. Lizzie realised that she was alert and listening, her body held rigid, fists tight in the small of her back against the wall, face taut.

'What is it?' she asked in a soft whisper.

'Shhh!' Maggie darted a look back at her which was full of hurtful antagonism. It was as if she was blaming Lizzie merely for being there.

She couldn't help herself and breathed 'sorry', but Maggie didn't turn and appeared not to have heard, or even to care what she might think or say.

A sudden noise from down the hall made her jump and even Maggie flinched. Then a door opened and Rod Viney burst through. He moved with such speed and purpose that he was oblivious to their presence; yanking open the kitchen door at the far end so forcefully that it juddered on its hinges. It revealed the silent interior where Lois was standing, her arms braced, leaning against the kitchen sink. She was turned away from them so that her face was not visible but her body hung loose, like something deflated.

Viney flung something onto the kitchen table and shouted. The sudden boom of his angry voice so shocked Lizzie that she felt herself start, and the lingering fright left her unable to even recognise the words that he then spoke. He took hold of Lois's shoulder and wrenched her round, at the same time thrusting her backwards, her body limply complying, while the other hand swung forwards and struck her across the cheek with a loud crack so that her head jerked back.

'Get out!' hissed Maggie tersely, and Lizzie realised she was being manhandled to the top of the stairs and pushed over the top step, in danger of losing her balance and tumbling. With trembling legs she fled downwards, stopping only when she found herself out in the brightness of the yard. The shock was still reverberating inside her and she felt a sickness down in her stomach, but was astonished to see that Maggie had followed and was now standing behind her.

'Quick,' she commanded, and ushered Lizzie to the cover of the sheds.

She obeyed without demur, but once safely inside in the enveloping gloom, she turned to her friend. Maggie stood where the light from the doorway fell upon one side of her face. The haunted look had faded, but had been replaced by an expression of resolve and bitterness. On one temple there was a dark swelling and her forearm bore the red marks of large fingers.

'What're you staring at?' Maggie snapped.

Lizzie recoiled, confused by the feelings of guilt churning within her at the brutishness she'd just witnessed.

'Nothing...' she whispered, but Maggie aggressively challenged her back.

'What?'

'Only...' But she didn't know what to say, and simply gestured aimlessly with one arm.

'It's none of your business!' and Maggie turned away, scrutinising the empty yard, as if in search of something.

'Did he hit you too?'

Maggie remained motionless, looking steadfastly away. It seemed that she would again ignore Lizzie, but then she shrugged with an abrupt jerk of her shoulders as if she were shaking something away and rubbed briskly at her forearm, glancing down at the imprint of a vicious grip. She made no proper reply but, eventually, abstractedly murmured, 'Mmm,' in acknowledgement.

'What was it all about, Maggie? Does he do that a lot?'

Maggie turned sharply and accusingly, but then her look softened a little and she seemed to reflect for a while; finally she seated herself on one of the logs. With relief, Lizzie followed suit, settling herself opposite. The other girl's face bore a harsh expression and there was a wild look still in her eyes.

'Bastard,' she muttered, 'Bleeding, bleeding bastard,' and she rubbed her hand vigorously in her hair as if to dispel the awfulness.

'Where're the others... your brother, the little ones?'

Maggie gave a brief, humourless laugh. 'Stephen? He keeps clear you won't find him around. He looks out for number one. The others're hiding. I pushed them in the bedroom.' She'd placed her elbows on her knees and now sank her chin into her cupped hands, eyes cautiously surveying Lizzie.

'What was it about? Why's your Dad so angry?'

'Because he's a bastard,' and abruptly she kicked out at a shovel that stood propped up, so that it clattered noisily to the tiles. 'I hate him,' she said with cold loathing. 'I hate him.'

VI

The truck had the same smell always; sawdust and dustsheets, linseed oil and wood shavings, a dusty, resinous mix that stayed with Ann long into adulthood, so that even a newly-puttied window would evoke memories of its comforting, cramped clutter. It was cream, or once had been, the back now rusted and chipped through daily use, but *'S. G. Dewberry, Carpenter'* still adorned the cabin doors, neatly sign-written in florid maroon script.

Her father's heels had worn the mat smooth and thin by the constant scoring from his feet on the pedals, revealing through flimsy holes the metal floor beneath. Sweet wrappers, lists, notes and receipts all littered the cubby and door pockets, tucked behind the visor and beneath the hand brake, spilling out to join the pencils that rolled about on the floor whenever he heaved the truck into a corner, leaning elaborately to help it round, pencil stub behind one ear, winking across to her with a conspiratorial grin. All the while, in the back, the saw horses, canvas bag and boxes of tools, levels, clamps, saws and jigs all jumped and clattered, for ever sentinel to his arrival and departure.

The truck was set high off the road. To clamber in, Ann had first to place one foot on the plate and then give a little hop until she could clutch at the door handle before swinging herself into the cabin interior, bouncing onto the worn and sagging passenger seat, the leather delightfully sun-warmed against the backs of her legs.

'There you go,' her father would say and, leaning low across her, smelling of hair oil and sweat and dusty work clothes, he'd heave the passenger door closed. Then they were in there together, just the two of them, sitting side by side in the small cabin; the outside world shut out, surrounded by the detritus of his daily activities, testimony to the hours he spent away from them whenever he drove off. The truck would clatter out over the cobbles, everything jangling and clanging in the back. '*S. G. Dewberry*': Sidney George. George after his father, a carpenter too. '*Carpenter*' – but also a father; and a husband. It didn't say that on the side.

Sid winked at Ann as he leaned the truck to the left, steering round the Horse & Hounds corner, his shoulder almost touching her head. 'Help her round,' he'd say and she'd lean too, the both of them laughing. It was a joke they shared, their little game. The pencils all chased one another across the floor, lining up against the curling mat, and a toffee plopped from the shelf below the steering wheel onto the floor. He reached down to retrieve it and tucked it behind her ear. 'How'd that get there!' he'd joked. Just the two of them: father and daughter, his proper daughter, as her mother said.

It was an all-too-brief time together that morning. Sid yanked the truck to a halt alongside Wheelwrights' yard entrance, snatching on the handbrake and stepping out before opening the heavy passenger door for her. He was already leaning into the back, pushing tools around and selecting what he wanted by the time Ann had jumped down. She waited, in no hurry to find Lizzie, listening to him rummaging in the back, his muscles and shoulders stretched smooth beneath the check shirt.

From along the street, several bicycles swept past, their riders unseen behind the high side of the truck. With a sudden explosion of sound that sent her heart pounding, they banged their fists against the metal panels so hard that Ann jumped with fright. A raucous voice yelled 'How's yer sister!' and she turned sharply to see the riders speeding away, their knees splayed wide, while twisting round in their saddles to look back over their shoulders; faces pinched with spiteful laughter.

She recognised Malcolm Draycott, Neville Potter, Jack Duckett and Squinter Brazell and watched them, bewildered, trying to calm her breathing and not reveal her fright. Her father was staring after them too, but he showed no reaction.

Joe and Ted Rose had emerged from the yard in their working overalls, but they seemed not to have noticed the incident and, after an exchange of greetings, Sid lifted some tools they were borrowing from the truck while Ted loaded in several lengths of timber. Lizzie and her mother meanwhile, came from the house and joined the small group. The adults went on to briefly converse.

'You're looking very nice today, Sarah,' Sid Dewberry had said, smiling his boyish smile to Lizzie's mother who, going into Cullingham, wore her Spring coat and a felt beret. She lightly laughed away the compliment, although it was clear it had given pleasure.

When he left, leaning across to the passenger window from inside the cabin, Sid gave a cheery wave with an outstretched hand, fingers spread wide, smiling. Pushing his cap back on his forehead, revealing a peak of light brown hair, he swung the truck back out into the road, not leaning this time.

Lizzie and Ann watched it drive away along Main Street until it was no longer in view and then followed the Rose brothers into Wheelwrights' yard.

'He's a charmer, that one,' Joe was saying as the two men stepped through the open door and into the workshop.

'You don't learn his ways in charm school,' Ted replied, dryly.

The girls at first stayed in the yard. It was a pleasant April morning and they were in no hurry to go indoors.

'Who was that yelling?' Lizzie had asked.

'Malcolm and Neville and some of the others.'

'Who were they shouting at?'

Ann shrugged. She didn't know, but their voices still boomed in her head, echo after echo; the shock of the unexpected sound from their harsh blows on the truck, making her start each time anew.

They went to Swallow's in search of the others but, once in St Mary's Churchyard, they found no one around. Instead they made themselves comfortable in a hollow amongst the soft tussocks below the stone tomb, their legs stretched out amongst the brass-yellow dandelions which studded the lush spring grass. Lizzie related how her Grandpa now spent his time watching his sons at work or else Lizzie's mother in the kitchen, when he wasn't stretched on the settee asleep, snoring softly. For hours he'd brush his thumbs and fingers softly over one another, perpetual and restless, his mouth working quietly, sounding their tasks; 'Rubbing it down, that's it, soft now, with the grain. Feel it... Put the pan on, light it, shake it about, careful now... Follow the line, watch it now, bow saw, straight now, that's the way...'

His sons largely ignored him, having grown used to his constant presence, tolerating the benign intensity of his watchfulness, his ever-vigilant, soft steps always behind them.

He was attentive as Lizzie's mother made the beds, or cleaned and tidied; quietly explaining, reminding, directing. She would step back into him while she cooked, exasperated to discover him two steps behind her at the cooker, crying, 'Father!' as she juggled with hot pans that she fought to avoid spilling. Whenever he saw Lizzie, he'd laugh and whistle.

They heard the familiar squeal of the Churchyard gate's hinge, but it was some time before a figure came into view; a man, clearly elderly from the slowness of his gait and the way that he stooped. He wore a long dark overcoat with a heavy cap and walked with an ungainly lurch, one foot scraping the ground as it drew forwards with each lumbering step. They watched with interest as he progressed awkwardly along one of the paths before turning to pass, some yards away, between the rows of headstones. He hadn't seen them, and Lizzie and Ann shrugged to one another their ignorance of his identity.

At another junction of paths he turned, now moving away. From their position beneath Swallow's, the old man's sagging head made it appear that his cap lay directly on his stooped shoulders. In one hand he carried a cloth bag, but it hung seemingly empty. Curiosity stirred, they rose and edged forwards, their advance concealed by headstones, slipping from one to the next, crouched down and then peering cautiously round.

Ahead he'd stopped, bent yet lower, and was scratching at one of the headstones with a long yellowed fingernail. From deep in his chest he produced a rumbling phlegm-thick cough. Ann glanced over to Lizzie and she pulled an expression of distaste. Then he pulled something from his bag, which appeared to be a handful of limp weeds, and he scattered these across the uneven ground in front of the headstone.

Then he turned towards them as if he'd heard a sound. There stretched across his temple and cheek a blood-red spider clung. As one, Lizzie and Ann recoiled in horror and fell back from view below the headstones.

From the man's throat rose another thick growling noise, and then they heard the crunch and scrape of his tread; they peered cautiously round to see that he was now moving away towards the further Churchyard gate. A short time after that he slipped from their sight and then they heard the gate out to the lane open and close with a sharp clang.

Later, Ann left Lizzie, who was going on to the pond in further search of Robbie, while she made her way back homewards through Church Piece to the bottom of The Green. Once alone, the ugly shouts of the youths resounded again within her head and she wrapped her arms across her chest for comfort, hugging herself reassuringly, holding the fright down and inwards. Removed from Lizzie's happy chatter, she was glad that the fields below the Church were small and could be swiftly crossed so that she would not be alone in their expanse for long but, as she mounted the second-most stile, she realised that the field before her wasn't empty. A short way ahead, close to the path, a dark stooping figure was bent over, tugging up handfuls of herbage which he was stuffing into a bag. As she dropped from the stile to the ground, the figure turned and she recognised the elderly man from the Churchyard. Her stomach tightened and legs stiffened. She hesitated, undecided by turn whether to flee or to walk on as if all was normal.

It was clear the man had noticed her. He straightened up as far as his misshapen back permitted, and was now observing her. The spider on the side of his face was turned away, which gave her some courage. Fearing the panic would overwhelm her if she acknowledged the dread to herself, Ann resolved to walk briskly forwards, keeping to the path and a little to one side of him. She didn't look at him directly, but kept him in the periphery of her vision; in the very corner of her eyes, sensitive to any movement he might make as she approached.

He was watching. At first she walked slowly, but then gathered pace as she drew closer, ready to break into a trot to pass him by as quickly as possible. But then he raised his arm, the one that held onto the bag, now bulging with weeds, as if he were hailing her, and he called out, 'Hello my moppet,' in a voice that was dry and cracked.

Fearing to show outright rudeness, Ann hesitated, her breathing quick and shallow with alarm.

'Hello, little moppet,' he croaked again. 'I know 'e, don't I?' The tone was friendly and beseeching, and he seemed both surprised and puzzled. 'Don't I know 'e?'

She froze, lost for what to say and too fearful to speak. She finally breathed a denial and broke into a blind run, not looking back until she was half way along Back Lane, and The Green was safely in sight just ahead.

VII

Word of money donated to the Church in curious circumstances, moved quickly through the village. While many attributed the gift to a generous benefactor there were those who were guardedly suspicious, and many who simply thought little of it, one way or the other.

It was some weeks after the event that the Vicar called on the Bird household, his dark shape an unexpected silhouette visible through the front door pane, bobbing and shuffling restlessly on the doorstep. The brothers, at play on The Green, had watched with casual curiosity as he'd turned into their front path to stand with hands behind his back, one cupped within the other palm, gently slapping time.

They'd watched as their mother had come to the door with a vague and slightly perplexed smile upon her face, and then she'd slipped back inside to be replaced by their father who'd stood stiffly, nodding occasionally before stepping to one side and, with a cautious glance out onto the street, permitted the Vicar to enter.

It was unusual since the Vicar, while a common sight around the village, was not a regular visitor to their house. In fact, neither brother could ever remember his calling on them, except once or twice to deliver a leaflet asking for donations for the Church bring-and-buy sales, or some such. They watched the house but its blank exterior gave no clue as to the business within, and shortly they grew tired of the matter, choosing to involve themselves in football with other boys who'd drifted out onto The Green.

It wasn't until they'd returned for their tea in the kitchen that they learned the purpose of the visit. Their mother's eyes were watchful, and their father a distant presence in the front living room, identified only by the remote rustle of the newspaper pages as they were turned or shaken smooth, and a gruff clearing of the throat. As they'd finished their tea Norma had slipped quietly from the kitchen, then when she returned they heard their father's voice summoning, 'Andrew'.

The twins exchanged looks. Neither was aware of any misdemeanour. Finch looked questioningly to his mother, but her expression was firm and she merely indicated the route to the living room with her eyes. Then Frank called again, 'Nigel, you come too.'

Their father was seated in his armchair, the newspaper now roughly folded on his knees, steadied by one hand, with his palm down. The brothers entered the room, one after the other and assembled before him, observing that their mother had come to the doorway where she stood now, alert and a little tense as if in readiness, her hands held against the lap of her apron.

Frank cleared his throat and took up his pipe from the low table beside him.

'The Vicar came to see me today,' he began, studying the boys who gazed back, their identical expressions apprehensive but questioning. He coughed again. 'He said that he saw you, Andrew, in the church,' and he raised his eyes to look steadfastly at Finch who shuffled uneasily before glancing across to Nid. Meanwhile Nid betrayed no emotion.

'Is that right, Andrew? Did Mr Pettigrew see you in St Mary's?'

Finch was like a startled rabbit in the headlights. He was acutely aware of Nid, motionless beside him, and of his mother, silent and breathing shallowly, standing poised in the living room doorway. His heart began to pound in his chest and his thoughts raced; mostly about his retrieval of the envelope of money left by the Bradbury brothers, and of later stealing back in while Nid kept watch and dropping it back into the wall box; hearing it fall softly onto the few coins within. He looked to Nid again, and Nid's eyes briefly flicked left towards him, and then returned to gaze unfocussed towards their father.

'Andrew?'

Beside him Nid flinched and pulled at a thread from a buttonhole on his shirt-front.

'Andrew? What do you say? I'm waiting.'

'I might have gone in there sometimes... I think. Maybe. I didn't break anything!'

'No...'

'I didn't. I...'

'It's not a place to play, you know.'

The boys looked glumly down at the carpet, avoiding their father's direct look. Frank cleared his throat again.

'Mr Pettigrew has told me something and I want to hear it from you. I want to know from you what you might know, and what you've been doing. Do I make myself clear now?'

'We don't play there.' This was spoken by Nid, and all three turned to look at him. Finch's breath escaped with relief. He hadn't even realised he was holding his breath.

'Something's been reported to the Vicar, Andrew. Something that concerns you. Something that was observed. Now I want to hear it from you. Is that clear?'

'What...?'

'I want you to tell me. You too, Nigel. Anything you know.'

Frank Bird saw his two sons, his second-born boys, blond and youthful, tongue-tied and evasive, shuffling and mumbling; his half-twins, one heart-felt yet wayward, the other studious and intense. He thought, deep in his heart, of the beautiful boy who had once combined the best of both.

VIII

As he thudded down the steps to the yard, Viney almost knocked Ann from her feet. Close behind was Jim Fellowes; a swarthy, broad-faced man who ran the village garage and was a regular at the pub. The pair had emerged from the dark passage to a door that revealed the countertop of the bar, surrounded with its shelves of glasses and pipes from the cellar to the bar-top hand pumps. It was a dark, alien world, unknown to Ann who'd never been inside a pub.

Viney, who moved with remarkable ease for such a large man, took in the three downward steps and the expanse of the yard within a few brisk strides. He was moving with grim purpose and so rapidly that Fellowes, no small man himself, was obliged to break into an awkward trot to keep pace.

'Top brass is coming,' Viney flung out over his shoulder. He was flustered and puffing from his recent exertions. 'There's three. Take it now, you can sort it later.'

'I've got it on me...' Fellowes clutched at his jacket pocket, folding the material in his hand.

'Later...' Viney spoke dismissively, and the two men disappeared into one of the sheds. He reappeared almost immediately and strode back across the yard to the pub, face darkly flushed and with an expression of distraction and agitation. His lips soundlessly formed words, and all the while his thick fingers worked restlessly across the fleshy pads of his thumbs.

'Lo!' he barked.

Ann jumped back, shrinking under his momentary unseeing glance.

'Lo!' He paused, one foot on the top step, finger tips resting lightly on his hips with little fingers extended, almost effeminately. 'For Christ sake,' he muttered, exhaling with exasperation. Up above, the flat door unlatched and he heaved forwards, moving determinedly along the inner passage towards the bar without once glancing upwards. 'Get down here and clean will you, I haven't got all day.' From behind the bar came the sound of glasses and bottles hurriedly being stacked. All the while, he puffed and cursed, breathing heavily with rage and frustration.

Shortly afterwards, Ann heard the sound of a vacuum cleaner from beyond the counter. Viney paused and leaned over, resting upon one forearm.

'What the fuck have you been doing? Put the chairs back... Here, give those glasses over and empty those ashtrays. Not in the fire! Quick will you! Then sort out this lot.'

He piled a tray of glasses and bottles onto the counter, then turned and began to march back along the passage.

'They'll be here at three,' he bellowed back. 'I'm getting the accounts out. Do you hear? Do you hear! It's got to be ready by three.'

Beyond him Lois came to the counter and heaved a tray of empty glasses onto its surface, her eyes flicking up to his retreating back. She wore a faded pinny and her hair fell limply across one eye.

Viney pulled open the cellar door and clumped heavily down the concrete steps to his office. Ann stood motionless by the yard door, while down below Maggie was in her secret hiding place where, only a short time before, Ann had left her.

***

She went the long way home, round past Luff's and up the sunken footpath behind the cottages. Here, the sides of the path foamed with cow parsley and May blossom bloomed so thickly that the hedges appeared to be coated with whisked egg white.

This was Ann's world, not the harsh bright light of the pub yard or the big open skies of the hill, but this enclosed little-used path, that made its hidden way behind the gardens. She'd begun to recognise the changing patterns of growth and flowering, and the berries that followed before winter stripped everything away, although even that dark skeletal world bore a familiarity that comforted and reassured her. She let the ugly scene she'd just witnessed back at the pub gradually drift away as she slowly ambled her way towards home.

Once she'd reached the end of their garden, she turned into the narrow side path that brought her alongside the boundary wall of home, and noticed with surprise, the cream roof of her father's truck parked at an angle in the front yard. Normally he'd be out at work during the day although, on occasion, he would call by if he needed to collect something or was simply passing. He hadn't said he'd be back today, which made this unexpected return all the more pleasing. As she drew alongside the cottage she could see that the front door stood open and she guessed that he must be just arriving or leaving.

Sid emerged abruptly and hurried along the front garden path towards the truck. She could see now that the passenger door hung wide open and that he casually swung a bag onto the passenger seat.

'Why?'

The eeriness of her mother's cry stopped Ann in her tracks. Nellie stood, only partly visible, an indistinct form just inside the front door. It was a beseeching wail and it pierced Ann's heart, chilling her to the core. She'd never heard or seen her mother like that. It didn't sound like a word; more a howl of despair.

At the truck Sid didn't turn and showed no sign of having heard, or even of being aware of Nellie. There was just silence, and then she repeated her question, but more quietly this time so that it hung in the air, desolate and unanswered.

He turned and walked back to the house, but his eyes were not on her, although she stood within the front door just ahead of him. He was looking instead from side to side at the flower beds bordering the front path. He didn't break step at the door where Nellie still stood, but merely twisted sideways and walked resolutely through, so that the gloom of the hallway quickly swallowed him up.

Ann saw her mother turn, her slim body rotating so that she remained facing towards him as he breezed past, and then she too slipped deeper into the house. Ann stood motionless, trying to disentangle the harshness and anger from the pub which now came flooding back, with what she'd stumbled upon between her parents. And all the while her mother's distraught voice; *Why?*

She hastened towards the cottage, glancing across to the normally comforting familiarity of the truck, waiting as she so often had in the yard, and then trotted up the front path seeking reassurance from her parents that all was well. She didn't look from side to side like her father had, but ran straight to the front door and bounded into the safety of home, although once inside she stepped softly along the hallway as if she were trespassing.

At first there was nothing to reveal where they were within the house; there was merely a hollow and empty stillness. She strained to hear, soaking in the silence, and then came the sounds of people moving about, and finally her mother's desolate, 'You never even think!'

'Give it a rest, Nell.' Sid's response was terse.

A moment later he burst into the hall making brisk strides towards the front door, his face set with an uncompromising expression that Ann had never seen before, and which alarmed her. Only then did he notice his daughter. For a fleeting second he registered surprise, but then collected himself and quickly smiled his usual boyish grin, his eyebrows tilting, blond against the browned skin which furrowed softly about his light blue eyes.

'Twinkle. You're back early!' His easy smile was broad and puckish, wide mouth open at the corners revealing strong but slightly uneven cream-coloured teeth. A coil of his sun-bleached wavy hair spilled onto his forehead. It was the same coil that forever escaped from his cap.

From somewhere in the room behind came Nellie's counter, 'No she isn't. It's the time she has her lunch.' Her voice was unnaturally thin and tight, but she spoke in a tone that assumed proprietorial rights, of pride in responsibility, of nurturing and protection. A triangle of protection and possession.

'In you go, then,' said Sid lightly to his daughter, stepping back to allow her past.

'Are you staying for lunch, Daddy?' asked Ann.

'Your father's got to go.' Nellie only now emerged from the back room and walked quickly across the hall to the kitchen, not looking towards them. She pulled an apron from a hook behind the door and tied it about her waist, all the while turned away.

'Can't you stay...?'

'Got to go, poppet. Busy afternoon ahead, lots to do.' He ruffled her hair playfully.

In the kitchen Nellie took up a loaf and began to cut slices, her skirt jiggling as she vigorously sawed.

'Can we play ball later?'

'Not tonight.'

'Why..?'

'Because I've got to work.'

'Later tonight?' she persisted.

He gave a slight laugh, 'No, I'm working. Maybe we'll play tomorrow evening, if it's dry.'

'Will you be back?'

'No, not tonight.'

'Why?' As she spoke, her mother's tragic outburst echoed in her head.

'Come and get your lunch,' Nellie called flatly from the kitchen.

'I'm off, then,' said Sid, but Ann could tell that he spoke only for effect and anticipated no response. Her mother didn't look up and merely placed a roughly-assembled sandwich on a plate before Ann as she clambered onto a chair at the kitchen table.

'Why can't Daddy come back?'

She spoke suddenly into the silence that had settled into the room. She knew she was venturing into forbidden topics, but everything today felt wrong, and there was no longer a pattern for how things should be. Nellie scraped crumbs from the breadboard into the sink with the blade of the knife. Her eyes glanced upwards to look blankly out through the window to the garden. A potted pelargonium on the window sill, softly dropped carmine petals. She made no move to answer.

'Mum..?'

'Mmm?' Nellie murmured distractedly, as if she hadn't heard.

'Why isn't Daddy coming back tonight again?'

'He's busy.'

'Where?'

'Working.'

'Why?'

'Ann!'

Nellie let the breadboard fall noisily into its place on the work counter and then turned to face the room again. She smoothed a frown from her forehead. 'Stop asking questions, that's all,' she said and busied herself, removing lunch things from the kitchen table across to the sink. 'He's got work to do, as you very well know.'

Her mother had cut off any further enquiry on the subject and Ann fell silent. The only sound now in the kitchen was that of Nellie washing up plates.

'Who's the man with the spider on his face?' she asked after a while.

'The what!'

'Lizzie and me; we saw a man with a red spider on the side of his face... here,' and she gestured with one hand as her mother turned over her shoulder to watch. Mother and daughter surveyed one another for a few moments.

Finally, Nellie turned away. 'Where did you see him?' Her voice sounded different now, firm and inquisitorial.

'In the Churchyard, then later in Church Piece. He was gathering weeds. We saw him in the Churchyard spreading something on one of the graves. He was in Church Piece when I came home and he said he knew me.'

'When was this?'

'A few weeks ago.'

'You didn't say?' Nellie seemed to be trying to sound casual.

'I forgot. Why did he say he knows me? Who is he?'

'You forgot? He's just someone around. Leave him alone; stay away.'

'Who is he? Why's he got a spider?'

'It's a scar, from the war. Stay away from him, do you hear me?'

'Yes, but why does he go to the Churchyard, Mum?'

'Someone he knew is buried there, who was killed in the war when he was injured himself. A bomb blew up near them. He's a bit disturbed, so don't go near him.'

'But why did he say he knows me? I've never even seen him before, neither has Lizzie, and I asked Maggie and she hadn't either and Maggie knows everyone.'

'Doesn't she just. You won't have seen him because he lives the other side of Netherington. Just stay away if he comes here again, do you hear?'

IX

Mayflies, rising and falling like smuts over a bonfire, hung thick in the air; so many splats of ink against the bright June sky. Striding away ahead of the others, Finch was walking with exaggerated steps, galumphing his way through thigh-high buttercups. Their golden pollen had stained all their sandals and socks to the colour of sulphur. Robbie was behind Jonathan, following in the broad swathe formed by his brother's heavy and purposeful tread, while Nid, seeking to evade all but the most open areas, left a narrow meandering trail, like a rabbit-run through the wavering stems of golden bloom. They'd been walking for some while, skirting the lower slopes of the hill through the damp meadows, and their route now brought them across the final field.

Finch was full of enthusiasm. He had in his pocket the new Swiss Army knife that was a birthday present and was filled with a sense of optimism and hope, as indeed he often was. He now scarcely thought about the episode with the envelope of stolen money. For a time after it had happened, he'd burned with curiosity about the money's origins, about what the Bradbury brothers were doing with it and why they'd acted so covertly, but Nid had impressed upon him the importance of maintaining secrecy. At least in order not to reveal the hand he himself had played in the matter, and now he'd long since consigned the whole episode to indifference and acceptance.

If he thought about it at all, and he scarcely did, it was to assume the money had been taken by John at the dance, and which Robbie, being John's best friend, must have hidden for him. The whole matter now felt fully explained and occupied little of his thoughts or concerns.

A clamber over the final field gate brought the four of them out into the narrow lane that passed behind the Manor. Its tall stone chimneys could be glimpsed beyond a belt of mature trees away to their right. In the opposite direction the lane made its way into a shallow vale to end finally at a farmstead, which lay at such a distance that it was in the next Parish. The Manor, a large and ancient house with a massive stone porch, stood in walled grounds with neatly-kept gardens and had been the residence for many years of Colonel and Mrs Benbow. With a keen interest in village affairs, the Colonel had always made it his business to ensure that his long military experience was brought to bear in village matters, and that all events benefited from his attendance, which was, as he would assert, right and proper; by which he meant that it was his duty, and therefore his right to officiate in all matters of village importance, whether invited to or not.

On that day he was walking the couple's two small terriers, Sadie and Bella, on their regular foray along the peaceful lane. Robbie noticed them emerging from the Manor's back yard, from in between the stables and carriage buildings, and beginning to amble towards them; the two small dogs streaming endlessly about the Colonel's ankles.

Robbie had also consigned the anxiety and drama of the stolen money to the past, although from time to time he recollected how John's trust had painfully compromised him. Mostly though he looked forwards, wondering if his friend would return again that summer, and hoping that he would. As the days lengthened and the air felt warmer, he remembered, ever more vividly, the happy days that they'd spent together during those last three summers; at least he remembered them as happy. Would John come again, he wondered? And would things be just the same if he did?

The Colonel was walking briskly towards them; smartly erect, a loose cravat about his neck and a stick swinging from one arm.

'Good day to you all,' he hailed, as he drew close. 'Ah, Mr Bird's' twins,' he concluded, having surveyed the four of them. 'How's your father, well I hope? Good chap. And the Bradbury boys, isn't it? Excellent. Out for a walk, hmm? Lovely day.'

They made as much response to this as was possible, mumbling respectfully while the dogs excitedly herded them. The Colonel then leaned back and gestured over one arm with his stick, towards the Manor's stable yard.

'Fancy a bit of wood? Always handy, some wood; you can make all kinds of things. Box-cart, that sort of thing, just get some wheels, hmm? How about that? Over in the yard, hmm? See George Rowe, tell him I sent you, he'll sort it out. Bits of old pallet and packing cases, not wanted, hmm?' And with that he nodded courteously and departed on his way.

'We'd better take it as he offered,' said Nid.

'Yeah, c'mon, let's get it!' Finch was all for it and began to hurry along the lane towards the stable yard.

'How're we going to carry it?' Nid called after him, ever pedantic.

'We'll manage,' Robbie said. 'Come on!'

The wood was easily found, heaped into the open front of one of the old carriage buildings at one side of the cobbled yard. Robbie and Finch quickly began to sort through and haul out the best, tossing the pieces into a rough pile in the yard. Before long their noise and chatter brought handyman-gardener George into the yard, but he was quickly satisfied with their explanation of the Colonel's offer and even helped them sort the wood.

'Where're you going with this lot, then?' he said once they'd finished.

'Tree house,' said Finch, quick as a flash.

'Right, see that barrow? You can use it to carry the wood then bring it straight back here, mind. Off you go.' And with that he strode off, back to his work.

The loan of the large wooden barrow was of immense help. They transferred all the wood into it and then, with much pushing and huffing, the four of them manhandled the heavy old barrow up along the lane to the field gate. From there it took the rest of the day to move the wood, armful by armful, across two fields to an ancient oak. Broad and stag-headed, it provided the perfect support for a tree house, a point agreed upon by all four boys.

When finally they lay under the tree's shadow, the wood carefully stacked out of sight, under the hedge, they felt pleasingly exhausted, but satisfied with their day's efforts.

X

The ink ran smooth and even, dark as night and glossy as the Vicar's car. It streamed from the pen nib, forming the letters and shapes unbidden, and Nid let them flow, spreading like a stain that slowly seeped into the crisp white page. The elegant ellipse of the pen weighed lightly in his hand, held between thumb and forefinger, resting on his middle finger and slipping easily across the paper's surface like a skater. A present from his parents for passing his piano examination, the youngest by far to reach that stage; it marked him out, the first boy in the class at school with his own expensive fountain pen. 'Excellent work,' his father had said. 'Keep it up, Nigel.'

He let the bright gold nib describe words as they sounded in his head, rendering them onto the page where they began to have a life of their own, a world that existed outside of him, but which he could conjure up by thought alone.

A sharp crack startled him and he ran to the window. Finch stood below in the front garden, arm drawn back with a second pebble held in his hand, squinting upwards to their bedroom window. Nid heaved up the sash window and leaned out.

'We're gonna play cricket. Aren't you coming?' his brother yelled from below.

'You know you shouldn't be throwing stones at the window. Mum'll be cross if she catches you,' he chided, although as he said it, he wondered why he was reinforcing his parents' strictures as if they mattered equally to him. Finch ignored the rebuke. Shielding his eyes from the sun, he was peering up. In his other hand he held a cricket bat.

'You coming or what? We're going down the field.'

'No. Later... maybe,' said Nid.

Finch shrugged and walked off, leaving the front gate wildly swinging as he crossed The Green to where a group of boys stood waiting. Nid choked back the temptation to call down to him to shut the gate and not leave it swinging. The other boys glanced upwards to the window, and then they all turned and walked away.

Nid slid back onto his chair before the small desk in the bedroom he shared with Finch and seized the marbled chestnut brown pen again, but the moment had passed. Perhaps he should have joined the others and participated in their game, but he was restless and felt disinclined to join in with all their banter and boisterousness. For a short time he took up a book and began to read, or rather pretended to himself he was reading, but the words swam meaninglessly before his eyes and he found himself staring emptily beyond the page and into the room. He cast his eyes about but nothing took his fancy or captured his interest or curiosity, although he ached with the desire to bury himself in some activity or purpose.

Eventually he went downstairs and seated himself at the piano. It wasn't so much that he wanted to play it, but he knew that at least he could play; he had the exam certificate to say so after all, and the approbation of his parents and teacher, and it would fulfil a sense of purpose and give meaning to activity.

He began with a few scales and practice exercises and then played one or two simple songs. After that he took up the long piece that he'd recently begun to learn. He played mechanically and without pleasure. Behind him he could hear the mantle clock ticking, contrapuntal to his playing. For a while, he felt himself listening to the clock rather than the music, which he finished without satisfaction or effort.

The afternoon sun, high in the sky at that time of summer, sent a deep beam burning onto the carpet so that he could smell the warm fibres and dust. Finch would be playing with the other boys now, batting no doubt, sending the ball forever skywards, screaming, *'Six!'* and flinging himself full-length back to the wicket. They'd all be shouting and running at once, yelling instructions and encouragement, or else name-calling, 'Nit wit! Stupid berk, piss-head!'

The house was silent, save for the mantle clock that dully marked the afternoon's passing. His parents must be in the garden enjoying the sun, or perhaps gardening. He strained his ears but could hear no sound from the back. The front window sash was raised a little and a gentle breeze occasionally sucked at the net curtains and then bellied them back into the room. From time to time a voice drifted in; someone walking beside The Green, to or from the shops at the top, their voices rising then falling as they approached and then passed by. But no, it was Saturday; the Baker's would be closed by now. Visiting perhaps then, or just strolling.

Children's voices, laughing and calling, came from The Green where a group of girls was skipping and playing ball. He could make out the bright colours of their clothes through the mist of the net curtains.

His fingers began to pick out a tune, a few simple notes that rang lyrically into the stillness of the room. It was a few moments before he realised that it was Maggie's tune, the one she'd brought them to play, the notes scribbled onto a scrap of brown card.

The creak of a floorboard just beyond in the hall made him jump, and he turned with guilty haste to see his father at the door, arm outstretched, one hand clasping the door handle. Nid tried to read his expression. It was blank, but also somehow accusing.

'What's that tune you keep playing?' asked Frank, steadily surveying him.

'I don't know.' Nid's words came out quickly and defensively, although he didn't know why. His father made him feel deficient and, in some way he couldn't fathom, guilty.

'You keep playing that tune. Why is that?'

'I don't.' Nid stared unseeing at some music lying open on the stand before him.

'Don't say you don't, Nigel, when I've just said you do. I've heard you play it before. Several times. Where did you learn it?'

Nid, at a loss to understand his misdemeanour, shifted uncomfortably on the piano stool. From the kitchen he heard the sound of a kettle being filled. It seemed remote and unreal.

'I'm speaking to you and I'd like an answer, Nigel.'

'I can't remember.'

'What is it?' Norma had come to the door and now stood behind her husband, peering perplexed into the room, another pair of eyes upon Nid, who felt himself liquefy under their dual scrutiny.

'Well, Nigel?' requested Frank in a tone that invited the truth while seeming to impugn.

Norma looked from one to the other, her head held close to Frank's as she turned questioningly to him. 'What is it?' she repeated, and then, 'Oh.'

They both looked to Nid again and he fumbled his fingers over the keys, silent now.

'I'm waiting, and I shan't ask again. Nigel?'

Time seemed to slide away, like a rush of water pouring over the lip of a waterfall. Nid felt himself pulled into the current, beginning to eddy, helpless in its inexorable rush.

'Nigel!'

'Frank... please! Can't you see he's getting upset. Come on, leave it. I've put the tea on. Nigel, come into the kitchen; I'll get you a squash and a biscuit. Come along now.'

He took his refreshments upstairs, in his bedroom now warm and stuffy from the sun which blazed onto the front window panes. Outside the world was dazzling, seeming to illuminate the entire room. He went into the bathroom at the rear of the house, cool and refreshed by the shaded air outside the raised sash. He washed his hands at the basin, touching the cool white ceramic. Down below, in the garden, his parents were seated below the apple tree, a tray of tea things between them; patterned china cups with little pink roses, a matching teapot and milk jug and a small plate with digestive biscuits. His mother sat in profile, her face partly shaded by the tree while his father was obscured by its lower branches. Nid could just see his legs, stretched out. He was wearing his gardening trousers. Beside Norma was a basket full of spent flower blooms and a pair of scissors. She wore flat open-toed sandals.

'Frank, really....'

'But it's so odd. You said so yourself.'

'I know, but...'

'Why can't he just say how he knows it? That's what gets me. It's simple enough.'

'You were rather hard on him.'

'What's so hard about a simple question? If my father asked me a question, he expected an answer and I gave it, whether it was difficult or not. If I didn't answer promptly it would be the belt, but I always did. I was brought up that way. They've got to know the difference between right and wrong.'

'Of course...'

'Why won't he say? What's the matter with him!'

'Darling...'

'Give me another tea, will you?'

'Here...'

'Thanks. Don't you think it's odd? It was you that said so in the first place.'

'They pick up so many things at school and from each other. Especially at that age.'

'I shouldn't wonder it's Andrew behind this. At least Nigel's got a sense of responsibility.'

'Oh, now that's a little harsh!'

'Is it?'

A hand reached across and snatched up a biscuit and silence fell for a moment.

'You've been so wound up lately,' she said.

No reply came to this remark and Norma sipped reflectively on her tea, and then delicately placed the cup back on its saucer on the tea tray.

'What is it? Is it that loan business again? Frank?'

'Mmm?'

'Is it the loan?'

'Oh, that...'

'Is it? Something's upsetting you.'

'I wish I'd never....'

'I did say....'

'What?'

'About him. How I've never liked him.'

'It's not about liking.'

'Yes, I know, but...'

'You don't do it because you *like* someone, or don't. It's a business decision. There are factors to be taken into account.'

'I know...'

'How would you know! It's Bank business. Anyway, it all made the grade.'

'Well, there you are.'

'It's my neck on the block!'

'You said it all came up to the mark, or whatever it was for the loan, didn't you?'

'So?'

'So what have you got to reproach yourself for?'

'It was my recommendation.'

'You made it with....'

'It's irrelevant what I made it with. It's gone belly-up and I'm the one responsible.'

'Oh, I don't think so...'

'Norma, don't assume you know how things work in a Bank. You don't!'

With that he launched himself from the garden chair and strode to the flower border where he once more took up the garden fork and began to prise it vigorously into the earth.

Nid returned to the bedroom, flinching in the harsh glare of sunlight. On the small desk that he and Finch shared lay the single sheet of paper covered with his writings, the neatly formed words that had flown free from his pen like another life. His eye took in the first few words and then his hand snatched up the page and crushed it to a crumpled ball which he pressed deep into the waste bin beneath the desk, burying it under the rejected jottings and drawings idly tossed there by his brother.

His mother's voice from the stairwell brought his awareness back to the room.

'Nigel, whatever are you doing indoors on a lovely day like this? Go outside, do. Come on now! Andrew's out playing cricket, go and find him or something.'

She couldn't help herself from smoothing his fringe back from his forehead as he passed her at the bottom of the stairs, and gently patted his shoulder. Her eyes said not to worry, but her gestures of affection and apology merely deepened his anxiety.

The warm air in the front garden billowed round him and the brightness made his head hurt. The girls that had been playing earlier had left The Green, but a few adults now strolled with younger children, or were sitting out on the grass or bench. Two doors along, a woman leaned on her front gate talking to a mother who held onto a small child wearing pale blue reins. The child, a little boy, was leaning into them and had learned that, in doing so, it could swing from side to side until his mother, in sheer irritation, yanked it back onto its feet, only for him to do it again just a few moments later.

A man cycled past; the owner of the garage, and he greeted the two women with an airy wave. Opposite, Morris's Greengrocers was shut, but a small group of children had emerged from Mrs Patterson's at the corner. Nid knew them all; two of the girls were in his class at school and one he was sometimes quite friendly with. They mingled outside for a while, offering up their sweets to one other and taking bites from each other's ices, but they soon disappeared around the corner and out of sight. They were replaced by some older boys, and then by a woman with a young child. The boys, who had been scuffling, parted to allow the woman through and then they too drifted away from sight. Nid supposed they were all going to the playground behind. Perhaps his brother was there too.

Outside the Jug & Bottle to his right, the landlord's black and white cat was asleep in the road, luxuriating on its sun-warmed surface. Nid let out a small snort of amusement when a dog burst unexpectedly from a garden nearby and the two faced one another off, more in surprise than aggression before tacitly agreeing to avoid further contact.

Looking back to sweet shop, he saw a bike bearing two figures come round the corner, swinging out to avoid the young woman who had now emerged with her child and was unwrapping an ice cream for him. The child was standing, expectantly; one arm stretched up, fingers twirling impatiently. His mother, who Nid now realised was Grace Rose, had to lick the melting ice cream as it was beginning to run down her own wrist. She glanced up as the bike swept past; it sped up the lane on the far side of The Green, in front of Morris's with the rider standing on the pedals to take the incline and the passenger, a smaller figure, slumped casually on the back. He seemed an extraordinary shape, but then Nid realised that he held between them a rectangular bag. The rider he now recognised, was Robbie.

The bike came to a halt outside Violet Ward's narrow brick house, almost opposite to the Bird's, and the two boys stepped off. Robbie carefully rested his bike against the wall and the two faced one another. Clearly they were talking and Nid saw that the passenger was John Norbert.

He hesitated, undecided what to do, when a commotion nearby heralded the return of the cricketing party. His brother was amongst them, breezily waving the others off with upraised bat. He began to turn as if to return to home but then noticed the two boys opposite and broke into a run towards them. Nid watched as they all greeted one another. Their quick and animated movements showed that they were talking and laughing, taking pleasure in meeting up again after nearly a year.

Eventually, Nid pushed open the front gate, patting its top decisively as he stepped away across the dusty lane towards the three on the far side. The cat slowly stretched out towards him, pleasurably flexing her claws.

He could hear Finch's laughter and raucous remarks from half-way across The Green and then came John's unmistakeable voice, hoarse and grating, not like a child's voice at all. They were clearly swapping stories, probably trying to out-do one another.

'Wha'cha!'

It was John who saw him first, standing as he was with his back to Mrs Ward's, looking out across The Green with hands thrust deep in trouser pockets.

'I just picked him up,' said Robbie by way of explanation. He was looking pleased, almost proud. They'd all been eagerly anticipating John's return since word had got round. The stories and recollections of past escapades with him had grown with repeated retelling, and each of them now looked forward to a summer of fun and entertainment. Somehow, without John, it wouldn't have been the same.

Finch in particular was excited. He'd long-since cast from his mind the matter of the stolen money; whatever wasn't tangible had little meaning to him, and it had all slipped from his consciousness as of no further interest or relevance. Now he was breathlessly relating to John a whole string of stories and events, not all entirely true or accurate, but that was due to his eagerness and not any wish to mislead. Nid refrained from interrupting to correct his brother; he could see that would be unwanted, and instinctively knew they'd rather hear Finch's entertaining version than any truth he might contribute. Robbie was laughing, carried along with the momentum of the tales, interjecting with points of clarity or adding colour, which was itself all the more ammunition for Finch.

John was going along with it all, laughing and capering, imparting short anecdotes of his own and encouraging Finch and Robbie to ever more stories and nonsense. Standing a little apart, watching and listening, Nid was able to observe John closely. He noticed that he seemed taller than last year, although still considerably shorter than any of them, and would have been an inch or two below even Lizzie's height, although perhaps not Ann's. His face was older, but not older like his and Finch's was, not like growing up older; just older, like ageing. His skin had a tired flakiness and fell easily into creases, while his wild hair now seemed dry and matted. Encircling one arm, above the wrist, was the remains of a large sprawling bruise, like the ghost of a harsh grip.

But above all, he saw a wariness in his eyes, a kind of watchfulness that Nid hadn't seen before. He would notice it often that summer; a cool gaze, furtive and appraising.

XI

John was at the lean-to even before 9 o'clock that first morning, impatiently rapping on the glass and rattling at the handle, cupping one hand over his eyes to peer in.

'He's back,' Sally flatly remarked, nodding a directive to her younger son to open the door and put an end to the noise from without.

'I'll get it,' called Jonathan, who was on his feet. He released the rear door from its lock, letting in the sweet smell of a summer morning.

'Alright then?' remarked Sally to John, glancing up at him as he stepped hesitantly into the small rear dining room. It was less an enquiry as to how he might be, than an acknowledgement that he was now returned, and with all that that might entail.

Meanwhile he was seeing the Bradbury family engaged in their Sunday morning relaxation; Tom was silently reading the newspaper, Jonathan had just finished clearing the breakfast things and was preparing to wash up, and Robbie was browsing through a comic. Susan was still in her shortie dressing gown, standing ready to go upstairs and get herself dressed. John made a noise, but not actually a reply; he avoided speaking to adults as far as was possible, and inclined his head in a gesture of invitation for Robbie to accompany him back outside.

Once in the garden John came back to life, puffing himself up with the satisfaction of his return and the attention it garnered.

'Orright?' he began, face scrunching into a grin. 'Wha' we gonna do, goin' up on the 'ill or sommat? Where's them others, they comin'? Wha' d'ya reckon? Where we gonna go then, eh?'

'Don't mind,' Robbie said, shrugging.

He was eager to be with John but, in truth, it took a while to get used to his disruptive presence once again. There was always something slightly unsettling about his friend's unfettered waywardness, his desire to push things too far.

'Shall we go and find Lizzie?' he suggested, falling back on the reassuring calm of his childhood companion, and led the way out to the side passage.

Grandpa Rose was in the yard at Wheelwrights. He was standing by the kitchen door, looking out across the cobbles to the workshops and old stables. In his mouth his unlit pipe drooped, and both hands were sunk deep in his trouser pockets, stretching his braces so that the buttons that held them in place looked likely to spring off. He was rocking slightly on his heels, but turned sharply when he noticed the two boys come round the corner into the yard. Expressionless, he watched them approach for a moment and then snatched the pipe from his mouth.

'You fed that 'orse, Joe?'

The boys faltered and John looked to Robbie for explanation, but Robbie could only mime a puzzled face.

'Don't you give me that look, boy. You fed 'im or not?'

When Robbie looked up, he was startled to see that it was to him that Grandpa Rose's question was directed, his pale blue eyes staring, unblinkingly straight at him.

'I'm not Joe,' he began, 'He's John,' indicating his friend who stood behind him.

'What's that? Come out, boy. What're you doing back there, what're you about? You ain't been and mucked out. Look! You haven't got no muck on your shoes. Look at me when I'm talking to you, boy.'

John stepped clear of Robbie and the two stared up at the old man, confused but also a little bemused. Grandpa settled himself squarely in his heavy boots, establishing his balance somewhat uncertainly, and then jabbed with the pipe which he held gripped in one knobbly fist.

'It's an hour after first light and you ain't even started. Where've you two been? You been out round that Thomas's again? You been there I'll tan your hides, the pair of you. Don't you go lying to me telling me you've seen to that 'orse when you ain't done a thing. Look at you both!'

'It ain't 'alf light, it's after nine,' John interrupted scornfully.

'You cheeking me, Ted, and I'll 'ave you, boy, now you get in there,' and he made a lunge forwards, sweeping one arm round the yard with a wild flourish, like a drunken man attempting to signal a direction.

'I ain't Ted, I'm John!' John sneered back.

The old man's face had reddened and his eyes were staring fixed and hard upon Robbie.

'What! Joe, you get your brother and you in that stable and see to that 'orse this minute or I'll tan both your hides for you, soon as you like.' He lurched towards them, making to seize their collars, but both jumped back, easily evading his stiff and awkward movements.

'I'm John! 'e ain't Joe, I'm John. I dun told ya!' yelled John, and then muttered to Robbie, 'stupid ol' fucker.'

'What you say, boy!' Grandpa's anger had risen uncontrolled and he was shouting now.

'Silly fucker! Stupid ol' fucker!' shouted John again.

The old man took a wild swipe with one arm, his outstretched hand aimed at John's head, but the boy merely swayed effortlessly back evading the blow and Grandpa stumbled forwards, falling heavily to his knees. Across the yard the kitchen door flew open and Sarah rushed over, stooping to her father-in-law who, semi-prostrate, was on his hands and knees, breathing heavily and beginning to crawl blindly across the cobbles like a sightless old hound.

'Robbie, go in; take your friend and call Lizzie's Dad, will you. Joe! Joe!' and she shouted back across the yard for her husband who was already emerging from the house, breaking into a run.

'What's he done? Dad...!' The two of them began to try and restrain Grandpa who, still on all fours, pushed blundering against them, as if he were a draught horse straining in its harness, while they wrapped their arms around his waist calling instructions to one another. Finally, Joe Rose managed to clasp his father under both arms and haul him struggling to his feet, where he continued to stumble and blindly lash out.

'Go in, Robbie!' shouted Sarah, puffing from the exertion as she hooked her shoulders under her father-in-law's arm to bear his weight.

The two boys, silent with confusion, went into the kitchen where Lizzie stood, her face small and anxious, peering through the open door to observe the commotion beyond.

'Grandpa thought you were my Dad and Uncle Ted,' she said.

***

The three of them walked to The Square and into the pub yard where they found the back door wide open. Lizzie mounted the few steps and peered into the gloom of the ground floor passage. The door from the rear of the bar was open and she could hear noises from beyond. Soon Lois's head came into view, bent low and bobbing, her shoulders working vigorously, and then Maggie appeared, lugging a heavy bucket. She struggled, bent-legged, along the passage and down the steps before slooshing the grubby water, sending it fanning out across the yard. As she did so, her eyes took in the others and, in particular, John.

'John's back,' Robbie said, unnecessarily.

She made a small noise in her throat and walked to the outside tap where she began to refill the pail. John strutted about, cool and confident as he always was, and the two looked at one another wordlessly.

'Can you come out?' Lizzie asked, a small frown on her forehead, but a hopeful tone in her voice.

Maggie paused, hand upon the gushing tap, eyes measuring the water as it rose in the pail. 'Maybe.'

As she spoke her brother Stephen emerged from one of the sheds, wheeling a heavy old bike and nimbly swung one leg over its dark frame, winking at the others while grinning in an absorbed and self-satisfied way to himself. Maggie watched as he turned out into The Square, swallowing her spite as he conspicuously revelled in his own freedom. They could all hear his voice as he greeted the other boys out there.

'Wait here,' Maggie said, and hauled the pail back indoors.

While she was gone the others chatted. Lizzie laughed at John's nonsense and the two boys ribbed one another as they made their way about the pub yard until they were opposite the exit that led directly onto The Square. Across, stood a group of boys; Stephen and another boy with bikes, then two others of a similar age. Robbie and Lizzie knew who they all were, and even John instantly recognised one.

'That fucker Draycott.'

'He's away at Senior School now,' explained Lizzie. 'We don't see him that much.'

'Or his friends,' said Robbie. 'That's Neville and Jack, remember them?'

As they watched, the group broke up and Stephen and his friend rode off on their bikes, leaving the other two who remained talking for a while and then they too began to amble away, making their way slowly towards the corner by the yard's other entrance. By this time Maggie had returned from the bar with another pail of grubby water and would have slung that across the yard also had John not darted across and wrenched it from her before she could.

He began to struggle with it towards the sheds, calling to Robbie to follow and help, all the while slopping grimy water all over his own feet. By the time the girls had joined them, the boys had pulled across an old stool from the doorway of the open shed and John was standing upon it attempting to raise the pail which Robbie, struggling, held up to him.

'Hang on,' called Maggie, and disappeared into one of the further sheds, quickly emerging with a battered stepladder which she leaned against the wall alongside of them. John clambered up to the shed roof, hauling the pail from the three sets of hands that raised it towards him, and then crept with it, along the corrugated iron roofs towards the corner. Malcolm and Jack Duckett, still in conversation, were idling on the pavement nearby.

'They're too far away,' whispered Lizzie, but at that moment the two lads turned and began to walk fairly quickly forwards to the corner. As Malcolm and Jack passed beneath the end wall, John swept the bucket back and flung the grimy pub floor slops over the two of them.

There was just time for Robbie, Lizzie and Maggie to register the astonishment and shock on their faces before all three of them were forced to race for the safety of the pub, pulling the rear door firmly shut behind them. Even before he could be seen, John had slipped down from the shed roof into the safety of the cottage gardens beyond, leaving the pail to tumble noisily to the yard floor.

XII

That summer John was wilder and more savage in his unruliness, with a crazy viciousness and aggression that belied all sense. He picked fights with bigger and older boys which, to everyone, it was clear he'd no chance of winning. Yet he'd needle and taunt them, punch and spit until aggression turned into violence and then within a blink, he'd be biting and scratching, leaping onto the back of his intended victim, swearing, kicking and throwing wild punches until finally, pummelled and knocked to the ground, he'd be left writhing, bloodied and bruised.

It wasn't long before some of the gangs began to target John, baiting him until his barely suppressed anger erupted. Then, blindly raging, he'd fling himself into futile contests of strength; mocked and jeered by those watching, just waiting for the moment when he'd be pounded into battered defeat.

None of this seemed to affect or in any way deter John. In fact, in many ways these bouts served only to feed his aggression that boiled just below the surface. He continued to seek out enemies for senseless brawls, much to the entertainment of the many who gathered around for amusement to watch him take yet another beating, from which he'd nevertheless emerge belligerent and cocksure, acting more like the victor than the utterly vanquished.

Repeatedly Robbie tried to dissuade or reason with his friend but John saw no cause to modify his reckless behaviour, shrugging off attempts to mollify or distract him when yet another fight seemed inevitable.

Yet, despite these frequent outbursts he remained a firm friend to Robbie; closer even perhaps than in the previous summers when, younger then, they'd simply larked and fooled around in one another's company. Now a bond of companionship held them together, binding the homely, uncomplicated village lad to his ferocious and troubled friend.

For three weeks John had made no mention of the cache of stolen money, and then finally, one day as they all roamed the hill, the two of them walking a little apart from the others, John suddenly said, 'Ya spen' i' then?'

Puzzled, Robbie asked, 'What?'

'The dosh.'

He'd been waiting for that moment, both expecting and dreading it. He frowned, drawing together both his brows in apprehension, and glanced sideways to John hoping to read his mood. Unexpectedly, he found his friend both relaxed and unconcerned, and not at all as he expected. 'No,' he responded, aggrieved at the accusation.

'Go on,' John jibed, disbelieving.

'Honest, I didn't!'

'Ya ain't said nuffin'.'

'Neither did you.'

John shrugged diffidently but cocked his head, expectant. 'Wot you dun wiv i' then?'

'Why d'you say that? Who says I've done something with it?' Robbie felt himself playing for time.

'Well, you ain't said nuffin, 'ave ya? You'd 'a said somethin' like, wouldn't ya?' John was smiling slightly, almost flirtingly like a girl, playing Robbie along but with no malice in the game. 'C'mon... wot ya dun?'

'I gave it back.'

'Ya dun wot!' He reeled back on his heels, hoarse voice cracking as it rose in pitch.

Robbie evaded the look thrown at him, choosing instead to study the pineapple weed beneath his feet that was releasing its pungent scent with every tread. He took in the sweet spicy smell and paused, reluctant and delaying his answer once again.

'I gave it back,' he repeated.

John stared at him, completely dumbfounded.

'I put it in the Church.'

'Ya wot?'

'I put it in the Church; that's where money for the Parish goes. The money from the dance was for the village, so I gave it back.' Then, after another pause, 'It's what Hugh said to do. You remember Hugh? Jonathan and me, we saw him at the Netherington Hall, at an engagement party; it's where Dad works.' These last items of information were superfluous, and treated as such by John, who cared little for such matters.

'Someone'll 'ave nicked i' from there,' he said airily.

'No they won't, it goes into a box; in a safe in the wall. No one knows who puts money in, and anyway, we were very careful; we made sure no one was about. Actually,' he added, 'Mr Pettigrew thought it might have been Finch, but it wasn't, and anyway he didn't see me and Jonathan put it in.'

John gazed coolly back and then shrugged and made a small gruff chuckle in the back of his throat, and that was that. The money wasn't mentioned again and seemed to be of little matter to him now that it was gone. His only comment, after a moment's reflection, was, 'You've gone soft, you 'ave. It's them girls,' and he shortly turned the conversation to a rude discussion about one of the village shopkeepers he'd taken a particular dislike to.

The group was by now making its way through the fields on the further side of the hill, towards their tree house, concealed within an ancient oak whose broad spreading branches provided the ideal support. For weeks leading up to the summer holidays, the friends had laboured to erect it, bringing old tools, nails and lengths of rope borrowed, begged or pilfered from their fathers, to attach and secure the pallets and wooden spars.

Their chosen tree stood sentinel at the lower corner of a sloping wedge-shaped field where three hedges intersected and formed a broad thicket of Blackthorn, Hazel, Spindle and Guelder rose. The old oak, its broad trunk fissured and leaning, was split from ground level to the point where its elephantine limbs spread out, sweeping wide and low across the field. Ancient in its standing, it marked the parish boundary.

Provisions had arrived, much as had the building tools and materials, with or without their parents' knowledge. Two tins of baked beans and one of pilchards, two bottles of dandelion and burdock, a bag of broken rich tea and digestive biscuits, a small jar of fish paste, a tin of pineapple chunks, a packet of chocolate fingers, some toffees, aniseed balls and lemon bon bons and three bags of crisps. They'd procured an old tin opener, a large serving spoon and two forks, along with three glasses that had surreptitiously been removed from the pub by Maggie, along with the crisps. All this was stowed on the tree house platform in an old tin box. Today they'd brought a large loaf of bread.

To reach the platform it was necessary to clamber up through the great cleft, first by placing a foot against one side of the damp gape, and then by bracing against the other edge and working upwards until it was possible to reach a large burr that swelled half way up. It then offered sufficient hand and foot hold to enable the climber to reach upwards and clasp the platform edge. From there it was a simple scramble to clamber up onto it. First up would reach down and help haul up the more awkward, like Robbie and Ann, and eventually all would be safely installed.

Seen through the foliage, the encircling countryside was spread about them like the full skirts of a summer dress, the fields now richly golden with ripe cereals and the desiccated grasses of high summer. They'd been planning this feast for days and eagerly fell upon the food, indiscriminately gobbling down pilchards and bon bons, pineapple and baked beans, and passing round glasses of dark, syrupy dandelion and burdock.

The sun had swung right across the sky by the time they'd descended from the tree and begun their walk back home, choosing this time to follow the narrow lane past the Manor. They were a lively group, chattering amongst themselves, full of the success of their elaborate picnic as they passed the big old house where the lane began to drop away, back down towards the village. Settled below the swell of the hill, the roofs could be seen through the gaps in the high hedges.

The dipping sun cast long shadows on the dusty road surface, throwing every loose pebble and hole into sharp relief. It wasn't until they were approaching that they discerned an odd shape on the lane ahead, lurching strangely. They walked forwards, cautiously at first, but could soon see that it was a rabbit, lumbering and seemingly unaware of their presence. It looked back with dead bloated eyes, its head bulged with swellings, and was now crouched and motionless.

'It's got mixy,' stated Nid, and they all silently agreed. Apart from John who knew nothing of such things. 'It's got myxomatosis,' Nid explained. 'It's a disease which kills rabbits. Lots of them have had it; that's why the warren on the top's empty.'

The group stood looking at the hideously distorted creature when John suddenly lurched, making violent gagging noises.

'Lurgy!' he yelled. 'I's go' the lurgy! Ugh, yuk! Ge' away,' and he scooted backwards, blundering into several of the others and knocking them sideways.

They all joined in the theatrics for a while, touching to 'infect' one another. Perhaps conscious of the noise, the rabbit began to stumble forwards once more, making towards where John stood. He kicked out at it but was reluctant to make contact, perhaps genuinely afraid of its illness, but then poked at it with one toe. It quivered and crouched low in fear, but then John flicked at it with one foot so that it was flung over, falling onto one side, leaving one filmy fish-eye gazing, sightless, back to them.

He shuddered with revulsion and stepped back, stooping, and then came forwards and lobbed a rock. It fell upon the creature's flank and it let out a wail. He picked the stone up again and raised it to his shoulder before hurling it downwards again, this time at the rabbit's head, bursting open the tumours that bloated its eyes. The rabbit shrieked and convulsed and lay twitching, blood and bubbles oozing from its nostrils and eye sockets. John made noises to show his revulsion and hate for the thing on the ground, but he looked satisfied with his achievement.

Behind him, the twins, Robbie and Maggie were silent but felt a thrill of horror. Only Ann and Lizzie mourned the dying creature and turned away.

'Got 'im!' cried John.

XIII

The bamboo was streaming in the hot, dry August wind, flaying the air with leaves that wrapped and warped like serpents. Ann loved the sound they made, their familiar soft rustle comforting as she lay in bed at night, hearing their whispers, seeming to talk to her, telling her things, secret things, and all the while murmuring soothing reassurances. The stems were swaying rhythmically, like serried dancers while the sage-green leaves coiled around her thoughts. Her mother paused from sewing and gazed up, her attention taken by their restless movement.

'There'll be a storm,' she said, snapping the thread between her teeth, tucking the needle safely into the fabric of her bodice.

Storms, now they were violet in colour. Secrets were silver-grey, tinged with faded lilac, like pewter and the lustrous depths of a shell. Fathomless, with no surface and no base, insubstantial, as liquid as mercury, thought Ann.

Mother and daughter were in the garden, idling away a long summer afternoon. They were used to one another's company and spoke only occasionally. Ann lay on the grass reading a book, or rather staring beyond the page at the creatures in the lawn, the warm fecund smell of the grass and earth in her nostrils making her drowsy. Both started at the noise from beyond the house, the abrupt clatter and rattle that announced Sid's arrival in the truck.

'There's your father. He'll be wanting his tea.' And Nellie rose, discarding her needlework onto the low table beside her garden chair.

Ann waited in the hall by to the front door, watching as Sid hauled his tool bag from the open back of the truck and walked up the front path towards her. His shirt sleeves were rolled to above his elbows and he wore a dusty white cap, pushed high on his forehead which was shiny with perspiration. The sun had turned his skin a deep rich golden brown. He smiled as he saw his daughter. 'Another warm one,' he said as he passed and, dropping the tool bag inside the front door, placed a hand which was heavy and warm on the top of Ann's head. 'Let's have some tea, Nell, I'm parched.'

Sid heaved himself onto a kitchen chair, snatching the cap from his head and flung it onto the table before wiping the back of one hand across his forehead, leaving a smear of grime. He let his forearms and large hands land palm-down on the table's surface with a loud smack and stretched out his legs, easing off his heavy work shoes. 'Warm one,' he said, again.

Nellie didn't answer but placed the tea things on the table, silently setting out the cups and saucers, teaspoons and tea strainer, milk jug and sugar bowl, systematically and meticulously arranging each within perfect reach as she seated herself opposite. She smoothed the table's surface to sweep away any vestiges of crumbs.

Ann took her place at one end, her father to her right and mother to her left. Sid scraped his cup and saucer across the table towards himself, measured in two heaped spoonful's of sugar and extravagantly stirred, swirling the tea into a deep golden vortex.

'Hotter tomorrow,' he said, then turned to Ann. 'What've you been up to today then, missie?'

Ann liked her father's attention and interest, and related her day; the morning with Maggie and the afternoon at home with Nellie, because Maggie had to help at home with the younger children and housework. Somehow Maggie always had to help with the household.

'She'll be running that pub soon,' mused Sid.

'She's just a child,' remarked Nellie tartly.

'Wise head that one all the same.'

'She knows too much for her own good.'

'What's 'too much for her own good'?' asked Ann.

'It's just a saying.' Nellie poured more tea and returned Sid's cup heavily so that it rattled in its saucer. She glanced at her daughter but declined to say more, and then gazed out through the kitchen window to the garden beyond.

'She's wise beyond her years, that's what it means,' said Sid.

Ann reflected on this. It hadn't occurred to her that Maggie might be clever; sharp and sassy, yes, but she didn't excel at school, or indeed try very hard. She just did what she had to, to avoid getting noticed or into trouble. But she did have an air of knowing and she liked to be right, that was undeniable, and she had a way of getting you to do things her way.

'Job's going well,' Sid offered brightly. 'Should be finished next week, Tuesday at the latest. Ted's coming down to give me a hand.' He glanced up to ascertain that Nellie was listening but she was still gazing away. 'Nell?'

'Mmm.'

'Back to Stevens' after. Got a cupboard to put in.'

'You'll be away then.' Her tone was clipped.

He pursed his lips and gave a barely perceptible shrug.

'I said you'll be away, won't you,' she repeated.

'As necessary.' Sid's reply was terse.

He rose from the table and walked to the kitchen sink where he washed his hands and arms before bending down to scoop water up over his face and the back of his neck and hairline, all damp with sweat. Snatching up the kitchen towel he dried himself vigorously. Ann was watching but, on the periphery of her vision, she could see Nellie studiously sipping at her tea with dead eyes, eyes that were like the rabbit's. She shuddered at the memory. Since that afternoon Ann had avoided the company of the boys but the creature's death shriek refused to leave her and would intrude, unbidden; its final terror suddenly haunting her quiet thoughts and activities.

That day she was happy to simply have her father home early and kept company with him throughout the late afternoon, probing him for entertaining tales about his daily work and customers. Nellie prepared their evening meal but there was a coolness in her manner and a brittleness that Ann had observed before and, when she spoke, which was infrequently and only when necessary, it was as if she were addressing someone not in the room. It dismayed Ann; she wanted to feel the reassurance of her parents around her and was unsettled by her mother's icy detachment.

Later, with the long summer evening still ahead, Ann crossed The Square to find Maggie. The pub's door and windows were flung wide open, letting in the warm evening breezes and releasing onto the pavement the gentle burr of conversation and pungent odour of beer and cigarette smoke. She was aware of Rod Viney in the open doorway. He was leaning against the door jamb taking in the evening air, his large body and white shirt bright from the low sun but his face was hidden by deep shadow. He was in conversation with Nodder Potter and talked and gesticulated with one hand while Potter stood at the edge of the step with his heels overhanging, hands in pockets and cigarette in mouth, nodding vigorously and croaking an occasional brief reply.

She found Maggie in the yard, furiously chalking on the wall of one of the sheds, her skirt jiggling with the effort. In the shade of the pub, seated on the rear step, was Lois, and the two younger children were amusing themselves in the gravel, noisily flinging stones about. Ann tried to talk to Maggie about the rabbit but her friend merely shrugged. 'It was gonna die anyway,' was her only response. Later they noticed that Lois had drifted back inside.

With a sharp noise that made both turn in alarm, a phalanx of bicycles suddenly swept through the yard scattering gravel, their riders whooping and shouting and laughing loudly at the fright they'd caused.

'Stinking idiots! Shit faces!' yelled Maggie as Malcolm, Neville, Squinter and their usual associates swung out into The Square, leering back over their shoulders.

Later, Sid stood at the yard entrance, a handsome man silhouetted against the sinking sun, a haze of insects above his head.

'Be back in half an hour,' he called to his daughter before turning to go into the pub.

'Who's he to say?' snapped Maggie.

Ann was taken aback by her friend's reaction. 'He's just reminding me,' she protested.

But Maggie was scarcely listening. 'Don't you hate him?' she asked. He was too self-regarding by far, that Sid Dewberry, she thought. But then she added, 'My lousy stinking father won't even give me anything for the Fair.'

'You can have some of mine; my Dad always gives me plenty. It'll be enough for both of us,' Ann offered.

'If you like.' Maggie showed no particular gratitude and then half-turned and yelled to her younger siblings, 'Get up to bed you two. Now!'

The children pulled faces and poked out their tongues, but they obeyed. Maggie dully watched them go and then beckoned, leading Ann to a small outhouse attached to the rear of the pub, where she pulled back the jagged and broken wooden door which scraped noisily over the rough stones.

'What?' asked Ann, unsure what was being revealed to her.

Maggie merely nodded into the dimness within and, as her eyes accustomed to the gloom, Ann made out a broken and splintered chair and the back of a radio, both tossed onto the floor. She looked to Maggie for explanation. 'He did it,' Maggie remarked. 'Smashed them up.'

'Why? How?'

'Threw them against the wall. Smashed the chair over the radio. Kicked it.'

'Why?'

'Threw it at Mum,' Maggie continued to intone.

'At your Mum! Why?' Ann was shocked and her voice had dropped to a whisper. She retreated from the shed's interior as if to distance herself from its contamination.

'He gets angry, he fights. C'mon,' and Maggie led the way back across the yard.

Later, the soft chiming of the Church clock, drifting across the village roofs on the heavy evening air, told Ann that it was time to go home. The light had seeped away and the buildings opposite stood in dark profile against the paling August sky.

The voices from the pub were muffled now, although the windows hung wide-open still, and the light from within pooled onto the pavement. She avoided its glare and stepped softly out into the shadows. On the far side of The Square she could see a scatter of bikes abandoned on the cobbles. The raucous voices of Malcolm, Neville and other youths draped about the steps of the stone cross told her who'd left them there. They were bantering and laughing coarsely, their breaking voices rough-edged and harsh.

From the corner two figures appeared, both boys, and passed in front of the shops. They paused for a moment and then turned to one another. One stepped away and stealthily approached the heap of bikes and she watched as he bent down before opening his flies and then, with legs straddled, pissed into an opened saddle bag. The other watched for a moment and then followed suit, into a different bag. She knew she was watching John and Robbie and saw them slink away, unseen, in the fading light.

The passage was gloomy and silent, with the smell of warm dust rising from the ground and walls, while ahead the house described a perfect profile against the darkening primrose sky, such as a child might draw. An open window threw a square of electric light onto the front garden, revealing Nellie sewing in the lounge with the radio on behind her. All colour had drained from the garden and it was like a phantom of itself, rich with scent but bereft of all hues, save a deathless white.

Where does all the colour go, Ann wondered, before it reappeared in her own head to attach itself around her thoughts and words?

***

Maggie stayed in the yard long after Ann had left. She too had witnessed the boys' act of mischief and mused coolly at its effect on the bikes' owners. She pulled an old chair from a shed and sat with her back against the wall, silent and motionless, gazing out across the empty yard, watching the light fade and breathing in the cooling night air. Only the lightest of breezes now brushed against her cheeks.

It was almost dark when she heard steps and saw a tall figure striding around the corner towards the pub's front door. A flash of light from the door preceded the man's entry and she heard her father's voice, and a moment later both men came out into the yard, Viney walking swiftly ahead, conducting the other who followed behind, more reluctantly.

'Very hard to come by these days,' Viney was saying. 'Didn't want you to miss out. Only got a few. Good, though; the best. Here, look,' and he stepped into a shed. Maggie could hear him moving items around inside.

Frank Bird remained in the yard. Even in the half-light she could see that he stood awkwardly, as if he had no wish to be where he was. He started to speak but Viney had emerged energetically and was holding a bottle aloft to read the label in the dimness. 'That's the one. Kept it back for you, knew you'd like it. Just the thing, eh? Good one this. That's all right, you can give me five. Special deal, eh?'

Money changed hands and Frank Bird took the bottle, holding it loose from his fingers, letting it hang down as if it were barely in his possession.

'Put that one aside for an occasion, eh?' Viney was sounding pleased with himself and in no hurry to return to the pub, although Frank Bird had taken several steps away and stood on his rear heel, seemingly in readiness to retreat.

Viney clapped his hands with a sound that split the silence. 'Ah, lovely evening.' There was a pause.

'Kids well?' Bird was attempting conversation on neutral topics.

'Yes... yes, they're well. Monkeys the lot of 'em. You know kids.'

'Mmm.'

'Yours?'

'Mmm, both doing well.'

'You, err.... Didn't you lose one, Frank?'

There was another pause and Frank Bird shifted his balance. 'Yes... Yes, we did. A boy.'

'Terrible, terrible.' Another pause. 'What happened?'

'Meningitis.'

A sympathetic intake of breath from Viney who was little more than a ghostly white shirt in the gloom. Frank Bird, in his suit, had melded into the night, visible only when he turned and his face showed the faintest presence against the enveloping darkness.

'Yes... Hospital, wasn't it?'

'Yes.'

'Too late, was it? Awful, awful. What a thing. You want the best for your kids and then things go wrong. Terrible thing that, when things go wrong. My missus, I don't know what she'd do without them kids. She dotes on 'em, positively dotes on 'em. What was his name?'

'James.'

'Young was he?'

'Two.'

'Terrible thing to lose a nipper.'

There was no answer, but an intake of breath from Frank Bird was audible with the sound of his feet moving on the gravel.

'Well, go in shall we?' said Viney.

Maggie stayed out until all the stars had appeared.

XIV

When the two of them were together, just Robbie and John, and there was no audience or party of friends to impress, John was calmer, less belligerent, and not so aggressive. It was as if Robbie were his ballast, a counterpoint to his ferocity and destructiveness. He was still truculent and impulsive but there was a strong and fierce bond of loyalty from John to his summer-time companion. For six weeks he shared in Robbie's life; his family and friends, the village and community where he lived, and the countryside he knew like the back of his hand; every path and hedge, pond and copse.

Yet, despite this intense companionship, Robbie understood that he, by contrast, knew little of John's real life; the one where he spent the rest of the year, far away in London, with his own family. He mentioned them rarely, and then only briefly, and with an evasion or dismissiveness that precluded close enquiry. To Robbie, John seemed to exist only in Moreton Steyning, as if there were no other world that he inhabited beyond it.

After three weeks they were once again immersed in one another's company, spending every day together. Sometimes with the others, although increasingly without the three girls. Robbie had no preference but more often than not John would shrug off suggestions that they should call on the girls, or he would simply pull an expression of distaste.

'Whad'ya want them girls fer?' he'd scorn and, in their company, was frequently disdainful.

Once when Lizzie and Ann had talked about the spider-face man, reliving their horror and repulsion, he'd scoffed at their fright and mocked when Ann repeated with alarm what the strange old man had said, about knowing her, and that her mother had warned her against him. But he didn't forget the story. Later he prompted Robbie to ask his own father.

''E's from that place. Go on, ask 'im. 'E'll know, I bet ya.'

So Robbie did ask his father. 'What're you asking about him for?' Tom had said. 'He's just an old fellow, he's harmless. Poor chap took a hit in the war; it's not his fault.'

'Where does he live, then?' Robbie had asked.

'Out past Netherington somewhere. I've forgotten exactly.'

This seemed unlikely since Tom had grown up in and worked there all his life.

'But how does he know Ann Dewberry?' Robbie persisted.

'Who said he does?'

'She did. She saw him and he told her he did.'

'Well, maybe he does or he thinks he does. He's got family in Netherington anyway. Off with you now. I've got to get on.'

'He's something to do with her father, isn't he?' Susan, who was seated nearby reading a magazine, spoke without looking up. 'That's what I heard, anyway.'

Tom had taken the opportunity of her interruption to depart, evading further attempts at enquiry, and the boys turned their attention to their sister, rising curiosity only vaguely satisfied by Tom.

'How's he connected, then?' Robbie urged.

Susan cast her eyes about the room, attempting to recall.

'Sid Dewberry something, but I don't know exactly. Megan told me there was something and I asked Mum but she said she didn't know, but I think she did. Anyway, Ann Dewberry's father knows him, that's for sure.'

'So he does know Ann, then?'

She shrugged, 'I suppose. Now buzz off and leave me in peace.'

***

Nid had taken to playing the snatch of tune in order to observe his father's or mother's responses, but particularly his father's. Somehow he'd come to like the music's soft lilt, the way it soothed but then suddenly ended, interrupted in its gentle, wistful course where the notation on Maggie's scrap of torn cardboard simply finished. He even prompted Finch to play it, although he did so rather falteringly having largely abandoned practising the piano, so that he could better observe Frank's reaction. It was almost a game for him now, one of cat and mouse, and he would set his trap, quietly and deliberately fingering the familiar notes and then wait for the bait to be taken; the irresistible taunt that he knew must provoke a response. He was playing it again that morning.

His parents were still in the kitchen, relaxing over the newspapers after their breakfast, always a traditional English on Saturday mornings. He heard the flap and crisp snap of the newspaper shaken smooth and recognised the impatient restlessness of its sound, and in his father's clearing of his throat followed with the quietly spoken 'more tea?' from their mother. He played a little more loudly and presently the kitchen door softly closed. He heard the snug click of its latch.

Nid waited a few moments and then padded to the closed kitchen door, stretching out to place his fingertips on its blank surface, steadying and controlling his breathing; listening, holding himself motionless. No voice came from within for several minutes, and then Norma spoke.

'You shouldn't have taken it, you know.'

'What was I to do? He put me on the spot.' Frank's tone was brusque.

'Even so.'

'Easy enough for you to say.'

'Why must you go there anyway?'

'For Heaven's sake!'

'It's not as if it's the only pub...'

'I don't have to explain! I like the company there.'

'Rod Viney!'

'I don't mean him, of course.'

'I should hope not.'

'I think I can choose where to go in my own leisure time.'

'It's just... you can't avoid him there. I'm surprised at you, with that loan business.'

'Well, it's too late now. It would look odd. Actually, it's a very good Scotch.'

'He's twisting you round his little finger.'

There was silence for several minutes. Nid felt himself swaying but kept his finger tips on the door. After a while he rested his forehead softly against its surface, feeling his own breath, warm as it reflected back off the wood into his face.

'He was asking about James.' It was his father speaking.

'James!'

'Actually, he was very sympathetic.'

Norma took in a deep breath, it sounded like a sigh, or a sign of exasperation. 'Time's gone so fast.'

'Twelve years now.' There was a silence and then Frank spoke again. 'If only we'd known.'

'We did know. How couldn't we?'

'But so quick; so appallingly quick!'

'That's how it happens.'

'There was no warning. How were we to know? If only...'

'We can't keep going over it.'

'But, if I'd known... The ambulance... We wouldn't have waited...'

'I told you I was worried!'

'I didn't know! I thought...'

'He was so little, so helpless.'

'That's right, blame me!'

'I'm not blaming you!'

'You as good as said.'

There was another pause. 'Maybe it wouldn't have made any difference anyway, the delay. Perhaps it wouldn't.' It was Norma speaking again, in a firm voice now. She sounded nearer, as if she'd stood up.

'You can think that if you like, but we'll never know, will we? I have to live with it!'

'So do I... So do I...' she whispered.

'That damned tune!' A chair scraped back and Nid quickly retreated upstairs.

***

Finch found Robbie and John together in the garden of Woodbine Cottage, and the three soon set off in search of entertainment for the day; wandering along Main Street in the direction of The Square. Sitting in Wheelwrights' front garden and reading a comic, Lizzie watched the three boys approach on the opposite side of the road, chatting and larking amongst themselves.

Robbie was closest to her with John in the middle, easily half a head shorter, and Finch was beyond, taller and blond. She could see that Robbie had observed her from the periphery of his vision, but he didn't turn to look across and didn't acknowledge her. All the while John was chattering away, with Finch and occasionally Robbie interjecting. As they drew opposite, Robbie's gaze flicked across, almost imperceptibly, but he maintained his pace with the other two and remained turned towards them. She knew he'd pretended he hadn't seen her and watched wistfully as they continued to reel along the street.

By that time John was on a mission of revenge against the farm lads, seeking vengeance for the beatings he'd taken, or rather brought upon himself, and retribution for three previous summers of enmity.

For Robbie and Finch the old animosities had largely been put aside. Malcolm and his cohorts had moved on to Secondary School in Cullingham and had more interesting challenges to occupy their lives but, from time to time, old antagonisms resurfaced and enlivened life in the village. If it proved entertaining, Robbie and Finch were more than happy to fall in with John's schemes.

With no particular aim in mind they made their way up Rushwood End lane, past the outlying cottages and farms, and onwards towards the hill. At the half-way point John was irresistibly drawn into the Draycotts' Lee Farm, but the yard was empty and quiet save for a sleeping dog, too deaf or lazy to notice, and he found no opportunity for mischief.

It was quiet everywhere, the farmers away in the fields, attending to their animals or harvesting cereal crops while the good weather held. From the hill's summit, tractors and farm vehicles could be seen working the fields, cutting and carrying away the season's harvest. The boys watched, following the steady industry as the vale's fields slowly turned a dark hue with each golden row newly cut. Even John seemed interested for a while, until his general restiveness impelled them to move on.

Back in the village, Lizzie had remained in the garden, pretending to herself that she was still enjoying her comic, but in truth her spirits had sunk and she felt dejected and deserted. She'd been abandoned first by Grandpa and now by Robbie, whose friendship she'd trusted, her loyalty betrayed and displaced by John. For a while she mooched about, idly pulling petals off the blooms until she saw Nid passing by and he stopped to speak.

'I'm going to the shops,' he explained. 'Might see you later, when the others get back,' and he too hurried on towards The Square.

It wasn't to the shops he was going, however, but to the Horse & Hounds, his business being with Maggie. He was confident he'd find her there, knowing she had to help with cleaning after the busy Friday and Saturday nights, and so that proved to be the case. The casements were flung wide open and he could see her, inside the public bar, energetically sweeping the stone floor. He clambered onto the wooden bench beneath the window and leaned in through and, since there were no adults in sight, called out to her.

She snapped her head up quickly and shot a look straight at him, furrowing her brows, but didn't speak.

He was leaning in with his elbows on the window sill. 'I need to speak to you; you finishing soon?'

'What about?'

'When d'you finish?'

She shrugged, 'Later.'

'Can't you get away for ten minutes?'

Maggie planted the broom on the floor and leaned into the handle. Head turned away she called towards the lounge bar door, 'Mum! I'll be ten minutes.' Then she jerked her head towards the rear of the pub and disappeared behind the bar counter and into the dark passage beyond. By the time Nid had reached the yard, she was standing at the top of the back door steps. 'What?' she said.

She was an obdurate figure but Nid was resolute in his determination to uncover the mystery. He'd promised himself he would.

'You know that music?' he began.

Her response was staccato. 'No. What?'

'That music you brought on that bit of card.'

'No.'

'You do!'

'I don't.'

'Don't lie! Look – this,' and he pulled the fragment from his pocket. She looked at it for a few moments.

'What of it?' she eventually said.

'Where did you get it?'

'Can't remember,' and she pulled a doubting expression to emphasise the point, looking vaguely around the yard.

'Maggie!'

'What!' She threw her arms up in exasperation.

'It's important. Please!'

'Tell me why, then.'

'I can't.'

'Neither can I, then.'

'C'mon, please! It's something to do with my parents, I know it is.'

'How?'

'It just is. Look, can't you just tell me? Please...'

She took a deep breath, looked over her shoulder towards the back of the bar to check that it was empty still, and then inclined her head, indicating for him to follow. Stealthily she turned the handle to a door just inside, off the dark passage, and ushered him through. He found himself in a chill cellar, lit only by a cold, grey gloom. A short flight of steps dropped away in front of him and he felt Maggie's hand in the small of his back pushing him down them. Dark racks of boxes rose around him, blocking the light even further. She pressed on past him and then stood, leaning back against a large desk, arms folded across her chest in inquisitorial stance.

'Where did you get it from!' he'd raised his voice in exasperation, and she shushed him angrily.

'It's off something I found,' she said.

'What?' but she merely pursed her lips in a show of non-cooperation. 'Look, I'll tell on you if you don't tell me!' he threatened.

'Says who?'

'Please, Maggie.'

She regarded him coolly for a few moments and then seemed to change her mind. To his astonishment, she suddenly sank to her knees, then flipped over and slithered on her belly beneath the racking behind him and out of sight. He could hear her making her way across the floor, breathing hard occasionally, and then a scrape as she emerged clear of the racks, against the further wall.

'What're you doing?' he whispered.

'Wait!' she hissed, and the sound of struggling and scraping was repeated until she returned to his side. For a moment she stood with hands pressed into her thighs, her hands hidden by the folds of her dress. 'Put out your hand,' she ordered.

Nid raised his right hand and she covered it with hers, dropping into his palm something cold and hard. He looked down onto a small dull, dark grey metal object. Holding it up towards such faint light as there was, he realised it was a cigarette lighter.

'Read it,' she commanded.

He was puzzled at first, but then could feel under his fingers faint grooves. Maggie cocked her head, listening for sounds, then quickly ascended the steps, where she switched on the single electric light bulb in the room, and now he could see, even though the lighter was blackened with tarnish, that there were lines engraved around the base and that the lines had musical notes upon them.

He turned it round and around in his hand and recognised the notation of the tune. He could even hear it in his head. He looked questioningly back at her and she snatched it from his hand. He thought she was being proprietorial but she simply turned the lighter over and held it in front of his face, pointing. He read two inscribed initials: *FB*.

Nid looked up into Maggie's face and she stared back, expressionless. 'Frank Bird,' she said.

'Where did you get it?' he asked her, softly.

'Found it. Under a seat in the bar one day. I didn't know whose it was. I'd only just noticed the music when I brought it round to you. Didn't know what it was before.'

He was silent. 'You didn't give it back...?' he said after a while.

'No.'

Neither spoke. Nid felt the lighter in his hands and studied the engraved music. 'It's a song,' he said after a pause. '*There was a boy...*'

'It's about your brother.'

'Finch?'

'No. The one that died.'

And he knew, just as he'd always known. 'James,' he whispered to himself.

Above them at that moment there was a loud commotion and they heard heavy footsteps descending from the upstairs flat to the passage outside. There were voices from the bar and Lois was calling. As he passed the cellar door, Viney was shouting.

***

John was stirred up by the sight of all the heavy farm machinery, working away in every direction around the hill. He'd been telling the others again about the shunting yards and sidings, about riding footplate, about helping to shovel coal, about the different types of locomotive, the night-long clanging and crashing and squealing, the massive engines moving back and forth, building up long loads. The other two had heard all this before, many times, but still listened eagerly, envious of the image of power and might and travel that it all conjured, in a world so very different from theirs in a country village. They still unconsciously encouraged him and he stitched ever more elaborate scenarios for them. At times Robbie wondered just how plausible John's role was in the world that he described to them, but it was all too appealing and exciting to permit practicalities and scepticism to spoil it. Finch nevertheless remained transfixed.

A hot, dry wind blew up and large birds spiralled on the thermals, like debris sucked upwards in a twister. With the wind snatching at their clothes, they began to make their way back down. As they returned via Rushwood End, tractors were moving along the lane ahead of them, drawing loads of grain towards the farm barns, while others emerged, speeding past and out towards the fields to collect the next load. At the Potters' cottage there was no one in sight still but, at Lee Farm beyond, a tractor and empty trailer stood waiting on the track that led to the lower fields, obscured from the farmyard itself by the barns.

John sprinted to it and, by the time the others had caught up, had already clambered up onto the tractor seat and was pulling at the steering wheel.

''Ere, key's in i'. Le's go fer a ride,' he called.

'I don't know how to drive.' Robbie was hanging back.

'Yeah, 's'easy. I'll show ya.'

'I know!' Finch said. 'I've watched my Dad in our car,' and he climbed up alongside.

John immediately reached for the ignition and turned the key. The engine spluttered and then sprang to life, juddering the engine and blasting dark smoke from the vertical exhaust pipe at the front. He was pulling at the gears, attempting to make the tractor move forwards, but was too short to reach any of the pedals. Finch stamped on each in turn, while John pulled and pushed at any controls he could reach. Finally, and without warning, the tractor lurched forward with an abrupt jolt that snatched violently at the attached trailer, leaving the pair of them wrenching and fighting to regain control of the steering wheel as the vehicle began to move along the track.

Finch had no idea which of the pedals he was excitedly pressing was the accelerator or brake, and they headed off considerably faster than intended. They were bounced and jolted by the vibration of the engine, while the rutted and sloping ground and weight of the following trailer continually snatched the steering wheel from their grip as they both wrestled with it. Within moments they were veering towards the rear of the farm complex and looming ahead was the outer wall of one of the cattle barns. With great effort the pair of them slewed the wheel round to the right to avoid the building. The tractor abruptly changed direction and swerved, flinging them both heavily to the ground. Driverless, it gathered pace, following the steeply sloping ground into the farmyard.

Sprawled in the dirt, John and Finch scrambled hurriedly to their feet and sprinted back to the lane where they found Robbie, watching from behind the wall, crouching where he couldn't be seen. The three of them raced away and didn't stop until they'd emerged into The Square.

Meanwhile, the tractor and its load careered across the Draycott's farmyard to where, had anyone been about, they would surely have had their chest caved in before the tractor finally came to rest, lodged against a water trough, a deep jagged groove gouged along one side.

The Square was relatively busy and there was a general air of bustle and social interaction. Those few days before the annual Fair always held an atmosphere of anticipation and heightened activity. Within two days the business of preparation, of staking out on The Green, of assembling the marquees and stalls and building the stage would begin all over again. Bunting had already been strung from the lamp posts and several shops had already put out special displays in their windows in readiness for the visiting crowds. It was no surprise then to see activity around the Horse & Hounds although it was not yet lunchtime. Two men were at the front door, speaking to someone who stood inside, out of sight; presumably Rod Viney, or his wife.

The three boys climbed onto the steps at the base of the old stone cross, seating themselves casually. Robbie observed the men at the pub doorway. Both had on dark suits. One, who wore a trilby hat, stood back a little; the other, perhaps younger, was at the door and appeared to be doing the talking to whoever was indoors. He stood lightly and moved easily. He was at once both relaxed and yet fully engaged in whatever he was doing, with an easy but confident manner. Fairly tall, with dark hair and no hat, he was apparently leading the conversation. All at once he stepped back and turned to his companion, gesturing him to enter, whatever it was seeming to have been agreed or negotiated with the occupants. As he did so, this younger man turned three quarters towards them and Robbie recognised with surprise that it was Hugh.

He nudged at Finch and the three boys hurried over to the pub and, from a discreet distance, peered in through the still-opened windows. The two men had stepped into the public bar and Lois stood nearby, silent. Viney was behind the counter, leaning onto one fist. The sounds from The Square made it impossible to make out what was being said but the voices could be identified; Hugh's was educated, well-spoken, even-toned and calm, but also firm, quite unlike how Robbie was used to hear him. Viney's was gruff and coarse by comparison, his voice raised; sometimes pitched unusually high, often speaking at length in contrast to Hugh's short and precise sentences whose tone suggested reasoned authority.

In the cellar room below, Maggie with Nid, was also unable to make out the conversation but she could hear well enough to determine that the visitors were unfamiliar, and that her father was both flustered and angry. She switched off the light lest it be noticed and hovered behind the door, listening. Suddenly footsteps sounded loudly, approaching along the passage outside.

She bounded back down the steps in one leap and grabbed Nid by the shirt, thrusting him to the floor. He yelled with annoyance but she elbowed him roughly in the ribs and shoved his head down under the racks. 'Get under!' she hissed, pushing at him as she slithered beneath herself, dragging on his sleeve to direct him. They had barely reached her secret corner before the door opened, the light was snapped on and several sets of footsteps came briskly down the cellar steps and into the room.

XV

Everything had stopped for the Fair, just as it always did. Crowds had flocked into Moreton Steyning and now filled the streets, clogging every lane and thoroughfare, jostling good naturedly on their way to The Green. Ann had called for Lizzie, Maggie being vague about when she'd be ready, or more likely was delaying as she had no pocket money to spend at the Fair. The other two had therefore gone on ahead, pushing through the surge of people with money from their fathers in their pockets and wish-lists of what to spend it on.

Lizzie wore her best full-skirted summer dress with her long pale hair loose, hanging over her shoulders, almost to her waist. She was fizzing with excitement and eager to get to the funfair rides. Ann thought she was at her most sparkling and engaging, her eyes wide and cheeks flushed with happy anticipation, but then Lizzie was always luminous.

The noise and clamour reached a crescendo as they rounded the corner to The Green, the loud hubbub of music and blaze of colours thwacking into their senses with a thrill that almost lifted them from their feet. Within moments they'd disappeared amongst the stalls and marquees, the rides and exhibits. Pretty much everyone from Moreton Steyning was there, somewhere, and plenty more from Netherington and beyond. People even came from Cullingham, special Fair buses arriving from early in the morning only to depart in the early evening when all was over.

The boys were at the Fair also, hanging around by the rifle shooting, coconut shy and funfair rides. They were glimpsed from time to time by the girls and were clearly content to remain in their separate group.

It was as the girls waited for the official opening that Lizzie had pulled at Ann's arm and pointed away through the crowds. Initially Ann couldn't see what it was that she was meant to be looking at, but then her eyes picked out the strange hunched figure, incongruous in a long mackintosh and, clearly visible, the deep cherry-red streaks splashed across one side of his face. This time the old man wasn't alone; a woman stood with him, of a similar age to their mothers, although perhaps a little younger. She wore a colourful summer dress with a matching bead necklace and, to the other side of her, held the hand of a fair-haired girl of about eight or nine. The little girl was dressed like her mother, at least they presumed them to be mother and daughter, and she held firmly onto a pink fluffy animal that perhaps someone had won for her.

The old man seemed much less threatening or strange here, surrounded as he was by so many people and such noise and gaiety, the general exuberance lending an air of well-being and reassurance. Somehow he seemed now merely bewildered and not the figure of revulsion and fear from the Churchyard. They were soon absorbed into the throng as people pushed forwards for the opening speeches, and the friends quickly forgot about the old man. Performing official duties that year was the local MP, of little interest to Ann and Lizzie who seeped back into the crowds and took advantage of the diversion to go on their favourite ride, the richly ornate galloper.

They clambered on board and settled astride the vermilion saddles of two golden prancing horses and in no time were swirling round and round so that the surrounding crowds were a whirling, dizzying smear that encircled them. It was wonderful, but over all too quickly, and so they stayed for a second ride, moving to the outermost horses for the greater thrill of motion.

The Merry-Go-Round began again and the horses lifted them gently up and down in time to a lilting Viennese waltz. Soon the whirling and spinning began again, the faces and movements of the surrounding crowds frozen for an instant each time they passed them by. Ann clung to the golden barley twist pole and leaned out into the swing and rush of air; it was then that she saw the old man again, his spider-face peering up. She turned her head sharply but he was gone in an instant, until a few seconds later she once more swirled past and there he was again.

Twice more she spotted him and then she recognised, by their brightly-coloured matching dresses, the woman and child who stood together at a short distance from him, turned partly away. They were speaking to someone who was obscured by the old man, but the woman was smiling in a self-absorbed way and had pushed the little girl forwards. The child had her arm raised. When she came around again, Ann saw that the little girl held aloft the pink furry toy and was smiling up with pleasure.

The Merry-Go-Round was still building its speed and Lizzie turned back and waved, her long flaxen hair flying out like the mane on one of the golden horses, and she was laughing with delight. As they passed the section of crowd where the spider-faced man stood, he was there again, only now taking a step in the direction of the ride's movement, as if he were trying to follow Ann as she was swept past. All the while he was looking up, his mouth hung open in a toothless gape.

When she passed once again at the point where she'd first seen him, the crowd had now opened up, revealing the woman and child who were still standing chatting to someone, and she simply knew from the man's stance that it was her own father they smiled at. This time he held in his hand the fluffy pink toy and was admiring it for the little girl.

The tune seemed to increase in volume as the ride reached its fastest rotation. Ahead, Lizzie was standing in the stirrups and waving one arm as if to catch the rushing air. The hem of her emerald green dress coiled and fluted, lifting to show her golden tanned legs. She waved to Ann again before sinking back into the saddle. The old man had moved further on, following the direction of the round-about, still gaping upwards, his head moving from side-to-side, attempting to still-capture its motion. Ann's gaze sought and found Sid. He was still speaking, but he no longer held the toy, it was now clasped again by the little girl whose attention had wandered and she too was gazing up at the ride, her expression one of delight and wonder.

Ann was starting to feel nauseous from focussing at each rotation into the same point of the crowd, but she felt impelled to continue her watch. The ride had begun to lose its thrill and pleasure and was merely the point from which she must observe, like someone peering through the slots of a zoetrope, watching the unfolding actions over which she had no control.

She recognised the frock, a blur of blue and green away on the opposite side of the galloper, and knew it to be her mother's, her Sunday best, although Nellie hadn't yet changed from her everyday wear when Ann had left the house that morning. She watched as the frock span across her vision, as if floating quickly across the grass, opposing the ride's rotation, until it came to rest, close by where the others stood.

The ride's headlong speed had begun to slow now and the blur of colours and faces gradually took on shapes and distinction. Nellie was on the complete opposite side of the Merry-Go-Round to the spider-faced man, but she stood just a few yards from Sid, and the two women, both in their Sunday best, faced one another.

Ann saw her mother's expression with shock. It was pinched and ugly and her arm was raised. Sid was turning about sharply. When she passed again, he was now facing Nellie, who was speaking and animated. The other woman stood behind Sid and seemed to be saying something but then placed her arms over the child's shoulders and began to turn her away. Sid had raised one arm towards her mother and had taken a step in her direction. The ride's motion was slow now, and the music of the waltz swelled back into her ears, filling her with its lyrical sound. She realised she hadn't been aware of it for some while.

The galloper glided slowly past the old man whose gaze was in her direction. Ann could see his eyes begin to focus as she drifted past, rising slowly up and then down as if in a dance. She twisted her head quickly, preparing her eyes and concentration as she was once more carried past her parents.

Nellie was hurrying away, her arm raised and extended behind her as if warding something off. Sid was marching towards her, his eyes evading anything from his left or right. She could only see the back of the other woman who was hurrying away in the other direction, ushering the child ahead of her. Ann could see only its arm, still holding onto the furry animal.

The ride took one final stately circuit, sweeping slowly past the old man before settling to rest. As she began to climb shakily from her mount, he pointed across and called, 'I know 'e, don't I, little moppit?'

XVI

There was something about the way the grass was spread about and flattened, about the way it was bruised and trampled down. They knew it long before they saw. There were the swathes through the long grass, purposeful and straight; not meandering and distracted like their own, flowing through the meadow like the currents in a stream, merging and diverging at will. These others were direct, the grass trodden beneath or kicked to one side.

The big old oak cast a broad shadow, dark as the depths of a muddy pool, but they knew already what it hid. Finch, Jonathan and John began to hurry forwards, quickly overtaken by Lizzie and Maggie who ran and leapt over the long grass. Before them the tree house lay destroyed; scattered about the crushed and darkened grass, the pallets smashed, the supports torn from the tree's branches hanging crushed and splintered. Everything was broken, every part destroyed and useless, reduced to a heap of worthless scraps. Finch took a wild kick, propelling a broken spar away into the hedge, fighting down his emotions. John seized up another and beat it against the trunk as if the old tree were somehow to blame for allowing this thing to happen. The others variously gazed about at the unrecognisable remains or silently attributed blame, for which there seemed little doubt.

When later they arrived at home, the twins were uncharacteristically silent, each absorbed in their upset and resentment. Nid took himself up to the bedroom and gazed angrily out over The Green. As with the meadow, only dark traces on the grass gave the clue to what once had been – the Fair and all that had come with it only a short time before; the noise, fun and laughter. He felt a deep emptiness and loss which he could scarcely explain to himself. After a while he slid across to the desk and took out from the drawer his notebook, the one he'd begun to write in. He hadn't meant to keep it a secret, it was simply that he'd neglected to talk about it. In truth he didn't know what he could say or how he'd explain what it was he wrote. He didn't really know himself and it wasn't the sort of thing that Finch would understand, or even be interested in. No matter then.

He began to write, slowly at first, but soon the words slipped from his pen as easily as the world about him slipped from his consciousness. He was unaware of the passing afternoon, or of the faint strains of his brother's piano playing below until shouts wrenched him back into the room. Within moments the door was snatched open and Finch stormed in. Behind him from downstairs came their father's voice, imperative and angry.

'Come back down!' he ordered.

Nid looked questioningly at Finch and could see that his brother, normally so happy-go-lucky, was rattled and close to tears. 'What is it?' he whispered, but received only a resentful shake of the head.

'Andrew!' Their father's angry shout came thundering up the stairs.

The brothers exchanged looks again. 'What?' mouthed Nid, more urgently this time.

'He says I stole it!' Finch whirled abruptly around as their father's figure loomed in the doorway.

'I told you to come downstairs. I expect you to do so. Running away will not do you any good and does not help you in the least. It's a sign of guilt. Now... you have one minute to get downstairs and explain yourself. Is that clear?'

Without pausing for a response, Frank Bird returned downstairs. Finch looked helplessly at his brother and then feebly followed.

It seemed several minutes before Nid heard their voices again, away in the living room below. Finch's was shrill, his tone rising and aggrieved. Uncharacteristically he was beginning to shout, his evident bewilderment only feeding his distress. Nid walked softly downstairs and into the front room. Frank was standing, arms folded in the small of his back, leaning out over Finch whose pose mimicked that of his father, although his fingers intertwined constantly, like a restless nest of snakes.

'It wasn't him,' said Nid.

Both snatched their heads round to look at Nid. 'What do you mean?' said Frank.

'It wasn't Andrew...'

'What do you mean? What do you know? I want an explanation. Why do you keep playing that tune both of you? Tell me,' he demanded.

'It wasn't Andrew.'

'So it was you that took the lighter then?'

'No!'

'My silver lighter, with the music engraved. Where is it? How do you know that tune?'

'It's Maggie's... she's got it.'

Frank stared thunderously at Nid. Finch began to breathe again and gazed at his brother, a glow of gratitude flowing from him.

***

It was too early for the evening's opening when Frank Bird knocked at the Viney's upstairs front door, but he'd chosen the hour deliberately; a time when Rod Viney would be at home but not working in the bar. The door was opened, not by Viney, but by Lois. She was like a startled rabbit, frozen under his gaze, staring back as if, in the very act of opening the door, she'd uncovered something appalling.

Frank affected bonhomie in an effort to reassure her and asked for her husband. The two younger children had emerged from one of the rooms into the long hall passage and stood behind her, staring unblinking and curious at him. He smiled a little at them and the girl giggled. A half-naked toddler waddled out to join them.

Lois glanced back but appeared not to have noticed the children. When she spoke to him again, the words barely escaped her mouth and were scarcely audible, as if she feared to expose them in public. It was as if she were swallowing herself bit by bit. After a moment she turned and walked along the hall, disappearing into one of the rooms. Maggie's head poked out from a door from further along, but only for as long as it took her to identify the visitor and then she was gone again, having shown no reaction.

Frank smiled again at the children. The girl looked brazenly back and then poked her tongue at him before laughing impertinently. The boy copied and they both rushed back into the room they'd come from, leaving only the toddler who sat heavily down on her bare bottom onto the lino floor, her fat legs splayed at him. Frank cleared his throat in embarrassment and stepped back, turning away to gaze back down the dark stairwell. He heard no sound from within the flat, only the noisy play of the young brother and sister, but then he heard a door open and footsteps along the hall, followed by the appearance of Rod Viney at the doorway.

His dark hair was awry and shirt open at the neck and cuffs, and there was a puffiness around his eyes and cheeks. It was clear to Frank that he'd been woken from his afternoon sleep.

'Frank,' Viney greeted the caller in a rough, sleep-edged voice. 'What can I do for you?'

The other man shifted a little uncomfortably. He felt in the right, certain of his ground but this man, rough and unsophisticated that he was, always set him at a disadvantage, always seemed to be one step ahead.

'Bit awkward this,' he began weakly, but then stiffened his resolve. 'Fact is, Rod, that lighter I lost three or four years back. You'll remember, the silver one Norma bought me. Considerable sentimental value, very considerable. Not just the actual value, although it was sterling silver you understand. Much more than that. Anniversary present, after... well, anyway... my boy tells me your oldest daughter's got it.'

Viney's fist was against the door jamb at head height, nearer to Frank Bird than to himself, and he was leaning onto it, his large head hanging forwards, framed by thick, dark curls. As Frank spoke these last words, Viney's eyes raised to the other's face. Frank was aware of the long eyelashes that were almost troublingly feminine.

'My daughter? That's quite a thing to say, Frank.'

'I don't say it lightly. There's reasons I'm pretty certain, a tune engraved. I can't see any other explanation.'

Viney pushed himself upright and looked fixedly back at Frank Bird. His face was stern and the puffiness had faded. He turned his head to one side and called over his shoulder, 'Margaret!'

Maggie's head appeared, just her face once again, at the edge of a door.

'Here!' he summoned, and she stepped sullenly out into the passage and walked slowly towards the two of them.

'Now, when I tell you to!' he barked, and slapped the back of her head so that it was jerked forwards. Her eyes stayed hard and cold and she stared up at Frank.

'Maggie... Margaret,' Frank began. 'Nigel tells me you've found something that belonged to me. A silver lighter.'

'You better not be thieving,' growled Viney.

The girl looked at them both, but she didn't speak. Viney took her by the upper arm and shook her vigorously.

'Steady, Rod,' said Frank. 'Let the girl speak, shall we?'

They both looked at her but Viney didn't relinquish his grip, holding her arm at an awkward and painful angle above her shoulder. 'Well?' he barked. She stared back, helpless in his grasp, but with a look of resentful hostility, determined not to show any outward sign of the pain.

'I found it,' she said, insolently. 'In the pub.'

'Thieving little bitch...!'

'Rod..!'

Maggie's dive to one side was too quick for the rough blow aimed at her.

***

There was nothing to be done about the tree house; no way that it could be repaired or rebuilt from the broken and smashed wood that remained. Even their makeshift ladder into the tree had been pulled away and stamped into the dull earth. No one had the heart to begin again. It had taken so much time and effort and sheer enthusiasm to build in the first place. Somehow it felt that there was no going back; that it couldn't be recaptured and, however hurt and vengeful they felt, the tree house was lost. After wandering dejectedly and aimless for a time, they'd abandoned their plans for the afternoon and the three girls had left the boys to their own devices and headed together back down to the village.

They returned along a path they used only infrequently. It dropped down between the long sloping plots of two old cottages which were set some way back from the lane. Their gardens extended upwards towards the fields, and the footpath followed a narrow stony gully between the high fences, along which a spring periodically broke out so that it was frequently muddy and wet underfoot, whatever the season. The pathway emerged right into one of the gardens, passing the end wall of the cottage itself, before following a broad grass track to the lane, which it joined almost opposite their school.

The girls dropped into single file and picked their way along the wet path, jumping between the stone slabs to keep their feet dry. When they reached the cottage they discovered Morris's trade bike was propped against the end wall, its basket full of green-groceries.

They quickly realised, from the conversation they could overhear at the front door, that this was Neville Potter making his delivery round.

Wordlessly, they made a pact of revenge and Maggie pulled out the bags of fruit and vegetables and the tray of eggs and carried them all to the narrow path where she strewed the contents and ground them into the muddy water with her feet. The other two quickly joined in and soon the area was a mess of broken eggs, pulped fruit and bruised vegetables, all barely recognisable.

They scarcely had time to race down to the lane before Neville returned from the cottage door and, even at that distance, heard his anguished roar. A few seconds later he came racing out on the bike, frantically looking from side to side in search of the perpetrators. The girls had taken up a position seated upon a front garden wall in the lane opposite, affecting a look of innocence despite their muddied legs and feet, in order to fully enjoy his reaction, confident he'd be unable to retaliate somewhere so public.

Neville came to an abrupt halt and stared at their laughing faces. They knew he'd be unable to tell Morris he'd lost his deliveries, or admit that a group of girls had taken them from him, and he knew that too. He kicked at the bike in anger and frustration. Both Ann and Lizzie felt a thrill of danger from the situation, even when he approached, having furiously slung the bike into a hedge. He glared conspicuously at their muddied feet.

'Muddy path that,' goaded Maggie. 'Can't think why we came that way.'

'It's because we like all the fruit along there,' chirped Lizzie. 'There's so much, it's all on the floor!' and they all laughed.

'Think you're so clever, don't you,' he snarled, but they laughed all the more, feeling for the first time since they'd left the tree house, deliciously light-hearted and cheerful.

'Finished your round, have you?' trilled Ann. 'You'll be home early today, then.' As she spoke her father's truck rumbled past and Sid tooted and waved from the window. She waved back with her fingers and there was a momentary pause as they all turned to watch, including Neville.

When he looked back to them, they were discomfited by the self-satisfied smile that had replaced his expression of fury. 'Off to his girlfriend's then, your Dad?' he remarked. 'Going to see your sister, eh?'

He paused for effect, content at having provoked the reaction he'd intended. Ann sat shocked and silent, a cold shudder gripping her insides, while the other two looked on, startled. He grinned to himself and retreated backwards towards the bike, all the while nodding knowingly. 'Your sister, eh?' he repeated. 'You just ask him.' Confident now, he mounted the bike and rode away, pausing only to spit out a great gobbet of shiny mucous which landed near them.

'Faggot!' yelled Maggie.

***

The twins having gone home, the three remaining boys had made their way from the wreck of the tree house, up to the broad summit of the hill where they sank heavily down upon the soft turf to gaze out across the vale, all verve for the day long dissipated. The steeper slopes dropped away behind them, down towards the village where, from time to time, the cries of children at play drifted up, while in every direction the countryside, in its green and gold with the ripening of summer, extended to the indefinable horizon. Two buzzards flew high above them, suspended on broad outstretched wings, before abruptly sweeping across the sky with wings inverted, calling their lament.

John leapt up, restless and still enraged, but the Bradbury brothers remained, sitting shoulder to shoulder. Jonathan joined the friends less often these days; he was, after all, now fourteen and had been going to his special Senior School for two full years, but he still liked to join in with the others occasionally, especially during the school holidays. The two brothers had remained close, their bond unaffected, despite the distractions and pressures of growing older.

Behind them John was roaming about, snatching up wind-broken branches and flinging them into the hedge top or thwacking clods of cow dung, sending each sailing far away over the hillside to where they would land with a crash amongst the bushes below. Robbie and Jonathan were aware of the disruption but had become so accustomed to these outbursts that they easily distanced themselves from the commotion.

'Why'd they have to do that?' moaned Robbie. 'They didn't have to pull it all down.'

'You have to ignore it, put it to one side. It'll only upset you otherwise,' said Jonathan, wisely.

'It's so unfair, though. We never did anything that bad.'

'No, but maybe they didn't know it was ours.'

'Malcolm knew. You can bet they knew! One of them must have seen us go there or something.'

'Perhaps. Anyway, you'll find something else soon, I'm sure.'

'I doubt it...'

'Of course you will. I lost my best pen at school last Spring and then I won one in the drawing prize, do you remember?'

'Mmm.'

'See, things happen like that.'

'Mmm, maybe.'

'You'll see.'

A faint breeze blew into their faces and a great roll of clouds tumbled across the paling sky, like a huge skein of grey wool.

'Look,' said Jonathan. 'Hugh.'

Robbie looked upwards to where his brother's gaze was focussed and there was the small plane, at such a distance that it could scarcely be recognisable, but he didn't doubt Jonathan's skill for identification and when, some minutes later, it passed them overhead, its distinctive chequered wing pattern was clearly displayed.

XVII

Ann crouched in the back garden, hidden from the house by the wood shed, and pressed her face against her knees. Thoughts swam in her head but she felt a kind of security knowing that she was unseen, a comfort blanket of concealment, a refuge from having to see, and then from knowing. She didn't want to go into the house, she didn't want to go in and see how different it all was; from that which was familiar to now a place bleak and removed of meaning. Above her she heard the whisper and slew of the bamboo leaves, their gentle restless movement in the faint breeze a constant reassurance, but also a reminder.

'Why?' her mother had wailed, shrill and ugly.

After a while Rags approached and softly sniffed with her wet nose at Ann's tear-salted cheeks, the dog's almond eyes regarding her kindly, but enquiring. She breathed in the smell of her coat; fetid, animal and comforting, her breath like wet leaves and fungi, the tang of the earth itself.

Ann rose and quickly crossed the garden to the side gate, quietly calling, 'I'm taking Rags out,' neither wanting or trying to be heard. The two of them hurried down the side to the rear footpath where she turned right, up towards Rushwood End, the little dark whippet bounding beside her, happy merely to be going out. Girl and dog hurried along behind the gardens, heartened by the emptiness of the sunken path and its atmosphere of a forgotten place, as if it belonged to no one, and therefore to her alone.

Thankfully, the lane at the end was empty and she crossed unnoticed, selecting the secluded route back to the hill rather than the open pastures, even though that way passed the Rushwood End farms. It was quiet enough and the big oaks and elms cast such shade that it was easy to slip unseen beneath them. The sunshine of earlier had faded, and the light had a drear colourlessness now beneath the greying skies. She was grateful for the change, feeling somehow undeserving of the sunshine. Secrets; in her mind they were pearly-grey, anyway.

'We'll go up the hill,' she whispered to the dog, who softly laid back her ears in response. She craved its vast, dwarfing skies; just to be nothing, a mere spec in its cradle.

A movement ahead caught her attention and she hesitated, unwilling to be seen. It was a small figure, a child not an adult, moving swiftly towards her. She soon recognised John, his swinging bandy walk unmistakeable, and he'd already seen her. Surreptitiously she wiped the moisture that clung still to her eyelashes and hesitated as he bounded towards her. He seemed to have forgotten all about the anguish and fury of the tree house that afternoon and marched up to her, full of energy and intent.

'Wha'cha. Where ya goin'?'

'Just up the hill.'

'Walkin' the dog, eh?' Rags was beginning to sniff around John's legs, causing him to recoil, mildly disconcerted by the animal's proximity and attentions.

'You know Rags...?'

'Yeah, 'course.'

She'd hoped he'd go on past after a short greeting, but John appeared to be in no hurry. On the contrary, unlike most other occasions when he seemed merely to have tolerated her presence, he was clearly now keen to chat.

'Them Draycotts,' he said, inclining his head back towards the farm from which direction he'd just come. 'They'll ge' i', they'll ge' wha' for, they will. I'm gonna see to i', I am. I'll 'ave 'em. They'll be sorry, right, they will,' he strutted. 'Yeah, them bastuds. They won't know, right, but I'll 'ave 'em, I will. Fuck 'em, all of 'em. Fuck 'em.'

'You should mind they don't see you,' said Ann, more for something to say than for any other reason. There was no likelihood of John listening to what she or anyone else cautioned, and she felt little connection to what he was saying. In fact she had scarcely been listening, so preoccupied was she with her own distress.

'Them fuckers is too stupid a see me,' he swanked. 'Stupid fuckers, all of 'em. See, in there?' and he jerked his head once more in the direction of the Draycott's farm, 'I've got my eye on 'em, I 'ave. I've found stuff, I'm watching 'em. They won't know, right.'

She scarcely followed this stream of babble. Her eyes were unfocussed, sliding off his face, which was animated as he jabbered and ranted, but also pinched with hatred. When he came to an end, she stepped sideways, indicating to pass him and continue her walk, but he turned back to her.

''E's gone off then, 'as 'e, yer ol' man?'

She was puzzled and a little discomfited by the question, and evaded it with a vague 'mmm'.

'Only, like, Lizzie, she sez... Anyway ya know, ya don't wanna take no notice of 'im, what 'e says, that fucker Potter. Maybe 'e is... well, I reckon 'e is, but wha' of i' anyway? 'E don't 'it ya, right? An' 'e comes 'ome, dun 'e.? Well, there ya are then. 'E ain't all bad, I reckon. Not like some of 'em, eh? That's right, innit? I mean 'e gives ya stuff, right? Christmas like, an' birthdays, an' ya goes on 'olidays 'n' stuff. I reckon 'e ain't so bad. It ain't right like, but i' ain't near as bad as i' could be, I'm tellin' ya. Don't get upset like; I reckon 'e, ya know, like 'e cares for ya 'n' stuff. S'right innit?'

Taken aback, she shrugged in response. John had never paid her much heed, and certainly never invested so much time and energy in speaking to her, and not about something that concerned her so directly. His words snagged at her distress and a sob caught in her throat. Humiliated, she stifled it and saw that he looked away, seeming to want to avoid her embarrassment or shame.

'It ain't worf i', getting' all upset like,' he said. 'There's plen'y worse'n your ol' man. Right, I gotta be gettin' on. See ya, then.'

And, with that, he gave a breezy wave and continued on his rollicking way, down the lane.

XVIII

'I'm not saying it was deliberate, you understand... It's important to me... to Norma and me... of very considerable sentimental value.'

Viney grunted in response.

'It's very significant for both of us, after the boy.... And we thought it was lost, and then Nigel got hold of that tune.'

Another grunt.

'Although I... we couldn't understand how it could just go missing, that it wasn't found, you know?'

Grunt.

'No. Well, what I'm saying... it must have got dropped. That's all I can think. Dropped on the floor, you know. Easily done.'

Viney looked over his shoulder to Maggie and his grim voice reverberated in the dank air of the cellar. 'Right! Now fetch it.'

She avoided looking at the two men who both stood before her in the narrow section of floor space. Her father's presence dominated the room, standing coldly impatient with suppressed anger, but an anger she felt wasn't so much directed at her for the misdemeanour, but at the position he now felt himself in with Frank Bird; at a disadvantage, guilty by association. Frank, by contrast, hovered edgily. His tension was tangible.

Neither spoke again and Maggie turned her back, unable to endure facing them when she gave away the access to her secret place. She slipped down beneath the shelves, as she had so many times before, and struggled beneath to her corner, the effort so much greater than usual. Once there she hauled herself up and stood before the small shelf, taking in her special possessions, the treasures she'd amassed over so many years and which she now felt to be sullied. She'd sat here so many times and heard her father across the room; she'd laughed and hugged to herself the comfort and triumph of knowing that she alone had her special corner, unknown by anyone. Now it was despoiled. She seethed with loathing for him.

'Get a move on!' he barked, and she heard things scraping. He was moving boxes on the shelves and attempting to peer through a gap to see where she was and what she was doing.

The afternoon was gloomy and only a dreary light fell from the small high window. It picked out the lighter, carefully positioned in pride of place beside the doll Alice who looked back at her, its expression serene but kindly; a mere child's toy. They were, she felt, all children's toys and trinkets, the mementos and treasure trove of her childhood, already slipping away. She took up the lighter and pressed her fingers around its hard surface, feeling the cold metal against her palm and then dropped down beneath the racks again.

Ahead was the box of ledgers beside which she and Nid had sprawled just four days ago, unseen and unheard as the two brewery officials had obliged Viney to provide the pub accounts ledgers for their scrutiny. It was Hugh, she'd known that. She'd recognised him, although he'd seemed much altered from the assured but casual young man she'd met with the others at the Hall two summers ago.

This Hugh was formal and authoritative. Her father had been angry then too, but it had been a different kind of anger; a raging but turned inwards anger. She'd been able to see and hear it churning within him, and all the while he'd affected a relaxed demeanour and charming manner, but the shake in his voice gave the lie and showed his anxiety. Hugh had seen through that too, she could tell. It was on that day she'd lain outstretched, head against the box of real ledgers with Nid's shoulder pressed into her ribs, the two of them silent observers. She'd heard Nid struggling to control his breathing, fearful but curious, turning his head to watch as three sets of feet had come down the short flight of steps to the cellar floor; Viney's were firm, taking in the short distance to the desk in three long strides, followed by Hugh, stepping easily, laced black shoes polished and shining, the trousers of his dark suit neatly creased. Behind him another man followed and then stood, rising occasionally onto the balls of his feet.

'And are these all?' Hugh had said.

'That's it,' her father had replied.

She could tell that Hugh turned and shifted his weight as if handing something heavy to the other man. This man's knees dipped slightly as he took the weight.

'Alright then, Mr Viney, thank you for your time today, and you can expect to hear back from us.'

'And when will that be?'

'I can't say, I'm afraid, but I can assure you we'll give it our fullest attention. Mr Fuller, our accountant, will be dealing with the matter and either he or I will be in touch. Well, thank you and we'll see ourselves out.'

There'd been silence as the two younger men had ascended the stairs, the only sound was that of the scuff of their shoes on the rough concrete surface. The other man trod heavily while, behind him, Hugh ascended briskly, pulling the door to behind them both. Her father had remained standing by his desk. After a moment he'd hoisted his trousers from the waist and settled them around his girth. He swore under his breath and then there was a sharp noise and something fell, or rather was sent flying, and several pens and pencils were spewed across the floor. Two rolled under the racks and Maggie shrank back in fear that Viney would retrieve them, but he ignored them. She heard him mutter some more and then he'd mounted the steps and left the room, banging the door heavily behind him. Beside her, Nid let out his breath in one long gasp.

'Get out here now!' Her father now roared.

She wriggled forwards, painfully and awkwardly on her elbows, the lighter held aloft in one fist. Her shoulder nudged against the box of ledgers, the ledgers Hugh should have taken; not the ones her father had provided, lying crook that he was. She kicked out with her legs and wriggled her torso free of the shelves. Immediately Viney bent forwards and wrenched the lighter from her grasp.

'This it, Frank?'

'Yes, that's it.' He spoke softly, after an intake of breath, and then said no more. She knew he held it in his hand; that he was turning it about, looking at it, reading the notation, familiarising himself with it once more. Did it feel smaller after so long, she wondered? Did it look grey and tarnished? Was it how he remembered; how he'd hoped it would still look?

She emerged slowly and rose silently to her feet, briefly ignored by the two men. Frank was holding the lighter in his open palm, as if he were weighing it or it was a rescued fledgling, and he was nodding to himself. His expression was dense; it was as if he were unable to speak.

Viney had watched. Suddenly Maggie felt a juddering thwack on the back of her head that sent her stumbling sideways into the shelves, her elbow dislodging a box of cigarettes.

'Thieving little bitch.'

'I'm not a thief, you are! I didn't know it was his. You're the liar; I know about you!'

A stinging slap to her cheek sucked the breath from her lungs.

'You get up those stairs right away. I'll deal with you,' and he flung her violently forwards. Resolute that she shouldn't cry, Maggie darted quickly ahead and ran up the steps and out of the cellar room.

XIX

The early evening cast a coolness that was unseasonable for August, but Ann was outdoors after her meal, in the cobbled front yard where she'd clambered into the open back of the truck and now lay amongst the lengths of newly-sawn timber, smelling their sweet resinous scent and fingering the shiny-smooth coils removed by her father's plane which she curled and re-curled about her fingers. She heard Maggie's footfall before she saw her, the sound springing off the walls of the neighbouring buildings as Maggie ran along the passage into the yard.

'I'm here,' Ann called, raising herself to look up over the rim of the open back.

'Quick! Come and help me,' commanded Maggie. She had in her arms a large bundle, wrapped in newspaper. 'Hide this and then help me get the rest. Come on!'

Her manner was even more imperative than usual, and with an edge of fear that made Ann comply without demur. She led Maggie to their back garden where together the two of them pushed the heavy parcel into a gap behind the wood shed and then, since she was given no alternative, Ann followed her friend back across The

Square to the pub. Maggie was uncharacteristically jittery as she let them in through the rear door.

Immediately the steady hum of conversation and acrid odour of cigarettes drifted up from the public bar and along the passage towards them, even though the door behind the bar counter was pushed to. Maggie stealthily turned the handle of the cellar door to their left and propelled Ann down the few steps and then, as Ann had seen her do before, sank to her knees and reached beneath the shelves to pull out the box which Ann recognised as containing the ledgers Maggie had once revealed to her.

With some effort she heaved out two large books, instructing Ann to take one, and covered both with newspaper sheets she had ready. Having returned the box to its usual position concealed beneath the shelving, she led Ann from the cellar room as cautiously and silently as they'd arrived. At the front of the pub Maggie peered in at the public bar window and would only cross back over The Square once she was certain her father was absorbed in conversation with his regulars. Back at Ann's garden, they heaped the two ledgers on top of the first bundle, and Maggie pulled foliage from the compost heap to further conceal them.

All this time Ann had obeyed her friend's orders, impelled by the other's determination, although she felt herself inwardly struggling to cope with her own anguish; her desolate, incommunicable hurt. The two girls now sat back upon the grass. Maggie's expression was rigid.

'You've got to take the books to Frank Bird,' she instructed.

'Me? Why?'

'You've got to! I'm supposed to be babysitting; I can't go out, right? It's important; say you will.'

'Alright, but why?'

'They're the real ledgers, okay?'

'Yes, I know; you showed me.'

'Right, well Bird's got to see them.'

'Why? Your Dad'll get into trouble.'

'He's a cheating bastard, okay? He's cheating the brewery, he hits my Mum and he's cheating the Bank.'

'He hits your Mum?'

''Course he does, stupid! You know it.'

'My Dad cheats, too.'

'It's not the same thing.'

'It's still cheating.'

Maggie paused and was silent for a time, the only mark of her sympathy. 'Still, he looks after you,' she said, offhandedly.

'That's what John said,' Ann reflected.

'John?' Maggie looked puzzled a moment and then quickly returned to the task in hand. 'Look, I've got to go back now in case they notice I've gone. You've got to get the ledgers to Frank Bird quickly. D'you understand? You've got to do it tonight.'

'They're very big...'

'Ann! It's important. Promise!' she demanded.

'Okay, I promise. Cross my heart and hope to die.'

'That's kid's stuff,' she snapped. 'Just do it. Right?'

Stung, Ann murmured, 'Okay, but what do I say?'

'You don't say anything. Just leave them there without seeing anyone. He'll soon discover what they are.' And, with no further word, she hurried out through the side gate. Ann could hear Maggie's footsteps as she sprinted away, back through the yard and along the passage to The Square.

For a while Ann sat reflecting on how to carry out her instructions. Another half an hour at most and she'd be called in for bed; and the ledgers were very heavy, so much so she could manage only one at a time. But then, inspired, she pulled her scooter from the shed, balanced the first of the ledgers on its footplate and, standing upon the book, propelled herself towards The Green, still uncertain how exactly she would accomplish the rest of the mission in time.

A group of youngsters was playing ball while several of the boys rode their bikes, labouring to the top of The Green and free-wheeling back down, legs splayed. She paused, partly to get her breath back but mostly to gather her thoughts, and then recognised Robbie and John, speeding together down the nearside of The Green on Robbie's bike. She waved and they wheeled across, mildly curious.

'I've got to deliver this and two more to Mr Bird,' she said. 'Will you help?'

'Is it from your Dad?' Robbie asked and, as he referred to Sid, there was a look in his eyes that suggested sympathy and she understood that he too knew what Neville had revealed.

'No, it's for Maggie. She asked me to help because she had to go back and babysit; you know what her Dad's like. I don't know about it exactly, but it's something to do with the pub. Look, it's supposed to be a secret and it's urgent, and really important.'

The boys fell in easily, content to be absorbed in some project. They hid the first ledger behind Mrs Ward's front wall and the three of them then returned to Ann's for the other two. 'I don't want to be seen putting them by the Birds' house,' Ann confided.

''Sorright. I'll do i' after dark,' John offered. 'When all them's gone a' bed. I'll stick 'em on their doorstep and no bugger'll know who dun i' like. All sor'ed, right?'

The light had faded, leaching all colour and life from the world, save for the liquid song of a blackbird, high on a gable end as it followed Ann home. A soft glow from the open front door lay upon the front garden, leading her towards the hall. Ahead she could see her father in the kitchen. He was making tea, looking down into the pot as he spooned in the leaves, while the kettle could be heard bubbling away on the cooker behind him, out of sight. In some way that she couldn't quite fathom, his shoulders seemed hunched and his attention unduly fixed upon the teapot, as if it would move away if he weren't focussed entirely upon it.

'A laughing stock,' came her mother's voice, unseen from behind the kitchen door. 'The whole village!'

Sid heeled back, briefly hidden by the door, and then poured the water on, his eyes following it down into the teapot, before settling on the china lid. 'You imagine it,' he muttered.

Ann pictured it, the bellied pot bubbling merrily on the stove, its soupy contents rolling and gurgling a happy laugh, chortling and babbling away while coils of steam snaked upwards to fan out across the ceiling, spreading their enticing, appetising aroma. Happy soup, merry broth, jolly stew; like a big cheery red-faced cook in her kitchen apron, tubby and joyous with dimpled hands. Laughing stock. Ha ha ha.

'Do I! Do I!' Something banged; Ann realised the door had been struck by an unseen hand, perhaps in a sudden gesture of despair.

'Give it a rest, Nell; there's nothing else to say. Just leave it will you.'

He turned to take up the tray and his eyes fell upon Ann who stood hesitantly in the hall. 'Look, here's Ann,' he announced brightly. His proper daughter.

XX

A sharp rapping at the front room window, accompanied by the shrill, panicked tones of a woman's voice, startled them all at their Saturday morning breakfast. Nellie and Sid exchanged concerned, questioning looks as the knocking intensified, accompanied by frantic cries of 'Nellie! Nell! Nell!'

Nellie jumped up, glancing into the lounge as she hurried towards the front door to see who it was at the window in such a state of distress. The door revealed Lois, limp dark hair pulled back so that the hollow distress in her eyes was all the more evident.

'My baby, my baby!' she was crying.

Sid thrust back his chair which scraped noisily across the kitchen floor and sprinted to his wife's side. Nellie had hold of Lois by the wrists, attempting to calm and question her as she wailed and thrashed, 'My baby!'

'Calm yourself, Lois, and just tell me. What is it? What's happened to Laura? Is she hurt?'

'My Maggie,' Lois lamented, 'Nellie, my little girl!'

Sid had hold of one arm now and, together, they drew Lois into the hall where she slumped against the wall and covered her face in her hands. 'She's gone,' she moaned.

'Lois!' called Sid, taking her forearm and shaking it gently. 'What's happened? Tell us so we can help, for God's sake!'

But all vitality was gone from Lois and she drooped forwards so that she was obliged to support herself with one hand on her knee, while the other wrung across her face as she soundlessly mewled.

'Her room,' she whimpered. 'She didn't come out to breakfast; I went to her room to call her and she wasn't there. The little 'uns hadn't seen her and she's nowhere. She's gone off, I know it, Nellie,' and she seized her by the wrist.

'There was a terrible fight with her father last night. Rod, you know, he gets terrible angry, he lashed out at her with his fists. He was shouting and swearing, like he does, and... what could I do? She says she didn't and he's accusing her, and she does bait him, she's like that, she's spirited but wilful and he can't take it. He's a man, with a temper; it just explodes out. He thinks the kids should do everything he wants, but they're just kids, aren't they? You know what kids are; they can't help themselves sometimes. My Maggie, she's a strong-willed girl. He can't take that and she riles him something terrible.' Lois paused to catch her breath and pulled a handkerchief from the pocket of her pinny and dabbed at her eyes and wiped her nose.

'Where will she have gone, Lois?' asked Nellie in the tone of one speaking to a child.

Lois looked slightly surprised for a moment, as if she'd forgotten the trauma that had brought her there, and balefully shook her head. 'I don't know, she could be anywhere. She must've slipped out while the little ones was asleep. She's probably been out all night. She could've been gone for hours!' and she began to weep again.

Nellie ushered Lois into the kitchen and made her drink hot sweet tea, looking all the while over her head to Sid, her eyes seeking from him what they should do. He was pulling on his jacket and quickly hurried out.

'You're her best friend,' sobbed Lois, raising a tear-streaked face to stare across the table to Ann, who recoiled in fright before her stricken look. 'Tell me, where would she go?'

But Ann had no idea and merely shook her head blankly, wide-eyed with alarm. While her mother attempted to calm Lois and deduce what could best be done, Ann slipped away unnoticed and ran to Wheelwrights, only to find that Sid had been there already to enlist the Rose brothers in a search party and that Lizzie had left, gone across the road to tell Robbie the startling news.

On hearing, Tom Bradbury had gone off to see what he too could do to help, leaving his two sons with Lizzie. They stood in the garden of Woodbine Cottage; restless, anxious and shocked by the unforeseen drama of Maggie's running away.

'She could be anywhere,' Lizzie bemoaned. 'Maybe miles away. Oh, poor Maggie. She must be so upset, and all alone.'

Robbie had to agree it was true about being miles away. Maggie was fit and could out-run many boys of her age; and she wouldn't be daunted at the thought of covering long distances, or the obstacles that she might encounter. Or fearful of the dangers, for that matter.

'It's hopeless. We'll have to be ever so lucky to find her. If she doesn't want to be found, she could be anywhere.'

'She could be spotted from the air,' said Jonathan who, until then, hadn't offered an opinion. 'From a plane.'

'We don't have a plane.'

'No, but...'

'We can't ring Hugh, we haven't seen him for ages for one thing.'

'We saw him at the Horse & Hounds only a few days ago, Robbie. Besides, this is an emergency. He won't mind, I know he won't. Come on, let's ring him. It's a Saturday, he'll be at home.'

Hugh's voice on the phone was affable but cautious. He was surprised, although not displeased to hear from the brothers, and asked them about their schooling and what they were up to. They held the handset between them, both speaking into it, crushed together in the telephone box at The Square. Jonathan had to bend down or Robbie would have been unable to reach, but they both held onto the handset, taking turns to answer and exchange pleasantries for a few minutes until Jonathan could wait no longer. As he spoke, he straightened up, inadvertently pulling the phone from Robbie's reach but was so absorbed he failed to notice.

'Hugh,' he said. 'You've got to help us.'

'What is it Jonathan? Are you in some kind of trouble?'

'No, not us. It's our friend Maggie. She's run away and got lost and no one'll be able to find her because she went hours ago and won't want to be seen, but you'd be able to see her from an aeroplane,' he blurted.

'I see. Do you think so?'

'Oh, please Hugh! Please help. I know you can.'

'Where's she gone from, Jonathan, and when did she leave?'

'You know it. From the Horse & Hounds pub here, and we don't know when but it was last night some time and she ran away because her Dad hit her. He's very big.'

There was a silence at the other end, then Hugh asked, 'Is that Mr Rod Viney?'

Robbie had pulled the phone back down so that he could partake once more. 'Yes, Hugh. She's his daughter and our friend. You met her once at Netherington Hall, but you probably don't remember. She's the same age as me; eleven.'

'Okay, look. Here's what we'll do. I'll go over to Aston Haddon to get the Cessna. I want you two to go down to the station. You know that big field on your side of the railway line? Has it got any animals in it at the moment?'

'No.'

'Right. Well, go home and get a sheet or a large white towel or something like that and then go to the field. Make sure there's no one in there and that it'll be safe to land. As long as it is, put the sheet on the ground and stand well away by the fence and I'll aim to put down there. I'll be about an hour, I should think, and try and find out what she's wearing. You might need to ask her Mum. You can see colours from up there but that's all. I'll see you down on the ground in about an hour, all being well. Alright?'

They stood in the field and anxiously scanned the sky, their backs pressed against the railway fence, their father's decorating dustsheet spread upon the grass. Jonathan was the first to spot the plane; a mere spec in the distance before it approached and made a pass above to assess the field's suitability. The boys watched as Hugh banked and then made another circuit before levelling the plane which dropped rapidly towards them, parallel with the railway line, touching down some fifty yards away before taxiing rather bumpily until it came to rest. Hugh cut the engine and stepped down, one hand on the wing strut.

In contrast to the day at the pub, he was casually dressed in an open-necked shirt with the sleeves rolled up. He approached the brothers briskly, right arm extended to shake each in turn by the hand.

'Good visibility, fortunately,' he began. 'You both look well. Now, what's the plan?'

Jonathan was beaming and had prepared well for the moment. 'She must be wearing her red dress; that's what her Mum told our friend's Mum,' he announced, taking the lead in the matter, playing the older brother; talking to Hugh man-to-man.

'Well, that's something,' said Hugh. 'It'll certainly help to make her visible. Now look, I'm going to need another pair of eyes. I can't see out both sides at once, and anyway you'll know the local terrain better than me.'

Robbie hadn't expected this. He looked at the Cessna behind Hugh; glossy red and white with the black and white chequered pattern just visible beneath the wings. Seen now, in this context, it seemed rather insubstantial. Both brothers were silent with surprise.

'Well then,' said Hugh brightly. 'Jonathan? Will you come and help me?'

Robbie was conscious of his brother beginning to sway slightly beside him and he made a small noise, whether of fear, excitement or anxiety it was impossible to tell. Hugh was looking at Jonathan with a small, encouraging smile.

'How about it?' he said.

Abruptly, Jonathan stopped swaying and pulled himself upright, his big hands flexing at his sides. 'Yes,' he said and, with some effort, propelled himself forwards.

'Good chap!' said Hugh, and clapped him on the shoulder. As they walked away towards the plane, Hugh looked back at Robbie and gave a smile and nod of acknowledgement.

Robbie stood back by the fence and watched as the plane gathered speed across the rough grass and then held his breath as it swept upwards, climbing quickly into the blue sky until it was no more than a small mark once again. He waved wildly and hoped that they could see him. As he watched, an emotion swept over him, welling up from deep within, almost unexpected. Such a swell of pride and joy was flowing through him, he felt his heart must burst.

Half an hour later he was sitting, high on the hill, with John and the twins. They'd gone to the old oak, where the tree house had been before its destruction, inspired that Maggie might have chosen it to hide beneath, but she wasn't there and neither was there any sign that she had been. They were straining to discern any scrap of red in the sweep of countryside that wrapped around the hill, screwing up their eyes and squinting against the harsh August light. Robbie's eyes rimmed the horizon, vainly searching. He thought he saw the little plane returning, but it was merely his tired eyes playing tricks.

'If it was me, I'd get a train to London,' said Finch.

'But it isn't you,' Nid sharply retorted. 'Anyway, she wouldn't have had the money for the fare. No one's said she took any, have they?'

'She coulda 'opped on wivou' the guard seein' like. S'easy. I dun i' all the time.'

'Says you.'

'I 'ave dun! Wha' d'you know; you ain't dun i', ave ya?'

'She could be anywhere,' Robbie repeated, yet again. 'Why did she go? I mean, why then and not before, or some other time?'

'It's obvious, isn't it,' said Nid. 'The lighter. She took our Dad's lighter and her Dad punished her.'

'She didn't mean to steal it, though.'

'Yeh, she wudda!'

'I don't think so. I mean, she must have known whose it was.'

'Dun ma'er. Silver innit.'

'My Dad had it engraved. It's a song for our brother, but he died.' Nid was looking out across the vale, expression bleak, and yet he'd never met James, hadn't even known until recently that he'd existed.

''appens, dunnit.'

Nid said nothing for a while, then added solemnly, 'He'd have been fourteen now.'

'Same age as my brother,' said Robbie, and then remembered that his brother was somewhere out there, flying in an aeroplane; his greatest dream. Actually flying, and with Hugh, his hero and great friend.

'Anyway, it's alright for you. You haven't lost a brother,' Nid accused.

'I ain't got no bruvva.'

'I thought you had a younger brother and sister.' Robbie turned from his reverie to look round at John, who lay sprawled behind him.

''alf. I ain't got no real bruvva and sister.'

'But you said...?'

'They're 'alf, ent they. They're 'is.'

'Isn't he your Dad?' asked Finch who, until then, hadn't participated in the discussion.

'That fucker.'

John sprang to his feet and marched up and down with exaggerated briskness, scanning the countryside, one hand shielding his eyes.

'I can't see no ships!' he chirruped.

XXI

'There's dew on the grass,' his father had said that morning, 'The year's turning,' and it was then that Robbie sensed the summer's demise, bringing to an end once again the reckless, risky, unpredictable weeks with John that lit up and bedevilled his summers.

He could count the days that remained; the days to still enjoy their freedom together before the school holidays would be over and John would go back to London. But this year was different. Robbie wouldn't be returning to the village school; he'd be going to the Grammar School in Cullingham, taking the bus each morning and not returning to Moreton Steyning until the end of each afternoon. He even had the uniform, bought for him in Cullingham; taken there by his parents who proudly stood admiring him while he, overcome with embarrassment, fidgeted in the stiff fabric; the wool of the over-sized blazer rough against his neck, the cap rigid and unfamiliar. He knew now how Jonathan had felt that day when he too had endured the right of passage of a first uniform and a new school.

He went directly to The Green to find John and discovered him engaged, as so often he was, in a fracas with a group of older boys; lads who, Robbie reflected, would be a couple of years above him in his new school. The type perhaps to take the opportunity to pick on him, a new boy, bewildered and unsure, who didn't know the ropes; easy pickings. There'd be no John to draw their flak, swaggering and goading for all he was worth. Robbie beckoned him away from the group which continued to trade insults and jeers as John turned his back.

'There ain't no fucker gonna put one over on me, right. I go' their number, en' I?' he trilled, sauntering over.

Robbie feared for himself in the big unknown world of Senior School, but he feared even more for John whose vitriol and chippiness would surely mark him as a target. Even now he was a slight figure for his age and always bore the marks and cuts that were a legacy of his regular skirmishes with those older and bigger than himself. Indeed, Robbie had never seen John without bruises or signs of having taken a beating, even when he first arrived each summer, and he'd been coming for four successive years now. Would he still come once they were all established at their

Secondary Schools, he wondered, or would their worlds have all changed too much?

Whether John thought about this at all it was impossible to tell, but he showed little or no interest in discussing his future, or of talking about school at all for that matter. Robbie was left uncertain where his friend would go on to, or even whether it was a Grammar or a Secondary Modern School, although he suspected that, unlike him, John hadn't passed his Eleven Plus. Even assuming he'd failed, John was unlikely to be bothered. He'd never expressed a desire for any future job, except perhaps on the railways. Robbie supposed that John had always assumed that would be his lot in life, and that his schooling was therefore something of an irrelevance, merely to be endured and passed through. In some ways, despite his bravura, that seemed to sum up John's attitude to life generally.

The Bird brothers wandered over from their garden to join the two friends. Nid, of course, had also secured a Grammar School place and it was a matter of conjecture whether Finch had also passed the exams, but the twins couldn't be split and so both would continue to be Robbie's classmates and join him at Cullingham Grammar, a matter of glorification and triumph for Finch and yet somehow of resignation for Nid.

The four of them were headed for the hill when they came upon Jonathan, his face obscured behind an enormous jam doughnut, which he was eating with great relish although it wasn't long since his breakfast.

The Baker's shop was popular with the local youth, who called in daily for pastry treats. A crowd could just be made out, milling around behind the steamed-up windows. Soon half a dozen older boys spilled out and began to fan out along the lane, noisy and boisterous. Malcolm and Squinter were amongst them, tucking into sausage rolls and throwing bits of pastry at one another.

As the group passed Jonathan, they engulfed and jostled him, surging round him like a river in spate, leaving him in their wake with an astonished look upon his face. His cheeks and nose were smeared with bright red jam, while about his feet lay the sugary, broken remnants of his doughnut. They were all twisting back to look, mocking faces creased into leering grins. Malcolm and Squinter laughed uproariously with their gruff animal-like sounds of newly-broken voices.

'Fuckers!' yelled John. 'Cow-shaggin' tossers, ya mother's 'ad i' with a goat, ya spastic fuckin' twats,' and he aimed a gob of spittle towards them, but the group merely continued on their way, still noisily jeering.

'Here's my hankie,' and Robbie pressed it into Jonathan's hand as his brother continued to stand, dazed and hurt, absently licking the jam and sugar from his nose and chin. 'I hadn't finished it,' he lamented.

'Come with us,' Robbie suggested to cheer him. 'We're going up the hill.' But they got no further than Snake Pond.

As they emerged from the confines of the narrow path and into the pond clearing, the waiting Draycott gang came suddenly upon them, rushing out from behind the surrounding trees and shrubs. Robbie felt himself rough-handled and punched and tried to lash out and kick, but heavier stronger arms held him and he was thrown roughly backwards into the scrub. He could see Finch tussling furiously with Neville Potter and from further away came the shouts, yells and clamour of combat. But cutting through it all came John's wild, high-pitched screaming.

Robbie struggled free, slumping forwards onto his hands and knees, panting to catch his breath. Finch now lay sprawled on his front with Neville's knee planted in the small of his back; he was desperately attempting to club Neville by swinging a large branch backwards over his own shoulder. Nid had run a short distance away and was being pursued by a youth who had him by the back of his shirt, with Squinter in hot pursuit.

But it was at John that Robbie was staring at transfixed.

He was raised high above Malcolm and Jack Duckett's braced arms, kicking frantically, all the while screaming and bellowing. Jonathan stood close by trying to stagger forwards and help, although he was clearly no match for any one of the others, never mind two of the biggest, and his arms were being pinned behind him by Malcolm's elder brother.

Jack and Malcolm roared with laughter as they waded into the pond's shallows and, in unison, launched John towards the deep water. He soared, arms and legs cart-wheeling, shrieking in terror, and landed with a ferocious splash that sent up jagged walls of brownish water with a series of waves that rolled across the pond's surface.

As he hit the water, his shrill shriek came to a crescendo, only for the sound to be swallowed by the thwack of his body into the pond and the raining back of all the displaced water as it splattered across the already-churning surface. Immediately he thrashed and flayed about, sending up more sprays and spumes of murky water, all the while making loud choking sounds and repeatedly crying *'Help!'*

The gang stood about, helpless with loud and callous laughter, and then clapped one another on the back before they lumbered away, pausing only to mock their victims with maliciously laughing faces.

Later, John would say he'd given as good as he got; that he'd been giving the Draycott brothers a right good pasting and kicked that Jack Duckett a right good-un in the knackers, and had Brazell in the gut and knocked Potter's head off and he was getting the better of them all; yes, even though all of them had been there – and that throwing him in the pond had been their only way of stopping his attack, and had they heard him? Bellowing his blood curdling cry which had scared the fuckers witless, and how they'd all cleared off after and didn't come back for more? Too afraid to wait around and get some more of it once he'd got out. He'd shown them.

He didn't say that straight away though. He emerged from the pond, hauled out by Jonathan, who'd waded in thigh-high to rescue him, choking and wheezing, his face pasty white and wiry dark hair plastered flat to his scalp. He stood at the edge, a wretched sight, with arms held clear of his body like a cormorant drying its wings while the water cascaded from every inch of him, even off his finger tips and nose; his shirt and trousers hanging sodden and flapping. He seemed so pitiably slight, almost delicate, and had now begun to shake from the shock. He was making a pathetic low moaning sound which quavered with each tremble of his small frame.

Robbie wanted to help, but didn't know what he should say or do. The truth was he felt shaken at how feeble and pitiable John appeared. His lips were blubbering uncontrollably and Robbie realised with alarm that the water which clung around his friend's eyes was no longer from the pond, but tears brimming behind his eyelashes. Abruptly, John turned and hurried away towards the village, wobbling on still-shaky legs, calling in a quavering voice that he was going back for dry clothes.

***

They didn't see him again until much later. He called round and induced each of his friends to come to the hill after their evening meal. They all met up, as arranged, and took one of the many footpaths to the top, avoiding that which passed the pond, although no mention was made of the morning's events. They were all there, including Jonathan, and were led by John who forged ahead, striding robustly in front, despite the effort needed to ascend the steeper slopes. The village quickly dropped away behind them and the warmth of the streets gave way to a light breeze.

John was on good form, bumptious, energetic and full of banter and swagger, all hint of vulnerability dispelled. He took them to the far side of the summit and remained smug and self-contained as they all disported themselves, much as they would on any summer evening on the hill.

Presently, as the sun dipped towards the horizon and the light began to soften, he broke away from the others and ran up towards the old hedge. They turned and watched as he dropped to his knees and scrabbled beneath a hollow tree and then struggled to his feet, returning to them bearing a large box with a look of triumph and satisfaction.

'Si' 'ere,' he directed, gathering everyone onto the grass, at a spot looking out over the eastern vale.

The paling sky had faded into the western horizon in a softest primrose, while, before them, the heavens had deepened into an unfathomable violet.

He placed the box further down the slope, and they watched with casual curiosity as he rummaged inside before strutting away for a short distance, appearing to forage around in the grass. He pulled something from his pocket and a light briefly flared, illuminating his face and hands, and then he briefly bent down before pelting back up the slope to plonk himself down in their midst.

'Jus' see, eh,' he chortled.

The rocket fizzed and then whooshed upwards with a scream like a Banshee, exploding in an umbrella of gold and silver which showered down all around them. He ran down again and repeated the process and a large Roman Candle lit up the hillside with fountains of green, red and moon-white globules.

'Where'd you get them?' cried Lizzie, eyes ablaze with the thrill, but John merely flung himself back onto the grass, cackling loudly.

'Where?' pressed Robbie, shaking his friend by the leg. 'Come on! Tell.'

'I go' 'em; I go' 'em bastuds! I found 'em, didn' I, in them Draycott's place where they 'id 'em. Them's their fireworks fa Bonfire Night, ain't they? I found 'em an' I nicked 'em. They bin keeping' them, savin' up like, but I got 'em, the fuckers!'

He ran down and pulled another rocket from the box, propping it amongst the grass tussocks before lighting it. It fizzled and flared and, as it did so, toppled forwards so that it made a low arc across the ground and fell amongst the box of fireworks. There was a silent pause and then the entire collection of pyrotechnics exploded as one, bursting into the evening sky with a magnificent cacophony and spectacle of dazzling light and colour that lit up the night canopy like a million sparkling jewels.

Part Two

1975

Chapter One

Rob flicked the Library tickets restlessly against one leg, and tried to relax back into the deep red banquette whilst quietly surveying the Library.

Shelves of books fanned out from a central desk, the whole room illuminated from above by a dome; rather reminiscent he thought of a London Underground station, but from a different era of course. The librarian, a middle-aged, refined kind of woman, who wore her dark hair in a bun set high on her head into which she absently poked her pencil, put him in mind of a spider in a web, and he mused at the thought, observing her as she stamped the books of those visitors who'd made their selections. The firm clunk of the date stamp echoed in the large, hushed expanse of the circular room.

A young woman, one of the staff he surmised, since she carried in her arms a pile of several books, swept briskly through the lobby area, her long, straight fair hair lifting faintly like a curtain on a breeze. The Library was busy; perhaps that's why he was obliged to wait for the books he'd ordered. Probably they'd had to be brought in from elsewhere, he reflected; a reference section in all likelihood as they were all of specialist interest. He didn't mind at all. It was in fact rather pleasant to be sitting there relaxing in what was, after all, the firm's time. He gazed upwards, studying the building's design; the high windows which must, on a brighter day than this, send shafts of light down to illuminate the area below, the restrained classical plasterwork and the use of pillars and angles to define different sections of the room. Moderately successfully, he thought.

The woman at her central lair took advantage of a lull in the numbers of borrowers to move a trolley of books away towards the shelves, and the same young woman from earlier again swept past him, approaching from the same direction as before, making him realise that he must have failed to notice her return, or perhaps she was able to circumnavigate the room without crossing the central area? Yes, that was most likely, and she wasn't holding onto any books so clearly she wasn't bringing his. She wore hip-hugging, bell-bottomed trousers and platform shoes with a neat little top, all of which emphasised a trim figure and, he noticed, a rather peachy behind.

He thought it would have been nice to remain in the locality while he was there and take a look around, have a stroll, but perhaps not if he was to be carrying four or five heavy books and, anyway, Janice would probably expect him, knowing that he was getting off work early. It was a pity, all the same.

'Mr Bradbury?'

He jumped at the sound of his name. It was Mrs Spider in the middle, holding up a hardback book and peering from over the top of large, dark-rimmed glasses. He raised an arm in acknowledgement and walked across to the desk. She was piling his books one upon another, checking the titles and firmly stamping each in turn.

'*Principals of Architecture* by J G Ballard?'

'Yes, that's mine.'

'*The Classical Building Examined by* Alexander Waterhouse; *Architectural Drawing for Students* by Dr Margaret Heissmann; *Architects and Planning Law by* Sir Gilbert Jefferson?'

'Yes, all mine.'

'*Hand Stitching for Fashion: Ethnic Styles Made Simple* by Antonia Lipovetsky?' The woman looked questioningly over her glasses, bright red lips briefly pursed.

'Yes.'

He felt he was being judged. Well, at least Janice would be happy. Apparently she'd looked everywhere for that book. He piled them all up and cursed to himself that he hadn't thought to bring a bag, most especially as two were great tomes and Janice's was over-sized, allowing for lots of lavish colourful illustrations and patterns, no doubt. Now she'd get on and finish the skirt she'd been talking about for weeks, increasingly frustrated at the lack of available information on 'ethnic styles', whatever they were.

Rob bundled the books into his arms and turned away from the desk and into the path of the same young woman who was once again hastening across the lobby area, rather more lightly burdened than he now was. She had a long straight fringe that hung low over her eyes and tossed her centrally parted hair back over her shoulders. As they passed she gave a vague acknowledging smile of politeness and clomped briskly away to the Library shelves. He was conscious of small neat features, an oval face and curved lips with slightly irregular teeth, a small nose that tipped up a little. He'd never seen her before but there was something familiar about the general ensemble of her appearance, something he couldn't quite put his finger on.

He turned and watched her busying herself as she reached the shelves, stooping low now to return a book, then stepping sideways a few paces, peering high and standing on tiptoe to reach a shelf above, long hair hanging down to her waist as she stretched upwards. The books weighed heavily in his arms and he shifted them, cradling the bundle by leaning the pile back against his chest. There certainly was something about the girl's expression but she was too far away now. He waited for a moment and then she returned from another aisle, walking briskly back across the lobby towards him, arms swinging freely, eyes looking ahead to the area beyond him.

'Ann?' he said, stepping sideways into her path.

She stopped abruptly and looked up, puzzled. 'Yes?' she answered, questioningly.

'Rob,' he said. 'Rob Bradbury.'

'Rob?' She looked vague still, but by now he was in no doubt.

'Rob – Robbie, from Moreton Steyning. D'you remember? It's Ann Dewberry, isn't it?'

'Yes... Robbie? My goodness, I really didn't recognise you!'

'It's been a few years.'

'It certainly has!'

'Fourteen?'

'It must be.'

'I'm sure I've changed, lost a bit of weight,' and he patted at his stomach, briefly removing one hand from beneath the pile of books in order to do so.

'I can see it's you now,' she said, and smiled. 'Gosh. What a surprise! Whatever are you doing here?'

'Getting books!' and he laughed, indicating the heavy bundle he held.

'Yes, you are rather burdened. Goodness, what's all that lot for?'

'Oh, studies, I'm afraid.'

She leaned forwards and read off a couple of titles. 'Architecture. Sounds good.'

'Hopefully. I've a way to go yet, though.'

'Even so.'

'And you? Is this where you work?'

She pulled what can only be described as a rather resigned expression and smiled ruefully. 'Well, for the time being.'

'It's alright, isn't it?'

'Not too bad.'

'You don't live in Moreton Steyning anymore, then?'

'No, not for a few years now; not since I left College. Have you been back?'

'Not for years actually. What about you?'

'I go from time to time. It hasn't changed all that much.'

'Look,' he said, shifting the weight of books into the crook of one arm. 'It's been so long, it would be really good to talk to you properly, for a bit longer and have a proper catch up. Could we meet, you know, have a good chat somewhere? Have a drink or something, perhaps?'

'I don't see why not; that would be nice. Do you live locally?'

'No, Uxbridge, but I work not that far away.'

'We could meet for lunch perhaps?'

'That would be great. When're you free?'

'How about Thursday?'

'I could meet you here.'

'Okay. Twelve thirty?'

'Twelve thirty it is then, on Thursday.'

They exchanged smiles and goodbyes and Rob left the building, stepping out into the pale grey of a March day in central London. Ann Dewbury, he thought. Good grief, after all these years, and his thoughts flew back to Moreton Steyning; dear old Moreton Steyning, and the safe and cherished world of his childhood. So long ago, such a different life, although in so many ways it seemed it was only yesterday. He realised, through a wave of nostalgia, that he'd scarcely thought about the place these last few years, through the ever-accelerating progress of his own life, through school and College and now work, building a life and career for himself, ever looking to the future. His mother had instilled that in him at least.

By now the edges of the books were cutting uncomfortably into the skin on the inside of his wrist and he hurried away, down the broad steps and out across the teaming main road to the Underground.

He called Janice from home but left it until after he'd eaten, until a time when he thought she'd be unwilling to turn out to collect the book and he could plead tiredness. There'd be no harm in delaying and, although she'd sighed and said that, if only he'd let her know earlier, she'd have come round and would then have had time to at least look through it, she accepted the inevitability and remembered to thank him.

'Does it look good?' she'd asked.

'Well, I think so,' he said.

She proclaimed it excellent when he took it round to her the next evening. Sitting on the sofa, sunk deep in amongst the cushions, the book raised close to her face, she studied in detail the intricate designs for embroidery, crochet, macramé and appliqué work.

It was almost four years ago that they'd met at College and they'd been together now for three. She was a slender, purposeful girl, with a lively face and mass of shoulder-length golden-brown hair and a doggedness that awed Rob. Whatever she undertook she would be fully absorbed by and allow nothing to deflect from her enthusiasm. She was nevertheless loyal and committed. There had been a few boyfriends before Rob but she found him very much to her liking. For his part, he was never sure if he'd asked Janice out or if she'd contrived to be asked by him, but he found her to be an attractive and steadfast partner. She wasn't by any means his first girlfriend; there'd been several during his late teens and early twenties, but their relationship had settled into a steady regularity.

They lived about a mile apart and he'd helped her find the flat, or more accurately flatlet; a neat modern one-bedroom apartment in a fairly modern block, close to the shops and convenient for where she worked as a dental nurse. Rob's own accommodation was where he'd lived as a student; a first-floor flat in a converted Edwardian house in the older suburbs, which he'd shared originally with two fellow students, both of whom had since moved on, and which he now occupied alone. It was a quiet and leafy residential road and he enjoyed the general air of quiet and security it provided. It was the kind of street that had changed little in forty years. By good fortune, it was also a mere six minutes' walk to the station for his daily commute to the architectural practice in London where he worked and where he was training for his professional qualifications.

Since Janice appeared disinclined to remove herself from the Antonia Lipovetsky, he flicked for a time through a magazine she subscribed to and then finally, somewhat bored and restless, pushed himself from the armchair.

'Coffee?' he enquired.

'Mmm,' she murmured distractedly, and then, 'Yes please,' and tucked her legs up, slippers discarded and now lying lop-sided beneath the coffee table.

Rob entered the compact-but-adequate kitchen and put the kettle on. He emerged a few minutes late bearing two earthenware mugs of steaming coffee. Janice glanced up, sated now from her needlework and craft book, ready to resume her sewing project, feeling entirely equal to the task and with the necessary information now at hand and already partly digested.

She wouldn't have called Rob handsome but he had a pleasant face, neither overly manly or weakly feminine. He wore his light brown hair, which had just the slightest wave to it with a stubborn cowlick above one temple, long over his ears and collar, and his hazel-blue eyes had a soft way of looking at you, as if he were always on the point of apologising. Unfortunately his mouth was a little lop-sided, but she felt that could be forgiven, and the jawline was at least firm, if somewhat rounded. He was almost a year younger than her and retained a certain boyishness in his appearance, not helped by a tendency to the over-casual in his dress, but she undertook to encourage him in that department to be more presentable. It would help in his future career too.

He placed the mugs on the coffee table and eased himself back into the armchair opposite. She smiled encouragingly and mouthed a ‘thank you’.

‘Bumped into someone at the Library I hadn’t seen for years.’

‘Oh?’

‘Someone from Moreton Steyning I went to school with; Ann Dewbury. Must be fourteen years since I last saw her. I didn’t recognise her at first, or she me for that matter.’

‘Small world.’

‘Yes. I’m meeting her for lunch the day after tomorrow so we can catch up.’

‘That’ll be nice. You’re coming here in the evening?’

‘I may be late back, especially if it’s a long lunch and I have to catch up.’

‘But it’s Thursday.’

‘I know, but it was the only day. Look, I’ll try. Anyway we weren’t planning anything, were we?’

‘No, but...’

‘What d’you want to do tonight?’

‘Don’t mind.’

‘Shall we go for a drink?’

‘Could do.’

They saw one another several evenings a week. Not Wednesdays, since that was when Janice saw her older sister, and in any event Rob had an evening class. Not on Mondays since they were both tired from their return to work after the weekend's entertainments, and rarely on Fridays since he had day-release that went on into the early evening. On Saturday mornings Janice saw her parents and sister, and more often than not joined them for lunch. Generally, afterwards, Rob would call on her or collect her from her parents' house and the remainder of the weekend would usually be spent in one another's company, except when he had exams looming and was obliged to study. On Tuesdays and Thursdays and at weekends they went to local pubs, to the cinema, to see bands playing, or met with mutual friends. Their lives were ordinary and uneventful, but not unenjoyable.

In two years, Rob would complete his training and had every expectation of promotion. Then perhaps, one day, an architectural practice of his own, but, for now, his weeks passed much as they had for the last three years since he'd left College and he and Janice had become a couple.

***

'There's the pub round the corner, or there's a wholefood place which is nice, if you fancy that sort of thing.' Ann was waiting in the lobby when he arrived and offered her local knowledge.

'Wholefood would make a change; why not?' he said, and followed her outside and through the local streets to a small and bustling café on the corner of a fairly smart street which was busy with mainly younger people. Here, they collected their food from the counter displays and found a place to eat beside the steamed-up window.

'I can't get over bumping into you like that!' Rob began.

She laughed lightly in agreement and he saw in her face an expression he recognised from her childhood, a familiarity that shot him back to his own younger days. 'When did you leave Moreton Steyning?' he asked.

'After College. I went back home during the holidays while I was studying of course and then, once I got back after I'd graduated, I had a job for about six months in Cullingham; nothing special, just admin work. Then I went into the central Library there and looked around for something in London.'

'And when was that?'

'Oh, about four years ago. Yes, four years last December. Not in this Library; in Notting Hill, and then I got transferred here.'

'That was good was it?'

'Oh essentially, yes. It was a promotion, and this is more central too.'

'You like being in London?'

'I do, yes. There's a real buzz to it, don't you think?'

'Definitely.'

'I still go back to Moreton Steyning to see my parents, of course.'

'They're still there, then? Both okay?'

'Fine, thanks. Still in the cottage.'

'Dad still doing carpentry?'

'Yes, he always seems to find plenty of work. You know him; he's never ill. And Mum helps with the pre-school club two mornings a week, which gets her out. What about you? What've you been doing all these years? We never heard once you left and I often wondered.'

'We settled near Denham.'

'That's what I heard, although we didn't know where.'

'It wasn't a bad place really and the house was bigger. Pretty modern; not like the old cottage.'

'Woodbine Cottage?'

He felt a warmth hearing the old name again and smiled with the pleasure. 'Oh, yes, Woodbine Cottage. Who lives there now?'

'A new couple from outside; I don't know them, I'm afraid. They've got young children.'

'I wonder if they go running amok on the hill like we did?' he laughed.

Ann looked up and gave a light snort of laughter too. 'Happy days,' she said.

'Yes.'

'So... tell me,' and she looked into his face to draw him out. 'It was a nursery business, wasn't it?'

'Yes, in partnership with my Mum's brother-in-law. It took a couple of years or more to take off, but it's been pretty successful really; a living, you know.'

'It must have been awful for your father, though – he loved that place. He'd been there all his working life.'

'And my Grandfather; and Great Grandfather.'

'Terrible.'

'It was an awful shock; I don't think he's ever really gotten over it, but there wasn't the money any more. You know, different times. It was the Winter of 60/61 that did it. The Harrison-Bates just couldn't justify the cost of keeping on so many regular gardening staff. There wasn't enough work or enough money, frankly. Dad was the youngest, the most able to get other employment they decided, so they let him go.'

'Yes, I can see that.'

'My mother's thrived on the move. She likes the shops and everything and her sister's nearby; they're very close in age. I think she found the whole thing of setting up the Garden Centre a challenge. She really got a lot out of it, and she does all the business side of things; the accounts and everything. Dad mostly concentrates on the plants. It's a lot of work, though. They're open six days a week, so there's very little rest and they've expanded a couple of times already.'

'Wow, they must be doing well, that's good. So, you must have gone to school round there?'

'Uxbridge, where I live now; the local grammar. It was okay. Then College, and now the architects' office. That's what I'm training for – architecture.'

'I always thought you'd end up as a Biologist or something. All those newts and creatures!'

'Oh, God, yes. I had tanks of them, didn't I? Beetles and pretty much anything that moved. Jonathan and I used to collect them from Snake Pond.'

'Oh, gosh, Jonathan!' she recalled. 'How is he?' and she smiled warmly at the recollection of his big friendly face.

All the while they'd been talking, speaking lightly and easily, glancing up to one another while they ate and as they exchanged news, but Rob now put his fork down and folded his arms along the table's edge, leaning forwards onto them.

'I'm afraid...'

She caught the change of tone and manner and instantly adjusted her expression. Her demeanour had been happy with the anticipation of news, but now bore a look of empathetic concern and a small frown.

'Oh, golly, what is it?'

'He died, I'm afraid.'

'Oh, Robbie. No!' she realised, as she spoke, that she'd instinctively reverted to the familiar name of their childhood, but suppressed a slight jolt of embarrassment. 'Oh, no! When?'

'Eight years ago.'

'What happened?' she spoke quietly, partly from the shock and sadness, but also for the sorrow she immediately perceived in Rob.

'A weak heart. We didn't know; it'd never been diagnosed. He just collapsed, suddenly, without warning, and he'd died even before the ambulance arrived. There was nothing anyone could do.'

'Where did it happen?'

'Just outside the Nursery. He'd just finished for the day, next thing he was on the floor. Dad didn't see it happen, he just turned round and there was Jonathan on the ground, not moving. He just had a little cut on his forehead from where he fell, otherwise he looked just like he always did, but he'd gone, already gone when Dad got to him.'

'That's terrible, really awful. I can't believe it, he was always, you know, just there.'

She gestured into the air to convey in some inadequate way the significance of his genial presence but, as she did so, realised the haunting accuracy of her words for Rob and the 'no longer there' that for him remained.

'My father's never got over it.'

They were silent for a moment, respecting the sense of loss behind Rob's words.

'I'm so sorry,' she said softly, leaning forwards to show empathy.

'Thank you.'

It was hardly recent, eight years, but he'd never got over it either – and he knew he never would.

'So… what exactly do you do at the Library?' he asked, to restore a lighter tone to their conversation.

'I manage the non-fiction area,' said Ann. 'That was my promotion.'

'Very good,' he smiled, nodding to show that he was impressed.

'Oh, it's not all that, although I do have two junior members of staff under me. What I hope to be is a journalist.'

'A journalist?'

'Mmm, that's always been my aim, but I got a bit side-tracked. A need to feed body, if not soul. The admin job in Cullingham was on the local paper but it didn't materialise into anything further, and the Library paid more than twice as much, even in Cullingham!'

'So, how do you plan…'

'I'm studying one day a week. I go to College every Wednesday on a Journalism course.'

'That's great.'

'Well, we'll see. I've had a handful of pieces accepted for local and specialist magazines.'

'Wow!'

'Oh, nothing grand… really! Don't get too excited.'

'Even so, you're making a start. So, what does the course cover? I mean, how do you get to be a Journalist?'

'It covers everything from news to sport and technical writing. It's news and features I really want to do, but the others are handy in case I can't hack it,' and she looked up, coyly smiling, acknowledging the joke.

He chuckled, abashed, having failed to notice. They'd both grown up from the games and scrapes of fifteen or twenty years ago and this was something of a different Ann. No doubt he appeared altered to her as well.

She glanced at her watch.

'Need to get back?' he asked, conscious that the time had passed quickly and there were so many more topics he'd like to have covered.

'Soon,' she said. 'In another five or six minutes, as long as I walk fast.'

'I haven't kept in touch, what of all the others? Are you in contact still? What did they all do? How's Maggie, do you still see her?' and then he laughed, acknowledging, 'Sorry, lots of questions!'

Ann smiled, in the small, quiet way that he remembered. 'That's alright. There's a lot to cover, isn't there? Well, Maggie's okay. She's a Financial Manager now for a large Hospital in Nottingham.'

'That's excellent.'

'Yes. And Andrew, you know, Finch? He runs the village garage; Fellowes's, as was.'

Rob's face told of his admiring surprise and Ann smiled back, nodding in acknowledgement. 'Yes, I know, and doing very well at it too.'

'Good for him!'

'I don't know about Nid – Nigel. He disappeared at some point during the university years. The family were always a bit cagey.'

'Was he okay?'

She frowned and shook her head. 'I really don't know. I tried to catch Andrew when I was passing the garage a couple of visits ago, but he was busy and just waved. They must be in touch but I don't know where Nigel went, or what he's doing now.'

'And Lizzie?' Rob tried to control the hesitation and eagerness in his voice.

'Well, Lizzie too in a way. She's well as far as I know, and we all went through 'A' Levels together at Cullingham, but I lost track of her after we both went off to College. Maggie and I stayed close, we still are and I see her regularly when I can get up to Nottingham or she comes down; she's always busy, though. A right career woman, she is!'

'Fancy that. Where did Lizzie go to College?'

'London, as far as I know. History, I think it was. She was always very good at it, wasn't she? I'm sure she goes back to see her family but our visits home have never coincided.'

Suddenly she flicked her wrist over and looked at her watch again. 'Oh gosh.'

'Time to go?'

'Mmm.'

Rob accompanied Ann back to the main road from where he could catch a bus to the vicinity of his own office. They paused at the foot of the Library steps.

'Edwardian Graeco-Roman classicism,' he said, indicating over his shoulder.

She looked round, puzzled. 'Oh! The building?'

'Yes. Oh God, here's my bus! Look, we've hardly touched on some of the things I wanted to chew over with you. D'you fancy doing this again?'

She gave a light shrug, agreeable. 'Sure. Call me at the Library.'

He waved cheerily and raced off to the stop, his arm raised to hail the bus before it sailed past. Ann watched him go, reflecting on how pleasant it was to share memories of their childhood together in Moreton Steyning. Robbie had always been such an amiable companion, if a little bit of a mother's boy. She found him pleasant company still, and rather a slimmer and taller individual than perhaps might have been expected from his younger self, but still essentially the Robbie she'd known.

***

The lunch had been a welcome highlight and distraction for Ann. She always disliked the days when Mark came; they unsettled her, reawakening old let-downs, and disturbing the otherwise smooth flow of her life. She hurried up the broad steps and across the lobby to the small office that she shared with her team, and swung herself in behind her desk. The others, a willing but careless girl in her first job from school, and a mature woman who'd had many supervisors before herself, both glanced up and the latter left the room to resume attendance within the Library itself.

Ann's desk was neat and tidy and she pulled the paperwork from her in-tray, settling down for the afternoon's duties, glancing up towards the clock above the door. It was almost 2pm. Sure enough, a few minutes later Mark bustled in through the heavy swing doors to the lobby, visible to her through the open office door. He wore his long dark overcoat and his dark brown hair was neatly cut. She followed him with her eyes and noted that he didn't look towards her office, but merely strode across to the second set of doors and disappeared into the Library.

Chapter Two

Janice had cooked a special meal for the Saturday evening when they entertained four of their friends. The look in her eyes across the table, her mood enlivened by the wine and boosted by what she felt to be her triumph as a hostess and cook, told Rob he'd be staying the night. That wasn't unusual but he knew the signals of expectation and permission, the sly looks and little performances of charm put on for him to savour.

She was talking and laughing, relishing her hostess role, seated opposite him at the further end of the table, the bloom in her cheeks reflecting the colour from the slinky coral pink maxi dress she wore. She'd been making it specially, in secret she'd said, as a surprise for him, and it undeniably suited her, flaring from her narrow hips, the bodice hugging her long slender torso. She'd braided the collar, she told him, deriving the ethnic design from the book he'd collected from the Library.

He smiled back in response to the winning gaze she flashed at him over the tops of their guests' heads as, together, they cleared the plates away from the main course of chicken casserole.

'I think they liked it,' she whispered to him back out in the kitchen.

'It was delicious,' he complimented.

His own contribution had been to chop the vegetables, prepare the cold starter and set the table. Apart from the male host's customary duties of serving the drinks, that is. Janice liked things done properly.

Their guests stayed a little longer than she would have liked, being eager to clear away once the performance of the meal was concluded, but everyone had relaxed and remained chatting over coffee and mints for another hour or so. It was considerably later than Rob would have liked too, but Saturday night was Saturday night, and their guests all wanted to have a good time. Rob had other ideas on how he'd achieve his.

The following day they stayed in bed until mid-morning and then, taking Rob's car, drove out to the woods for a walk. It wasn't like the countryside of his childhood, but he was well-used to the comfortable and accessible Green Belt, and they came regularly to take the fresh air and exercise for a few hours. They found lunch at a nearby pub and returned in time to grab an early sandwich and then go to the cinema in the High Street for the evening.

He was resigned to another week's commuting by the time he was seated on the Underground the next morning, being jogged and jolted, pressed into the customary rush-hour crush between others who, like him, were blearily returning to work. It was ten days since he'd seen Ann. Last week had been out as he'd had clients to see, but he'd made a mental note to call her as soon as he got in today to see if she could make a lunchtime to meet up again.

The phone rang for a time and a brisk voice answered. He asked for Ann and, after a few clicks and two brief rings, he heard her small, clear voice answer 'Hello'.

'Hello, Ann.'

'Hello?'

'It's Rob.'

'Rob! How are you?'

'I'm fine, fine thank you. I was wondering, have you got time to meet up again?'

'I'm busy Thursday this week, I'm afraid, but I can do tomorrow if that's any good.'

'Perfect. Twelve thirty again?'

'Yes, and I won't have to rush back quite so much, unless you have to that is.'

'I'll stay on a bit tonight to make up.'

'Great, I'll see you then.'

During the evening, he thought of many questions to ask her, and yet more still while travelling in by train in the morning; things that hadn't come to mind during their previous lunch. The weather was fine, a mild day in early April when the sun shone softly and the daffodils and early tulips had already supplanted the crocus. He bustled eagerly across the main road and found her standing on the steps outside the Library, observing his approach. He smiled bashfully, knowing that he had been watched. She was a diminutive figure still, but now bore herself with a sense of her own individuality.

'Hi there,' she called, making her way down to join him.

'Hello again. How're you?'

'I'm fine, thanks. What a lovely day! We could go to the park and sit outside. What d'you think?'

'That sounds an excellent idea.'

They collected sandwiches from a café en route, and found a vacant bench which overlooked the lake where Canada Geese and white swans drifted, unconcerned and aimless. Rob threw a few crumbs to them.

'They'll never leave you alone,' she warned.

They'll sting if you flap, he thought.

'So...' he began. 'Tell me more.'

'Where do we begin?'

'So much. After we met, I was thinking about Moreton Steyning and everyone. I kept remembering things and people.'

'Do you miss it? Did you, after you moved away?'

'I suppose I did, but everything was so strange and so different then. I wouldn't say 'missed' was quite the right word, because everything I knew was changing.'

'Everything does change at that age though, doesn't it?'

'Well, that's it. There was so much else going on. New school, new house, new friends. The new business.'

'It must have been quite an upheaval.'

'It was. Worse for my parents probably, especially my Dad. I had cousins nearby; my Mum's sister's kids, it was her husband we set the business up with, so at least I knew someone.'

'Oh, of course.'

'There was a boy nearly my age – Clive – and a girl that was Susan's age.'

'Oh, your sister! I'm sorry, I forgot. How is she?'

'Married, two children; not far away so she keeps an eye on Mum and Dad.'

'They must enjoy the grandchildren?'

'That's one way of putting it!'

'And the business, the Garden Centre, you say it's going well?'

'Definitely. It'll see them both out. It has its ups and downs and it's a bit seasonal, of course. Although they do Christmas trees and holly wreaths, that sort of thing in winter, but overall it does very well. They've expanded twice and there's five staff now.'

'That's terrific. You know, I was thinking after we met before, about Nid. He went to Scotland, I think. I think that's what Andy said. It struck me later.'

'Doesn't Andrew like being called Finch anymore?'

'I don't think he minds, but most people seem to call him Andy now. He's a real businessman, you know; everyone takes their car there. He's a very good mechanic apparently.'

'You see, he just had to find his niche!'

'I know. It's a pity his Dad didn't see it that way. Still, it never seemed to bother Andy much, did it?'

'Not that I could tell; he was always the happy-go-lucky one. So, Maggie... what's her set up? Is she single?'

Ann threw back her head and laughed. 'You'll never guess,' she said. 'See if you can guess who she married.'

'Malcolm Draycott!'

'Not exactly, but close.'

'Go on then.'

'Neville Potter.'

'No!'

'Yes! And she used to bait him like mad. Actually, I think she always rather liked him.'

'Kids?'

'No, not Maggie. She's a career girl all the way. It'll be a while yet, if ever.'

'Is she still the same?'

'Oh, yes, just as forthright. She's got a good heart, though.'

'And that father of hers?'

'Prison. Or was that before you left?'

'It was. Two years wasn't it?'

'Something like that.'

'And what happened to the family? It was just before we left the village and we rather had our own concerns at the time. They were still in the pub flat when we moved away, but there was that new Landlord.'

'Council house in Cullingham. Did them a favour, actually, there was much more room for them all and no one knew them there or what'd happened.'

'So, where is he, Viney? Did he go back?'

'No, he didn't. She slung him out, wouldn't have him back. Can you believe it? Poor Lois finally stood up to him. Actually, I think it was Maggie really, but once they got settled into the new place and Lois claimed benefits and everything, I think they found they could manage on their own. Good riddance, frankly.'

And she turned and smiled, and he smiled too.

They were silent for a few minutes and gazed out over the water, both having finished their sandwiches. The early Spring sunshine felt gently warm on their faces and everywhere the trees were bursting with a vivid green from new leaves and growth.

'What about the shops?' he asked, turning back to Ann. 'Are they all still there? Surely not?'

'Some. Your Uncle's went, but you know that, and Luff retired. The Jug & Bottle's been done up and is quite smart now but the Horse & Hounds is much the same.'

'But without the off-sales...?'

'Yes! At least, not the out-the-back ones. Oh and Mrs Patterson's still there!'

'No! She must have been about a hundred!'

'Well, she's about a hundred and fifty now.'

'That's amazing. D'you remember us all crowding in there after school?'

‘Of course. Everyone jostling and spilling out onto the pavement. Those awful bright orange lollies.’

‘Loved them!’ exclaimed Rob. ‘Fancy that. Incredible. I’d have put money on it that she’d have retired years ago, maybe not even been alive anymore.’

‘I know. Thank goodness some things remain, and just as you remember them. D’you remember the day Malcolm and everyone caught us in the school playground and tied us up in that rope?’

‘We got well and truly caught, didn’t we?’

‘I had the scars from those wheals for about two weeks after. I had to try and hide them from my Mum or she’d have had a fit.’

‘What about when Finch broke his arm. D’you remember carrying him down from the hill. Didn’t we make a stretcher out of jumpers and sticks?’

‘Yes we did, but d’you remember the look on his mother’s face when we brought him to the house?’ said Ann. ‘Like she’d seen a ghost.’

‘Well, you know why that was, don’t you?’

‘Oh God, yes. After losing the first one, it must’ve been an awful shock. She didn’t know Finch’d only broken his wrist. You know the twins didn’t know? Their parents had never told them there’d been a child before that had died?’

‘I didn’t know either. My sister said she did but I suppose she’d have remembered, being that much older.’

‘None of us did, growing up. It was kept a secret. They were ashamed I think, or too traumatised. It was Maggie who found out.’

‘It would be!’

‘Yes…’

‘What’s the story then? What did you hear?’ asked Rob.

‘Only that it was a little boy and that he had meningitis and died very suddenly, before they could get him to hospital even. The Bird’s never got over the shock.’

‘According to my mother they doted on the boy and used to say he was exceptionally bright, although how they could tell when he was so young I don’t know. But that’s the thing, you see. Jonathan would've been a similar age, just a bit younger, I think. They'd have been bringing them both up at the same time, my Mum and Norma Bird. I don't know what my mother would have thought, given the circumstances. Given the contrast.'

'She never minded though, did she? I never felt your parents believed, well, you know,' Ann shrugged, somewhat embarrassed, struggling to find an appropriate way to express herself. 'I don't think they believed Jonathan was someone they should ever treat any differently, or value less as a person. I always thought highly of them for that.'

'My father always called Jonathan his 'special boy'. I admired him hugely for it. Still do. He treated him as if he were a blessing on our family.'

Ann saw that Rob's eyes shone with moisture and that he looked away for a bit, affecting to study the ornamental birds.

'Mandarin ducks, aren't they?' she said to deflect any awkwardness.

'Mmm, I think so.' He paused and then, as a memory came to mind, asked, 'D'you remember the twins' kite; the one they had for their birthday? It seemed absolutely massive to me.'

'Do I! You all wanted me to go flying on it. I was terrified!'

'You didn't show it.' He laughed lightly.

'Didn't I? I was absolutely petrified at the thought but I didn't dare refuse in front of you all. I couldn't, could I? You were all waiting, counting on me to do it.'

'You did, though, didn't you? I seem to remember that you did.'

'Yes, but the wind dropped and saved me, thank God. John rode on it in the end.'

'Oh yes, he did, didn't he.' Rob's voice dropped into reverie. 'Gosh! John...'

'He took over with your brother, didn't he? With Jonathan?'

'Yes.'

'He was fearless, wasn't he? John, I mean.'

'That's one way of putting it!'

'Did that really happen?' she suddenly said, trailing off. 'John, I mean, riding on the kite like that, getting carried away across the hill?'

'That's how I remember it.'

'Me too. Seems unreal...' and then she added, 'Do you see John at all?'

'No. We lost touch after I left Moreton Steyning. I often wondered what happened to him.'

'He was crazy, wasn't he? I mean... I'm sorry, I know he was your friend, but he was pretty wild.'

'He was that alright, but I looked forward to his coming back every year,' said Rob, and then he paused. 'Did you remember anything further about Lizzie?'

'No, but I'll make a point of checking when I next go back.'

'It would be really good to see her again.'

'You two were really close, weren't you; when you were younger particularly.'

'Yes, we were.'

'Lizzie said you wrote for a while. That's how I remembered where you went to and about the business.'

'I did, I'm sorry to say it tailed off. You know, teenage boys; not very good at letter-writing. I regret it though, losing touch. I feel I've lost a link to my childhood, you know?'

'I'm sure she's somewhere. She won't be hard to track down.'

'I guess not.' He hesitated as Ann was looking at her watch. 'Time to go back?'

'I'd better. I have to do a stint on the desk at three and I've a couple of calls to make first.'

They rose and moved away from the lakeside, heading back towards the park exit and the busy city streets beyond.

'You know, you should go back,' said Ann. 'To have a look. Andy would love to see you, I'm sure. And there's other people you'll know.'

'They say you should never go back...'

'Do you believe that, though?'

'Not really. Actually, I would like to see the old place again. See what's changed; see if it's still as I remember it.'

'You should. My parents would love to see you too. You should call in if you go.'

A thought struck Rob. 'Is Mrs Ward still there?'

'No, she died. A couple of years ago, I think it was.'

They parted at the main road; Ann to return to the Library and Rob to the tube. He realised he'd be quite late back to the office, but that was too bad. He'd stay on later that evening to make it up, although that would mean putting off Janice from their regular Tuesday evening. He sat in the train, aware of, but oblivious to, the bounce and jolt of the carriage while a steady succession of memories, and the feelings they evoked, streamed unbidden through his half-conscious mind. There was so much he hadn't thought of for all these years, so much that was no longer a part of his life; recollections long-buried and no longer refreshed through recall, abandoned and uncherished for so long.

What of Lizzie, he wondered. Sweet-natured, open-hearted Lizzie. When he'd been a child he'd assumed they'd marry one day, when they were grown up; that that was the way these things happened. Of course, it wasn't that simple, but yet some degree of guilt gnawed at him. He had, in so many ways, taken her for granted and abandoned her without so much as a backward glance. He remembered with discomfit the evening they'd stood in Main Street, gazing eye-to-eye, her hurt and solemn expression, her pitying, betrayed look when he'd sought to explain his gloom at John's premature departure. Why hadn't he taken her into his trust and told her about the stolen money? He comforted himself with the thought that perhaps he'd sought to protect her from the responsibility.

Just at that moment he became aware, through the window opposite, of the name of the station where he should alight and the harsh *shush* sound of the doors about to close. He leapt to his feet, hurling himself just in time from the carriage as the doors swept to close behind his back.

Chapter Three

Maggie's voice was strong and clear over the telephone. 'Come up,' she'd said. 'While I'm there. Why don't you, and then we can all meet up? It makes sense.'

It was, as usual, more of a directive and Ann smiled wryly to herself but recognised it wasn't actually a bad thought. Rob had said he wanted to go back for a visit so she felt there was no harm in asking. It was a quiet afternoon at the Library and, thankfully, there'd be no Mark this week, no interruption to the hard-won steady flow of her days. No reminder that left in its wake that gnawing disquiet, unsettling the fragile equilibrium whose delicate fingers daily stitched her life back together.

She took up the telephone and dialled the number on the business card he'd proffered and which she kept in her bag. A woman answered with the architectural practice name and, after a pause, Ann heard an uncharacteristically business-like, 'Rob Bradbury, good afternoon.'

'It's Ann,' she said.

'Hi there!'

'Hello.'

'I didn't make you late back the other day, did I?'

'No, it was fine. Look, I've just had a call from Maggie. She's coming down to Cullingham to see her Mum the weekend after next. I'm going up anyway and I'll meet up with her, but I told her I'd seen you and she suggested you might want to come too and then we could all meet up.'

'In Moreton Steyning?'

'Yes.'

'Next Saturday?'

'Saturday week. I'm staying the weekend at Mum's, but we wondered if you fancied joining us for a day. You know, have a look around, have a chat and a catch up. We might find some of the others you knew.'

‘It’s a great idea; I’d love to, I really would. I could drive us, or do you have a car?’

‘No, I can drive but I don’t have a car, not living in London. I generally get the train out to Cullingham and then the bus.’

‘What if I drive us? I can come back in the evening and... would you be okay coming back on the train?’

‘Of course, and that would be lovely. As you’re in the suburbs shall I get the tube out to you and then we could go on from there?’

‘Perfect,’ said Rob.

***

After lunch at the park with Ann, Rob had found himself unable to focus on work, his thoughts wandering unbidden to the corners of his childhood and the landscapes of Moreton Steyning; the fields and lanes, the woods and hill, the smell of the air that swept the top of Lullington, bringing with it the scent of the fields, the tangy odour of manure in the dusty lanes where cows had passed, and then the clamour from the village children recklessly running down The Green or playing at the pond. Snake Pond. ‘They’re only grass snakes, they won’t hurt you.’ He remembered those words, Lizzie’s excited laughter. And John; he remembered John.

At seven o'clock he realised he wasn’t going to get back in time to see Janice. It being a Tuesday, she’d be expecting him for the evening, so he telephoned instead. He’d interrupted her cooking and her voice was somewhat terse.

‘But where are you?’

‘I’m still at work.’

‘Still at work! It’s after seven.’

‘I know... I got delayed.’

‘Whatever were you doing! You met up with Ann, didn’t you?’

‘Yes, we had lunch; we went to the park. I’ve had a busy afternoon too and that didn’t help either. Look, I’ve got to make up the time; and I can’t stay on tomorrow because of classes.’

‘Oh Rob, really!’

'I know. I'm sorry...'

'You knew we were going out for a drink. We agreed. We're supposed to be trying out The Albion.'

'I'm sorry, but it can't be helped. There's still Thursday.'

'That's not the point. I was expecting to go out tonight. I've got everything ready. Honestly, you could have said earlier.'

'I'm sorry. I was hoping to catch up more quickly, but I can't.'

'There's nothing on television either.'

'Look, I'll never get away if we keep talking. I'll be round on Thursday as usual. We can go to the pub then if you like.'

'Mmm. Maybe.'

She wasn't pleased, much as he'd anticipated. Replacing the receiver he unconsciously released a sigh. Janice inhabited a position at the heart of the world of her own construct, with a sense of order that bordered on the doctrinaire. There was a how and a when to be followed, and she resented any disruption to her routine. Had it occurred to him he might have said she was rather like Mrs Spider at the Library, but it hadn't and perhaps that was just as well.

He reflected that, by Thursday, the day's let-down would largely be forgotten and, after a period of clipped exchanges, she would slowly soften until normal communications could be resumed. Oftentimes such froideur was followed by a period of heightened affection and she would become attentive, even kittenish, skittishly teasing and enticing him. He smiled at the thought.

Nevertheless, Rob chose not to tell her immediately of his planned visit to Moreton Steyning. It was disingenuous of him he knew, but she'd be unwilling to forego her routine of Saturday morning visits to her older sister. The two were close, more like best friends, and appeared to depend upon their weekly get-togethers when, as far as he could gather, they exchanged information and news about the minutiae of their lives. Heaven knows what she revealed about him and their relationship. Frankly, he'd rather not think about it, but instinct told him she was unlikely to hold back on detail, the sisters sharing an intense bond, plus a familial closeness with their parents that was similarly unyielding.

When finally he revealed his plan it was on Sunday, as they strolled through the nearby woods, searching for the first bluebells. Janice halted and turned towards him, hands thrust deep into her jacket pockets.

He'd said, 'I forgot to say, I'm not going to be around next Saturday. One of the old friends from Moreton Steyning is going back there and she and Ann have invited me to join the two of them for a look around and see if there are any of the others we can find.' He'd been rehearsing the speech in his head and hoped it sounded light. 'As it's a Saturday you'll be seeing Joyce, won't you? And you won't know any of them anyway, so I knew you wouldn't want to come.'

She'd adopted an expression of surprised resignation. 'If that's what you've decided.'

'You'll be seeing Joyce... I knew you wouldn't want to miss that.'

'Couldn't you have made it for another day?'

'Maggie's coming down from Nottingham specially. Anyway, you don't know them. We'll be talking about old times and people you don't know. I meant to mention it,' and he shrugged to communicate vagueness and how it had simply 'slipped his mind'.

'When did you decide?'

'I didn't decide, I was asked. Only a day or so ago,' he lied. He felt that was in her interests as much as his. He didn't want to upset her, any more than he wanted a row about it. 'Ann just rang me at work when she heard from Maggie. I forgot as we were having such a nice evening yesterday. In all likelihood I'll be back in the evening anyway, so it won't make much difference. Why don't you have lunch with your parents? You often do.'

'Thanks, I can decide for myself.'

'I was only suggesting.'

Despite his casualness, Rob found himself keenly anticipating the visit. He'd deliberately let it slip from his mind, perhaps so he could fib more truthfully, or more convincingly, but he now tried to picture how the village would appear, how his old friends and acquaintances might look. Would they recognise him; be pleased to see him?

At their Tuesday and Thursday evening meetings that week Janice asked a few questions; about Ann, about the format of the day and their travel arrangements, about Maggie and who else it was he hoped to encounter, but he felt it was a box-ticking exercise and her questioning was factual rather than out of interest or empathy. He hoped she'd be more interested when he returned, when perhaps he'd have stories and news to impart. Maybe they could visit together afterwards and he could show her round his childhood haunts. 'Here's Woodbine Cottage; it's where I grew up,' he imagined himself saying as he escorted her around the once so familiar streets.

Nevertheless it would be strange to go there with Janice; like mixing one life with another. From what she'd told him, he knew she must have been a rather controlled and proper child. He simply couldn't imagine her running riot over Lullington Hill, building tree houses or flinging manure at other kids.

Chapter Four

The arterial roads quickly gave way to a succession of rather dusty, traffic-blown settlements that hugged the route, all familiar but anonymous as they flashed past, one-by-one. Before long, hills rose gently on both sides and a succession of quaint red-brick villages followed, each with tiny cramped cottages that jostled the roadsides. Fields now lined the route, interspersed with patches of darker woodland staining the lower folds, while isolated spinneys topped the rounded hills. The trees stood bare against the sky, although Rob noticed that their colour was tinged with the mossy green of rising sap and that the first leaf buds had begun to break. A small market town with half-timbered buildings and a wide thoroughfare, which he knew well from family Sunday afternoon drives, drew them out into a broad shallow valley, the road accompanied by a marshy stream edged by stumpy, pollarded willows. Sleepy cows grazed indifferently in the passing meadows.

Ann was watching the passing countryside through the car window, a faint smile on her face as the pale sun gently warmed her skin through the glass. They spoke occasionally, but mostly were content just to observe the world slipping by. For a time they kept pace with a train that ran parallel to them; raised above the fields on an embankment before it sank from view in a deep cutting and was then lost to their sight.

'It's the route I take when I go by train,' commented Ann, breaking the silence. 'There, that's the Church steeple I always notice. The station's nearby, but only if it's a stopping train.'

'Do they stop now?' Rob asked.

'Yes, some do.'

'Not at Moreton Steyning, though?'

'No, not any more.'

'Shame.'

For a while the hills hemmed close about them, the red roofs of occasional farmsteads clearly visible amongst so much green. Then they shot clear of the Downs as if they were soaring, and all the vale was spread out in front and below, exactly as Rob remembered it, like a frail and ancient tapestry, extended to the violet-coloured hills at the horizon. He felt a swell of pride, of re-arriving.

'Wow,' he said, although he'd seen the view many times before.

'It is lovely, isn't it,' said Ann. 'There's Cullingham,' and she pointed to the indistinct blur of the small town some two or three miles distant, where the darker hue of buildings replaced the soft springtime green and olive of the fields and trees. Beyond, in the haze, Rob strained his eyes, peering into the pale sunlight, to pick out Lullington Hill. Somewhere, at its feet, lay Moreton Steyning.

For a while the car seemed to convey him onwards, unbidden, and the sights and feelings rushed towards his senses more quickly than he could assimilate. He felt himself willing it to hold back, to delay, to permit him more time to grasp all that assailed him. Alongside, Ann sat in quiet enjoyment of their arrival, calmly looking about her as they travelled.

'Oh, there's Mrs Dodd,' she'd exclaimed, although Rob had hardly heard, and in any event didn't recognise the name, or indeed notice the bearer.

It had begun as they'd skirted Cullingham, now the possessor of a small ring road. Even before he could comprehend that he'd arrived at the old town after all these years, he found himself on the road that led out again, through the vale and onwards to Moreton Steyning. Fields and farms and two or three more hamlets, had all rushed past in a blur, each more joltingly familiar than the last, and all the while ahead rose Lullington, swelling from the very earth, upwards to meet the cheerful April sky. Already he could see the hedges that latticed its flanks, foamed white with blackthorn as if whispered over by frost. How many times had he pricked himself on their vicious thorns or stained his fingers from the bitter purple-black sloes?

Now came the first houses as the road ahead funnelled, drawing him forwards, sucking him into the village itself. The buildings flashed past, familiar but altered; new paint, new curtains, new doors, new windows. All the same, but somehow changed. That's when Ann had spoken, craning round to confirm to herself the woman she'd recognised.

'Mrs Dodd?' he said vacantly, hardly aware that he'd spoken.

'Mmm. They run the Post Office now.'

And there it was; The Green, a broad triangle of undulating grass tilted up from its apex, rising upwards to Lullington Hill which rested protectively across its broad top. Along each side the assortment of old cottages and houses, the Jug & Bottle with a few tables outside. A few shops, even Morris's, yes Morris's! and Mrs Patterson's sweet shop still on the corner, and even now children at the doorway, two counting money into each other's hands, looking to see if they had enough, no doubt. Was it Black Jacks or toffees, or those syrupy orange lollies?

There was the farm still at the bottom with a tractor in the yard, engine idling so that the seat vibrated. Then there was the twins' house looking out across The Green, its front gate still closed upon the neat front garden, although he couldn't see that from where he was sitting. It still had that dead-eyed look about the windows, the kind of stillness that makes you wonder if anyone can be inside, although you know there must be. It looked out across The Green and there, pretty much opposite, was Mrs Ward's. He hadn't recognised it at first. The front door had been replaced and was now glazed, and there was something brightly-coloured in the front garden. Was it a child's three-wheeler bike? The dusty old shrubs that had crowded the path were no more and sunlight shone into the front windows.

'It looks the same, doesn't it?'

Ann's voice startled him back to awareness.

'Yes...'

'Places have changed hands of course, but the houses are the same, aren't they? And the shops, even Lower Farm.'

'Yes...'

He heard her laugh a little, a light laugh of sympathy.

'It must be very strange, a bit of a shock coming back after all this time?'

She was now seated facing him, turned slightly sideways in the passenger seat, smiling encouragingly. 'It's more than half your life since you were last here.'

'Is it?'

'Yes, it must be. It's fourteen years.'

'God, yes. I suppose it is.'

'We've grown up in that time. People have got married, had children.'

And died, he thought.

'We've all got our own lives now,' she said.

'Do you think we could walk from here?' he asked. 'I can't drive and take it all in. Can we leave the car? I'll come back and pick it up after lunch.'

'Of course, good idea.'

He pulled over and they climbed out into the bright spring air, the breeze ruffling their hair and stroking at their faces. Rob stepped onto the grass and turned round and about, taking in each view, measuring it in his mind against the images he held there, finding both change and continuity.

'Where d'you want to walk?' asked Ann. 'Along Main Street?'

They walked together, passing close by Mrs Patterson's, and the view along the street ahead fell into place, both vision and remembrance colliding for Rob. He felt his chest tighten as he looked across to Woodbine Cottage and there, almost opposite, was Wheelwrights, much as he remembered it. His steps faltered as he gazed at his old home and Ann instinctively hung back, allowing him space to observe. It hadn't been whitewashed for a while he noticed, and on the dining room's front window sill was a child's toy, much as there might have been when he was growing up, except his mother wouldn't have allowed such casual untidiness.

'It looks much the same.' Ann's voice from behind briefly startled him.

'Yes, not much different.'

'The Rose's are still at Wheelwrights, of course. Grandpa Rose died, but perhaps that was while you were still here?'

'Just after.'

'Lizzie was so upset, wasn't she? She doted on her Grandpa and he spoiled her terribly. It was awful how he went downhill so fast.'

'Did he?'

'Yes, he had senile dementia. He didn't recognise anyone for the last few months. Didn't she tell you?'

'I think she mentioned it when she wrote.'

'It was a big funeral, lots of people. Everyone here knew Grandpa Rose. I think the family were all very touched.'

They were standing now in front of Wheelwrights and Rob looked up at Lizzie's room, to the upstairs window where she'd lean out and wave across the street to him at his own bedroom, the one he shared with Jonathan. He looked back across to his room, but different coloured curtains now hung and he felt no particular connection to it.

They walked on, past houses with doors, and windows with curtains, passageways and gates with glimpses of gardens with fruit trees and shrubs, and all familiar in a way that didn't compare to where he lived now, or where he'd lived since Moreton Steyning, and probably never would. Ahead, he saw the corner of The Square and the first couple of shops. To his right was the high wall that bounded the rear of the pub yard against which leaned the old sheds.

As they turned the corner he was struck by an unexpected quietness and lack of activity.

'Luff's has gone,' remarked Ann, although she'd told him that before. 'And the shoe shop, of course.'

'And I don't think the Drapers does much by the look of it. Gosh, the Bank's still there!'

'Yes, people always need money.'

'And there's the passage to your house. It's just the same, isn't it?'

'Yes, not much different. Shall we go into the pub? I said we'd meet Maggie about one.'

A few people occupied the lounge of the Horse & Hounds, although it was clear from the noise beyond that the public bar was by far the busier. They settled themselves by the front window where the sun cast a gleam across the table's surface and brought a comforting warmth. Apart from new covers to the window bench seat, the room seemed, as far as Rob could tell, pretty much unaltered.

'That door wasn't there,' Ann pointed out. 'The back stairs from the flat used to come straight down here into the bar.'

'I never saw them; I didn't even know there was a second staircase. I was too young to be in here, I guess.'

'Maggie used to bring me down sometimes, in the afternoons. We weren't supposed to be here, but we'd creep down while her father was asleep. It felt really adventurous, and rather scary, for a child being in a pub where you're not supposed to be. Very much an adults-only world. It had that odd smell; you know, all stale beer and ashtrays? Oh look, there's Maggie!' and she smiled towards the door where a young woman had entered.

Rob put down his pint and briskly took the few steps across to her. Maggie was still considerably taller than Ann, but no longer the lanky boyish girl with straggly hair that he remembered. Dressed in sober but smart clothes, and with her dark hair cut to a sensible bob, she had an aura of cool self-assurance and competence.

'Maggie!' he cried, leaning towards her in warm greeting and clasping one of her hands while she, with the other, gripped his upper arm, her response catching him off guard.

'I'm so sorry to hear about your brother,' she quietly said. 'We all loved him.'

He took an involuntary step back to see her face and she gazed directly back at him, her eyes steady but expression kindly while she rubbed gently at his arm. 'Ann told me; it's so sad. Twenty, was he?'

'Yes.'

'What an awful thing. Thank goodness your parents have you and your sister. Are they all well?'

'Yes very, thanks.'

'Good. And look, here's Ann,' she said, raising a hand to wave at her childhood friend who sat quietly observing their encounter, and she walked briskly across to the table where the two briefly embraced. 'How are you, you rat bag?' Maggie greeted.

'Oh, fine,' said Ann.

'Oh well, never mind. Get me a drink anyway, I've been driving for ages.'

'So,' said Rob when they were all settled. 'Neville Potter!'

Maggie was gazing around the bar with a casual but detached curiosity, her intense eyes roaming steadily through each portion of the room. She didn't react initially, but instead took a long drink from her glass before replacing it on the table and only then did she turn to him.

'He couldn't resist me, could he?' she said with a sideways look that was at once both self-mocking and thankful.

'No one else'd have you,' Ann dryly remarked. 'Actually, she led him a merry dance, poor Neville, before she finally gave in, didn't you?'

'Me?'

'Poor Neville!'

'So, where is he?' asked Rob. 'I'd have liked to have seen him.'

'Nev? At home, playing football this afternoon and no doubt he'll stay out too late with his mates and finish up with a curry somewhere and a headache. He's well, doing okay at work, I'll give him your best. He was interested to hear I was seeing you and asked to be remembered.'

'That's good. No hard feelings then?'

'No! That was just kids stuff wasn't it? More fun than anything.'

'It wasn't fun when we got wrapped up in that rope,' remarked Ann.

'We gave as good as we got though, didn't we?'

'Sometimes.'

'So... where's Malcolm Draycott?' interrupted Rob. 'Is he still around?'

'He's a plumber, married with children,' answered Ann. 'I see him around occasionally, and he speaks to me. He's alright actually... and it seems such a long time ago all that.'

They ordered sandwiches and continued to chat and exchanged news about their lives, and about friends and about others they'd known from the village. As they talked Maggie appraised Rob and found him more adult and confident than she'd expected, and wondered if perhaps that owed something to the loss of his brother. There was nothing like tragedy for engendering self-reliance she reflected. She remembered him as credulous and rather naïve, and observed that there remained an uncertainty about him; a tendency to falter, a certain insecurity. He was, of course, considerably taller now, a few inches taller than her, whereas once she'd always overshadowed him, and he was no longer plump. In fact, she decided, the visual impression was generally pleasing.

'You're not married then?' she asked.

He blushed slightly at the directness of her remark, or rather the directness of its delivery. 'No...'

'He's got a girlfriend; Janice,' explained Ann, although no one acknowledged her interjection.

Maggie didn't turn her gaze from Rob and he was conscious of her scrutiny.

'We've been together about three years,' he explained. 'It'll be three years this summer in fact. She's a dental nurse and we met at College.' He remembered how Maggie had always made him feel deficient, her strength of will and resolve overwhelming his own capabilities.

She merely made an acknowledging noise in response, and he found himself talking about his and Janice's respective flats, although he hadn't intended to, and it added little, although both girls nodded in response.

'You should get somewhere like that,' Maggie said to Ann who shrugged a little. 'Her place is really small,' she added by way of explanation to Rob.

'I live further in,' Ann protested. 'You don't realise, places cost a lot more in central London.'

When they left the pub they began to wander, strolling first about The Square where they gazed in at the shop windows. They looked down the passage to Ann's house and then walked to the bottom of Rushbrook End and looked along its narrow lane towards the farms and to Lullington Hill rising up beyond.

Finally they turned along the top road which led them past their old school. As Rob knew it must, it appeared small compared to his childhood memories. Ann made no further reference to the incident with the Draycott gang and the rope, but instead pointed ahead remarking that it looked as if the garage was open and perhaps they would find Andrew in there.

Rob found himself buoyed at the thought and hurried forwards, stopping at the entrance to the cobbled passage that led to yet another of the village's many rear yards, with a metal trestle sign advertising *BIRD'S GARAGE, proprietor: A. Bird*.

He began to walk down the passage to the yard where several cars were parked with the brick workshop beyond. From within the building he could hear a radio playing, and the occasional chink of a spanner or tool dropped onto the concrete floor. He was conscious of Ann a little to one side of him and turned, smiling questioningly to her. She smiled back and shrugged and then walked forwards into the workshop and he heard her call out, 'Andy?' her small voice echoing in the stark interior.

After a moment a voice responded, 'Hello?' and a fellow in greased blue overalls emerged from beneath the up-raised bonnet of a car. 'Ann!' he called. 'How're you?'

'I'm fine,' she replied. 'Look who I've brought,' and she looked back over her shoulder, indicating to where Rob stood at the entrance, framed in the wide doorway.

Finch looked at the silhouetted figure, squinting against the glare from without, a spanner still clenched in his right hand, wiping at the dirt on his forehead with the cuff of his overall and spreading it still further across his brow.

'Hello mate,' said Rob advancing forwards, arm outstretched. 'It's Robbie.'

Finch took a step towards him, then tossed the spanner to his left palm and seized Rob's hand with a fierce grip and vigorously shook his arm up and down.

'Robbie!' he cried. 'Robbie... Robbie! Well I never.'

Finally the two laughed and embraced, clapping one another on the back, Finch narrowly avoiding clumping his old friend between the shoulder blades with the spanner.

'Well,' he said, pumping Rob's arm repeatedly. 'Christ almighty!' He turned to Ann who stood by, beaming. 'Where did you find this one?'

'By chance,' she said, although he gave her no time to explain further.

'God,' he said. 'Look at you. Slimmed down a bit, eh!' and he gave Rob a firm punch in the gut that made him step back and clutch at his belly. 'You're looking well!'

'You too. It's great to see you!'

'Time for a cuppa?' Finch jerked a thumb behind his head towards a small glazed office in one corner of the workshop.

'Sure,' said Rob, observing that Ann was smiling and nodding. He suddenly noticed that Maggie wasn't with them and indicated such to her.

'Oh, we'll pick her up later,' she said.

They squeezed into the small grimy office, which smelled of grease and engine oil, and Finch pulled a couple of stools from beneath a desk whose surface was piled with paperwork and mugs grimed with dirt and tea stains. Car keys hung from hooks on a board and invoices and other items of paperwork were pinned over every wall space, save that occupied by a calendar whose April page showed a heavily-breasted blonde leaning forwards across a car bonnet. Rob noticed that Ann's eyes took it in but that she then avoided the picture, seating herself on the stool Finch offered, with her back to the calendar.

'Sorry about the mess,' said Finch. 'Keep meaning to clear up but I'm always busy, you know how it is. Tea alright? Well it'll have to be, I haven't got anything else. Christ, I can't get over this! Robbie Bradbury! Must be fifteen years isn't it?'

'Nearly.'

'Christ! You look well. God I'm repeating myself; must be the shock. What're you doing with yourself?'

'Training to be an architect. I work in London at an architectural practice; it's how I met Ann. We bumped into one another.'

'An architect... what about that! Good for you.'

'I'm still studying. I've got to qualify yet...'

'Still...'

'You look as if you're doing alright for yourself?'

'Can't grumble.'

'Business good? You look busy.' Rob indicated to the cars parked in the workshop and beyond.

Finch nodded. 'Yeah, very.'

'Andrew's got a good reputation as a mechanic,' chipped in Ann. 'Everyone brings their car here,' and she smiled warmly at him.

He shrugged, abashed. 'Doing alright,' he said, scrubbing away at his forehead again with one grimy cuff. His fair hair, stiff with grease, stood almost on end and his blue eyes seemed to stare out of a darkened face amongst all the dirt. 'Christ,' he said again and poured the steaming kettle onto the three mugs, vigorously stirring the teabags before squeezing them between his bare fingers and flinging them into an open bin, above which tea splatters fanned up the wall.

'When did you start up?' Rob asked.

'Oh, 'bout two years ago on my own. Started working here for old Fellowes when I was sixteen, then when he got sick I more or less did it all, then finally took on the business when he retired. Yeah, it's been okay,' he affirmed, and perched on the filing drawers, one leg raised up, tea mug resting upon his thigh.

'Good for you,' said Rob. 'Family?'

'Missus and a nipper. Three this month.'

'Anyone I know?'

'Probably not, Rose Anderson; Cullingham lass. You?'

'No.'

'Girlfriend though?'

'Oh yeah.'

'Good catch you, eh? Architect!'

'Well… one day, maybe. How's your brother?'

'Nigel?'

Rob had forgotten Ann's remarks of a few weeks ago and was conscious now of a slight shifting in her position, of a pause and stiffening from the normally relaxed and affable Finch.

'He's in Scotland, mate.'

'Scotland?'

'Yeah, 'bout eight years ago, something like that.'

'See him?'

'Not a lot.'

'What's he up to?'

'Poet.'

'A poet!'

'Yeah, he writes stuff.'

Rob and Ann exchanged surprised looks.

'A poet?' said Rob. 'Successful?'

'Can't say I know. Not my kind of thing,' and Finch shifted from the cabinet to stand in the middle of the room, looking down at Ann. 'What brings you up here, then? Family alright?'

'Yes, fine thanks,' said Ann.

'How's that brother of yours?' Finch asked, turning back to Rob. 'I was thinking of him only the other day.'

'I'm sorry…' Rob began.

Finch drew in his brows, perplexed at the response, but then began to comprehend. 'There isn't something… what's the matter then? He's not been…?'

'He's died, Andy,' said Ann softly.

Finch stared at her for a few moments, then stared at Rob, mouth hanging slack, mug hanging empty from his crooked forefinger. 'Dead?' he said, looking from one to the other. 'Jonathan?'

Rob nodded. 'I'm afraid so.'

'No! When?'

'Eight years ago.'

'Christ!' And he sank heavily back onto the filing cabinet.

'I'm sorry,' said Rob.

'Not your fault, mate. Christ, that's awful. Fuck me.'

'It was his heart,' said Ann as neither of the others could bring themselves to speak. 'His heart failed. I can't believe it either.'

'Fuck me. Terrible thing, mate. Jonathan... Christ! I can think of him like it was yesterday; grinning, you know, like he did, big happy face. God, it's not right, is it?'

'No, it's not right.'

'Maggie's down,' Ann said after another pause.

'Yeah?'

'She came over to meet Rob. We just went to the Horse & Hounds for lunch, the three of us.'

'That old place, eh!'

'Do you live in Moreton Steyning still?' asked Rob.

'Down by the station, mate. 'Ere! What about that fella John?' He'd suddenly recalled the episode at the station. 'D'you see him, he was from London? Cricklewood wasn't it?'

'That's right,' said Rob. 'No, I haven't. We lost touch after I moved away. I never had an address for him, and he wouldn't have had mine once we'd left here. We never wrote to one another anyway, he just used to turn up, didn't he?'

'Like a fucking bad penny! Laugh, though.'

'Yes, he was. He never came back, then?'

'No mate, not after that last summer you were here. Not after we all went to Senior School.'

'And Mrs Ward's died?'

'That's right.'

A while later Rob and Ann found Maggie sitting on a bench looking out over The Green, legs casually crossed, smoking a cigarette. She acknowledged their approach and waited as they walked over.

'Seen him, then?' she said.

'Yes, you should have come in,' Rob admonished.

She flicked away the ash and gave a vague shrug, but no answer. 'You're here now,' she said, rising.

'Well, how about an ice cream?' he suggested, and treated them all at Mrs Patterson's for old time's sake. They stood together outside the shop, laughingly eating their cornets and retrieving with their tongues the sticky melts that ran down the sides of their fists.

'God, they're every bit as awful as I remember!' said Maggie. 'Rob, that was wonderful. Thanks so much. I'd better get going now and see Mum. I've left my car round the corner. It's been good to see you again,' and she briefly embraced both him and then Ann before departing with a casual wave, leaving the two of them standing alone at the corner of The Green.

'And that was Maggie!' said Ann with a grim laugh.

'No change there!'

'She's alright, very kind, actually,' said Ann as they began to move towards his car. 'She's always there for me.'

He let her in on the passenger side and then heaved himself inside; it was warm and fuggy, the interior warmed from the earlier sun.

'Why didn't she come to the garage?' he asked.

'Bit of bad blood there,' Ann explained, as he turned the key and the engine came to life. 'It's something to do with Nid and when he left. Something she said, you know what she can be like. Anyway, she just dismisses it if I ask so I don't bother now, and if I mention her to Andy he becomes evasive. Clearly there was a falling out; that's all I know.'

'Seems a shame.'

'Yes.'

'I'll run you down to your folks',' he said.

They drove back along Main Street, past his old house and Wheelwrights, pulling in briefly to let a bus pass, and then turned into The Square where Rob parked on the cobbles. He turned to

Ann, ready to say a farewell, but she was gazing out of the window, thoughtful.

'You know, when I was young,' she said, 'I thought everything had a colour. Not just things; I don't mean that – obviously things have a colour, but words, like... oh, you know, days of the week and concepts, abstract things. In my mind, they all had a colour.'

She glanced to him, a little uncertain of his reaction, cautious lest he should fail to understand or think her odd, but he was smiling and interested.

'It was lovely, really,' she continued. 'It brought things to life in a particularly vivid and magical way. And it was always there, in my head.'

'It does sound rather amazing...'

'Sadly, it's faded as I've got older, but I still get flashes of it. Like just now – when we drove back here. It reminded me of being in the truck with Dad and coming home. He used to lean extravagantly at the corners to amuse me and you did it a bit then too!' She laughed briefly and Rob smiled, somewhat abashed.

'Sorry,' he said.

'No, it was nice – really! It's just that it did briefly make me feel like a kid again, coming back here, sitting in the passenger seat as we came round the corner into The Square... and I thought 'home' and instantly this most intense yellow glowed in my mind.'

Chapter Five

The flat, little more than a bed-sit really, was indeed cramped, just as Maggie had rather tactlessly reminded Ann, like a parent insensitively trespassing on a growing child's need for its own identity. She was right though; it wasn't just small, as Maggie had said in that disparaging way of hers, it was poky and mean and distinctly shabby. Ann had made it as personal and cheerful as she could, using lengths of oriental fabric and ornaments found in junk shops to give it an individual feel and enliven its general gloominess with colour and texture and a sense of individuality. But, however much she dressed it, there was no denying that it was a poor substitute for the bright and airy, and distinctly rather smart mansion block flat that was Mark's, and which had once been her home too.

That loss, and the dispossession, still hurt. Through time she'd learned to live with the shabby flat-let, managing to tolerate day-to-day the room that the sunlight touched, if only for a few brief hours early in the morning before it was gone again. Until that magic hour when, fleetingly, it reflected off the windows opposite, just as it dipped low in the sky behind the brick terraced house. All the houses in the street were brick terraces; all of them cheaply and quickly-built, and each now filled with flats and bed-sits for immigrants and students and low income workers.

She'd had to move fast, not because she'd been expelled; no, Mark was decent enough and had told her to take her time in finding somewhere else to live. It was just clear that, what he meant, was for this to be as quickly as possible.

No, it was the banishment, the sense of having been discarded and considered of no further interest that cut so deeply. The realisation that, for him, she had only been a passing interest. That's what had really hurt, although in truth it was something of an escape. At least that's what Maggie had tried to convince her of, and probably she was right, just as she usually was.

Nevertheless, the sense of exile and feelings of loss overwhelmed her often and, at such times, she thought of her mother's grievance; how she felt herself to be a laughing stock, not the jolly bubbling pot Ann's childhood imaginings had innocently fashioned. Her plight had been shaming and demeaning, and Ann understood that.

As her District Manager, Mark had secured for her the new job at the central Library, presented persuasively and encouragingly, as if it were an achievement for her and an offering on his part, and yet it was merely more evidence of his coercion in her life. It was another means of banishment too; a removal from Notting Hill Library so that he would no longer have to see her, except on those days when his responsibilities brought him to her new branch. On those days he would stride purposefully and business-like up the broad steps to meet with the Senior Managers while she sought refuge in her office, unnoticed and disregarded.

It's a lucky escape, Maggie had said. He's controlling, he wants someone he can dominate, was her assertion; charming and handsome but ultimately selfish. Not worth it. You're better off without him.

All that was nine months ago and now she was settled and largely coping well, although at times the feelings of rejection welled up still. A laughing pot alright, that's what she'd been at Notting Hill. Taken for a ride, swept up and flattered, picked up like a foolish pretty thing and seduced by a glamorous and privileged world, but ultimately cheated on and found to be not good enough. Not up to the mark.

Chapter Six

Janice was leaning against Rob's shoulder and he could smell the shampoo in her hair as it softly touched his face. After a time she slid down his arm and settled her torso upon his lap, legs curled up amongst the settee cushions, her palms reassuringly anchored between his thighs, warm through the fabric of his trousers. The film they were watching had absorbed them pleasantly for an hour or two, part-adventure story, part-romantic comedy. Rob let his hand fall onto Janice's shoulder and rest there, sensitive to the texture of the silky fabric of her blouse and her smooth and lithe shoulder beneath. They laughed in unison at an amusing episode in the film and he felt her flanks judder and her warm breath sharply exhale onto his leg. He squeezed her shoulder softly, acknowledging their shared amusement.

When the film was over they drank beers and Janice coiled herself into the corner of the settee while he relaxed, one arm extended along the back of the cushions, eating peanuts from a bag balanced on his knees.

'I saw that at the Cullingham Odeon,' he said. 'About 1958. Mum took Jonathan and me one afternoon in the school holidays.'

'Yes?'

'I only remember the adventurous bits, none of that romantic stuff or anything. I thought it was fantastic. Jonathan and I acted it out for days after; we even built a hideaway down the garden.'

'Typical boys.'

'I suppose so, but it seemed incredibly exciting to us, all that fighting and leaping about. We used to pretend the hill was enemy territory and go stalking them up there.' He laughed at the recollection. 'Actually, I thought we might go to Moreton Steyning this weekend, you and me, so I can show you round. What d'you think?'

Oh, Rob... you are they end! I told you I wanted to go shopping. I did say so.' And she heaved a theatrical sigh of exasperation.

He'd completely forgotten. 'But you can go shopping any time...' he said, disappointed.

'I need to go on Saturday; I need a new dress, don't I? I did tell you...'

'Can't you go next week?'

'No!'

Janice sprang from the settee and padded to the kitchen where she snapped on the kettle switch and stood glowering as it creaked and banged while steadily heating, feeling her chest rise and sink beneath her folded arms at each new deep breath.

Why didn't he listen? He was too wrapped up in his own world, that was it. He had Wednesday nights at classes, and he was frequently delayed on Fridays after his day-release, and even then she rarely protested, but it was always her fault if she wanted do something specific at the weekend.

She surveyed his kitchen, reflecting on the out-dated décor and odd assortment of crockery and cooking pots. The sound of the television in the lounge was now drowned out by the rising hiss and drumming of the kettle. Snatching mugs from the wooden mug tree, she tossed coffee into them and poured on the boiling water and milk. As the bubbling in the kettle subsided, the sound of voices from the TV returned to her ears and she recognised a comedy that Rob liked. After a few moments she heard his bellow of laughter and tutted to herself, irritated that he'd cast from his thoughts so quickly their disagreement of a few minutes before.

He looked up with a brief distracted smile as she placed the coffee mug on the coffee table before him; she sought his eye for thanks, but his attention was on the programme. He was chuckling again at a lame joke but finally glanced up and said 'ta'. Janice coiled herself back into her corner of the settee, tucking her feet up amongst the cushions, observing with hostility the side of his face, turned in profile away from her, concentrating on the television, smiling with amusement at the foolish old programme.

'So... are you going to take me shopping then, like you said you would?' she enquired after a suitable interval, during which he'd shown no response or inclination to talk.

Rob paused, waiting for a break in the dialogue. He sighed and turned to her, sensing how she'd wedged herself into the corner of the sofa, intractable and cross.

'I suppose so. If you're set on it.'

'It's just that I said. You know I did.'

'Yes, alright. I said alright, but I don't see why it can't be another day.'

'When? I can hardly go on Sunday, can I? The shops aren't open. Anyway, we can go to Moreton another week. It's not like it's going anywhere, is it?'

'Neither are the shops. What's the urgency anyway?'

'I need new clothes for Spring. I've hardly got anything.'

'I'm not sure that's true.'

'Like you'd notice!'

'That's hardly fair. Anyway, I thought you'd like to come. I thought you'd be interested to see the village.'

'I am, but not this week. You've never bothered before, what's the panic?'

'No panic, I just wanted to go back again and I could show you. It's no big deal. We won't bother if you're not interested.'

'Okay, we won't bother then.'

Janice smouldered to herself and sipped too speedily at her coffee so that she burned her lips.

They spoke no further until the comedy had finished and then Rob turned and invited, 'Lift home then?'

They travelled silently in the car for the short drive from his flat to her own. Janice looked out of the window as the suburban streets slipped past, light from the street lamps flashing a succession of vignettes of semi-detached houses and quiet streets. She let her focus soften and allowed them to flood past, the light pooling across her cheeks, each golden glow illuminating the curls of her hair.

Their leave-taking was brief and Janice was soon upstairs in her own neat flat. She heaved a sigh of irritation and flung her bag down upon the settee. A hint of guilt only inflamed the annoyance that still burned within her from the evening's dispute, but she held fast to her resentment.

There was no harm in a new set of outfits for the coming season, after all; she liked to look nice and took pride in her appearance and having an up-to-date look. There was nothing wrong, or very little, in attracting a little flattery; especially if you hadn't set out to achieve that in the first place, even if it was the accidental result. It helped the days pass pleasantly; it gave them some meaning and purpose, and it was all innocent, she assured herself.

Fiona would, of course, be making an effort, she mused and she couldn't have Fiona out-doing her on that front. Not with Brian next door.

Fiona had come rushing into work a few weeks ago, breathlessly bursting into their small work kitchen one morning, the one just behind the consulting room where Janice's dentist worked.

'Have you seen?' Fiona had gushed, barging Janice to one side while she poured herself a coffee to take back to the reception desk.

'No, what?' had been Janice's reply, expressed rather testily in the light of having been thrust aside.

'The new chap next door? In the Estate Agents? He's a real dream! An absolute heart throb.'

'No,' said Janice coolly. She found Fiona's enthusiasms and immaturity generally rather tedious.

Janice knew the staff in the neighbouring office, just as did Fiona, the pair of them having worked at the dental surgery for three years. It was routine to meet staff coming and going from 'Humbold and Stewart'. The two businesses had front doors that were set at angles to one another, so that they shared a small lobby from the street. You could see into the Estate Agent's every time you left the dental surgery – going out for lunch or leaving in the evening. And, of course, Humbold and Stewart's staff were always coming and going through the lobby, visiting properties or taking clients round.

'Just wait till you see!'

'Well, what does he look like?'

'Tallish, dark wavy hair, *gorgeous* brown eyes, slim but really well-muscled, long legs, moustache, *really* smart...'

'Sounds alright.'

'He's divine,' crooned Fiona. 'I can't stop looking out so I don't miss him every time he comes in or goes out.'

Two days later she rushed in at coffee break to tell Janice he'd caught her eye, through the glass door. The following day it was to say he'd winked at her. After that she made a habit of tidying the magazines in the rack near the door at any time she estimated he might be about to arrive or leave.

Before long she'd established when he had his lunch hour and contrived to leave at the same time. Once or twice Janice herself had bumped into him and he'd smiled and said hello. Two days later Fiona arrived with the news that his name was Brian and she'd spoken to him outside the surgery.

'I said he was new, wasn't he? And then we got talking,' she enthused. 'Then, he said why didn't we meet for lunch sometime!' Her cheeks were pink with excitement.

That sometime was later the same week, when Brian walked into the surgery waiting room and leaned casually against the reception desk, his long legs extended. Janice had been coming from the consulting room to collect her dentist's next patient and Brian had nodded and smiled at her.

She could hear that a lunch was being discussed, and was surprised when Fiona caught her between patients to tell her that Brian and a colleague had suggested the two of them meet her and Fiona for a bite to eat that Friday lunchtime at the pub on the corner.

'You've got to come!' shrilled Fiona. 'You've got to! So I can see Brian. Say you will! Rob won't mind, it's only lunch. Anyway, you don't have to tell him.'

That was the way Fiona lived her life and, while she didn't exactly approve, Janice didn't pay a lot of attention either. Fiona was younger and fairly juvenile – Janice thought her scatter-brained – and had spent much of the past three years in pursuit of various young men and boys.

She'd sighed in response. 'Okay, I'll come,' she'd said. Lunch hours could be dull, and it was good to round off the week with a lunch out.

Brian proved to be as charming as he was good-looking, with impeccable and attentive manners. He was also amusing and effortlessly kept the conversation going between the four of them. His colleague, who both girls knew well by sight, was rather dull by comparison, or indeed by any measure, and proved more interested in discussing sport.

Janice shuffled awkwardly when he tried to engage her in a discussion on football while the other two chatted animatedly and Fiona flirted and giggled. When the lunch was over and they all strolled back to their offices, the two boys had said 'we must do this again' and Fiona had eagerly agreed, then giggled again.

Janice was reluctant and assured Fiona she would stand a far better chance of a romantic liaison with Brian if she met him alone, but the younger girl was lacking in self-confidence and inveigled her to once more join them; all the more so, she said, since Alan (for that was the colleague's name) was hoping to see Janice again.

The lunch in question was on a Wednesday. It was the day following Rob's extended lunch with Ann in the park, the one from which he'd been home too late for their usual Tuesday evening together. Janice hadn't known that when she'd agreed to the lunchtime meeting, but it gave her a sense of justification when the day came. Alan was as dull as she'd recalled and Brian as much the opposite. This time they went to a rather smarter bar, about ten minutes' walk from their workplaces.

Fiona had prepared specially for the occasion and wore an extravagantly frill-necked dress in a brightly coloured satin fabric with platform shoes, all distinctly unsuitable for work wear. Her hair was newly curled and she'd made a particular effort with her make-up, especially around her eyes. Janice watched as Fiona simpered, smiled and laughed in all the right places, and talked far too quickly and loudly. Alan was telling Janice about his hobbies of collecting beer mats and brewing home-made beer, neither of which seemed to her to have much to commend them. She also noticed that his suit, which she guessed was the only one he possessed and was pressed into service for workdays alone, smelled none too fresh and she leaned away from him, trying to avoid his eye so that he might stop talking to her.

After a while Alan was obliged to make a trip to the bar for more drinks and Fiona asked Janice if she might not want to go to the ladies. Janice didn't, and was puzzled at the look her answer received. Alan returned to the table with their drinks and Fiona flounced off on her own, looking back with consternation when Alan departed to the bar again to collect his change, leaving Janice and Brian briefly alone together.

Brian smiled to Janice and rearranged his pint on the beer mat, one hand settled loosely on one hip so that his crooked elbow extended casually to one side. He wore a gold signet ring on his little finger. They sat in silence for a short time and he cast his eyes down into his pint and Janice observed that they were indeed attractive, with long dark lashes.

'She's a girl, isn't she, Fiona?' he said, snorting with amusement.

'She's alright,' Janice replied, trying to sound supportive to her work colleague, although Fiona wearied her.

'And what about you?' he asked, and settled a look on her face that she felt was a little too personal.

'Me?'

'You don't say much.'

'Oh...' She shrugged, mildly flustered by the attention.

'Live near here?'

'Not far.'

'We should get together some time.'

Before she could respond, Alan was back with his change and Fiona had arrived at speed from the ladies. As they walked back to work together, Brian allowed his hand to gently swing against Janice's.

Chapter Seven

A few weeks had passed since Rob's visit to Moreton Steyning with Ann. In the intervening time, work and study for his architectural exams had occupied both his time and attention. He'd even had to miss the odd evening with Janice in favour of revision, and occasionally when they met he'd been tired, and perhaps he was tetchy too since they'd argued a few times. He was both sorry and annoyed that they'd been unable to go to his old village home together. For one thing he'd been looking forward to showing her around, and it was both typical and unreasonable of her to be so dogmatic about wanting to go shopping for clothes instead, as if that couldn't wait. Her inflexibility could be positively maddening, he reflected.

He thought of Lizzie and her sensitive and compassionate nature. Why had he let their correspondence slip? What fools thirteen year-old boys are. He wondered where she might be now.

All about him lay his books, the ones he'd collected at Ann's Library amongst them, scattered about on the floor, across the coffee table, one open on his lap and more still on the table. His notes lay open on the arm of the settee and a pencil hung loosely between his fingers. The remains of his morning coffee had gone cold in the mug, but he ignored his revision and tried to picture how Lizzie would look. Like him, she'd be aged twenty six. Would her hair be soft and pale still? Clearly she wouldn't wear it in long plaits any more, but would her grey eyes gaze out from beneath those level eyebrows, beneath the smooth forehead where soft coils of hair curled at her temples?

He shook the thought from his mind, telling himself it was all too absurd and a long time ago, but memories clawed at him; his father at the allotment, bent over the furrow, seeds trickling down the deep crease formed in his palm and into the soft ripe earth; sitting with Lizzie on the old grey log at the pond while insects darted in the heavy air and grass snakes slithered through the silky brown weed; the view from Lullington with all the vale spread about; and John.

The pencil slipped from his grip and fell onto the floor and he thrust himself, with resolution, to his feet.

Almost before he knew it he was driving along the dual carriageway, speeding away from the suburbs and out towards the hills. He'd have to cancel Sunday with Janice in order to catch up on his revision, but that would be for then. For now he was on his way. Cullingham came and went, the Downs left behind as the vale, rich now with spring flowers, surrounded him. Ahead was Lullington, little more than a low swell on the horizon until he was a scant two miles away and then it reared up, its flanks a vivid green now with lush grass. Even from here he could discern the grazing cows and sheep.

He finally throttled back and cruised slowly into the village, pulling up just as before at the base of The Green. A working day now, a Friday, the atmosphere was different and there was a distinct sense of activity. He walked straight to the top of The Green and around the corner, where he found the Baker's still in business, and bought himself a pasty and cold drink. It was cloudy, but felt mild and rather humid, so he sat on a bench to eat with the view of all The Green and the cottages along its sides set out below him. A few minutes later he was walking along the top lane and down the passage to the garage.

He found Finch – Andy – in his office, completing the week's paperwork, and was immediately hailed and offered tea.

'Back again,' said Finch with a cheery smile, slumped in a swivel chair, legs untidily outstretched.

'I hardly had a chance to look around last time,' Rob replied, sinking onto a rickety stool opposite.

'Easier on your own?'

'Well, maybe. I was going to bring Janice but she's busy.'

'Too bad, mate. Day off then?'

'Actually, I should be revising for my exams.'

'Bunking off!'

'Sort of. I'll have to catch up at the weekend. So, tell me, what's the news on Lizzie? We didn't get a chance to call in there last time and Ann didn't really know where she was. Heard anything?'

'Your place, mate.'

'My place?'

'London, far as I know. She went to College there, didn't she, and then stayed? After that I don't know,' and he heaved himself up in the chair with his elbows on the arms, tea slopping over the brim of the mug onto his overalls. He casually brushed it away. 'Didn't someone say she got married or something?'

'Did they?'

'Dunno, mate, not sure. Thought I might have heard it but I haven't seen her for... oh, years, it must be. Shame. You've not bumped into her up there, then?'

'No!' laughed Rob. 'No, it was quite something bumping into Ann, I can't imagine it happening twice.'

'No, I reckon not. Awful thing, your brother.'

'Yes.'

'Couldn't stop thinking about it after I saw you. Fucking terrible. Must've hit you hard.'

'It did.'

'How old were you when it happened?'

'Eighteen. He was twenty.'

'Christ, what a thing,' and Finch slowly shook his head from side to side.

'Tell me more about Nid.'

'Nid?' Finch looked up sharply, as if he were being asked to recall someone he couldn't be expected to remember, and then he looked over his shoulder as if in search of the past. 'What's to say?' he said.

'Well, how come he's in Scotland?' asked Rob. 'That's a long way!' and he laughed to lighten the moment.

'Well... he took off there, didn't he.'

'Why there?'

Finch pulled the corners of his mouth down and shrugged. 'Dunno. Fancied it, I guess. Can't see it myself, all them Jocks, eh?'

'Where in Scotland, then?' Rob persisted.

'Dumfries way. He's in some sort of commune.' Finch rose and placed his mug by the kettle from where he retrieved a pack of cigarettes and held it out to Rob.

'No thanks.'

He took one himself and jabbed it into his mouth, then struck a match which he discarded to the floor, stamping on it with heavy boot to ensure it was extinguished. 'Shouldn't smoke in here,' he said, 'but I do.'

'A commune? That doesn't sound like Nid.'

'Doesn't it? You'd be surprised.'

'I would. He was always the studious one.'

'Nah, mate. Didn't give a shit for all that. It was the old man, wasn't it? Wanted his sons, or one of them at least, to follow him; chip off the old fucking block and all that. Nid, he couldn't be doing with it, couldn't handle it. It was pressure, pressure all the time to be something he wasn't, and all just because he was bright. Me? I didn't give a toss. I was never going to be a bloody Bank Manager, was I? But the old man, he wanted Nid to follow in his footsteps, thought he should be the one to carry on the family profession and all that crap. Nid, he could never see himself in a bleedin' Bank. He fucked off. It was all too much. Just gave it all up and pissed off.'

'When was that?'

'Few weeks after he started University.'

'How did your parents take it?'

'How d'you think?'

The two of them were seated now with their elbows on their knees, Finch's hand dangling with the smouldering cigarette held between two fingers, the smoke coiling between them. Their heads were close together and both looked up to one another in silent acknowledgement.

'So,' said Finch after a few moments, pulling himself upright and placing his cigarette between his lips again and speaking with it held there, waggling on his bottom lip. 'It was left to me to make a mark,' and he laughed grimly and hoarsely. 'That fucked the old man's mind up a bit.'

'You've made a success, though? That must please him.'

'Oh yeah,' and he laughed again, with evident satisfaction.

'Right, mate,' said Rob slapping his thighs, 'I'd better be off and let you get on.'

Both rose and shook hands firmly. 'Good to see you again, mate,' Finch said. 'You come back, eh?'

'I will. And if you speak to Nid give him my best.'

Finch nodded but didn't speak, and Rob left the office exchanging a wave with his old friend. He found his way back out into the lane which was quiet now. The sun had filtered through the low cloud and cast a gentle warmth onto his head and shoulders. He looked both ways then turned to his right and found himself at the top of Snail Path. With a smile of simple pleasure he began the descent. On his right the steep bank still rose up while the backs of various yards and gardens formed the boundary to his left, just as they always had. Beyond the bank was the children's playground and from there he could hear their laughter and shouts. Stooping to the ground he plunged his hands into the damp undergrowth, and in no time found a couple of banded snails; he smiled with satisfaction.

Further on down, he came to the rear of Morris's Greengrocer's. He paused, turning to look back up the slope and his mind formed an image of the dam they'd constructed and his eyes followed the course of the wild flood, down the steep path and into the back of Morris's yard and shop. He could see John ripping at the bank and hedge, tearing out clods and rocks and bits of branch, his sinewy legs and arms straining with the effort, hoarse voice barking commands. Then there was that crazy ride on Morris's trade bike. He laughed to himself and emerged out into Main Street at the bottom where he couldn't help but look around in fear of a bus bearing down upon him.

***

A young girl of about ten, with soft flaxen hair that curled about her shoulders, darted across Wheelwright's yard at his approach. He started with a jolt of familiarity that practically took his breath away. Collecting himself, Rob approached the kitchen door and knocked, looking over his shoulder to where the child skipped away, seeing in his mind's eye the boy he'd once been, the boy who'd played there so often, running alongside of her.

There was silence for a few minutes before a woman pulled open the door and stood half-smiling in uneasy part-recognition.

'It's Robbie,' he offered.

'Robbie!' exclaimed Sarah Rose and called over her shoulder into the house beyond, 'Joe! It's Tom and Sally's boy. Look, it's Robbie Bradbury. My goodness Robbie, but you've grown up a bit. Come on, come in,' and she stepped back to allow him into the big old kitchen that he knew so well.

As Rob entered, Joe Rose came in from the hall behind and greeted him warmly. Rob didn't like to comment that they too seemed older, while also appearing smaller and more inconsequential. Just adults now, like himself; simply people and no longer the figures of authority of his childhood who'd seemed to inhabit some other, more important world, not yet accessible to him.

They continued to welcome him warmly and asked repeated questions of his circumstances, his family and what had passed since they'd seen him last, when he'd been a new grammar school boy about to embark on the first stage of his future life. They provided tea and biscuits and sat with him at the big kitchen table, where he'd sat so many times before, the old pine planks smooth as skin beneath his palms.

When the inevitable shock of Jonathan's death had been imparted, discussed and condoled, and his life and work and education told and retold, and the health and well-being of his parents and sister reiterated and confirmed, only then could he come to the real purpose of his visit. But first he asked, 'Who was the little girl I saw?'

Sarah looked puzzled for a moment and turned to Joe with a frown, but then realised.

'Emma, that was Emma, our grand-daughter: Ron and Grace's third.'

'Your granddaughter?'

'Yes, second one. She's got an older sister, plus her brother, of course. He's at secondary school now. Hopes to be a carpenter, like his Dad and Granddad, and Grandpa too of course.'

'She gave me a shock, running across the yard like that. She looked just like Lizzie did at that age.'

'Mmm, perhaps she does.'

'How is Lizzie, then? We lost contact. We used to write and, well... it's my fault really. You know, boys, they're no good at letters...'

'Oh, not so bad...'

'I'd heard she's in London now.'

'Yes.' It was Joe who responded this time.

'Anywhere near me? I'd love to see her again.'

'Sort of...' Joe furrowed his brows thinking, then he glanced at Sarah. 'She's north London way, isn't she, girl?'

'Yes, that way,' said Sarah, raising the heavy teapot and looking over to Rob questioningly. 'More tea?'

He pushed his cup forwards. 'Yes, thanks. And she's well?'

'She's been a little under the weather lately, but coming on.'

'I'm sorry to hear that. Nothing serious I hope?'

'She's fine,' said Joe.

'And she did history at University, was it...?'

'Yes,' Sarah readily replied, with pride. 'At the University of London.'

'Work?' Rob persisted. 'What did she do after?'

'Local authority,' said Joe. 'Got it straight away. Good grades you see, snapped her up. She did well there.'

'Excellent, and she's still there is she?'

'Having...' began Joe.

'Taking a break,' Sarah said.

'Short break, then she'll be carrying on, pick up again like.'

Rob hesitated, somewhat uncertain as to how to interpret this information. 'And ... does she have plans for the future? Any particular career?'

'Sort of planning and development, that sort of thing,' said Joe, as if he were speaking a foreign language.

'Oh, my area then!' exclaimed Rob, and they both nodded and said yes, but with scant conviction.

'Well, I'd love to see her,' he repeated, and smiled warmly at them both.

'Yes,' said Sarah. 'That would be nice.'

'Is she... do you have an address? Somewhere I could contact her?'

'She's moving, probably about to move,' Joe replied. 'Bit uncertain at the moment.'

'I see.'

'She'll be sorting a few things.'

'She's fine,' said Sarah rather unnecessarily.

'But she's been unwell?'

'No!' Sarah laughed.

'She just needs to sort herself out,' said Joe again.

'Perhaps you could pass a letter on, if I write?' Rob suggested.

'Yes, of course,' smiled Joe. 'We can do that, can't we missus?'

'Yes, of course.'

'I'd like to contact her. We were best friends for pretty much all of our childhood.'

'You were, weren't you? You played together so beautifully for hours. You were never any trouble.' Sarah beamed at him. 'Well, my dear,' she said. 'I have to see to a few things but don't let me rush you out. Joe here isn't going anywhere,' and she stood up. 'It's been really lovely seeing you Robbie, it really has. And give our love to your family. And please, you must come and see us again next time you're in Moreton Steyning.'

'I will,' he said, rising.

Joe clasped his hand firmly and shook it for slightly longer than was strictly necessary.

'Good to see you, boy.'

The yard outside was empty and the Rose's young granddaughter now nowhere to be seen. The sun had finally melted away the last of any clouds, and oblique shadows were now flung from the outbuildings' many angles. From the carpentry shop, the sweet resinous scent of wood brought him right back to all the times he'd spent there. He gave the yard one last look and then returned to The Green where his feet carried him towards the hill. He turned the corner in the direction of St Mary's Church and there, on the left, he found the old path; the cow parsley and nettles already tall, hemming him in, and the thorny branches of May blossom forming an arch above his head.

Avoiding the muddy and damp sections, he pressed his way upwards towards the brightness ahead. He finally emerged into a broad glade that was fringed by tall oaks and horse chestnuts, and where the first buttercups had already supplanted the dandelions.

To one side was Snake Pond with its luminous seaweed-brown water lit up by a broad fringe of marsh marigolds. From the shallows, soft reeds and flag iris rose stiffly, awaiting their moment to bloom. In the brightness he was conscious suddenly of the sounds of birds which, in that enclosed space, seemed all the more intense and, as he stepped forwards, he disturbed a foraging blackbird which flurried away, scolding him loudly.

He didn't remember it being so hemmed in, and indeed the encircling trees seemed bigger and the sense of enclosure more profound. It all felt strangely at odds with every other experience he'd had as an adult returning to a child's world. His shoes he realised were wholly unsuited to the conditions, and already muddy from the footpath, but he was unconcerned. He walked slowly, not willing to intrude upon the sense of balance and order that he found in the clearing.

Initially he hesitated from approaching the pond itself, reluctant to come upon it too quickly in case it should in some way fall short of his memory, but eventually he stole slowly forwards, stepping through the rich meadow grass until he came to within a short distance of its margins.

The sun was reflecting off its mirrored surface, sending out glints that hurt his eyes. He stooped down and then leaned forwards onto his hands, peering into the clear brown water, silky as an eel, and slipped his fingers below its surface, swirling its luscious weedy depths about. He stood abruptly and looked around and then saw along the margin the ancient, sun-bleached silver of the log, ossified by so many summers that it was shrunken, half-submerged by foliage, one end sunken into the sediment at the pond's edge.

He waded through the thick undergrowth that clasped at his ankles, heedless now of the marshy ground, until he came to the great trunk that wallowed at the shallows, a mere spectre of its old self, as much a part of the pond itself.

Nevertheless, he sank down upon its smooth back. The view before him was more familiar and welcoming than his own room, more than his own face even. Every tree and bush, although larger now, was exactly right. The form and curve of the pond just so, the rise and sweep of the hill as if he'd never left it; even the air felt right; warming the top of his head, reflecting from the pond's surface up into his face.

Pond skaters were darting and their rapid movement sent flashes of sunlight to his eyes. He leaned forwards and combed the water with his fingers, seeing that as he did he disturbed a myriad tadpoles and, away to his right, a black beetle dived, its legs rowing it rapidly downwards. A shadow flitted across and he saw that a swallow had swooped low to feed.

He remembered Lizzie laughing, her brown legs dangling into the water; and he remembered John lying on his back, cackling with his coarse laughter. Above all he remembered Jonathan.

Moisture pooled in his eyes and for several minutes he allowed himself the quiet solace of tears.

Chapter Eight

Janice knew that she looked attractive. The new trouser suit and platform shoes she'd bought, in that shopping trip she'd promised herself, displayed her lissom figure to its best effect, and the emerald green of the fabric was a perfect foil for her russet-gold hair. She knew that Fiona's eyes followed her about the reception area, wide and hollow with admiration, and Janice revelled in the consciousness of her own superiority.

Two or three times a week Fiona had impatiently rushed to share her coffee break with Janice, and then feverishly relate her date with Brian of the previous evening, their drinks and meals out and the smart new places he'd taken her to. She'd never visited such places before and her head was dizzy with the excitement of it all. More recently her accounts were of nights spent with him, nights when they didn't emerge from her room at all; nights that left her bed awry and her hair a sweaty tangle, the room un-tidied and coffee mugs ring-stained. Nights when Brian would wordlessly slip from her bed in the early hours.

Janice saw that Brian continued to glance in at the surgery window, his deep brown eyes peering across the reception, a slight turn of his lips whenever there was a look of recognition, sardonic rather than joyful, thrillingly enticing. Once he winked at her, his fingers silently snapping.

There were several weeks at that time when Janice didn't see Rob until the weekend, weeks when he rang her late just as she was already drowsing in her bed, and he tired from his prolonged revision, grateful for a sympathetic voice. They'd talk quietly, their voices soft against the night. He was slumped upon his settee, mind fogged by tiredness and effort, their conversations bathed in a dream-like unreality.

***

At last, after three more weeks, Rob's exams were completed. He walked from the College building with an untroubled airiness, out into the June sunshine with a sense of freedom he hadn't felt since his schooldays at the break-up of term. He telephoned his mother and assured her all had gone well; he would simply have to wait now for the results.

In the evening Janice came to his flat straight from work. He hadn't seen her all week and thought that she looked particularly alluring. She'd had her hair restyled and, although he couldn't have said whether he'd seen them before or not, he noticed that she wore clothes that especially flattered her. She saw all this in his eyes and it excited her.

When later they went out to eat to celebrate the end of his exams, Rob again suggested that they go together to Moreton Steyning, and this time she said yes.

***

'Oh, but it's so quaint!'

Janice was standing on The Green, beaming across at the older cottages. 'You never told me,' she exclaimed, with a note of criticism that Rob felt was rather unjust. 'I'd no idea it was so pretty. Look at those! Aren't they lovely? And just look at that thatch, you don't see that much now, do you? And that one; all those beams. They must be hundreds of years old. And that old pub, real *oldee worldee.* Golly, fancy growing up here. I'd no idea.'

'I must have showed you a picture of it at some time.'

'A real English village green. There's even a pump! I wonder how you could bear to leave it.'

'I didn't choose...'

'And what's that? Up there, look! In the trees at the top.'

'It was a Windmill.'

'A real Windmill!'

'It was. It's derelict now. Hasn't worked for decades.'

'Fancy. But no shops?'

'Yes, round the corner in Church Lane, and then several more down at The Square. I'll show you,' he assured her.

'You must. And is there a pond? There's always a pond.'

'Not like you mean, no.'

'What a shame; but this is gorgeous. I love that one; there, with the thatch and the little windows, and that one there. We could live there, couldn't we? I could just imagine us there, Rob. Or that black and white one, or that one; such a pretty garden, a real cottage garden. Don't you think?

'I suppose.'

'I don't like that one, far too plain.' She was pointing away, opposite.

'I went to school with the boys from there.'

'It's not as nice as the others. Too modern and ordinary.'

'Twins actually...'

'I went to school with twins. You know, I told you; Helen and Hazel Coombs. D'you remember?'

'These were boys.'

'I haven't heard from them for ages,' she said, somewhat distractedly.

'One's still here, actually,' he continued.

'I think one went to work for London Transport. Hazel I think it was. Where's the Church? I'd love to see the Church. I so love old buildings, don't you?'

'Up here.'

As Rob led the way, he could feel his past and present colliding, the one like a rip current to the other.

***

Passing the Almshouses, a gate clanged to behind them.

'Rob?'

He heard his name exclaimed with a mixture both of surprise and questioning. It was a female voice and he turned to see Maggie standing at the gate, one hand still on its latch.

'What're you doing here again? You can't stay away!'

'Maggie! Hello. Here, this is Janice. I've brought her here to show her round the old place, to see where I grew up.'

'I've been dying to come,' Janice lied. She'd stepped forwards, almost too eagerly, and both women now stood discreetly appraising one another. 'It's so pretty, I simply can't believe we hadn't come here before. Rob's been keeping me away all this time. I just love all the little cottages round The Green! So pretty. Did you live in one, or do you live here?'

Maggie looked round to see where Janice gestured to.

'No, these are the Almshouses,' she replied.

'You're a bit young!' Rob joked.

'Mum's visiting a friend here, so I gave her a lift in. I'm just going out to get some cigs. Know I shouldn't, but there you are.'

'We're going for a look at the Church,' Janice said. 'It looks wonderful from here, so ancient.'

'Standard village Church,' Maggie remarked.

'I'll walk down to The Square with you, if that's alright,' Rob suggested. He turned to Janice. 'It'll give you time to have a good look.'

'Okay ,' she said and tripped on down the lane towards the Churchyard, her wavy hair springing upon her shoulders with each step.

He and Maggie fell into step and took the route along the top lane towards The Square.

'Your other half, then?' she said, after they'd walked a short distance.

'Yes, that's right.'

He was silently conscious of Janice's reactions to the village and how she must appear, with her stylish and colourful clothes that contrasted so conspicuously with Maggie, dressed in a practical skirt and cream blouse, short sleeved and open at the neck. He noticed a small locket, the only item of jewellery she wore, apart from a wedding ring.

'Tell you the truth I had to get out for some air,' she said. 'They rattle away, nattering about people I don't know and things I've no interest in whatsoever.'

'Down for the weekend again are you, then?'

'Just overnight. Nev's on a footie beano.'

He nodded in acknowledgement. 'How's it going with you, then?'

'Fine thanks. You?'

'Mmm. I've just finished my architectural exams so we've got a bit of freedom, hence the trip here. It really is a nice surprise bumping into you again like this.'

'You too. Seen Ann?'

'No, I've been too busy revising. Is she well?'

'Yes, I think so. It's a couple of weeks since we last spoke.'

They'd turned into The Square and he followed her across to the Newsagents, waiting outside while she bought her cigarettes. She emerged already smoking one.

'So, you two... getting married?' She exhaled the smoke upwards.

Caught off guard, Rob laughed and shrugged, a little embarrassed although he couldn't have said why.

'It's not so bad,' Maggie remarked. 'Although some would disagree; like my Mum, or Ann's.'

They stood side by side, looking across to the pub. It was early July and the swallows wheeled above their heads, owning the sky.

'You know, that day,' he said, and he didn't know why he'd said it, not now after so long, although perhaps that was the reason in itself. 'That day you ran away. What happened?'

Maggie didn't speak and she didn't react for a while, so much so that he wondered if she'd heard him, or if she was simply going to ignore the question. After a few moments she led the way across The Square to the benches outside the front of the Horse & Hounds and sat down, leaving a space for Rob to seat himself alongside her. The pub was closed and The Square had settled into that quiet period of afternoon, at rest in the early summer sunshine.

She took a long last drag on her cigarette and stubbed it out into the cobbles by her feet before relaxing back, one leg crossed over the other.

'I was actually on my way back when your brother found me.'

'Were you? But what made you go on that day in particular? Whatever happened?'

She made gestures of exasperation, raising both hands from the wrist, letting them slap back onto her thighs, a brisk shake of her head, mouth turned down with helpless anger and frustration.

'You know all that,' she said quietly. 'It was him, like it was always him, knocking my Mum and us kids about when it suited him; his rages and lying and toadying, the way he was so useless and thought he was such a big-shot, and all that double-dealing and greed. My Mum always just taking it and never, not even once, standing up to him, and my selfish self-seeking brother, and never a word of kindness, not ever. Even if I didn't mind it, doing stuff for the others when they were just kids, and then him accusing me of stealing. Him! Accusing me! Like he was some paragon of fatherhood and standing up for what's right.

'Him and Frank Bird together, who'd driven his own son away after he'd near as damn killed the first one. I'd had enough, enough of being taken advantage of, and living in that... that awful atmosphere of fear and hopelessness. She was just going to keep right on taking it, my mother, and Stephen, he'd be out first chance he got, not that he was ever around or did a thing to help anyone except number one. I'd just had it, had enough.'

She glanced up at the windows of the pub behind their heads. 'Funny, isn't it? I don't feel a thing for this place. Not a thing.'

Maggie paused and Rob thought she would say no more, but after a while she continued.

'I went down the old track, in the evening, quite late on, while they were all in the pub, well, my Dad was. Stephen was out I guess, Mum was helping in the bar; it was a warm evening so it was busy in there. The little ones were in bed, so I just walked out. I hadn't actually decided I was going to run off but I also knew I wasn't coming back. He kept an emergency stash of cash in the cellar, so I got that and then I just walked out and across The Square and onto the track and just kept going. I'd taken crisps and nuts and a bottle of lemonade from the storeroom and I walked for about an hour until dark, and then I went in that barn, you know the one on Birch's farm at the corner of Fox Covert?'

Rob nodded.

'I slept in there, really peacefully as a matter of fact. I just felt so light and free, like all my troubles were gone. It felt like a whole new life was starting. I couldn't believe it, I couldn't believe it was so easy. Why hadn't I done it before? The next morning I had to dodge people, of course, making sure I wasn't seen. I wasn't foolish or optimistic enough to assume people wouldn't be looking for me, trying to bring me back, so I hid under the hedge if I heard anything. I circled round Netherington to avoid people, crossed the main road out at Stebb's Cross, waiting until there was a long break in the traffic so I wasn't seen, and then went on round the back of Marsh Nethering.'

Rob knew it; it was a scruffy hamlet beyond Netherington. Nothing more than a collection of half a dozen farm workers' estate-built brick cottages, the farm itself and a Weslyan Chapel.

'I went through a cornfield because I knew I'd be well-hidden but I couldn't get out through the thick hedge at the end so I had to double-back onto a track round the farm, which was quiet fortunately, and then along behind a pair of the cottages.'

She stopped and glanced up at Rob, perhaps to assure herself he was still listening and that he wanted to hear all of her story. He nodded to encourage her.

'I don't really know it, but I know more or less where you mean,' he said.

'Yes, well that's why I came back.'

He looked at her quizzically.

'One of the cottages had a garden facing me as I approached and I could see that there were people in it, three adults and a child, so I walked in the shade of the hedge because I figured they were talking and absorbed and they wouldn't notice me under there, in the dark; which they didn't.

There was a woman, about my Mum's age, a few years younger probably, and the man maybe a bit older. He was sitting in a deckchair, the woman was standing up, and there was an old chap. I'm not sure what he was doing but he was watching, I think, because the younger man, the chap in the deckchair, he had a child on his lap, a girl two or three years younger than me, and I could hear them talking and laughing. The little girl was chattering and the younger man and the woman were laughing, you know, like parents do at children's chatter, and then the child ran off and came back with a ball or a toy or something, I forget exactly what.

She ran up to the man and presented it to him, saying, 'Here you are, Daddy', or something similar and I realised then it was Sid, that the man was Sid Dewberry, Ann's father. The old man was the other adult, I could see him then. He had red scars all down one side of his face. That's what did it, really. I knew he was Ann and Lizzie's spider-faced man and it just seemed obvious to me. Grandfather, mother, daughter, and daughter's father, and that father was Ann's Dad. See? I knew all along somehow, I knew he was up to something. Always away, coming and going like he did, and Nell, Ann's mother, she always had that stricken look, didn't she? Like my mother, she had that haunted look. So I knew.'

Involuntarily Rob glanced across The Square to where the cobbled passage led to the Dewberrys' house, its roof and chimneys just visible beyond the shops.

Maggie let out a sigh of resignation. 'So that's why I came back.' And she turned to Rob, but he frowned and looked a little vague. 'For Ann,' she explained. 'She needed me, see? And my mother. She needed me, she was never going to manage on her own, was she?

'I was walking back up the old track when the plane flew over. I was making no attempt by then to hide myself and I suppose I must've stood out pretty clearly on the track, red dress and all. I saw the plane come over and thought nothing of it, but then it circled and when it came back it was much lower and tilted over on one side. And then it disappeared behind the tall hedge next to me and next thing I knew it was coming towards me, above the track, really low, head-on towards me. I knew then it was Hugh and I just stayed there. I made no attempt to hide and he tilted it over again, like he was looking out of the side window at me, and I could see faces looking out. I heard the engine really loud and I knew he was low and looking for somewhere to land.

Next thing is he's circling round and is back ahead of me and then he drops really low and down below the next field hedge up ahead, and then the engine noise stopped and I knew he must've landed. Then Jonathan's running along the track towards me with his arms outstretched, his big feet flapping on the ground and he's thundering towards me and he just keeps running, running up to me calling my name again and again, and I can see his face, how relieved he is, and how happy, and he runs right up to me, arms outstretched, really wide, face all red and puffing with excitement and the effort, he wasn't much of a runner, was he? And he flings his arms around me and knocks all the air out of me so I can't speak and can hardly breathe, and he pulls me right up off my feet and he's saying 'Maggie, Maggie, I've got you. Maggie, it's alright. I've got you, you're safe'.

'And behind him, there was Hugh approaching, smiling.'

Chapter Nine

Fiona bore an expression of great tragedy, despite it being Friday and the final day at work before she went away on holiday. Admittedly it wasn't a Mediterranean trip with Brian, but instead a week away in Cornwall with a group of girlfriends, but her huge cow-eyes and constant doleful expression exasperated Janice each time she caught sight of the girl behind the reception desk as she came to collect the next patient. At their morning coffee break she found Fiona hunched on a stool in the kitchen, shoulders stooped and hair hanging down so that it obscured her face. She neither looked up nor spoke when Janice entered.

Deprived of the incessant chatter and detailed chronicling of her colleague's exploits with Brian, Janice made her coffee in welcome silence and then settled herself on the other stool. For several minutes Fiona remained uncharacteristically silent, delivered with such meaningful intensity that, with a regretful sigh, Janice found she had no alternative but to ask eventually if something was the matter.

This elicited a low moan, but it was impossible to tell whether or not it indicated illness or pain.

'Are you alright? Do you need a paracetamol; I've got some in my bag?'

Janice watched dispassionately for some kind of reaction, but Fiona didn't move. Grimacing to herself with impatience, Janice drank some more coffee before once again attempting to draw her colleague out.

'What's wrong?' she said, with an edge of irritation in her voice to disguise any sympathy, or indeed amusement, that she might find in the situation. 'Fiona?'

'It's over,' the other girl mumbled, words barely discernible.

'What is?'

'Brian.'

'Brian?'

'And just before my holiday!' and with that, Fiona turned a stricken face to Janice, and then her features crumpled and, with a choking sob that convulsed her entire body, was left so utterly limp that she was barely able to support herself on the backless stool. 'The bastard.'

'What d'you mean; what're you talking about? What before your holiday?'

'He packed me in. Last night, he packed me in,' she wailed. 'He said he'd wanted to leave it right until before I went away so we wouldn't have to see each other after, so it wouldn't be awkward. Her moaning searching for a higher crescendo. 'More like so he wouldn't see me! And I sucked his dick every time he wanted.' She flung this out with a particular emphasis on the 'and'.

Janice inwardly shuddered as Fiona presented her gaping, wailing mouth, before snivelling back into the crumpled tissue she held clasped in one hand.

'That's too bad,' Janice replied, trying hard to think of something vaguely sympathetic to say. 'Better if it was going to happen that it should be before you'd got too used to him.'

'We'd been going out for nearly three months too,' Janice lamented, merely plaintive now. 'He never gave any warning. I thought he liked me! We did it all the time. He must've, mustn't he?'

'I don't know. I suppose so.'

'He said I was too young, too immature. That's not fair, is it?'

Janice inwardly sighed. 'No.'

Brian himself was absent from the office that day, his unoccupied chair and desk visible across the shared lobby. The following Monday, when Janice walked to the waiting room to collect a patient, her eyes sought and found him; half turned away from her, bent slightly over his desk, leafing through a brochure. She could clearly see his strong profile, the straight nose, full but firm lips, dark curly hair that hung over his collar, always immaculately groomed, long sideburns and dark moustache, fashionably drooping at the sides.

Later in the morning he was walking across the office, jacket removed so that his finely-toned torso was clearly apparent through the fitted shirt, accentuated all the more since he wore his suit trousers at hipster level and they were buttock-huggingly tight. All this Janice saw and noted.

***

'Nice day.'

As she heard the words she felt a light flick at her hair that sent a lock swishing forwards across her right cheek. She looked up through her eyelashes as Brian drew alongside of her, striding fast to catch up, left arm still raised from where he'd playfully tweaked at her hair. Despite her surprise and pleasure at his unexpected appearance, she managed to smile only faintly and in a manner that suggested she wasn't to be trifled with. She kept up her pace, maintaining a discreet silence, awaiting his opening gambit.

'Not speaking, then?' he asked.

'Yes, it's a nice day,' she enunciated with deliberation.

He laughed, making it clear that he was enjoying himself and was in no way deterred by her lack of response. 'Nice enough day for a lunchtime drink?'

'I have to go to the shops.'

'But time for a quick one?'

'No.'

'You prefer evening drinking, do you?'

'I can't say I'd thought about it.'

'Well, you look like a woman who knows her own mind.'

'Perhaps. Why wouldn't I be?'

'I'd say you definitely are.'

He paused, causing her to also come to a standstill and obliging her to turn from her direction of travel, back towards him. He was smiling down at her, head slightly to one side, jacket held casually over his right shoulder, one finger looped under its collar.

'It's written all over you,' he said. 'In the way you stand, the way you dress, the way you conduct yourself, your hair, your make-up, your voice.'

'Oh?'

'It says, I'm a sophisticated young woman and I know what I want out of life.'

'Really? What's that, then?'

She was toying with him now, enjoying the dance of their exchanges. She liked the music of it too; it buoyed her up, stirred and moved her, and it enticed her in a way she felt she should be enticed.

He shifted his coat to the other shoulder, his weight from one leg to the other, standing loose and relaxed, his eyes narrowed slightly against the sunlight. His tanned skin glowed and it was almost perfect, save for a small area of blemishes on one cheek, but she didn't feel that mattered, or deterred in any way from the overall effect of his masculinity and experience.

'To live life to the full, enjoy the best it has to offer; good food and wine, travel. Fill it with experiences, take the occasional risk, fulfil your potential.'

He had a slight smile, which was cool and questioning.

'Isn't that a natural way to be?'

He shrugged. 'Depends.'

'And you?' she said. 'What do you want?'

'Me? I want it all. What're you doing tomorrow night?'

'I'm busy.'

'Too bad.'

'I have a boyfriend, you know.'

'I'd expect nothing less, an attractive woman like you. What about Wednesday night?'

Janice paused. She'd be seeing Rob as usual on Tuesday, but her sister was away on holiday so she wouldn't be seeing her that week.

'Wednesday could be free,' she said, noncommittal.

'That's it, then,' he said. 'I'll take you out to dinner. Meet you outside the station at seven thirty.'

With that settled he winked, then spun on his heel and strolled back towards the office, turning once to look back at her with a knowing smile and admiring nod.

Chapter Ten

'I hear you've finished your exams.'

Ann's call came during a dead afternoon as Rob idly stirred his tea, willing the telephone not to ring, dully awaiting the hour when he could reasonably leave for the day. Outside the window a light breeze casually stirred the leaves of the trees. It was neither sunny nor dull, one of those days of indeterminate light that tires the eyes, but fails to stimulate.

'How did they go... okay?'

'I think so,' he replied. 'It's hard to tell, but no disasters at least.'

The colleague he shared the office with was out for the afternoon and he relaxed back into his chair and swivelled so that he could plant his feet on the radiator beneath the window, grateful for a diversion from the tedium.

'I'm sure you did fine,' she brightly replied. 'Is that it then, or is there more to come?'

'One more year then I'm done, all being well. How about you? You've had exams too, haven't you? How did yours go?'

'Oh, okay too, I think. As you say, it's hard to tell but they seemed to go alright. That's it for me now. Fingers crossed I've passed.'

'That's great. So what's it to be now, then? Arts correspondent on The Guardian, News Editor on The Spectator?'

He smiled as he heard her laugh at the end of the phone.

'Oh, I'm going to submit a few feature pieces to some magazines and local newspaper groups,' she said. 'Then maybe I'll try applying for some jobs. I've had a handful of pieces published...'

'Well done you!'

'It's nothing much, just odds and ends for magazines only too grateful to have some half-decent copy from someone who can spell and knows what a semi-colon is. Still, it's all good experience.'

'Sure...'

'You went back to Moreton Steyning, I hear. My spies caught you out!'

'Yes, she did. I was taking Janice for a look around.'

'Did she like it?'

'I think she did. She thought it was pretty.'

'Well, it is, isn't it, on the whole?'

'I suppose so. I'd never thought of it like that; it was just home.'

He recalled how he'd rejoined Janice that day, after his conversation with Maggie outside the pub, and she'd expressed great admiration for St Mary's Church, that is, once she'd ceased complaining at how long he'd been. I'm sorry, he'd said. We got talking, you know how it is with old friends you haven't seen for ages. Janice hadn't responded to that but later had pronounced the Church to be 'possessed of a special atmosphere' and 'of Norman origins'. She must have read that somewhere, he'd reflected. She'd never passed an opinion on building history or architectural styles before, and had temporarily overlooked the fact that it was his own area of expertise.

Afterwards, he'd shown her his old school and they'd walked to The Square, and there she'd cast an eye over the remaining shops, wondering that people once managed to exist on such basic supplies. After that they'd gone into the pub yard and he'd told her it was here where Maggie had lived and where they'd all played.

He'd taken her along Main Street, towards Wheelwrights and Woodbine Cottage. There're the allotments on the right, he'd told her, where my Dad had a plot (where he endlessly tumbled the rich soil, calmly, patiently, with simple dedication and pride, in time-honoured accord with the changing seasons). That's the back of the school, that high wall over there, and there's where my best friend Lizzie lived, at Wheelwright's, and her back yard where we played all the time, where her Dad, Uncle and Grandpa worked; they were all village Carpenters and occasionally still made or repaired cart wheels. And that's my old home over there, nearly opposite; Woodbine Cottage. That was mine and Jonathan's room, that one at the top on the right looking out over the street to Wheelwright's, from where I could see Lizzie's room and she used to wave to me, her sunny face ever-smiling.

'That's nice,' she'd commented, but he knew it wasn't as 'quaint' or 'pretty' as the cottages by The Green.

For weeks beforehand he'd visualised taking Janice to Snake Pond, to show her where he'd spent all those hours as a child, so many happy hours searching for pond beetles with Jonathan or chatting with Lizzie, but it wasn't the pond of her imaginings, not a circular pool where pure white ducks bobbed and dabbled and children threw bread. The path to it was steep and would be overgrown at this time of year, and was always muddy from the springs, and she'd been wearing high-heeled shoes. No, there was no point, best to leave it. Her disappointment would only pain him, and he'd no wish to try and explain or excuse its wild and unmanicured state.

'That's what Maggie would say,' Ann said, laughter in her voice still. 'She doesn't do pretty.' And then, as if with resolve, 'She's okay , though.' After a brief pause she added, 'did you see Finch again while you were there?'

'No, I didn't feel I could impinge on Janice's patience any further after talking to Maggie for so long.'

Janice had declined his suggestion that they go and eat at a well-regarded restaurant which was offering a special mid-week tasting menu. With his Wednesday night classes finished for the summer, and Janice's sister who she usually saw each Wednesday currently away on holiday, he'd expected her to be enthused at the idea.

'I want a rest, what's wrong with that?' she'd complained.

'I thought you'd be really keen, especially as we can't usually go out on a Wednesday.'

'I do want to go there, but just not then.'

'What do you need a rest for, we've hardly been anywhere for weeks while I've been revising?'

'Why do I have to explain myself? If I say I need a night off, I do. Honestly, Rob!'

He'd been hurt and disappointed and had snapped back, 'What's the big deal?' He was looking forward to a good meal out after all the hard work of study, and her disinterest and unresponsiveness was both frustrating and illogical.

'There's no big deal, I just...'

'Oh well, suit yourself.'

So instead he'd spent most of that Wednesday evening indoors, at home and on his own, only walking to the corner pub for a pint at about ten where he'd found a chap who lived in the same street who he could at least talk to for half an hour.

'How about meeting for lunch again?' he asked Ann.

'Yes, that would be lovely,' she said.

'Tomorrow?'

'Yes, certainly.'

***

She seemed a little different when he spied her some distance away, and he realised that he hadn't seen Ann in summer clothes before. A soft, floaty sapphire-blue dress swung about her knees and she wore strappy platform-soled sandals. She walked rather briskly for one so diminutive, so that her straight hair, which hung almost to her waist, swept from side to side behind her back with each swinging step. As she saw Rob, she raised one hand and wiggled her fingers in acknowledgement, and then walked across the grass towards him.

The brass band struck up once again as he pushed himself to his feet at her approach. She was stepping smartly between the office workers, enjoying a leisurely lunchtime around the bandstand, and his words of greeting were lost to the opening bars of music.

'You look well!' he said, as she reached him.

'It's always good when summer finally arrives, isn't it?' she smiled and sank to the ground, alongside of him. 'Oh, they look good!'

He'd brought sandwiches and bottles of fruit juice to share and a bag of large glossy black cherries. 'I hope you like cherries.'

'Oh, goodness, who doesn't? So... you had a good day going back to the village?'

'Yes, but it was rather strange, being there with Janice, but remembering it all how it used to be.'

'Well, we can never be an adult in the world of our childhoods, can we? If only we could... how different it all might seem.'

'Maggie was on good form,' he observed.

'Good.'

'We were talking about the day she ran away.'

'Oh, God, that was awful, wasn't it? Poor Maggie, that awful man.'

'Rod Viney?'

'Her father, yes.'

Did she know, he wondered, why Maggie had come back that day and what she'd seen? And how much did she know about her own father? But it wasn't his business to tell her, or to comment on it.

On the ornate Regency Bandstand, which rather resembled a child's Merry-Go-Round, a military band dressed in vivid crimson jackets struck up a vigorous marching piece. Rob and Ann ate in silence, listening to the music and watching the conductor who resembled a toy soldier, his arms moving automaton-like in time to the rhythm. When the tune had finished they joined in with the ripple of applause from the relaxing onlookers, at least those who stirred themselves, if only briefly, to show appreciation.

Perhaps prompted by the similarity, Ann suddenly remarked, 'I used to love the Fair; especially the Gallopers. All that excitement and the crowds. It seems silly now, but I used to look forward to it for weeks. We all did, didn't we? D'you remember John there? He was always up to something.'

Did he remember John? How rarely he thought of him now, his special companion of those distant childhood summers.

'Did you ever try to find him?'

Her query brought him back from his reverie, just as the band began another number, a slow waltz this time.

'No, no I haven't. I wouldn't really know where to start.'

'It's probably easier than you think, you know.'

He turned, questioningly.

'Don't forget I work in a Library,' she continued. 'There's a reference section with directories and access to electoral rolls, and all that sort of thing. People are always coming in wanting to track someone down they've lost contact with.'

'I wouldn't know where to start,' he said.

'No, but I would.'

'Really? Would it be possible?'

'It's possible, certainly. It just depends what sort of tracks his family have left. But I could have a look. Where was it you said he came from?'

'Cricklewood, but he never mentioned a road name. Oh, hang on… he was always going on about the railway and the marshalling yards. It couldn't have been far from them I would imagine.'

'Anything about family members?'

'He was always vague. Paddy something, but that wasn't his father. He once said his father had cleared off. There were two other children too.'

'Older, younger?'

'Younger.'

So, it's a second marriage, or at least a second relationship.'

'The only name we have is Norbert.'

'Okay . Shall I look?' she asked.

'Alright, why not? If you don't mind.'

'I don't mind,' she said.

Chapter Eleven

Outside the window the night was drawing in, etching the trees across the road against the faded sky. A moth had flown in through the opened casement and was now dashing itself repeatedly against the lampshade, the soft bumping of its body drumming in the heavy night air, reminding Rob of another such night.

Tom had let them in at the lean-to door, and it had yielded easily to the push of his hand, the wood shrunken in the dry air. He switch on the lean-to light which abruptly illuminated the softly darkening evening and a moth flustered into the light bulb. Tom and Sally were quickly swallowed up by the house's dim interior, appearing like characters on a stage as they moved from room to room, ordering their things, preparing a final pot of tea before bed.

The boys hung back outside, unwilling to leave behind the fading evening. They wandered onto the lawn, feeling the thickening evening air and coolness of the grass beneath their feet. The first bats were but brief movements captured against the huge canopy of violet-hued sky and they counted the first stars of the night.

A noise at the gate alerted Robbie and he saw a red point of light that bobbed beyond the greenhouse, and which then intensified to a rich carmine glow before it swept down towards the ground, swinging slowly a foot or so above the path. A sharp noise, like a creature calling in the dead of night, at first startled him, but was quickly followed by a rasping summons and John stepped from the shadows and onto the lawn, a lit cigarette held between his fingers.

'Whotcha. Woz up?'

'Nothing. We just got back.'

'Right. Comin' then?'

'Where? It's after nine-thirty.'

John merely inclined his head and led Robbie out through the side gate. Behind, Jonathan called softly to his brother that it was almost bed time.

'Won't be a minute,' he replied.

At The Green John paused, drawing slowly on the cigarette, holding it at the filter end between in-curved index finger and thumb, sucking in his lips and dragging hard upon it. He ejected the smoke in one long, steady plume that settled about them, directionless in the breathless night air.

'Orright?' he said, adopting a casual stance.

There was no point in questioning John; Robbie knew what his response would be. He'd have slipped out while his Aunt slumbered in the armchair, the radio still chattering cheerfully beside her, unheard and unnoticed.

It was often this way with John. While Robbie slept, oblivious beside his softly snoring elder brother, John roamed the village, secretive, watchful, observing; creeping into gardens and prowling about the cottages.

'Got this,' he pronounced, holding up a half-used packet of cigarettes.

'Where?'

'Pub. Them fellas,' and he chuckled throatily, jabbing his thumb back towards the table of village men seated outside the Jug & Bottle. 'Stupid fuckers, eh? Weren't watchin'.'

He always had his pockets-full of cigarettes; loose usually, in twos and threes, but occasionally there'd be a part-full packet and a box or book of matches. Invariably there was also a handful of coins, sometimes even a note, and perhaps a pen or pencil or some sweets, all stuffed deep into the pockets of his trousers, their openings frayed and grimed, dragging on the already shapeless garment so that it hung ever more loosely from his thin waist.

During the daytime, his eyes were dark-ringed and hollow.

'Fuckers, eh!' he cackled.

***

Railway Terrace, reflected Rob. He should have remembered.

'I've found something,' Ann had said. She'd called him at work, a few days after their lunch at the Bandstand.

'There's a D Norbert listed at 73 Railway Terrace in Cricklewood, just at the time John would have been first coming to Moreton Steyning, and remains there for several years after,' she'd said. 'The last record is two years ago, so it's worth trying. It sounds likely it's his family. What d'you think?'

He sat in the flat, absorbed in motionless reverie, recalling those summers of his childhood. John's memory, so long forsaken, was increasingly vivid now; his unkempt appearance, the swagger and wildness, the air of danger and risk. He was a creature of mystery to them as children but, as Rob looked back, he saw now a strange and burdened child, furtive and unnaturally alert.

That night he dreamt again of Jonathan.

Chapter Twelve

It was a curious one-sided street; a single, long terrace of uniform, plain-brick houses that stretched as far as the eye could see, chimney after chimney, front door after front door, rows upon rows of windows, all identical. Rob stood at the entrance to the road and gazed down, uncomfortable now to be in such close proximity. They'd walked from the station, beneath the noisy flyover, past the grimy industrial units and dusty weed-infested waste areas. Away to one side came the occasional noise of a train. *You can 'ear 'em shuntin' 'n' stuff, loadin', goes on all night like,* the voice in his head said, hoarse and rasping.

He was the first to speak.

'Number seventy three?'

'Yes. There're no houses opposite so perhaps the numbers run consecutively. I think they must do.' Ann was frowning. She was also standing with an air of slight reluctance.

They fell into step and soon reached the beginning of the seemingly endless terrace. After a short time, they realised that the apparently unbroken run of houses was in fact punctuated at intervals by passageways that led through to the rear. The houses themselves were narrow, the width of one small room only, and each had a narrow strip of garden at the front, divided from its adjoining neighbour by a wooden fence, and from the street by a wall of ugly concrete planks. Purely functional cement paths led from the street to each front door.

The overall appearance might have presented some kind of harmony, and yet each house somehow managed to dissociate itself from its neighbour by the random alteration of a front door or window, from the untidy clutter of rooftop aerials, or by a careless choice of curtains, hanging loose from missing hooks flapping unnoticed from an open window, or through a lack of paint on the woodwork.

Some had paved their front gardens and these were filled with vehicles, partially obstructing the view along the front where otherwise each dividing garden fence followed the next, one after another, seemingly forever, much like the gills of a mushroom, until in the distance they were indistinguishable.

Along every few houses a window had been replaced or was broken and covered by boards. Dustbins and discarded items, old mattresses, a plastic washing basket, broken children's toys and carrier bags of who knows what all spilled through broken front walls and onto the pavement.

They'd reached the start of the terrace and began to walk along its length, noting as they passed the number of each house running, as Ann had suggested, sequentially. Both had their heads turned towards the houses, letting their eyes rove over the features of each. Rob felt a sigh escape and his own chest heave with the dismal sorrow of it all.

'They're a bit grim, aren't they?' said Ann, who must have heard, or perhaps sensed his disquiet.

There was little sign of life, no sight or sound of children and no people walking, although several cars and motorbikes were parked in the road or had somehow been squeezed into front gardens.

'Number sixty,' said Rob, reading off the number from the nearest house that had its number displayed, and felt his heart begin to thud.

'… Sixty eight,' said Ann, noting the number of the house alongside the next side passageway they passed.

Just five houses to go. Mentally they both scanned ahead, working out which was number seventy three. Rob felt his chest tighten and he struggled to draw his breath. Involuntarily his footsteps slowed; he even found it difficult to walk and was aware of a trembling weakness in his limbs.

'This is it,' Ann said, softly.

She'd noticed that Rob had scarcely spoken the whole time they'd walked the length of the terrace, and now saw that his face was tense.

They both stood at the garden gate. It hung partially open, painted in a dull green that was repeated at the front door and windows. Large patches of bare wood were exposed from where the paint was worn or had peeled away in narrow strips, some of which still hung loose, coiled back upon themselves. The usual concrete path led to a front door and the garden area was a tumble of dry crumbs of earth amongst which seeding weeds grew with a few desultory, fading poppies.

Rob felt that his legs were numbed and immobile and was unable to propel himself forwards. He looked at the windows, two small rectangular ones upstairs and one larger downstairs that faced out over the front garden. Curtains of indeterminate colour hung limply and it was impossible to see inside for the dimness of the rooms, despite the bright day.

'Shall we knock?' asked Ann.

She stood a little apart from Rob, and had also been peering up at the blank windows. She turned now to face him, presenting an uncertain and questioning look.

'I suppose so,' he heard himself say.

'We've made the effort to come all this way,' she said. 'Shall I knock?' she sounded uncertain, seeking his consent.

He nodded and watched as she pushed at the front gate. It caught upon a raised patch of concrete path, forcing her to edge sideways through the narrow gap. There was a bell beside the front door which she pressed and both automatically strained to hear its chime. There was no sound or response from within and Ann took a couple of steps backwards and looked across to the living room window, waiting. She glanced back to him and then rapped on the door with her knuckles.

Out in the street, Rob shifted uneasily and found himself focussing on her long hair; anything to still his anxiety. Hanging like a silky curtain to the small of her back, it was no longer the pale straw colour of childhood but russet and golden-toned, like the ripening multi-hued seed heads of meadow grasses. He stared into its depths as if he were focussing in meditation, his mind deadened to all else.

Her voice brought him abruptly back.

'There doesn't seem to be anyone in.'

'No?'

'No... nothing. I can't hear or see a thing indoors. I'm pretty sure there's no one around. I suppose we could try next door. What d'you think?'

The house to the left, with a window ajar upstairs, seemed to display the most obvious signs of habitation. This time both walked up to the door and knocked, but nobody came. Dismayed they went to try at the house on the other side of number seventy three. Several cardboard boxes occupied the front garden and a motor bike filled the remaining space so that they could reach the front door only by stepping awkwardly around it.

At first their knock drew no response, but then a window was flung open above them and a woman poked her head out.

'You won't get no answer there.'

'It's next door we wanted to ask about actually,' Rob called up.

'That's what I said.'

'Have they gone out?'

Ann tilted her head back to see the woman, who leaned upon one broad forearm which she rested along the window ledge.

'Gone,' she said abruptly.

'When will they be back?' Rob asked.

'Gone ent they. Ain't bin no one there fer two years, gotta be. Never sin anyone.'

'Do you know where they've gone to?' asked Ann.

The woman pulled an exaggeratedly doubtful expression, looking away down the road, observing something further along the terrace that had caught her attention.

'Nah,' she said after a pause. 'Try 'er,' and she indicated back the way they'd come. 'Sixty eight,' she said and pulled the window shut with a firm thud.

Number sixty eight proved to be a house beside the passage. They glanced at one another and then made their way along it. It was more a tunnel than passage, as the upper floors of the houses continued above, so that their footsteps briefly echoed as they walked through, and it smelled damp and unpleasant. At the rear they found the houses had small back gardens or yards, and a long pathway ran the entire length of the terrace behind. Beyond were the railway yards.

The view of the rear of the houses was every bit as unprepossessing as the front. Each had a back door and two small windows. Washing hanging in a few of the yards, and one toy bike flung onto the back pathway, gave scant evidence of life. They turned to their right and, counting, found their way to the rear of number seventy three. A tattered and mouldy carpet and some rusted empty tins was all that occupied the rear garden. Ripped curtains were pulled across the ground floor window obscuring any view of the indoors.

They returned to the street and when they rang the bell of number sixty-eight. It was a thickset man of about sixty that came to the door, shirt rolled to the elbows and opened at the neck, revealing a matt of greying hairs at his throat. In response to their enquiry he summoned his wife, all the while keeping them both under scrutiny, his bulk blocking the doorway which he only relinquished when she appeared.

'She's gone,' the woman said. 'Went last year.'

Rob felt a surge which could have been disappointment or was perhaps relief. He really couldn't tell, but found himself breathing more easily.

'Do you have a forwarding address? Or have you any idea where she went to?' Ann was being exaggeratedly courteous, trying to draw out any information that the woman might possess. 'We were friends with her son when we were children; with John. We'd really like to trace him, if you could possibly help.'

The woman stared at them for far longer than was polite, eyeing them up, perhaps curious, or merely suspicious.

'He weren't there,' she said after a pause. 'I ain't seen 'im fer a long time. They went, the rest of 'em; I don't know where. She said they was goin' East.'

'East? Did they say where East?' Ann persisted.

'Jus' East,' and the woman took a step back as if she were about to close the door on them.

'That's Mrs Norbert, is it? John's mother? Was she friends with anyone else along here? Is there someone who might know more, or did she mention any relatives perhaps? Or did John have any friends who're still in the street?'

The man's voice came from within and the woman twisted round, calling, 'Not them, the Norberts was five houses down. You don't know!' Then she turned back to them. 'She weren't from 'ere and I didn't know that fella; they went off soon after anyway. I 'ent seen the grown-up kid but 'e were a right one. What you want a look 'im up fer anyway?'

'We were friends,' said Rob lamely.

'Well, you know yer own business,' the woman replied, and this time she did close the door on them.

Rob and Ann stood back in the street, discouraged and dispirited.

'I think we're going to have to give up,' he said after a while.

He'd tried to imagine John as he would be now; like himself, aged twenty six. Would he still be small of stature, with that same crumpled face that wore too many years for his age? What sort of man does a grimy, uncontrolled boy become? He'd begun to walk away, back along the terrace to where the street rejoined the more familiar roads of semi-detached houses, back towards the station and home, and Ann had followed in silence.

After a few minutes an older woman passed them from the opposite direction, walking slowly, carrying bags in both hands. Ann turned and watched her casually and, a few minutes later, turned again to monitor the woman's progress.

'She's gone in somewhere near seventy-three,' she observed, and it was only with some difficulty that she was able to persuade Rob to go back with her and try the house.

It proved to be three doors beyond the Norbert's, a less untidy place than some, suggesting someone who might have been resident for a number of years. Rob would as soon have left, but he joined Ann as they knocked on the door and the same woman appeared before them.

'Oh, the mite,' she said, when asked about John and then invited them in.

It was a small but neat living room, and they were obliged to crush together into a narrow settee whose sagging springs tipped them one against the other. The woman, who was younger than their first impression had suggested, even brought them welcome mugs of tea.

'Out all hours,' she said, unprompted.

'He liked to roam about late when I knew him,' Rob remarked. 'He was always out playing late into the evening.'

'She couldn't care, that one. Always out drinking, drunk as you like; shocking it was, pair of 'em. Out all hours, he was. Shut out, nothing to eat more often than not, and nothing to him.'

She took a long draught of tea, indicating the room at the rear of the house so that Rob and Ann found themselves gazing at it, but without knowing quite why.

'He use to sit in there. I called 'im in, if I saw 'im. He could be out there any time; after nine, after ten, after eleven. Kid like that, sat outside, never knowing. He had more meals in here, I'm telling you, than ever 'e had with 'er. Skinny 'e was, like you never saw. All skin an' bones, nothing to 'im. A breeze would blow 'im away. Mind, you wouldn't leave yer small change around or he'd have it, the little blighter; light fingered 'e was, but you can't blame 'im for that. Terrible she was, that mother of 'is. Soon as she took up with that Irish...'

'Would that be Paddy?' Rob found himself asking.

'Big fella; muscles, scrapped all the time 'he did. Always used his fists. Used his fists to sort anything, even the boy. Always had a bruise, he did, ain't that right?'

'That wasn't his father though, was it?' said Rob.

'Norbert upped and went years ago. The boy was only about five, maybe four. She took up with that Irish fella and before you know it she's got the other two, one after the other, straight off. The boy don't get a look in, do 'e? He was a right bastard, 'scuse my French, but I call it how I see it, knockin' the kid around. Wasn't his, see? Left to hisself all the time, roamin' about all hours of the day and night, pilferin' for food.

'The kid was always neglected. Don't get me wrong, kids round here, they're a bit on the rough side but they've got 'omes, even if they go short a bit, and most of the men, they're all off the railway, they all likes a pint or five. But this Paddy, he was rough. Big, violent man. He'd as soon as hit you as look at you. He frightened me, I don't mind saying. The kid though, John, I swear he wasn't frightened, never was frightened of him, not of nothing, but he took some beatings, the poor little mite.

'He just used his fists, didn't he, that Paddy, even on the kid, scrawny little bugger that he was. I said to 'im one day, pick on someone yer own size, and if looks could kill, I wouldn't be here now I can tell you. He was a 'orrible man, and she never stood up to 'im, not even for her own son, she just let it happen. Terrible mother, treating her child like that.'

There was silence as they all drank their tea. Rob's mug was empty, but he held it to his face to cover up for the fact that he didn't know what to say. She'd told him everything he'd known already, but somehow he hadn't known, hadn't wanted to understand.

'Do you know where John is now?' he heard Ann ask.

'Married, isn't he, dear?' the woman smiled.

Rob and Ann glanced to one another, astonished.

'Yes,' she said. 'Nice girl, too. And a baby, I'd heard.'

Chapter Thirteen

His father was invariably to be found in the storeroom, a long dark shed at the rear of the public sales area where they stored the sundry items sold at the nursery, and it was there he could be found, engaged in piling up sacks of compost and peat, ordering and checking, counting, sorting.

'Hello, boy,' he'd always say on seeing Rob, and his face would fall naturally into the creases of his smile.

He spent many hours organising that stock, assessing the shortfalls and future needs; logging, moving, lifting. At other times he'd be in the glasshouses, meticulously pricking out hundreds of plants, all identical, ready for the spring and summer market, all the day long. Row upon row in their little round pots, all set out upon the wooden staging, organised by colour and type. Once it had been Jonathan's job, the arranging, watering and checking; he was naturally methodical and conscientious. No plants ever died on his watch; none strayed into the wrong batch. Now it was the contract staff who helped – students and seasonal workers, some of whom scarcely even spoke English, or who merely talked amongst themselves about their own interests.

Tom rarely commented on the changes forced upon him as a result of Jonathan's death, still less on the immense transformation brought about in his life since they'd left Moreton Steyning. Rob knew and understood that his father had born the adjustments and compromises with quiet fortitude, yet the pain of that loss was with him every second of his life, a hollow bereavement that always remained.

From his fingers sprang many thousands of plants, each healthy and bearing that vigour and uniqueness necessary to charm and satisfy its new owner. Hundreds and hundreds of cuttings, many thousands of seeds all sown and nurtured, each and every season, carefully tended and brought forward to please and delight, and yet not one satisfied his own needs, that dignity and satisfaction of tending and growing his own, for his own.

***

The sun was strong now, high in a deep blue sky and warm day followed another warm day. Summer was upon them and a lightness and carefree air suffused London. People paraded in casual and brightly-coloured clothes, such that they wouldn't wear at other times of the year but which seemed entirely appropriate now. Rob craved a break away from the city; a few days in the country or by the sea perhaps. But somehow he and Janice had failed to organise anything. She'd been evasive or distracted and always the topic had been put aside. Now he suggested it to her again – a few days away over the weekend while the weather holds; it would be foolish not to. She sighed heavily and insisted that he knew very well how busy she was. Staff at work were away and she had to cover for them. It simply wasn't possible.

'You always say that. Don't you want to go away?' he complained, conscious that he was raising his voice down the phone.

'Yes, but I can't,' she snapped back. 'I keep telling you. What's the matter with you!' Her tone of late had become hectoring. She never wanted to go anywhere or do anything.

He groaned inwardly, suppressed his own rising anger and told himself he should simply go on his own, but knew he wouldn't. Just how busy could a Dentists' be, he muttered and almost knocked over his coffee. There was a message from Ann which he'd delayed answering in the attempt to organise a trip away with Janice. Now he took up the scrap of paper and dialled off her number. It wasn't the usual work one so he wondered if she was at home. Lucky her, he thought.

There was a delay and she answered rather breathlessly.

'I was just going out,' she said.

'Not working?'

'No, I'm using up leave. I left a message for you, didn't I? Look, I've checked to see if there was a birth registered, but I couldn't find anything. I'm talking about John, by the way. Then I thought... there may be a record at one of the maternity hospitals if there's been a baby. There're only a couple in that area of London. Could be worth a call, you never know. Someone might have info they can pass on. What d'you think? Worth a try?'

He'd given it little thought since their visit to the Railway Terrace, his thoughts more absorbed in the matter of a break away from work. Although he realised, if he was honest with himself, that he'd deliberately avoided thinking about John. The woman's description of his friend's childhood had unsettled him.

'I suppose so,' he answered vaguely.

'Do you want to, or shall I?'

'It might be better from a female friend,' he said, using it as an excuse.

He booked the end of the week off anyway and had scarcely arrived home from his final day's work when the phone in the flat rang. It was Ann with news.

***

He was taken aback by the building; a monolithic Victorian brick edifice which might once have been a workhouse. It stood amongst parched weedy lawns, partly secluded behind heavy-limbed trees. Behind it ran a railway. So that's fitting, he thought.

'It took three calls,' Ann had explained. 'I had to be persistent; I said we're childhood friends of many years and had lost touch after moving. All I know is there's a Mrs Norbert who's been here a while after the birth of a child and the father's name is John. After that I think we'll just have to wing it and hope we don't make too much of a fool of ourselves.'

Ann was happy and relaxed. Another article had been accepted and she'd been able to take time off to work on another. The paper had seemed satisfied and held out the hope of a follow-up and, now that summer had arrived and students had other matters than study on their minds, the Library was pretty empty. She'd been working on a series of features to write and was also able to devote time to the search for John. She sensed that, unless she gently helped and encouraged him, Rob wouldn't have the heart or will to pursue it himself, and yet he needed to. There was something deep down that he had to resolve.

He wasn't quite his usual self that afternoon and seemed a little distracted. Ann was conscious of having to prompt him, but he followed her directions readily enough. Eventually they found the Maternity Wing, approached through a series of long corridors that seemed to take entirely random twists and turns. There were windowless passageways without any reference to the world outside so that, completely disorientated, they had no idea which part of the building they were in, when eventually, the double doors before them announced that they'd arrived at the Harriet Windsor Maternity Ward. In the distance a series of side wards could be glimpsed, but there was no staff in view and a strict notice informed them that visiting was permitted only within official hours.

They lingered uneasily until, eventually, a Nurse approached along the corridor from behind them. Ann explained their purpose, apologising that they were ahead of visiting hours, but could they ascertain that a Mrs Norbert was, or had been, a patient. The Nurse, a brisk and sinewy Asian woman who was clearly anxious to move on, listened distractedly and strode away through the double doors, muttering something inaudible. They waited a long time, so long that they began to wonder if she would return at all, but eventually she burst back through the doors and announced that Mrs Norbert had been transferred and was in Dahlia Ward. Finally, as if under duress, she indicated distractedly away behind them and to their left before marching back into the ward, leaving them in no doubt that she had no further time for them.

Ann began to lead the way and Rob fell in beside her. They eventually found a long and multi-coloured direction board which mentioned the ward by name, in a wing that contained several other functions, including the departments of Haematology, Psychological Medicine and Urology.

Their route took them through echoing stairwells, along high-level bridges that connected one section of the hospital to another and even, at one point, out into the bright sunshine before they were plunged once more into the tense artificial light of yet another corridor. The only difference between this and the many others they'd passed along being the colour of the paint; this one was a dull pale green and not the cloying yellow of before. They finally reached an open and bright reception area where there hung another multi-coloured list of departments and wards, one of which indicated an area to their left, through Psychiatry, where there was listed a series of wards all afforded the names of flowers.

Rob might have allowed the sheer effort and tedium to have deterred him but Ann pressed on and he kept to her side; admiring her complete resolve and energy. The overwhelming size and unsettling blend of odours from the hospital made him feel slightly nauseous and dizzy. That, and the combined warmth and airlessness in the long, windowless corridors.

Eventually, after nearly twenty minutes, they found themselves entering through double doors, the area of wards with jolly floral names, each leading off a brightly-lit central lobby. Dahlia Ward seemed to be the smallest, approached down a short length of corridor.

By now, the general visiting times had begun and they felt able to enter, albeit walking rather self-consciously along a broad central area off which there was a series of side wards, each with half a dozen or so beds. They glanced discreetly into each as if they might, by some mysterious means, identify, just by appearance, the young woman to whom John could be married. Rob didn't know what to expect but he walked with great trepidation, making an effort to breathe deeply and evenly, trying to suppress the nervous queasiness in his stomach.

A Sister at a central desk looked up as they approached and, to their relief after their earlier experience, smiled encouragingly.

'Mrs Norbert?' asked Ann, as if it were the most normal thing.

'Is she expecting you?' the Ward Sister asked.

'Probably not, but we're old friends of her husband's,' said Ann brightly, smiling to convey that their presence was a natural and good thing. She had a particularly sweet and charming smile, Rob noticed. No one would disbelieve her.

The Sister, who was a fairly heavy woman, pushed herself from her chair and walked off down the corridor, disappearing into one of the side rooms. She emerged in a short while and waved her arm indicating that they should go in. She passed them in the corridor as they advanced and gave them both a pleasant smile.

The room itself was surprisingly bright and cheery compared to the rest of the hospital that they'd seen, with a large window opposite the door; bright yellow curtains at both the window, and at each bed and a colourful picture on one wall. There were four beds in the room, two to each side, each one occupied by women of varying ages.

Ann scanned them quickly and assessed that only two, the one beside the window on the right and the woman immediately to their left, were of the right age. Rob was standing frozen and immobile, as if overwhelmed. She was just able to make out the name on the hospital notes at the foot of the first bed to their left, sufficient enough to determine that it couldn't be Norbert, and so walked confidently towards the window-side bed on the right, aware that Rob slowly followed.

A young woman of about twenty-five was seated in the bed, her legs brought up under her chest and one arm wrapped around them. The other was placed upon the bedcover which she softly stroked with restless fingers. Her face was turned partially away and she was looking out through the window. Ann saw that she was of slim build, a little too thin perhaps, with fair hair that had a slight wave but was oddly styled, cut short just below the ears in a rather abrupt and unfinished way.

They both walked to the foot of the bed and Ann saw that the name upon the notes was indeed Norbert. Mrs E. Norbert. After a few moments, the young woman in the bed turned her head towards them with an evenness and regularity of movement that was both poetic and odd, and her eyes swept across their persons, softly, flutteringly, like a moth in flight. She had grey-blue eyes, although they didn't look directly at Ann and Rob.

'Hello,' said Ann and her voice sounded small, like she was.

The young woman in the bed parted her lips slightly, but didn't speak. There was a questioning look about her expression and a beauty that had been in her features but which was now overwhelmed by the appearance of distraction and great weariness. She raised her eyes and looked upon the faces of her visitors, flicking swiftly between them, back and forth.

Beside her, Ann was aware that Rob's stance suddenly stiffened.

'Lizzie!' she heard him whisper.

Chapter Fourteen

They found a café. It was on a busy road, but at least it offered shade and there was some seating outside. They were hot, the air swollen with enveloping warmth and suffused with the soapy perfume of a nearby lime tree. Rob flapped his shirt at the open neck and Ann mopped at her brow with the back of one hand. She sat with her hands hanging loosely from the wrists, drained of all effort. They both ordered cold lemonade.

Neither spoke while they waited for their drinks to come, and both silently watched as the girl set the bottles and glasses on the table before them.

'I had no idea,' said Ann at last. 'No one did. The family said nothing.'

Rob made a small noise in his throat and, with some effort, pushed himself forwards in his chair sufficiently to reach his glass, which he filled from the bottle as if it required great concentration.

Ann looked over to him and briefly brushed the back of her hand against his.

'You okay?'

'Yes,' he sighed. 'It's just so sad; such a shock. I mean, Lizzie... she was always so carefree. At least she was as a child.'

'She was as a teenager too.'

'I can't believe it... it seems incredible.'

'Me too.'

'Did you get to read the notes? I saw you looking.'

'It said *postpartum psychosis*; that's post-natal depression, I believe, but much more severe.'

'Poor Lizzie.'

'Yes, poor Lizzie.

She'd recognised them even before they themselves had realised that the woman in the bed before them, the woman whose face bore an expression of vagueness and distress, was their childhood friend. When she saw them, her features had disintegrated and, dropping her brow onto her knees, she'd helplessly sobbed.

At once a Nurse had bustled into the room and, pulling the curtains around Lizzie, had ushered them both out into the corridor where side-by-side they'd sat, just as they had at the café, forlorn and in stunned silence, straining to hear the reassuring murmurs of the Nurse and the soft wails that emanated from behind the curtains.

After a time the Nurse had reappeared, sweeping back the curtains with a brisk swish and Lizzie had turned towards them, a hesitant smile upon her face, and with one slender arm she'd beckoned them back in.

'It was the shock,' she'd said in a frail voice, but her expression had radiated a hungry pleasure and, as they approached, she'd reached out with her arms and clasped each by the hand.

'So lovely,' she'd whispered. 'So lovely...'

***

It was early evening when Rob drove home. The pavements were thronged with people walking, enjoying the warm sunshine, stopping at pubs and bars for the evening. Ahead, the road surface was burnished bronze from the low reflected sun and he was forced to drive with one arm raised to shade his eyes from the glare. The car windows were open on both sides and the heat swept in, bringing with it the snatched hubbub of conversations and drone of slow-moving vehicles. His elbow lay upon the lowered window, fingers casually on the steering wheel as the traffic edged along the main road which was unusually busy for that hour; due, he surmised, to people leaving early, or simply going out straight from work. In his shirt pocket was the scrap of paper that bore John's address.

He rather envied the crowds and the couples parading along the pavements or seated in groups, drinking and clearly having fun in the way that people do on hot summer evenings. He'd had to drop Ann at the station since she was meeting friends later on but it was, he felt, rather a waste to be headed home alone when it was so lovely out. He'd made no prior arrangement to see Janice. This was unusual, exceptional even, since they would invariably meet on a Friday when he had no classes, but she'd cried off the previous night and he was still infuriated with her over her negative attitude to their taking a break away. She'd also been thoroughly disagreeable lately and he was only too pleased to withhold contact from her for a few days.

There was a long delay at the traffic lights and he let his arm swing down from the elbow, brushing the hot metal of the car with the palm of his hand until the queue began to creep forwards and stretch out. The road turned slightly to the north from here, leaving the sun further away to his left so that he was able to see ahead more clearly now and could drop his shielding arm. He pulled into the inside lane as a queue began to build up at yet another junction; fortunately the last before he reached his own turn-off. Ahead people were milling around a wine bar with outdoor tables, standing with glasses of wine in their hands, skin glowing, sunglasses on. They all looked more attractive and glamorous than their normal selves.

His gaze was drawn by a movement around one table, the crowd parting a little as a couple came to their feet, pushing their chairs back, forcing others to move apart, and then the pair gathered their things and made their way through the throng and onto the wide pavement beyond. They were an attractive couple, both stylishly dressed and one or two people turned to look. She wore a tangerine floral halter-necked catsuit, cut low behind to reveal her sinuous back, right down to the curve at her hips, and wide so that it showed the first swell of small, neat breasts, while platform-soled sandals and wide flared trousers emphasised her long, slim legs.

The male emerged onto the pavement first, dressed in emerald-green flared trousers and patterned shirt with a butterfly collar. His movements were leonine, a measured and stealth-like stride, head held high; he was considerably taller than most around him, with well-groomed dark hair and stylish drooping moustache. Beneath his tightly-fitting shirt it was clear he was well-muscled and toned. She followed him out, her lean hips swivelling as she twisted and sashayed between the tables, a handbag hanging from the crook of one arm. As she stepped out to the pavement, falling in with his long stride, Janice shook loose her bronzy hair which tumbled about her bare shoulders and she slipped her arm through Brian's, her head inclined against his firm shoulder.

Chapter Fifteen

'He was like a talisman for us, wasn't he? I mean things were different when he was around. It was all more fun; dangerous too sometimes.'

'I used to look forward to him coming back for weeks ahead and then, when he was due, part of me would begin to dread it, but in an excited way still. Being with him always involved some sort of risk, that's for sure.' As he spoke, Rob was aware that his remarks could equally apply to how he felt now.

They were making their way along a cosmopolitan high street, the pavement restricted by the many shop displays that had encroached upon its width; Greengrocers mostly, with exotic fruits and unfamiliar vegetables, the shops themselves pungent with spices. Between them bargain stores, barely visible behind the piles of assorted plastic containers for sale and the cardboard boxes of cheap socks, plastic washing lines, pressed cutlery and china seconds.

The proximity of heavy road traffic and the lingering vehicle fumes combined in making it not an especially pleasant experience, but every now and then a shop window displaying the jewel-coloured fabrics of saris brightened the otherwise rather shabby scene.

For the third time in as many weeks, they were both in a corner of north west London unfamiliar to them, seeking an address, stepping upon the elapsed world of their childhoods. Rob consulted the London A-Z in his pocket and directed them to a side turning from which led, at right angles, a series of roads of terraced houses constructed of London stock bricks. Despite the generally impoverished feel of the area, it didn't have the same hopeless air of Railway Terrace, and appeared to be a busy and flourishing community, albeit a rather transitory one of many cultures.

They located the road quickly enough and walked along until they found the house. It was subdivided into two flats and they rang the bell for the lower one, then they knocked as the bell didn't appear to work. There were no telephones, so they'd been unable to call in advance, and at this point, they had no idea if Lizzie would have had the opportunity to tell John that they'd be visiting. Rob held his breath, feeling light-headed, not quite believing that he stood with certainty upon the doorstep where his old friend now lived. Ann could feel her heart beating hard and her chest constricting. She was glad Rob was with her; she wasn't sure she'd want to call on John on her own.

Both shifted uneasily as they awaited a response. Rob steeled himself, estimating in his head how long it would take for someone inside to register the sound and then walk to the front door, perhaps first peering from the front window to try and identify an unexpected visitor, but that interval passed without a sound. Abruptly there was a rattling noise from within as the latch turned and the door was snatched inwards, sticking a little so that it juddered on its hinges, and then it opened to reveal a narrow section of hallway.

It was quite dark inside and it took a few moments before Rob could register that a figure stood at the opening; partially obscured by the door, a not very tall or well-built figure stood. A man's face looked back at him from the ill-lit hall and made a small guttural noise in the back of his throat.

'John?' asked Rob.

'Yeh,' said the figure, stepping a little sideways into the gap, the inflection in the voice questioning. He was looking straight back at them, directly and challenging.

Rob could barely squeeze out the words; he knew instantly that he was looking at his old companion.

'It's Robbie,' he said, rather breathlessly.

John shifted, stepping forwards into the greater light at the threshold. He was on the step and so appeared taller than he actually was, but his form was still lean and angular, his limbs wiry and connected awkwardly to his frame. The impression was of an ill-assorted individual. He looked straight at Rob and his expression revealed consternation, a mix of astonishment and disbelief through which filtered gathering recognition.

Rob took in his friend's face, the still-crumpled countenance with deep furrows that lined the cheeks, the small chin and lopsided mouth and the two deep, intense dark eyes that blazed back, hostile, shocked, vulnerable.

'It ent,' he said, his words in direct contradiction to both their acknowledging tone and the look of recognition on his face. 'It ent, can't be!' although he clearly knew that it was.

'D'you remember Ann?' said Rob indicating, and John turned to look as if he were witnessing something occurring in a dream.

***

The living room was neat, with largely modern, although not especially new, furniture. On a bookshelf stood a photograph that showed John and Lizzie on their wedding day. Rob looked sideways at it, focussing on Lizzie's pretty smile, the white flowers entwined in her soft fair hair, John spruce in wide-lapelled suit, one arm proudly raised where her small pale hand rested on his sleeve, wedding ring on her finger. His chin was raised, head tilted slightly back, and beaming proudly into the camera. Lizzie's head was inclined into his, her eyes directed at his face and she was smiling sweetly. She'd worn a traditional white wedding dress, lacy and full at the hem, and her feet peeped from below in dainty white shoes.

Ann had taken up a position near the window and John was standing just inside the door through which he'd entered, having ushered them into the room ahead of himself.

'We saw Lizzie,' Ann briefly explained, and Rob was grateful for her intervention; for the opportunity to take stock and to look about as she explained their sudden appearance on the doorstep. John himself was standing, hands on hips, head lowered, looking up at her from beneath his eyelids. He was breathing deeply and seemed in shock. Rob noticed that his dark hair was wiry but cut a little closer to the head than in childhood. Untidy coils still fell onto his forehead and over the collar of the dark polo shirt that he wore over faded bell-bottom jeans. He had on well-worn slippers, a detail that Rob found especially incongruous.

'We had a nice talk to her,' Ann reassured him. 'She was a bit shocked when she first realised who we were, but then she was glad to see us and we had a nice chat. She seemed very pleased,' she added, with an encouraging smile. 'I'm sorry she's been unwell, but it really was lovely to see her again. I think she enjoyed it too.'

John took a deep breath, so long and deep that it was clearly audible. One hand dropped and vigorously rubbed at the leg where it fell, then scratched at the side of his nose and rubbed at its tip.

'We didn't want to intrude,' she quietly added.

He let his head nod a couple of times and finally raised it, looking at the photograph and then directly at Rob.

'Guess you didn't know,' he said.

'No. When was it?' Rob was conscious that his voice sounded unnaturally thick.

'March '73.'

'Congratulations.'

'Thanks.'

'We didn't know she'd met you again,' Ann said. 'Although, to tell the truth, I hadn't seen Lizzie more than a couple of times since she went away to College in London.'

'Sure.'

'How did you come to meet up?' asked Rob.

'Jus' chance.'

They both nodded silently, waiting for him to continue, which he did, but only after a lengthy pause.

'I knew it was 'er. She didn't know me like, not till I said, but I'd a knowed 'er anywhere.'

'I saw the Roses a few weeks ago,' said Rob. 'They didn't mention anything.'

'They wouldn't. Not 'appy. It weren't what they wan'ed fer their daugh'er.'

He indicated for them to sit down and they each took the chair behind where they stood, which meant that Ann and Rob were on opposite sides of the room. John settled back into the sofa, facing towards the window so that the light fell onto his face, accentuating the creases and hollows. The settee itself was rather tired and he sank deep into it so that his knees jutted out oddly and he rested his sharp elbows upon them, clasping his hands together, looking awkwardly into the space between them both. Rob felt that he was observing once more the troubled companion of his childhood summers.

'You?' he asked, pointing from one to the other.

Ann and Rob glanced to each other, determining the appropriate response to the enquiry.

'Oh, no,' said Ann. 'We just met by chance too, about four or five months ago, and we've got together a few times, talking about old times and all that. Then we thought it would be nice if we could find you. We both remembered you so well; especially Rob.' And she smiled across to Rob who smiled vaguely back to John, abashed at this reference to past closeness.

'You ent there, then?' he asked, his voice hoarse and rough, the same as it always was. 'In More'on Steyning?'

They both said that they weren't and briefly explained their respective moves to London, and their lives since.

'You wan' a coffee?' he asked afterwards and went off to make them. It was as if it were to fill time, to evade or delay further discourse.

Rob and Ann exchanged looks, cautious glances to reassure one another, and both peered about the room, conscious of the trespass upon their friends' new lives in this different place, silent in their contemplation. John returned with three mugs, which he gripped in one fist like beer glasses, and set them unevenly down on the coffee table where they slopped.

'Long time ago, all tha',' he said, as though he'd been reflecting on it in the kitchen.

Rob wondered if it was wise to have come. Perhaps it was all too long ago for him to attempt to resurrect their shared past. Perhaps he should have kept his treasured memories as simply that.

'Four summers: 1957 to 1960,' he acknowledged.

'Christ.'

'Kids, weren't we?'

'Yeh, how old was ya?'

'Eight, same as you.'

'Born a same month, weren't we?'

'Same month, two weeks apart.'

'Yeh, them summers...' He tailed off and took a gulp of coffee, and Rob felt a shimmer of pleasure at the tone of reflection creeping into his old friend's voice. 'Changed much 'as it, then? Liz said it ain't.'

'No, not really.'

'Pub still there?'

'Yes.'

'Windmill? Ain't fell down yet?'

'No, it's still there.'

'The Green and the 'ill, woz its name?'

'Lullington.'

'Tha's right, Lulling'on. Christ, we 'ad some times up there. What was tha' geezer's name, ginger fella we was always fightin'? Dray'on weren' it or some'ing?'

'Malcolm Draycott.'

'That's 'im, the fucker. Christ, I'd forgot all about that! And you ain't there now?'

'No, we left in 1961; not that long after you were last there. My Dad got laid off from the big house and we set up a garden centre with some of my mother's family in Middlesex. Bit of a change really.'

He glanced up to John and saw that he nodded sympathetically, pulling down the corners of his mouth.

'Where's ya brother, the big fella? Bit... you know. Woz 'is name?'

'Jonathan. He died, I'm afraid.'

‘Fuckin’ ’ell, what ’appened?’

‘Heart,’ said Rob, and saw that no further comment was necessary.

‘I gather you’re a father?’ Ann interposed, seeking to steer the conversation and spare Rob from painful topics.

John merely looked sideways at her so that she felt obliged to continue in order to fill the silence.

‘We found a woman a few doors from your old house in Railway Terrace, she said she’d known you as a boy and that you’d married and recently had a child. That’s how we came to find Lizzie at the hospital in fact. We tried the Maternity Ward initially.’

‘Postna’al psychosis,’ he flatly said.

‘I’m sorry, that’s awful. Poor Lizzie, it must be really difficult for you too.’

‘I’m alrigh’,’ he rather tersely replied, and both Rob and Ann were conscious of a chilling air in the atmosphere.

‘When was the baby born?’ It was as direct a question as she felt able to pose.

‘April,’ he said. ‘April twen’y third.’ And he took up his coffee mug and drained it to the dregs.

‘A while back then. Boy or girl?’ She smiled encouragingly, leaning forwards with friendly interest.

There was a pause before John answered. ‘Boy.’

‘Is there a name?’

‘They’re jus’ babies ent they,’ he said sharply, placing the mug rather noisily on the coffee table. ‘They cry an’ they crap an’ they sleep.’

Rob and Ann laughed a little uneasily, and then she tried one more time.

‘Is he being looked after at the hospital; where Lizzie is?’ she spoke as lightly as possible, not feeling able to merely drop the topic in light of his testy response, not now that she’d broached it.

‘She couldn’t, could she? she weren’t well enough. Couldn’t ’ave it there.’

‘I suppose not, but people recover,’ Rob offered, feeling he must say something encouraging now that the conversation was so inexplicably tense. ‘It’s not that uncommon and it passes soon enough, I’m sure. Awful at the time, but it passes, and she’s in the best place, isn’t she?’

There was no response from John who continued to look at his hands which now dangled from their repose on his knees. After a while he said, ‘It weren’t ’er fault.’

‘Of course not.’

‘She blamed ’erself. Kept sayin’ it were ’er an’ tha’ she were no good.’

‘But she’s being looked after, they’ll know how to treat her there.’

‘She said it were ’er fault, the baby, like it were ’er doin’, but it weren’t. How could it be? She didn’t do nuffin’. Look at ’er,’ and he pointed at the wedding photograph, speaking quickly now. ‘See ’ow she looks, ’ow could it ’ave been ’er? I ask ya? There ain’t no sense, but she won’t ’ave it, jus’ won’t ’ave it, wha’ever I says.’

‘Don’t blame yourself.’

Ann glanced anxiously to Rob, but he was simply looking helplessly to John, lost as to how to respond.

‘Is the baby at the hospital?’ she asked, selecting what she hoped was a neutral question.

‘It were. She couldn’t manage ’im; too upset. I ’ad it ’ere after, when it come out.’

‘That must’ve been hard work,’ said Rob with an attempt at jocularity, trying to re-establish a rapport with John.

‘She wan’ed ’im ’ere, at ’ome, at ’ome with me like, so ’e could be at ’ome not in the ’ospital. She couldn’t look at ’im anyway; it were too ’ard... too upsettin’ fer ’er.’

He paused, and for a minute or two there was a hollow and awkward silence.

‘It weren’t right,’ he added after another pause, and he bent forwards to scoop up something from the carpet, some small thread or item that he rubbed between finger and thumb and then let drop again.

'That's very sad,' said Ann.

'It were a mongol.'

He looked blankly back at them, absorbing their shocked looks.

'A mongol,' he repeated, 'and spastic. Cried all the time. She couldn't cope, could she? She wan'ed it perfect… not like that, not all twisted an' messed up like that, writhin' an' cryin' all the time like it's in agony. Poor little fucker, didn't have no chance, did it? What chance did it 'ave in life? It was gonna need operations, lots of 'em… fer years an' years, poor little blighter. Wha' kind of a life, eh? Wha' kind of fuckin' life for a kid like tha'. Always 'elpless, can't even wipe its own fuckin' arse?'

He paused again and then continued. 'It were best, for 'er. It's wha' matters… for 'er, so she can ge' better.' He nodded vigorously, as if affirming it to himself. 'She couldn't help it, it were just too much, too much. I wan'ed what's best for 'er. It's best for 'im too. I knew tha'. And he were peaceful like, after.'

***

He followed them back along the hall, pulling open the front door for Ann who stepped out first. She turned to exchange goodbyes and convey her best wishes to Lizzie, but there was a discomfiture in her voice and her normally easy manner seemed strained and forced.

She walked slowly along the path, lingering at the front gate for Rob, who was on the doorstep still, with John at his back. The day was bright and balmy and both Ann and Rob were struck by the strength of the light and the pleasant warmth of the sun's rays on their skin now they were back outside.

'Cheerio, then,' said Rob, speaking backwards over his shoulder. 'It's been good to see you again, especially after all these years.'

'Yeh,' replied John, one hand on the latch.

'We must talk over old times again.'

Rob stepped backwards down onto the path, turning to face John for what he knew would be the last time.

'Best wishes to Lizzie. I'm sure she'll come through this.'

'Sure.'

'Bye, then,' He backed away, one arm raised in salute.

Standing on the step, John was immobile, but then abruptly he advanced down the step and stood before Rob, fingers tucked into the pockets of his jeans and, in the close proximity, Rob was aware of his old friend's slight stature, his frail vulnerability.

'We was best mates, wasn't we?' said John.

He stared away down the road as he spoke, his dense eyes scrunched against the brightness, forcing deep creases down his cheeks, but then he looked up at Rob and his face was uncertain and questioning, his eyes squinting and dense as asteroids.

'Wasn't we?'

'Yes, sure...'

'You was there fer me every year. You was always there, when I came back. You always remembered.'

Chapter Sixteen

'They seem okay, your folks.'

'They are, they're pretty settled these days.'

A few crisp, browned leaves crunched beneath their feet as they walked the dry, dusty lane of Rushwood End, a reminder that summer was now passing. No breeze stirred the warm late-afternoon air which hung motionless, held between the stone walls on either side of the lane.

'You've never been tempted to contact your half-sister?'

Ann flicked her hair back behind her shoulders and Rob saw that she drew her brows together. They'd spoken of her family's big secret a few times now. At first he'd raised it tentatively, testing to ascertain that it was a topic that could be broached. She'd smiled wistfully, grateful even for his broaching it; she knew Maggie had told him and was relieved now to discuss it openly.

'Maybe one day. Not yet, though. Anyway, they've moved away. The Grandfather died and I believe she got married and moved to the West Country somewhere.'

'You never asked your Dad?'

'No! I wouldn't want to. I'm just glad things are muddling along okay at home, and that they seem settled together.'

She turned and smiled briefly up at him and he wrapped his arm around her shoulders, pulling her in towards him, feeling her relax against his flank as their steps fell into easy rhythm with one another. Much shorter than he was, her shoulder nestled under Rob's arm and she slipped her arm around his waist. Lightly and easily, Ann had become a part of his life, her intuitive nature and ready empathy a welcome bond. He rarely thought of Janice now and had made no further contact with her since the day he'd caught sight of her with Brian.

Lunch at Ann's parents' had been a pleasant, sociable affair and they'd all spent the afternoon in the garden. The two of them had slipped out for a walk on their own now, through the yard and passage to The Square and up the lane which rose gently to the lower slopes of Lullington Hill. They passed through the farmyard at Rushwood End to the steep and narrow footpath that lifted them to the broad back of the hill, the countryside dropping away as they rapidly ascended the grassy slopes where the black cattle lumbered slowly from their path, eyeing them warily.

They settled down with the old hedge at their back, laden with blue-black bullaces and golden-green crab apples. The sun-warmed stalks of the grasses, all seed now spent, yielded to them. There was no one else on the hill. The first daddy-long-legs tumbled amongst the grass stems and swallows streamed over the slopes below. A silent, dreaming peacefulness not found at other times of the year had settled on the countryside; fructose, soporific, replete.

Far, far above a small aeroplane was a glint in the paling sky.

'Hugh never judged my brother, you know. He never saw his shortcomings. He could've done, but he never did, not once, ever. I feel bad about it, it was wrong, we should've told him when Jonathan died. We should've invited him to the funeral.'

'There's so much to do at a time like that.' Ann said, wanting to be conciliatory. 'You had to think about so much and you must've been in shock, all of you. When it's unexpected like that, you know... when someone so relatively young dies so suddenly.'

'We were in complete shock, all of us. It was awful; I'd never felt so alone in my life. Jonathan had always been there, I'd never known a day without him.'

'Hugh would've gone, I think, to the funeral.'

'I think he would too, if only he'd known.'

'Why don't we try and find him?' Ann suggested. 'It can't be difficult.'

'You know, we should. I'd like to do it for Jonathan, if for no other reason; I think that would be right.'

'...shall we then?'

'Let's.'

Above them swifts wheeled, scything the very air.

- END -